Riverboat Point

Also by Tricia Stringer

Queen of the Road
Right as Rain
Riverboat Point
Between the Vines

THE FLINDERS RANGES SERIES

Heart of the Country

Riverboat Point

TRICIA STRINGER

First Published 2014
Second Australian Paperback Edition 2016
ISBN 978 1760371777

RIVERBOAT POINT
© 2014 by Tricia Stringer
Australian Copyright 2014
New Zealand Copyright 2014

This is a work of fiction. Names, characters, places, and incidents are either the product of the author's imagination or are used fictitiously, and any resemblance to actual persons, living or dead, business establishments, events, or locales is entirely coincidental.

Published by
Harlequin Mira
An imprint of Harlequin Enterprises (Australia) Pty Ltd.
Level 13, 201 Elizabeth Street
SYDNEY NSW 2000
AUSTRALIA

® and TM are trademarks of Harlequin Enterprises Limited or its corporate affiliates. Trademarks indicated with ® are registered in Australia, New Zealand, and in other countries.

Printed and bound in Australia by McPhersons Printing Group

MIX
Paper from
responsible sources
FSC® C001695
www.fsc.org

Tricia Stringer grew up on a farm in country South Australia. A mother of three wonderful grown-up children and a devoted nanna, Tricia now lives in the beautiful Copper Coast region with her husband, Daryl.

Most of Tricia's life so far has been spent in rural communities, as owner of a post office and bookshop, as a teacher and librarian, and now as a full-time writer. She loves travelling and exploring Australia's diverse communities and landscapes, and shares this passion for the country and its people through her stories. One of Tricia's rural romances, *Queen of the Road,* won the Romance Writers of Australia's Romantic Book of the Year award in 2013.

Riverboat Point is Tricia's third book with Harlequin.

www.triciastringer.com
www.facebook.com/triciastringerauthor
@tricia_stringer

For Vivonne

CHAPTER

1

A tapping sound penetrated Savannah's dream. Something jabbed into her back and her hip was wedged firmly. She flung out an arm and hit the steering wheel. She was in a car. Her heart lurched. The car crash! A dog barked. It was loud and close. Her eyes flew open. A huge woolly head, mouth open, teeth exposed, was right in her face.

She jerked backwards. The gear stick dug deeper into her left thigh as she twisted out from under the steering wheel. There was a mist on the driver's side glass between her and the dog.

"Down, Jasper," a male voice commanded, then, "Are you all right?"

Savannah gasped. The dog was replaced by a man's face; unshaven, frowning. She glanced around. The grey light of early morning revealed the interior of her car. Not her parents' car, there had been no crash. She'd pulled over last night, lost and too tired to drive any further.

The dog barked. The man tapped on the window again.

"Are you all right?" he repeated.

Savannah straightened stiffened limbs and felt for the lever to raise her seat.

"Yes, I'm fine," she snapped, glad the closed window separated her from the large German Shepherd.

"Not a good place to stop," the man said. "Just around a bend."

Savannah ignored him. She had completely lost her bearings last night when she'd pulled to the edge of the dirt road. It had been pointless to keep driving.

The man walked on, the dog leading the way, eager to be off. She looked in the rear-view mirror but the back window was covered in mist, like the rest of the windows. She gathered up the towel she'd pulled over her as an extra layer against the cold and used it to wipe the windscreen. A stab of pain shot down her arm. Definitely not a good idea to sleep in her car overnight. She would be stiff and sore all day.

"Bloody Jaxon and his schemes," Savannah muttered. Her brother's desperate phone call the day before had enticed her out of the city to this shack of his, kilometres away from civilisation, on the banks of the Murray River. Trouble was, she'd only been to visit once before to check what she was going guarantor for when he'd bought the place. That had been a year ago and in daylight. Last night it was as if it had disappeared off the map.

She turned the key with stiff fingers. The engine roared to life. She lowered her window and stuck her head out. The crisp chill of early morning air flowed over her. She was parked just around a bend, the stranger had been right. Ahead the road was straight, bordered by wire fences on either side. It stretched on towards some tall gums and …

"Damn it!" Savannah slapped the steering wheel. She could see Jaxon's distinctive letterbox. The frame of an old pushbike with a box balanced on the handlebars. His idea of a joke. The only bike he ever rode was a Harley-Davidson. She pulled out and drove forward. She had been so close, yet last night in the dark she hadn't realised. Hopelessly lost once she'd left the main highway, she'd driven around for ages. There were no streetlights and not even any moon. When she'd tried ringing Jaxon, his mobile had gone straight to message bank and his landline was answered by his recorded message.

Now, as she approached his driveway, she didn't know whether to be angry or worried. She pulled up in front of the solid mesh gate. On it hung a large blue sign with navy-blue writing declaring "J&S Houseboats". The gate was latched with a chain and a locked padlock. She pulled a set of keys from her console. Jaxon had given her a spare of every key. "You're my guarantor," he'd said with that cheeky grin of his. "Everything here is yours until I can pay it off."

She tested half the keys before she found the one that opened the padlock. The gate swung free, shuddered against the fence then stopped. She drove through and on past the workshop and sheds to Jaxon's shack, perched high above the river. It surprised her now as it had the first time she'd come. The drive through the bush to get here gave no indication of the existence of the wide river flowing past Jaxon's door.

She pulled up under the carport at the side of the shack. There was no sign of Jaxon's bike. She climbed out, stretched her stiff body then stood still, listening. She heard nothing. How he could stand the isolation and silence she didn't know. Give her the sounds of the city any day.

She walked around her car to the verandah that ran the full length of the shack facing the river. All the blinds were closed and the middle section, which was once a wall with two small windows and a rotting wooden door, had been replaced by some kind of panelling, floor-to-ceiling windows and a large sliding glass door. She remembered Jaxon telling her on one of his visits to the city that he'd met someone who had a salvage yard and someone else who was a carpenter and he'd replaced the front of the shack. She tugged on the door handle but it didn't budge. She didn't have the keys for the new door. She knocked on the glass.

"Jaxon!" she called. "Hello!"

She listened but there was no response. She retraced her steps, past her car to the back. Once again the verandah stretched along the length of the shack but this time it ended in a room which was the laundry. The screen door was old and creaked open at her twist of the handle. The door beyond it was also old and weathered but solid. She hoped one of the keys in her hand would open it.

The first key she chose turned the lock. She had to give the door a shove to get it open. The handle slipped from her fingers and the door flung back, slamming into the wall.

Savannah paused on the doorstep and peered into the gloomy interior. The laundry window was filled in with cardboard. The only light came from the doorway and illuminated a large automatic washing machine that took up most of the small space.

"Jaxon?" she called again but with less confidence. Had something happened to him and she was about to find his body?

There was a faint rustle from inside the shack.

She pursed her lips and stepped through the doorway.

"Bloody hell, Jaxon, if you're playing tricks I'll throttle you," Savannah called as she turned right and went up a step, past the toilet and bathroom and into the kitchen.

With every blind closed it was gloomy inside. She wrinkled her nose. There was a smell of something musty. She reached out a hand to find the light switch and flicked it on. Where once there'd been a few old cupboards, a stove and a sink that served as a kitchen there was now a large U-shaped bench. In one corner of the U was a pantry cupboard with open benches joining it at right angles. Under the window a new sink gleamed along with an oven and cooktop. Jaxon had been busy. There must be a lot of work for electricians around the area. From what he'd told her the houseboat side of things ate money rather than made it.

She stepped further into the room but pulled up at a rustling sound. She spun and studied the pantry. It went from the floor nearly to the ceiling, the angled space between the two benches filled by a louvre door. She approached it carefully, her feet silent on the linoleum floor. At the door she stopped, carefully grasped the round handle and tugged. The door swung back, a light came on and a grey blur whizzed along a shelf close to her face. She shrieked and slammed the door shut. Not quick enough to contain the smell of mice.

Savannah clasped a hand over her mouth and hurried to inspect the bedrooms. The house was a rectangle. The kitchen and living area formed an open space in the middle. Jaxon's bedroom was the largest, taking up the side of the house in front of the laundry and bathroom. The bedclothes were pulled up, shoes filled a basket and scattered the floor around it. From the open wardrobe door she could see there were more clothes jumbled in a heap at the base than hanging from hangers. She walked around his double bed. The bedside table was covered in a layer of dust, coins and paper receipts but nothing to indicate Jaxon's whereabouts. Just a faint male smell remained. Better than mice at least, and hopefully it meant they weren't in here.

A picture frame had fallen to the floor. She picked it up. It was one of the last family photos they'd had taken. Their mother had displayed it on the small mantelpiece in their lounge room.

Savannah grew to hate the picture. Their faces smiling on a rare holiday at the beach, all she could see was her large body. How had her mother ever allowed her to wear two-piece bathers, the rolls of fat unrestrained by fabric? Puppy fat her mother had told her, but that's not what the kids at high school had called it. Savannah had hidden the photo. She wondered how Jaxon ended up with it. And where was he now? She put the picture facedown on his bedside table and continued her search.

Across the living room in the opposite wall were two more doors. The front one revealed a double bed and wardrobe and the room behind it was stacked with boxes and electrical gear. In one corner was a desk. Above it hung a pin board with papers clipped in rows and a calendar with an all but naked brunette astride a bike. Files were neatly stacked on the desk alongside the flashing answering machine. That was the house all checked; unless he was in a cupboard or under a bed, Jaxon wasn't here.

Savannah sighed.

"Where are you?" she murmured.

Suddenly desperate to use the bathroom, she went back across the living room. Beyond her the screen door swung open. Savannah turned to see the dog with the large woolly head. It bared its teeth in a snarl. She froze. A man stuck his head round the door. The same bloke she'd seen out on the road.

"Who the hell are you?" he growled.

"None of your business. Get your dog and yourself off my property."

The man's face relaxed into a confident smile. "Your property? You picked the wrong place to break into and tell that lie, sweetheart. This place belongs to my mate."

"Jaxon?" she said ignoring the "sweetheart".

His smile faltered.

She nodded at the keys still hanging from the lock. "They're my keys and I own half this place with my brother, Jaxon Smith."

This time his smile showed relief. "Savannah?"

"Yes but …" She shuffled her feet. The dog snarled again.

"It's okay, Jasper. The lady's a friend." He pushed the dog back and stepped inside, pulling the screen door closed between him and the animal. The dog barked.

"Sit, Jasper," the man commanded and turned back to her with a smile. "I'm Ethan Daly," he said. "Jaxon's neighbour. I've been expecting you. You're just not …"

Ethan put his head to one side and swept his dark brown eyes over her. Savannah felt naked. She wrapped her arms around her waist, ignoring his outstretched hand. He'd looked older out on the road. Now she thought he was a little older than her, perhaps not much more than thirty. The smile softened his features.

He grinned at her and used the hand to bat away a loose lock of dark hair that had fallen over his eyes. "You're not quite what I was expecting." He glanced over her shoulder. "I thought I heard a scream."

"I got a surprise. There's a mouse in the pantry."

"More than one by the smell. I can give you a hand if you like?"

He went to step past her. She pressed a firm hand against his chest. He stopped.

She dropped her hand. "I don't need help," she said.

His smile faded.

"Thanks anyway," she added.

He made a move for the door.

"Do you know where my brother is?" she asked.

"Gone on a holiday."

"A holiday?" That's not what he'd told her when he'd rung.

"I was expecting you days ago. Jaxon said you'd be up to take care of business."

"Business?"

"The houseboat bookings mainly. His other customers know he's away."

"Other customers?"

"His electrical business." A small frown crossed Ethan's face. "You don't know much about your brother, do you? Maybe I should see some ID."

Savannah drew herself up. "My brother's six foot – he got the tall gene. Blue eyes like mine, fair wavy hair – I dye mine – charming smile."

"You dye that too?"

Savannah ignored his dig.

"Jaxon rang me two days ago," she said. "He reckoned he needed my help urgently. I wasn't going to come at all but he sounded desperate and I'm … well, I'm between jobs."

Ethan raised an eyebrow. The dog gave a small whine.

"I don't know why he only rang you recently. He's been gone for over a week."

"A week?"

"Longer. I was beginning to worry. I know he's got a couple of bookings next week."

"Bookings?" Savannah rubbed at her forehead. She had so many questions. Ethan was right to some extent. She knew her brother but nothing about his life since he'd moved to this isolated piece of river. "There must be some mix-up," she said. "Are you sure you're his neighbour? Maybe I should be the one checking ID or perhaps ringing the police."

Savannah stared him in the eye. He looked down.

Guilty, she thought.

He reached around and drew a wallet from his pocket. He flicked it open in front of her to reveal a wild-looking likeness to his face on a driver's licence with the same street address as Jaxon's.

"You can ring the police if you like but as I told you, Jaxon's on holidays. I don't think the police will want to go look for him." He slipped the wallet back in his pocket. "I'll leave you to it. I'm just over the fence that way." He jerked his thumb over his shoulder. "Give me a shout if you need anything."

"I'll be fine," Savannah said. She was already digging her phone from her pocket as Ethan let himself out. She tried not to notice the firm hug of his jeans. Damn it, he was a good-looking guy. And he was fit and well toned, as if he worked out. She'd felt the strength of his chest under her fingers when she'd stopped him from going further into the house.

With her spare hand she tugged the keys from the door and shut it firmly on the nosy neighbour. There would be no chance to find out what was under that shirt. She'd track down Jaxon and hightail it back to the city. She wasn't going to stay in this backwater any longer than she had to. She scrolled down the screen and selected Jaxon's number.

CHAPTER

2

"She's here but I don't think she's going to go for it, mate."

Ethan pressed the phone firmly to his ear as he flicked on the kettle. The voice on the other end of the phone was breaking up.

"Okay." Ethan sighed. "I'll try, but don't blame me if it all blows up in your face." The voice crackled and the call dropped out.

He tossed the handset onto the bench and busied himself making some breakfast. He hadn't wanted to be a part of his mate's plan. Normally Ethan liked to mind his own business. It had worked for him this last year and he'd never had any trouble. Jaxon's houseboat trade had brought a lot more people to this quiet patch of river. Ethan had hoped his friend would lose interest in it and concentrate on the electrical business. But Jaxon had wanted his sister's involvement, said she needed a change of pace.

Savannah Smith was not what Ethan had expected. She had the same angular features as her brother but the feisty temperament was a total reversal of her brother's easygoing persona. Jaxon had had his fingers burnt a few times with his trusting nature. Savannah wasn't going to have the wool pulled over her eyes easily.

It had been stupid blundering into the place thinking she'd broken in. A year ago that could have got him killed. He was getting soft. From the start he'd been on the back foot. He should have realised it was her when he found her parked up the road. The photo he'd been shown had her with longer black hair not the short white spikes she sported now, but those piercing blue eyes were the same and the cute little nose. He shook his head. She could be trouble and this could all blow up in Jaxon's face.

Ethan carried his bowl of cereal and his coffee out to the front deck and settled at the outside table. Jasper padded after him and flopped to the wooden floor. Ethan drew in a breath, closed his eyes then opened them again as he slowly exhaled. The river stretched out before him. The mist that had clung to it when he'd woken was all but gone. The water looked flat and serene, belying the strength of its flow. Shadows turned it to deep green close to his bank but over the other side was the grey-brown of water in full sun. Birds of varying descriptions flew, swam, fished and sang. It was going to be a glorious day on the river.

He thanked his lucky stars again for the day he'd found this place. He'd bought it just before his last deployment. Having a place to call home had helped him settle. The only thing that disturbed his patch of the river was the houseboats coming and going from next door. He twisted to look at his neighbour's river frontage, where he could see glimpses of deck and glass. Four of the tourist attractions were moored there. He was getting used to them.

Ethan finished his cereal and settled back to watch the water as he drank his coffee. The peace of his surroundings had helped him relax. Without realising it, life almost felt normal again. The broken sleep bothered him less often. He thought about the little white pills in the bathroom cabinet. Perhaps the day wasn't far off when he wouldn't need them.

A bang, followed by another loud thud and a muffled yell brought a low growl from Jasper.

"Easy boy," Ethan said and reached down to ruffle the top of the dog's head. "Just our new neighbour chasing a few mice."

Jaxon's shack was separated from Ethan's pole house by only a few metres and a boundary fence. Ethan was glad to discover a good bloke like Jaxon had bought the place next door. They got on well. It had only ever been the two of them in the ten or eleven months since Jaxon had moved in. Now there was Savannah.

Jaxon had said his sister was a city girl. Ethan had imagined a high-heeled, lipstick-wearing office type who'd be pestering him for help at every turn in case she broke a fingernail. He chuckled. Perhaps it wouldn't be so bad having Savannah next door while Jax was away. As long as she minded her own business he'd mind his and they'd get along fine.

"Mr Daly?"

Jasper growled.

Ethan put down his cup.

"Mr Daly!"

Jasper raced to the end of the deck, barking as he went.

"Damn!" Ethan pushed back his chair and strolled after him.

Savannah stood below on her side of the fence, waist high in weeds. Jaxon really should have cleaned them up before he'd gone. It was coming into snake season.

"Sit, Jasper," Ethan said. He placed two hands on the railing and leaned forward. "We're not formal around here. You can call me Ethan."

She put her hands on her hips, tipped back her head and locked her steely gaze on him.

Ethan held her stare. She certainly wasn't the retiring type. "What can I do for you?"

"I wondered if you knew anything about hot water?"

He tried not to smile. "Depends on what kind of hot water."

"The kind that comes out of a tap when you turn it on. I don't seem to have any."

"Jaxon probably turned it off before he left."

"Off?"

"Saves electricity. There'll be a switch in the meter box under the carport. Would you like me to check it?"

"No." She put up a hand. "No need. I'll find it, thanks."

Ethan watched her wade through the long grass until she was out of sight around the corner of the shack. Then he allowed the grin to spread across his face. No, Jaxon's sister was certainly not what he'd been expecting. Damn Jaxon for involving him.

Ethan rubbed at the stubbly skin of his jaw, the smile dropping from his face. He went back to his coffee. He wanted as little to do with Jaxon's scheme as possible and that meant steering clear of his sister. He had promised to help if she had mechanical problems with the houseboats, that was all. Today he would work on his bike and maybe go fishing in the late afternoon, catch something for dinner.

Jasper sat up, ears pricked.

"Mr Daly?"

The dog growled. For a brief moment his deep brown eyes met Ethan's then he lowered himself to the deck and dropped his head on to his outstretched legs.

"Thanks for your support, mate," Ethan said. He stepped around the dog and walked to the railing again. There she was, hands on hips, looking up at him with that piercing stare of hers.

"Ms Smith." He raised his eyebrows.

"I found the switch but it doesn't seem to be working. Do you have any other ideas?"

"I'll come down."

He turned, ignoring her protest. "Stay, Jasper," he said as the dog got to his feet. "You only complicate matters."

Ethan walked through his house and padded down the stairs, hoping he hadn't been wrong about Savannah. Perhaps she was going to be the needy type after all. There was no way he wanted any involvement with her, no matter that she had a pretty face and if her shape under the clothes was anything to go by, a toned body. He needed no complications in his life right now.

He met her under the carport, where she was studying the open meter box.

"It's on," she said turning to look at him. Her eyes defied him to say otherwise but she didn't look too scary with a smudge of dirt on the tip of her nose.

"Yep," he agreed. "It's on." Annoyed now that his morning breakfast ritual had been disrupted.

"Well, it's not working." Her hands were on her hips again.

"What do you mean?"

"There's no hot water. I've checked the kitchen, bathroom and laundry. All cold."

He shook his head, not sure whether to smile or frown. "It's not instant," he said. "It heats up overnight."

"You're kidding?"

He stepped around her. "I can flick it over to heat now but it will take a while."

"What kind of place doesn't have instant hot water?" she snapped.

"I gather you have gas at home?"

"Yes."

"This is an old electric hot water service. It's set to heat at night when power's cheaper. Normally you wouldn't notice." He shut the meter box and turned back to her. "It'll take an hour or so then you should switch it back to night rate."

She glanced from Ethan to the meter box and back then let out a sigh.

He hesitated. For a moment she looked vulnerable. He felt bad about his churlish behaviour. It was obvious she didn't want to be here. This could well blow up in Jaxon's face.

"Thanks ... Ethan."

"No probs, Savannah." He gave her the briefest of smiles. "Call me anytime," he said, but not too enthusiastically.

He saw the steely look return to her eyes.

Good, he thought. Hopefully this had been a call for help out of desperation and she wouldn't do it again in a hurry.

Ethan returned to his house, disposed of the remains of the cold coffee and rinsed his few dishes. Keeping busy didn't banish the picture in his head of his new neighbour. His mobile phone rang. He tensed at the name that glowed on the screen and Savannah was forgotten in an instant. He thought about ignoring the call but it was such a rare occurrence perhaps there was something wrong.

He pressed accept and put the phone to his ear. "Mal," he said, trying to inject a casual tone into his voice. "What's up?"

CHAPTER

3

Savannah dumped her overnight bag in Jaxon's spare bedroom and shut the door on it. The mice appeared to be confined within the pantry but she wasn't going to give them any chance of getting into the room she was planning to sleep in.

She tested the hot tap again. The water felt slightly less cold or was it her imagination? She had to presume Ethan Daly knew what he was doing. She wasn't prepared to get her hands dirty cleaning out mice debris until she had a decent quantity of hot water. She'd done a search for cleaning products throughout the shack and as expected, Jaxon's supply was limited. In the laundry she'd found one old battered bucket that had a decaying mop stuck to its base and half a bottle of bleach. No other detergents other than dishwashing liquid, no disinfectant and no rubber gloves.

Similarly, the fridge held little of interest as far as food went. The cheese was mouldy, the milk out of date and the crisper revealed a few withered carrots and a bag of liquid that could once have been a capsicum. She closed the door. Again she cursed her brother and whatever he was up to.

She paced the living area. Back at the kitchen bench, she snatched up the keys she'd removed from the back door. She would make a trip into town for supplies. At least that would fill the time while she waited for the water to heat.

It crossed her mind she should check directions. She'd driven around in the dark for quite a while last night. She'd passed a sign that said *Riverboat Point* but how far back or which road she'd been on she couldn't remember.

She half turned in the direction of Ethan's place but stopped as she heard the sound of an engine starting nearby. Through the trees that followed the fence between Jaxon's and his neighbour's, she saw a bike drive away. Ethan wasn't hanging around to offer further help. Used to managing on her own, she preferred it that way. If it hadn't been for Jaxon's archaic hot water service she wouldn't have needed to ask for help.

Her car keys jangled to the concrete floor of the carport. Annoyed, she bent to pick them up, ignoring the dull ache in her left leg as she caught a glimpse of the river. She straightened, gazing to her right then to her left. Brown water as far as she could see in either direction. This was the mighty Murray River. Hard to imagine it was the lifeblood of the state and the centre of much political wrangling. Her gaze came back to the four houseboats tied up at the bank below. She frowned. What had Ethan said about those boats and bookings?

She climbed into her car. First things first. She had to find the town, get some supplies and tackle the vermin-infested house. Then she'd worry about the rest.

The early morning mist and cool air had completely disappeared, replaced by a bright blue sky and sunshine. Savannah turned out the gate and followed the dirt road back the way she had come last night. Daylight revealed little more of her surroundings. Thick trees and bush hugged both sides of the road. Every so often she came to a gate and a driveway and got an occasional glimpse of a roof or a wall. No sign of people or another car. For all she knew she was totally alone out here.

A couple of smaller roads ran off to the left and then to the right. Last night she probably took both of them when she was looking for Jaxon's place. Finally she came to a T-junction. She turned right and stopped beside the sign pointing in the direction she'd just come. The sign said Old Man's Landing Road but Jaxon had said there should also be a blue sign pointing to J&S Houseboats. It wasn't there.

She continued on and was relieved, after a few more twists and turns, to find the bitumen road ahead. A sign declared *Riverboat Point 3 kms*. Once more the J&S Houseboats sign was missing. Perhaps Jaxon had planned to put the signs up and hadn't got around to it. That would make sense.

She moved out onto the main road. Not much further to civilisation. A few minutes later she was revising that thought. She'd driven the extent of the small community made up of an assortment of old and new houses, some of which were obviously holiday shacks. Another houseboat business and a caravan park hugged the river close to a small jetty. Back from that was an old double-storey dwelling with beer signs out the front and a sign declaring *Accommodation Available*. She assumed it was some kind of hotel. Further on, tucked in a bend of the road as it followed the river, was a shop. She couldn't have missed it. Signs advertising everything from newspapers to fuel to Australia Post Agency adorned the walls or stood at various angles around the footpath. She pulled up across the road in the shade of a group of large gum trees. A patchy lawn spread away from her towards the river.

An old lady stepped out of the doorway carrying a shopping bag. Savannah noticed a large IGA sign. Posters listing specials filled the windows. This place was also the local supermarket. A young lad carrying a box and another bag followed the woman. Savannah watched as he placed the items in the lady's car and opened her door.

Savannah was impressed. That kind of service was rarely seen in the city. It gave her a good feeling about Riverboat Point. She took a bag from her back seat and crossed the road. The shop was housed in an old building, part of a row of three. Just inside the door was a supermarket counter and a selection of fruit and veg. There was no sign of anyone. Once she entered she could see that the supermarket took up the space in all three of the old shops. Adjoining walls had been knocked out to form access.

Savannah turned back to the counter as footsteps echoed towards her along the wooden floor. A woman emerged around a row of shelves carrying a bucket of fresh flowers.

"Hello, can I help?" she asked.

"I just need some groceries," Savannah said.

"Let me know if you can't find something you want. Otherwise help yourself. Trolleys and baskets over there." She pointed past Savannah, gave her a good look up and down then bustled behind the counter to place the flowers beside a *Fresh Flowers* sign, her interest in Savannah short-lived.

Savannah took a basket. She wasn't planning on staying long. A few cleaning items and some food staples would get her by.

It took her a while to gather what she needed in the unfamiliar layout. She had to backtrack several times. She came across the lad she'd seen carrying the old lady's groceries. He was unpacking cans of cat food. He glanced her way then went on stacking.

Perhaps Jaxon should get a cat, Savannah thought. Then she had another idea. She turned back to the lad.

"Do you sell mouse traps?" she asked.

"Next aisle." He pointed to the left. "Between the fishing supplies and the garden needs." He spoke slowly and politely. "There are signs."

"Thanks," she said but he'd returned back to his task. She noticed him pause and then straighten a can and turn its label to the front.

She went on to the next aisle and passed the sign that said *Fishing Supplies*. When the lad had said signs he'd really meant it. These were not like signs that hang at the beginning of the row in a supermarket; they were printed and laminated and stuck above each section. Savannah looked along the aisle. She'd been so intent on finding her groceries she hadn't noticed them. There were signs everywhere.

She found the mouse traps with the mothballs, flyspray and snail bait under a sign that said *Vermin Eradication*. Just for a moment a bubbling feeling welled up inside her. She clenched her teeth and looked up and down the aisle. She couldn't remember the last time she'd giggled. It was a strange sensation. She put a mouse trap in her basket and reached for a second. Beside them on the shelf were packets of steel wool. Someone had got their cleaning products mixed up with their vermin eradication. She bit her lip to stifle another giggle.

A sudden memory of her mother came to mind. Savannah remembered her plugging holes in the skirtings of their house with steel wool – to keep out the mice. She added a packet to her overloaded basket and headed back to the counter.

She could hear voices chatting happily as she neared the front. Two people were ahead of her at the checkout. Savannah waited beside a pin board that was covered in flyers and notices. The board had been divided into columns and once again someone had made signs for each column. The *Entertainment* column advertised an upcoming darts competition. The *For Sale* column was a bit busier with a car and assorted furniture listed. The last column was labelled *Public Notices*. Savannah's sweeping gaze halted at the name *Jaxon Smith Electrical*. It stood out in big bold print. Below it was pinned a note: *Unavailable until further notice*. There was the name and number for another electrician but it was the 'unavailable until further notice' that held Savannah's attention. She stepped closer and bent to look at the note as if an explanation might magically appear.

"Next, please."

The shrill tone of the woman's voice made Savannah spin. She bumped her basket against the counter and several items slid to the floor. She reached down for them, gasped as pain shot up her leg, and straightened quickly.

The woman stared at her. Savannah gritted her teeth. Sometimes it caught her like that, the pain sudden and intense, reminding her she was no longer whole.

"Are you all right?" The woman made a small move towards her.

Then the lad was there gathering up her items. Before she could protest he had put her basket on the counter in his steady manner.

"Thank you," Savannah said and stepped gingerly after him.

The pain was now a dull ache. She was used to that. It was the sudden sharp stabs that could still take her breath away even after all this time. Nerves still healing, reconnecting, the doctors said. Something she would have to live with. Easy for them to say. She managed fairly well but sleeping in the car last night hadn't done her body any good, or her nerves if she was honest.

"Do you have any bags?"

"Yes."

Savannah glanced at the woman whose badge said her name was Faye.

Faye had started scanning her items. She paused and they both looked from Savannah's pile of items to the one bag she'd placed on the counter.

"Get the lady a box, Jamie," Faye called.

Someone else stepped up to the counter. Faye became much more animated as she greeted the man she called Terry. He was an old bloke with a twinkle in his eye. He gave Savannah an interested look before Faye entered into a detailed conversation with him about the weather and the state of his vegetable garden.

Jamie returned with a box. In his slow, methodical way, he packed her items while she paid.

"Have a nice day," Faye said, with barely a glance at Savannah once she'd handed over her money.

Jamie picked up the box and waited at the door. Savannah gave him a quick smile and went ahead of him to her car. She popped the boot. He slid the box in and stepped back.

"Have a nice day," he said. His words followed the pattern and tone Faye had used – like a recording.

"Thank you," Savannah said.

He nodded. She watched him walk back across the road, not sure what to make of her Riverboat Point shopping expedition.

Seeing Jaxon's sign had thrown her. Not being available until further notice was so indefinite and yet not the kind of thing you'd write if you were going away for a week. And according to Ethan, Jaxon had already been gone for that long. She pulled her phone from her bag and tried her brother's number again. She sighed as it went straight to his message bank. She jabbed the end button and tossed her phone back in her bag. She'd already left him several messages. No point in leaving another. There'd be plenty she'd say to his face when he finally turned up.

CHAPTER
4

"What are you doing here?"

Ethan looked into the eyes of his older brother. Blake's face, prematurely weathered from a life of outdoor work, was pulled into a smile but his eyes showed his pain. Ethan had seen that look on other faces, set like masks determined not to allow the agony to the surface. Unless you were very clever, the eyes always told the true story. He pushed the memories away.

"Checking up on you, big bro," Ethan retorted. He nodded at Blake's arm encased in bright white plaster. "Still can't ride a bike."

They both grinned at the recollection of childhood days when Blake, always in the lead, often went a cropper off his bike. He'd broken a collarbone, been hospitalised with concussion and had too many cuts and bruises to recall.

Blake lifted his head. "Can you prop me up a bit? I hate lying flat."

Ethan shoved another pillow under Blake's shoulders. He heard the sharp intake of breath but there was no other sound of complaint.

"You didn't bring a beer, did you?" Blake's voice came out in a rasp. "I've got cocky cage mouth."

"That'd go down well with the painkillers. How about some water?"

Ethan held the glass to his lips. Blake took a sip and let his head fall back on the pillow.

"Damn!" he muttered. "I'll be out of here tomorrow."

"Not according to the old man. You've smashed yourself up pretty good this time."

"Mal rang you?"

"He was worried about you."

"Must have been."

They both lapsed into silence. Their father rarely spoke directly to Ethan. They had disagreed on many things for as long as Ethan could remember, but it was his joining the army that had nearly torn the family apart. Their parents were part of the anti-war movement during the early seventies. They had raised their sons to value democracy and freedom. Ethan did. He just looked at it from a different perspective. Blake understood that but Mal and Barb couldn't accept Ethan's choices. His call-up to Afghanistan had brought a slight reconciliation with his mother when she couldn't bear to let him go without hugs and kisses she hadn't bestowed for years. Mal was not there to say goodbye, nor did he welcome him home at the end of his final deployment.

Ethan walked to the window and looked out into the bright sunshine reflecting off the cars in the car park.

"I'm happy to help anytime," he said.

"And I'm happy to have your help. Mal's not as quick as he used to be."

"You know I love engines."

There was a pause before Blake spoke. "You should be getting a proper income from the place, not working-man's wages."

"We've been over this before." Ethan turned back. His brother's face looked haggard against the white pillowslip. "Anyway, a working man is what I am. Employed part-time as needed." He nodded at the cast on Blake's arm. "Which is right about now. Mal said you'd have a list of jobs for me."

"Damn it, Ethan." Blake slapped his good arm on the bed. "He can tell you just as well as I can what needs doing."

"I know, but you're his favourite method of communication when it comes to me." Ethan drew up a chair. "Don't worry about it. I prefer it this way. Fewer arguments."

A rattling sound was followed by movement at the door. A nurse entered. She towed a small machine with one hand and gripped a clipboard in the other.

Ethan moved out of the way while she poked and prodded at Blake and recorded her observations. She gave him tablets and watched while he swallowed them. Finally she straightened the sheet across her patient's bare chest and gathered up her things.

"You need some sleep," she said to Blake then raised her serious eyes to Ethan. "It's a bit early for visitors but you're obviously his brother. Don't stay long."

She turned on her heel and left, the wheels of the machine rattling after her.

"They say we look alike," Blake said. "I can't see it."

"Mal's height, Barb's colouring. That's about it."

They fell silent. Blake's hand fidgeted with the sheet.

"The old man's mellowing a bit, you know," he said.

"Not enough to accept a son who went to war." Ethan could feel the tension across his shoulders. He reached back and dug his fingers into the muscles.

"Barb misses you." Blake's dark look deepened. "I know what that feels like."

"We're a weird bunch." Ethan forced a smile to his lips. There was no point talking about all this stuff. It never changed anything.

Blake rubbed at his eyes. "That shit makes me light headed."

Ethan took a notepad from his pocket and the stub of a pencil. "Give me your list and I'll get out of here so you can sleep."

By the time Blake had finished his eyelids were drooping and Ethan had scribbled instructions across several pages.

"Get some rest." He stood up. "I'll ring you if I need to."

"I don't know where my mobile is," Blake said. "They've put all my things somewhere."

"You don't need it at the moment. I can always ring the hospital." Ethan gripped Blake's good shoulder. "Take care, bud."

Blake's eyelids fluttered shut then flew open again. He grabbed Ethan's arm.

"There could be someone at my place," he said.

"By someone I assume you mean a woman?" Ethan shook his head. Since his divorce Blake had chased anything in a skirt.

"Jenny's not like that." Blake's voice became a mumble. "She's a keeper."

Ethan watched as his brother's eyes closed.

How many times had Blake said that about the various women in his life including the one he'd married who'd nearly cost him the family farm? At least that union had produced grandchildren for Barb and Mal. Ethan had been besotted by his niece and nephew as they grew from babies to toddlers but life in the army meant he hadn't seen them much and hardly at all since the divorce. He'd thought about having his own. Slight problem of not having a partner long enough to make it permanent.

Ethan looked at the list he'd scribbled. No fishing this week by the look of it. He glanced at his brother, his face now relaxed in sleep.

"Rest easy, bud," he said.

Several hours later after a trip to swap his bike for Blake's ute, Ethan turned off the highway, the back of the ute loaded with spare hoses, oils and assorted machinery parts. He followed the dirt track up the hill to the homestead Blake inhabited. The property adjoined the original family land where Mal and Barb still lived, but their home was twenty kilometres away over the hills as the crow flies, further by road. The two properties were divided by the hills and a creek. East of the hills Mal managed the sheep country and on this western side, Blake's country was better for crops. They worked together but apart, which suited them both.

Ethan pulled in at the back of the house and rolled to a stop by the gate into the yard. The freestanding garage was open and empty except for assorted boxes and bags. There were no other vehicles about.

Ethan was relieved. He wasn't in the mood to make small talk with this Jenny.

The cat miaowed at him from the verandah. Blake wasn't into pets but he'd allowed a cat when his children were little. They'd called it Pookie. The wife and children were gone but the cat remained. At least a cat could look after itself for a while.

The cat called again.

Ethan went through the gate then stopped to take in his surroundings. The ramshackle garden had been tidied to the point where it actually looked like someone cared. Blake certainly never had. Ethan looked around as he slowly followed the path to the back verandah. The weeds were gone, roses had been pruned and lavender bushes trimmed. A row of annuals had been planted along both sides of the path.

A small cloud of flies buzzed around a red clump near the back door. He poked at it with his boot as the cat tried to rub against his leg.

"You've been catching rabbits, Pookie." He kicked the remains of the baby rabbit into the garden.

The cat let out a long complaining miaow.

Ethan glanced towards the bowls of food and water. All empty. Not surprising but they were pristine clean. Blake fed Pookie as if he was a hen, scattering dry food everywhere. The build-up of old food that usually littered the concrete around the bowls was gone.

Someone had given the verandah a scrub. Not Barb, she had trouble enough with her own house and she wasn't a fussy house-keeper. Her garden was cared for but ramshackle, no rows or order. Perhaps it was the doing of this Jenny that Blake had mentioned.

Ethan stuck his head through the back door.

"Hello," he called.

The only response was another wail from Pookie.

"Okay, cat."

Ethan picked up the empty bowls and refilled them from the supplies in the laundry. Pookie crunched on the dry food. Ethan left her to it. He shut the door to the house. He had no desire to look any further into Blake's private business. Perhaps this woman was the right one. Ethan hoped so.

He retraced his steps along the path, once more taking in the neat appearance and noticing smaller plants he hadn't known existed there. He shut the yard gate and went back to the ute. He would be spending his days in the sheds going over machinery left idle since last harvest. He gave a brief thought to Jaxon's sister. He'd prom-ised to keep an eye on her but she'd given him the impression she wouldn't take kindly to that. What was of more concern, there'd be no fishing for a while. He'd have to eat something else for dinner.

CHAPTER

5

Savannah lugged the bag and box of groceries into Jaxon's shack. The musty smell of mice greeted her straight away. She pressed her lips together and tried not to breathe deeply. She needed something to eat before she tackled the mess in the pantry.

She turned on the tap and was rewarded as the stream of water turned hot.

"At last," she whispered.

She washed down the bench beside the sink, gave a cup and a plate the same treatment and set about making herself some breakfast. Normally she started the day with freshly brewed tea but it was more like brunch time now. Coffee was what she needed.

Once the meal was ready, she crossed to the wall of glass facing the river and pulled up one of the thin venetian blinds that covered the sliding door. Light flooded the room. She pulled up a second then unlocked the door and slid it open. Fresh air flowed inside and she allowed herself to take a long deep breath.

She looked at the small dining table then back out at the verandah. The end closest to Ethan Daly's boundary was enclosed on
two sides, with a small wooden table and two chairs tucked part
way into the space. At least it was hidden from his house. Perched
up on its stilts, Ethan's pole house reminded her of her little place
in Adelaide with the block of flats so close to the side fence. She
decided it would be better to eat her meal out on the verandah than
inside. Broom in hand she swept off the setting, retrieved her coffee
and salad roll and sat down to enjoy them.

After several mouthfuls she sat back and picked up her coffee. She
took a sip and tilted her head back. Above her, thick wooden rafters
supported the tin roof. She remembered from her first inspection,
when Jaxon had been preparing to buy it, that the bones of this old
place were good.

She looked down at the concrete under her feet. It met lawn
that, in turn, stretched down towards the river. Between her and
the four houseboats below were a couple of shaggy trees, perhaps
peppertrees, providing some screening between the boats and the
shack. Large gum trees scattered along Ethan's side of the boundary down to the bank. Framed between the two lots of trees was
the river. Across the wide expanse of water, the low bank opposite
was dotted with towering gums and scrawny saplings and beyond
them the vegetation was thicker, forming a wall of varying shades
of green. Birds swooped and glided but other than their occasional
calls there was little other noise. Apart from Ethan's house she could
see no other signs of habitation.

She sighed, leant back in her chair and stretched out her legs. The
ache in her left leg had gone. Her eyes drooped shut for a moment.
The sound of an engine made her sit up, probably Ethan returning
from wherever he went. Savannah turned her head to listen. The
noise was coming from in front, not behind.

A small boat appeared from her left. There was one person huddled down at the back. She watched as the boat sped along then suddenly veered towards the houseboats. She jumped to her feet, grimacing as a sharp jab of pain caught her again. It looked like the guy was going to drive right into the moored boats then he disappeared behind them and continued on up the river.

"Maniac," Savannah called as the sound of the motor faded, replaced by the slap and bang of a series of waves hitting the houseboats and rolling onto the bank.

She walked across the lawn and stood on the bank watching the waves spread up the sandy slope then slide back. Parts of the low cliff were eroded. No wonder. There must be boats going up and down the river regularly, other houseboats among them, and she'd seen ads for paddle-steamers. She stepped back a little. The edge could be quite unsafe. Why hadn't Jaxon made a proper landing?

She turned back to the shack. She had no understanding of rivers and houseboats and houses that didn't have proper hot water.

"You'd better get back here quick smart, Jaxon," she muttered.

She gathered up her cup and plate and steeled herself to go back inside to deal with the mess in the pantry. The thought of those little four-legged vermin gave her the creeps. What if they ran up her arms or her legs?

Savannah went to her bedroom and opened her bag. She changed from jeans to trackpants, borrowed a pair of thick socks from Jaxon's drawer which she pulled on to encase the legs of her pants. Back in the kitchen she snapped on rubber gloves. Small broom in hand and rubbish bin close by, she stepped up to the pantry.

"Coming ready or not," she said and flung open the door.

The light flicked on but nothing moved. She reached in with the handle of the broom and shifted a cereal box that had chew marks on one corner. It revealed a trail of white flour from the packet next to it and some black blobs she assumed were mouse droppings. Feeling braver, she poked a few more packets and shifted some containers. No sound and no movement other than her own.

"Right!"

Savannah dragged the bin into the space beside her. She reasoned anything in a jar, can or unopened packet without chew marks should be okay. It didn't take long to get everything out. The ruined items filled the bin and the rest were stacked on the sink to be disinfected. She swept and scrubbed. When she was satisfied the pantry was clean she searched every inch for a place where a mouse could get in. On her hands and knees she found small gaps where the pantry supports met the wooden floor. The linoleum had also been cut away. She pulled the steel wool apart in tufts and used it to plug the holes, then she set the traps.

With the pantry clean she washed and replaced the useful items, added her own stash of groceries and started on the kitchen. She couldn't stop there. She opened all the windows and went through the living area with broom and then mop. She scrubbed the toilet and the bathroom. She tackled Jaxon's bedroom and even changed his sheets. The set on the bed looked and smelled like he hadn't changed them for a long time. She dusted the family photo but left it facedown. Her bedroom appeared tidy but she decided a sweep and mop wouldn't hurt.

She pushed the door to and froze. Behind the door, jammed between the frame and a rickety chest of drawers, was a full-length mirror. She saw the deformed angular person looking back at her and turned away. A wave of heat swept over her.

There were several sheets in the old cupboard where Jaxon kept his linen. She took one out, retrieved the packet of drawing pins she'd found in his pantry and used the heel of her boot to tack the sheet over the mirror's wooden frame. There was no way she wanted to catch a glimpse of her crippled body whenever she got dressed.

By the time Savannah had finished the cleaning, her legs and arms ached and she was soaked in perspiration. She gave a thought to Jaxon's office, but there was barely any floor space in there and she was well and truly over cleaning and needed a shower. She tugged off Jaxon's socks and sat back to wriggle her toes. The cool air around them was a relief. She'd dusted the venetian blinds that covered the front glass and left them pulled up and the door wide open. Once more she looked at the river.

While she'd been cleaning she'd been aware of motors as a few boats went back and forth, more sedately than the one she'd seen earlier, but now that she'd stopped there was silence. Leaves rustled, moved by the breeze, and there was the occasional call of a bird and buzz of an insect. She could be the only person left on earth and yet she felt so exposed.

She'd been about to strip off and jump in the shower. Instead, she shut and locked all the doors and windows and lowered the blinds. Only when she felt everything was totally secure did she take the shower she longed for. She didn't linger. She was in and out quickly and dressed in fresh clothes. She looked around the gloomy interior. Now the shack felt claustrophobic. She shook her head. She'd been living alone most of the time since she'd left school. What was so different about this?

She pulled up two of the front blinds and slid the door open a little. If she did that at her house in the city, the sounds of traffic and human movement and voices would flood in. She looked out at the river and the trees beyond. How did Jaxon stand the isolation?

She turned back to the living area. Now that she'd cleaned everything she had nothing to do. It was late afternoon already and her grumbling stomach reminded her she'd eaten little today. She went outside to retrieve the last of her things from the car – her tea-making gear and her exercise equipment. At least Jaxon's living area was a good space for her to work out and she could either watch his large TV or the river view while she did it.

She made herself a pot of tea and cut up some of the fruit she'd bought at the shop. Once again she sat out on the verandah. What was she going to do? There was no word from Jaxon and it appeared he'd been gone for at least a week already. She tried to recall the phone conversation they'd had just a few days ago. He'd begged her to come. Said he had some urgent business and needed someone to look after the place for a few days.

She had run out of excuses to stay away. He knew she was between jobs. She gave a snort. Between jobs was a polite way of saying she couldn't keep a job. After her accident the recovery had been long. It had taken her a while to find someone who would employ a partly crippled woman who tired easily. Her brother knew she liked to keep busy. He'd been so convincing, as Jaxon could be. It was only for a little while, he'd said, just to keep an eye on things.

"Well, here I am," she said aloud. "Now what?"

As if in answer to her question, Jaxon's phone began to ring.

Savannah struggled to her feet and swept a searching look around the living area. Where was the phone? The ringing was slightly muffled. She looked towards the closed door alongside her bedroom – the office.

She reached the phone just as the answering machine cut in.

"Hello," she said over the top of Jaxon's recorded message.

"Hello," a woman's voice responded. "Have I reached J&S Houseboats?"

It was hard to concentrate with the distraction of Jaxon's voice saying something similar.

"I'm sorry," Savannah said. "I don't know how to stop the answering machine." She glared at the flashing buttons. This phone was totally different from any she'd used before. She jabbed at one of them but nothing happened. A high-pitched squeal sounded and finally the line was clear.

"Hello?" the voice queried.

"Yes, I'm here. I'm sorry about that." Savannah tried to sound calm.

"I'm ringing to confirm a houseboat booking. I transferred the money this week but I haven't had a receipt or a reply."

"I'm sorry," Savannah said, although the only one who was going to be sorry was Jaxon. "My brother's not here right now. Can I get your name and number and I'll call you back?"

"Today?"

Savannah hesitated. It was already late and she had no idea how she was going to track Jaxon down.

"He's away for a couple of days. I'll try to contact him but it may take me a while. I'll get back to you as soon as I can."

"My money ..."

"I'm sure it's gone through fine." Savannah hurried to reassure the woman though she hardly felt confident to do so. "What's your name and contact number?"

She took the information, reassured the woman again and hung up.

"Damn it, Jaxon," she growled. "What are you up to?"

She tapped her fingers on the desk and looked around. The calendar drew her attention. It was already turned to September. She pulled out her phone. Today was the first of September. There was nothing written in any of the boxes; nothing to suggest appointments, work or any kind of commitment. There were tufts of paper around the staples where the previous months had been ripped off.

October, November and December were blank. He must have some way of managing bookings.

Then she noticed two large black books jammed between the phone book and a fat plastic folder. She tugged out the one that had *Diary* written on its spine. An envelope slipped from its pages.

Her name was written across the front in Jaxon's untidy scrawl. A sudden surge of dread welled inside her. She wanted answers and hopefully they'd be inside this letter, but would they be what she wanted to know?

She went back to the kitchen. She didn't drink often but she'd noticed Jaxon had left a few beers in the fridge. With one in hand, she sat at the dining table and ripped open the envelope. There were several pages inside. The top one was a letter and the rest appeared to be instructions, account numbers and diagrams.

It didn't take her long to run her eyes down the page.

"Damn it, Jaxon! You bloody idiot."

Stunned, Savannah flung the letter down and pushed back from the table. Her beer bottle teetered. She reached out to grab it but was too late. Beer frothed and spluttered onto the table.

She cursed as she righted the bottle and struggled to her feet to get a cloth. Her anger was temporarily diverted to cleaning up the spill. When she was done she snatched up the bottle and took a swig of the frothy liquid.

The letter lay on the table, its edges damp with a brown stain. The brink of the beer puddle had reached it before she'd got back with the cloth. She glared at the paper. Surely she must have misread it.

She lowered herself to the chair, picked up the letter and read it through again, slowly this time. Nothing changed with the second reading. Jaxon was an irresponsible little prick. He was going to be away a while, possibly for as long as two months. His electrical business was fine, all bills paid but without that income it was only the houseboat business that paid his mortgage. If it didn't make money he would default on his loan – and Savannah was his guarantor. Her little house was all hers but she currently had no job.

Their parents' death had left them both with a nest egg. Hers had been augmented by the compensation from the accident. She'd used it wisely. She had a home and money put away. Now that was all at risk.

She felt sick and angry all at once. Back on her feet, she paced the room. She had her own life to live. He was the one who'd wanted to make the change to living in the country. Now he was saying he needed to get away and stretch his wings, and for two months.

"How can you put this on me, Jaxon?" she raged.

CHAPTER
6

Somewhere there was a pulsing thud. Savannah stirred. The sound wasn't in her head but coming from beyond her body. She opened her eyes. A surge of panic coursed through her. Everything was black. She rolled onto her back. Then she remembered. This wasn't her bed. She was in Jaxon's shack. Her anger at her brother returned.

She lay still, waiting for her eyes to adjust. With no streetlights and no moon, the room around her remained firmly black. The distant pounding noise continued. She groped for her phone. It was only eleven o'clock. She felt like she'd been asleep for hours. After her early meal and short session in front of the television, the last of the sun's rays had still glowed behind the curtain when she'd put her head on the pillow. Exhausted, she'd fallen straight to sleep.

She pushed the torch function on her phone and made her way to the kitchen. At least the clock on the microwave gave a faint light to guide her. In the bathroom the pounding was louder and she could hear music. She unlocked the back door and stuck her head out. Definitely music playing somewhere close by. The cold night air made her shiver. She stepped outside. The concrete was damp under her bare feet. She wrapped her arms around herself, poked her head around the corner and looked up. There was a glow from a light somewhere at the back of Ethan's place. The music had to be coming from there.

She went back inside, shivering from the cold and wide awake. Damn! She hadn't had a disturbed night for a long time. Going to bed so early meant she'd had just enough sleep to get by. She flicked on the lamp in the living area and dragged the blanket from the end of her bed. Jaxon's couch was large and comfortable. She wrapped herself in the blanket and flicked on the television but she could still hear the pulsing thump emanating from next door. She surfed the channels then stabbed the off button. There was nothing of interest to watch.

The thumping was louder. She bunched the blanket around her shoulders and switched on the kettle. A nice cup of chamomile tea was what she needed. While she waited for it to brew, she dug her old beanie out of her bag. Immediately an image of her mother's solemn but gentle look came to mind. The beanie had been hand-knitted from assorted wool, leftovers from childhood jumpers, and handed over with insistence it be worn against the early morning cold of Savannah's winter runs. She had shoved the multi-coloured monstrosity into a bottom drawer. One of her friends must have discovered it after the car accident. It was amongst her personal items in rehab. A funny-looking thing, but it was a connection with her dead mother and warmth for her shaved head during that first long cold winter alone. She wouldn't describe herself as senti-mental and yet she hung onto it still and wore it when she could.

She tugged it down over her ears. Her head felt instantly warmer but it did little to muffle the thudding of Ethan's music. She took her cup of tea to the table and sat huddled under the blanket. She glared at the model motorbike in the centre of the table. It was an ugly red and black thing made of resin or clay. Jaxon's letter was across the table where she'd dropped it. Anger surged again. She'd tried to ignore it before she went to bed but it was still there and Jaxon was not. She closed her eyes, willed herself to be calm and took a sip of her tea.

By the time she'd finished the tea she knew its relaxing effect wasn't enough to settle her. Thoughts of Jaxon's absence and his letter kept going around and around in her head. She'd only given the extra pages a cursory look. She hooked one arm out from under the blanket and reached across the table.

This time she ignored the letter and took a closer look at the pages underneath it. The first was a list of what he'd headed "Important Information" – the bank account for the houseboat bookings, username and password, the log on for his laptop. She didn't remember seeing a laptop. It must be in the office somewhere.

The next page was all about managing the houseboat bookings. By the time she'd read through it her head was spinning. However was she to manage all that? She didn't know the first thing about boats of any description let alone a houseboat. On the next page were diagrams and instructions. She read it but nothing made much sense to her. The last page was partly stuck to the one above. It had come off worse for wear after the beer spill. She eased it away but some of the page stuck and ripped. On it was listed names and phone numbers, and towards the bottom Jaxon had scribbled a final note. She peered closer to read his scrawl.

You should find the contacts above helpful for various things. The community here is very friendly. Ethan knows lots about boat engines and Faye at the general store will see you are looked after.

Savannah paused her reading. Faye hadn't given her the impression she was all that friendly.

Have fun and relax. This is a special place.

Savannah gave a snort. "If it's that special how come you've left?" she said.

One last thing. I don't want you to worry but there have been a few … things late …

Savannah twisted the page. This was where some of it had stuck to the previous page and bits of it were unreadable.

Just keep an eye out. Not sure about the neighbour … ight. Could be nothing. Ethan can be … mo … but it sh …

The closer she got to the end of the note, the fewer words she could read. The rest made little sense other than it seemed Jaxon was warning her about the neighbours.

"Ethan can be what?" She moved the paper from side to side. Then she put on the main light and stared at it closely but the writing remained unreadable.

"Damn it, Jaxon, what are you telling me?"

On the previous page he'd outlined the process for the houseboats, what needed to be done before and after hire. Ethan was the one she was meant to ask for help there, especially anything to do with engines. Then in his next notes Jaxon was saying something about watch out for the neighbour. What did it all mean and what did she know about houseboats? Nothing! Once more she vented her annoyance. Swearing at the empty house made her feel better.

She scratched at her forehead under her beanie. The pages were laid out across the table. She glanced at each one. Her eyes stopped on the page with the usernames and passwords. She picked it up and went into Jaxon's office. The laptop was there on the desk under a pile of brochures. With its lid shut she hadn't noticed it. She read the instructions again. The black box had to be on and plugged into the shared cable with the phone. She read further then checked the correct lights glowed blue: internet and wireless. The laptop came to life quickly. Much faster than the computer she had at home.

She clicked on the link to his bank account. Perhaps something there might give her a clue about what he was up to. A few minutes later she sat back in the chair, disappointed. This account was with a different bank from the one that held Jaxon's mortgage. All the transactions appeared to be for the houseboat business. She could see where people had transferred money into it for deposits; the latest being the name of the woman who'd rung that afternoon. The black diary had her booking recorded in it.

Savannah opened the other book that was a kind of ledger. In it were the names of the houseboats, the dates, the name of the person booking and their personal details. She could see where she was supposed to record the $600 deposit paid. It was for the houseboat *Tawarri*.

Savannah paused, pen in hand. *Tawarri* had been the name of their family home. The engraved brass sign from her mother's family farm was fitted to the front wall of their home in Adelaide. She assumed the sign had still been on the house when it was sold. The other three boats were named *Our Destiny*, *Riverboat* and *River Magic*. It had never entered her mind that Jaxon might be sentimental about the name. He'd been a baby when the property was sold.

She entered the amount in the ledger then turned back to the instruction page and followed his steps to create an electronic receipt. She clicked on the desktop link to his email account. She hoped she might find a clue to his whereabouts there but once again when she logged in she could see the emails were all about hiring houseboats. Her enthusiasm ebbed away. The address was obviously just for the houseboat business, there was nothing personal she could see at a quick glance. She emailed the receipt to the address he'd recorded and ticked it off in the receipt column. Jaxon's processes were clear and easy to follow. She was surprised and just a little impressed. They had good bookkeeping skills in common.

She logged off the computer and closed the books. At least she was used to office work. She frowned as she thought about her last job working in a small real estate office. In hindsight it hadn't been a good idea to call the boss a dickhead to his face – even if it was accurate. Her frown turned to a smile. The look on his face had been worth it.

The result was there was no longer any job requiring her presence in Adelaide. That had become a bit of a pattern. It was six years since the car accident and she'd spent most of it in survival and recovery mode. She'd turned away from the fitness instructing she'd loved before the accident and taken whatever she could get that had nothing to do with gyms.

Her first job had been doing the books for a guy with a mowing round. She wasn't up to long hours at that stage. Turned out neither was he. He wasn't a hard worker. He went bust. But by then she was a lot stronger. Her next job was working the counter in a bakery. The other employees were silly young things with nothing to talk about but boys and what colour they were going to dye their hair on the weekend. She'd eventually become fed up with them and given them a mouthful – they'd called her a bitch. The boss had said they were overstaffed and as the last one in she was the first one out. There'd been a couple more short-term jobs and then office help in the real estate agency. Once again her inability to tolerate fools and her sharp tongue had got her into trouble.

She had no pets and what garden she did have could survive at this time of the year without water. No close friends would be wondering where she was. The block of flats on one side of her house meant she never knew her neighbours. Only old Mr Thomas on the other side might wonder if she didn't appear. She'd better ring him and let him know she'd be gone for a while. He would take the junk mail out of her letterbox.

She sat back and pulled the blanket close around her. Gradually she became aware of the silence. Ethan's music had stopped at last. She jumped at a loud clack from the pantry – a mouse trap.

CHAPTER

7

The sound of an approaching vehicle and yapping dogs drew Ethan out from under the truck. He was on his feet and wiping his greasy hands on a rag by the time the ute pulled up next to him. He dropped the rag. The two dogs tied to the ute's tray strained towards him, barking excitedly. He patted them both and ruffled their heads before turning his attention to their master.

"Mal." Ethan nodded at his father as he came around the back of the ute.

"How's it going here?"

"Not too bad."

"Blake give you a list?"

"Yep." Ethan patted his shirt pocket.

One of the dogs gave a small whine. Ethan looked at the pair of them flicking their watch from him to his father.

"Inconvenient time for Blake to have an accident," Mal said, peering under the open bonnet of the old truck. His long hair, almost grey now, pulled back in his customary ponytail, hung out from under his battered hat.

"I guess so."

"The crops are looking the best I've seen in a few years. If this warm weather keeps up we might have to bring everything forward."

Ethan remained silent. Farming was such a fickle business; wonderful one day, terrible the next. He much preferred working on engines. Things could go wrong with them but they made sense to him. The weather was too unpredictable.

"Much on the list?"

Ethan thought about the things Blake had asked him to do. "I haven't got to the harvester yet but I've changed the oil in all the engines, there's a tyre needs patching and I've replaced a couple of hoses."

"You've been busy."

Ethan looked at his father but Mal had already turned away, making a show of inspecting the truck's tyres.

"Gypsy didn't need much work," Ethan said following a few steps behind.

"Blake keeps it in good shape." Mal kicked the front tyre with the toe of his boot. "They made them simpler back then."

"She's slow to start, almost misses a beat then she purrs like a kitten."

"No." Mal ran his hand over the rusting front mudguard. "More like an old lioness."

They really only kept the old truck to shift field bins from one paddock to another but it had sentimental value as well. When Blake and Ethan were young, Mal and Barb would load it up with camping gear after harvest. They'd drive across country a couple of hours to a beach on Yorke Peninsula where they'd spend two glorious weeks, swimming, crabbing, fishing and living under canvas.

Blake had called it their gypsy caravan and the name had stuck. As they got older the two of them had learnt to drive it. Helping his father tinker under the old truck's bonnet was probably where Ethan developed his interest in engines.

"What are you smiling about?"

Mal's question brought him back. Ethan turned to look into his father's eyes. There was a softness in his face Ethan hadn't seen for a long time. Was he remembering those good times too?

"It's a wonder it still goes after what we put it through."

Mal slapped the door of the truck. "They were built to last back then."

They were both silent.

One of the dogs gave a short bark.

Mal stepped back. "Rust'll get her eventually," he said sharply. "Like a cancer, it eats away."

He strode back to the ute.

"Blake's coming out of hospital tomorrow," he said when he reached the driver's door. "He's busted his arm pretty badly and the burn on his leg was bad. He'll be staying with us for a bit."

"I'll keep an eye on things here."

Mal gave a sharp nod. "Don't forget to put your hours in."

Ethan opened his mouth then closed it again.

Mal was already climbing into the cab.

Ethan turned away as the dust from the moving vehicle swirled around him. "Nice talking to you, Dad." He tapped his hand on the side of the truck. "Where were we, Gypsy?"

By the time he reached home the cloudy sky was orange and pink and the trees across the river were throwing black shadows over the water. Jasper was pleased to see him. Ethan only locked him up if he was going to be away all day. The enclosure took up most of the space under the house and was kitted out with everything the dog needed.

"Come on, mate," Ethan said as he opened the gate.

He grasped the dog either side of its face and gave it a playful tussle.

"Let me check on the curry and we'll go for a quick walk."

Ethan could smell the curry before he opened the door. The delicious aroma from the slow cooker made his mouth water. At least tonight he'd be able to eat at a decent hour. He'd put in three full days' work at the farm since he'd left Blake in the hospital. The first two nights he'd been late home and it had taken a while to prepare his meal. He'd dozed in the chair and then he'd been restless, unable to sleep until the early hours of the morning. Determined to break that pattern and be more organised, he'd set the curry going before he left this morning.

He turned the cooker off then filled a glass with water and drank it down in a few gulps. Even though the outside temperature was still warm he picked up his jumper. Once the sun went down the night would quickly turn cold. Just as he stepped out onto his back landing Jasper began to bark in the tone that meant visitors.

"Damn," Ethan muttered.

He looked down the stairs to Jasper who was facing the side fence. Ethan sighed. Not visitors, he was guessing it was Savannah. His back steps were screened from Jaxon's shack by the little garden shed on Jaxon's side of the fence. The fence was only chicken wire. There'd been no need for anything permanent. It was just to mark the boundary for the dog.

"Jasper, sit," Ethan commanded as he went down the stairs. Once his head was lower than floor level he could see her outline in the fading light. She was standing back from the fence, no doubt wary of Jasper. There was no longer a jungle of weeds on her side.

He hadn't even noticed when he'd come home. She must have had the mower out.

"You've been busy," he said as he reached ground level. "You managed to start Jaxon's archaic mower."

"It took a while but I got it going."

Was that pride in her tone? It was hard to see her face in the gloomy last light of the day.

"I was just taking Jasper for a walk."

"I realise you're busy but I don't know when best to catch you," she said quickly.

"Do you need something?"

"No ... well, yes."

She took a step closer to the fence. Jasper stood up and she hesitated.

"Sit," Ethan said. "He won't hurt you. He's a big teddy bear."

Savannah glanced down at the dog. "I'm not an animal person."

Ethan patted the top of Jasper's head. Surprise, surprise, he thought. Out loud he said, "Drop."

Jasper immediately sank to his belly.

"You need my help?" Ethan asked.

"Yes." Savannah stepped a little closer.

Ethan could see her gaze flick between him and Jasper. The dog remained still.

"It seems Jaxon's gone for a while," she said, "and he's left me to take care of his houseboat business."

"I got that impression."

She stepped right up to the fence, her face suddenly lit by the sensor light at the corner of his house. She looked apprehensive. Surely not still about the dog? Jasper hadn't moved.

"That's where I need your help," she said.

"Something wrong with one of the engines?"

"No ..." She put her hands to her hips. "I don't know."

Ethan frowned. Now he was confused. "You don't know?"

"Damn it." She threw her hands in the air. "I don't know anything about houseboats. I don't know anything about any kind of boat, full stop."

Ethan's frown deepened. "Jaxon said you'd take care of the houseboats."

"I can do the paperwork but as far as actually doing things on the boats." She let out a sharp rush of breath. "I've read through the instructions he left me several times and I may as well be reading another language for all the help they are." She shook her head. "Jaxon can be so unreliable. I don't know what he was thinking."

"Neither do I, I'm afraid," Ethan replied. That was true enough. Jaxon had said he'd be gone for several weeks but Ethan had never thought of him as unreliable. He'd assumed Jaxon had called on his sister because she could manage in his absence and she had the necessary qualifications. Jaxon had wanted her to take a break from some issues she had in the city. Ethan could understand she wouldn't want to tinker with motors. That wasn't for everyone but ... He leaned closer. "You're saying you've never driven a houseboat and you know nothing about them?"

"Nothing. Zero." She waved her hands back and forth one over the top of the other. "Zilch."

"You don't have a ticket?"

Lines wrinkled across her forehead. "A ticket for what?"

"You have to have one to show people how to do turnarounds."

"Turnarounds?"

The puzzlement on her face told him everything. Ethan didn't like the comings and goings of people and boats so close to his little patch of river, but he hadn't imagined it would end like this. Jaxon had made a major stuff-up.

"Did your brother leave a customer list? You'll have to ring and cancel."

"Trust me, I'd like nothing better than to pack up and go home but … I don't have a choice."

"I'm not sure what you want me to do."

She took a deep breath. The harsh light highlighted a scar on her forehead just below her hairline he hadn't noticed before.

"I don't know where to start. Jaxon's left instructions about fuel, sewerage tanks, steering, mooring, cleaning – I think that's the only thing I understand."

"So you want me to …?" Ethan shrugged his shoulders and Jasper stood up. It was dark now and there was no moon, too late for a walk tonight.

"Jaxon said you knew lots about boat engines."

"I'm a mechanic." It felt good to say that. Mechanic was how he wanted to be known.

"Do you have this ticket?"

Ethan hesitated. He had done the training with Jaxon. It had been interesting at the time, something different, but he was only ever meant to be back-up in case of emergency.

"I was hoping you might be able to show me what he means for me to do."

Ethan could see it had taken a lot for her to ask for his help. She looked desperate and even though he wasn't sure what Jaxon was up to, he was a mate. There was nothing for it but to help.

"I can try," he said. "Although it's probably a bit late to start tonight."

"I don't expect you to do anything now," she said. "I just wanted to catch you. You don't seem to be home during the day."

"I'm working away at the moment."

"Oh." The worry lines deepened. "The first booking arrives on Monday."

"That's tomorrow."

She nodded.

Ethan ran his fingers through his hair. It felt greasy after being jammed under a hat. One of the downsides of letting it grow longer. He wasn't sure how this would work. There was still plenty to do at the farm.

"From what I understand the boat is ready to go," Savannah said. "But I have to be able to show the people how everything works and how to drive it. In a few days when they come back there will be lots more jobs to do."

"I could rearrange things," Ethan said. "Be here tomorrow to check all's okay."

"And be here when the people arrive?"

Ethan opened his mouth and closed it again. He could stay home, not go to the farm tomorrow. It didn't matter to him which days he worked.

"Sure," he said.

"Thank you." The relief in her voice hadn't removed the desperate look from her face. "I'll leave you in peace. See you in the morning."

"Sure," he said again.

She turned away then back. "You have a boat licence?"

"Yes, but you don't need one for a houseboat. Just as long as you have a driver's licence."

"That's one tick for me then." The hint of a smile crossed her face. "Thanks."

He watched her disappear from the edge of the light and round the corner. Jasper rubbed his head against Ethan's leg and he bent to give the dog a pat.

"What am I getting us into, old mate?"

CHAPTER

8

Savannah was up at first light the next morning. She did a quick work-out, showered and dressed and took her breakfast out onto the verandah. The air was crisp. A bank of fog clung to the river but above it there wasn't a cloud in the sky.

It was the first time since her sleepover in the car that she'd been outside so early. She stared towards the river. Trees began to appear, gradually becoming sharper as the fog slowly dispersed. The colourless sky was turning azure blue; funny how she didn't remember noticing those kinds of things in the city.

In the four days since her arrival she'd given the shack a total clean, mowed the rough grass and the lawn, weeded the tiny vegie patch and inspected the sheds. She'd read one of the Matthew Reilly novels from Jaxon's shelves and rearranged the rest of his books into some kind of order.

There had been no further sign of mice since the one she'd caught in the trap. The little devil had got past her steel wool.

She'd plugged the hole firmly since then. She'd gone over Jaxon's notes till she knew them by heart and worked out the system in his office. Yesterday she'd taken the keys from the hooks inside the cupboard door and she'd inspected the inside of each houseboat. She was surprised at how well-appointed each one was. They were floating motels with all mod cons. Another revelation had been the name *'Tawarri'* fixed to the front of the houseboat above the windows. Somehow Jaxon had ended up with the large sign that had originally hung on the gate to their grandparents' farm. She'd taken her pot of tea and sat on the sundeck of *Tawarri*, imagining herself on holiday and pondering her little brother's link to their family heritage.

A distant bark brought her back to the task at hand. No doubt Ethan was taking his dog for a walk. They hadn't made a time to meet, just said this morning. He could be over any minute. Apprehension gnawed inside her. Jaxon had obviously trusted him enough to ask for his help with the engines but what about the day to day? And what about this turnaround business? Jaxon knew she didn't have any experience with boats and certainly not the piece of paper Ethan had said was required. Why had her brother ever thought she could just turn up and know all there was to know about houseboats? She had to get help and Ethan was the only one available. She'd just have to keep an eye out for anything odd.

She went back inside, washed her dishes, made her bed and tidied away her gym gear. There was absolutely nothing more she could do until Ethan came. She picked up Jaxon's notes. She'd given up trying to call him but she knew exactly what she was going to say when she did get to speak to him. Anger was always ready to resurface when she thought about her brother.

A tap at the back door made her jump. She took a deep breath, counted to three and picked up Jaxon's instructions and the houseboat keys. She needed Ethan's help but she didn't want to appear too eager.

When she opened the door, the welcoming smile she'd planned barely stretched her lips. Ethan looked terrible. His eyes were bleary and his hair dishevelled. The light stubble that had given his face a rugged look a few days ago had grown into a thicker but ragged covering. It wasn't appealing. Perhaps this was the real Ethan coming out. Had Jaxon found him not truly trustworthy?

"Good morning," she said.

"Ready to check out these boats?" he replied.

With barely a look to see if she followed, he turned and set off for the river.

She pulled the door shut behind her. The cool of the early morning had been chased away by the sun and a swirling breeze of warm air. A set of keys fell from her fingers taking the paper with it. She made a sudden lurch forward to stomp her foot on the page to stop it blowing away and gasped as a stab of pain coursed down her leg. She stepped forward gingerly. The pain receded just as quickly, replaced by a dull ache. Ethan had disappeared around the end of the house. She gritted her teeth and set off after him.

By the time she reached the river he was inspecting the front of the first boat. It was pulled up onto the sloping bank just below Jaxon's lawn. Ethan was intent on what he was looking at and obviously didn't hear her approach. She reached him just as he stepped back, colliding with her. The force of his body knocked her backwards. Her feet went out from under her and she sat with a jolt on her bottom in the damp sand.

The pain that surged through her forced a guttural cry from deep in her throat. She closed her eyes against the wave of nausea. She took in a deep breath and held it.

"I'm so sorry." Ethan's alarmed voice reached her ears. "Don't move. Where are you hurt?"

The smell of stale alcohol and unwashed body odour worked like a dose of smelling salts. She flicked her eyes open. Ethan's face was close to hers, full of concern.

"I'm all right."

"You've lost your colour. Are you sure you're not hurt?"

"I'm okay," she snapped.

Ethan hesitated then offered his hand.

Savannah sucked in another deep breath. Damn her broken body. No matter how hard she worked it could still let her down. The pain was always there just below the surface ready to strike. It was hardly Ethan's fault she was a cripple.

She took his hand and used his strength to carefully ease herself upright.

"I thought you'd broken something," he said.

"I'm fine. The ground's soft." She let go of his warm hand and brushed at the back of her jeans. "Just a muddy behind, I suspect."

His eyes studied her, still full of concern.

She pulled her lips up in a grin. "Just an old war wound. It bothers me every so often."

The worry on Ethan's face turned to a frown.

"You've been in service?"

"Service?" Savannah rubbed her hand down her leg. He must mean the armed service. "No. It's just an expression."

Ethan pulled himself up straight. He was a good head taller than she was.

"Well, if you're okay we'll get on with it." His voice was distant now. All trace of concern gone.

Savannah frowned. People said she was prickly. Obviously Ethan had a dark side too. Maybe this was what Jaxon had wanted her to look out for. She'd certainly not seen signs of any other neighbours since she'd arrived.

"Have you got Jaxon's list?"

His voice snapped her out of her pondering. The paper and keys had fallen from her grip as she'd put out her hands to save herself. She eased herself down to gather them up. The ache went with her but no more sharp pains.

She looked into his eyes. Once more he was watching her closely.

"It's an old injury," she said. "Plays up every so often. I'm fine."

She handed over the slightly muddy, crumpled piece of paper. He looked down and studied it.

"Seems like Jaxon got them all ready to go before he left. Most of the work will be when the boat comes back. Which one's going out this afternoon?"

"*Tawarri*," she said and nodded at the boat directly behind him.

"Right, keys then. We'll take her for a spin."

"On the river?"

He gave her a look one might give a child then turned away to step onto the boat. "First we'll start the engine," he said.

"We?" The word came out in a whisper and was lost in the sound of the cabin door sliding open. She stepped carefully along the narrow gangplank and followed him inside to the open living area at the front of the boat.

"Make sure the throttle is in neutral," he said as she moved to stand beside him at the console. "Then you turn one key."

A motor sounded from the back of the boat.

"And then the other."

"Two keys?" she said as the motor sound grew louder.

"Two engines."

Ethan stepped around her.

"Now the ropes," he said over his shoulder as he went back outside.

Savannah followed him, watching as he loosened the ropes, coiled them and placed them aboard.

"Now the gangplank."

She shuffled out of his way as he dragged the metal walkway aboard and shut the gate filling the gap in the guardrails. She felt useless. Once again she wondered how on earth Jaxon had thought she could do this. It was as foreign to her as flying a plane.

"Let's go," Ethan said. "You whip down the back and check to see if anything's coming."

He winked at her and ducked back inside.

She made her way along the side of the boat and looked up and down the river. Nothing in sight. She retraced her steps. Ethan's wink played over in her mind. It had transformed his face. He'd appeared boyish, full of fun. Her thoughts spun in confusion. He'd greeted her in a surly manner, been both brooding and caring and now he was almost flirting with her.

"All clear?" he asked as she reached the door.

"Yes."

The blast from the horn startled her. She stepped back inside the cabin and looked around. There were couches in one area and near the front window a table with eight chairs. She wasn't sure whether to sit or stand. Behind Ethan there was a large swivel chair intended for the driver but he stood, his hands gripping the wheel. She opted to stand beside him. The sound of the motor changed. She put a hand on the console to steady herself as the boat reversed slowly from the bank. Ethan's look was now one of concentration.

Tawarri slipped past its fellow houseboats and out into the space of the river.

"You need to make sure at least one of the people hiring the boat is competent at driving it," Ethan said.

Savannah turned from the view through the huge front windows to look at him.

"You stay on board while they back out and make sure they can turn the boat around."

Savannah glanced out the window at the swirling water made by the turning boat and back at Ethan.

"Jaxon did this for every customer?" she asked.

"He did or I did if he wasn't able to."

Savannah watched as Ethan checked the river around him, moved a lever and spun the wheel. *Tawarri* did a complete turn and they were facing the other direction.

"This is the throttle," he said tapping the black levers in front of him. "This way's forward and the other way's reverse. Straight up and you're in neutral."

He moved the throttle then the wheel and the boat did a complete turn the other way.

Savannah watched through the glass as the scene changed from up the river to down the river.

"I could never do this," she said. She rubbed a hand across her forehead. How was she going to keep Jaxon's business turning over and save both their homes?

"I'm sure you'd learn but without your ticket it's no good anyway," Ethan said. "You have to be qualified to be able to supervise others in doing this."

Savannah gripped the back of the swivel chair.

"I guess I'm sunk," she said and grimaced at the irony of her words. "Figuratively speaking."

Ethan manoeuvred the boat back towards its mooring space. He cleared his throat and glanced her way.

"Not on my watch. I'm throwing you a lifeline." His lips turned up in a silly grin. "I can do this bit for you."

Savannah locked her gaze on his. Was he making a serious offer of ongoing help? "But there are so many other things to do besides driving the boats," she said.

"I know."

Savannah thought about Jaxon's booking schedule. "Maybe it won't matter too much. There are no more bookings until the weekend. Perhaps Jaxon will be back by then." Her voice projected a hope she didn't feel.

Ethan flicked a look in her direction then forward to the water. "I'm not sure you can count on that."

"Have you heard from him?"

She studied Ethan's profile. He wouldn't look at her. What was he hiding?

"Jaxon didn't tell me how long he'd be gone. I just got the feeling it would be a while."

"Damn," Savannah said.

"I'll help where I can but you're on a steep learning curve."

"Just what I need." Savannah had a sudden surge of self-pity.

"It depends on whether you're up to it."

Nothing in her life had been easy. Why would she expect this to be any different? She straightened. "I need this to work," she said. "I'm a quick learner."

"Good," he said. The houseboat nudged up onto the bank. "You're about to learn how to tie up a boat." He moved past her to the door. "Grab the rope on that side."

She followed him and watched as he cast his rope towards a large gum tree at the water's edge. She bent to pick up her rope. How hard could it be? The heavy weight of the rope was deceptive and her rope fell well short of the mooring pole on the riverbank that was her target.

"Doesn't matter," Ethan said as he slid the gangplank into place. "Just pick it up and walk it to the pole."

She watched how he tied his rope around the tree trunk then attempted to replicate the wrapping and knotting with her rope. Ethan helped her with the final knot. He tugged at the rope to test its strength.

"You'll soon get the hang of it," he said and left her to climb back on board.

He stopped the engines. Through the window she saw him pull his phone from his pocket, glance at the screen and put it to his ear. It was a short call. He came back out on deck stuffing the phone in his jeans pocket with one hand and jiggling the keys with the other.

"What time are you expecting the customers?" he asked.

"Three o'clock."

"I'll be back by then," he said. "In the meantime you should go over every room and make sure it's clean and ready, especially the sundeck."

He held the keys out to her as he passed and strode away.

Savannah sucked in a breath as she took them from him. She'd asked for his help with driving the boat but she didn't expect him to be giving her orders about everything. Jaxon's notes had indicated everything was ready. She turned to say the same to Ethan but he was already at the top of the path. She swapped the keys from one hand to the other, looked back at the boat then decided to leave it.

She followed Ethan's footprints up the slope. By the time she'd reached her back door she heard his motorbike rumble into life. She had a momentary pang of regret. She hadn't thanked him for his help. All the same she couldn't help the plea that left her lips.

"You'd better be true to your word, Ethan Daly, or I'm going to be in deep —"

The roar of the bike drowned out her words. Once more she felt vulnerable as the isolation settled like a cloak around her.

Ethan rolled his bike to a stop at the back gate of his parents' house. Both dogs had yapped at his tyres, now they circled the bike sniffing Jasper's scent. Ethan removed his helmet. He gave one of the dogs a nudge with his boot as it lifted its leg.

"You're a sight for sore eyes, little bro."

Blake hobbled along the path towards him. There was a small backpack slung over the shoulder of his good arm and a helmet dangling from his hand. The skin under his right eye was dark blue, a vivid contrast to his pale face. He didn't look strong enough to lift a cup of tea let alone look after himself.

Ethan shook his head. "Are you sure you should be going home?"

"I can't stand Barb fussing over me any longer."

Blake put the helmet on his head and slid the backpack from his shoulder. Ethan strapped it to the luggage rack then looked his brother up and down.

"I should have gone and picked up the ute but I'm short on time."

He couldn't see how Blake was going to get on the bike let alone hang on.

"So am I."

"Why don't I get Mal's ute? I can drop it back tomorrow."

"I want to get going. Mal and Barb will be back from town soon."

"A chance to say goodbye."

"I haven't told them I'm going."

Ethan paused doing up his helmet.

"I've left them a note," Blake said.

"We could pass them coming home."

"We can take the back way?"

"You're kidding?" Ethan shook his head again. "The ride will test you as it is without taking the back way."

"I'm feeling much better."

"Maybe from lying around all day. I think you should —"

"Stop fussing," Blake snapped. "You're as bad as Barb."

Ethan could see the determination on his brother's face.

"The back way it is," he said. "Get on."

"You get on," Blake said. "I'll be right."

Ethan stopped the head shake he was going to give and threw his leg over the bike. If Blake wanted to be pig-headed about it there was nothing to be done. He felt the bike shift under the extra weight as Blake climbed on behind him. A hand hooked into the top of his jeans and the corresponding knee wedged against his thigh. Looking down he could see Blake's right leg stuck out at an angle. This was going to be awkward. If only he hadn't promised Savannah he'd be back by three. Better still, Blake should have stayed another day with their parents.

"I'm ready." Blake's voice was brusque.

Ethan kicked the bike into life and eased it forward, turning in a long slow arc towards the track that would lead them across country, over hills and through the rough creek crossing to Blake's house.

The track was good in places and rough as guts in others. The creek crossing had been eroded by cutaways. Ethan tried to follow previous tracks made by the farm ute but it was tough going. Each time he had to stop to open and close a gate he took his time over it, giving his brother the chance to rest. At the last gate Blake got off the bike. They'd left the grazing country behind. This was his land – fertile cropping country. Hard to believe the difference a few kilometres could make. Blake took off his helmet and wobbled out into an almost waist-high paddock of canola. The long green stems reached skyward covered in buds promising flowers very soon. He bent over the stalks then slowly made his way back to where Ethan was waiting beside the bike.

A grin split Blake's face. With his black eye, pale skin and stubbly chin he looked ghoulish.

"All the crops are looking good but this canola is going to be a goldmine for us."

Ethan looked over the paddock of waving green plants. The strong sweet smell of opium poppies swamped him and he was back in the narrow fertile valley in Uruzgan. The survival of those crops was literally life and death for the poor farmers who tended them. While he understood his brother's delight, a low yield wouldn't bring about his death.

"Looks promising," he said.

"Don't get too excited, little bro."

Ethan gave a small shake of his head. "It's early days and farming's –"

"Not your thing." Blake cut him off. "I know."

He turned back towards the crop. Ethan followed his gaze. He'd been going to say unpredictable.

"It's got to be a bumper," Blake murmured.

Ethan remained silent. They always paid him for any work he did for them but other than that he knew little of the farm finances.

"I need this one to pay off," Blake said. "I nearly lost it with the divorce."

That was old news, Ethan thought. Blake's ex, Lucy, had been a bitch through and through. Blake didn't discover that until after he married her. Luckily their parents had made sure the two properties were in separate names, otherwise she could have wiped out the lot.

"You came to an arrangement. I thought she wasn't going to take the kids' inheritance?"

"Not until she'd bled it dry. Lucy's been playing that card ever since." Blake looked back at Ethan. "Now she's found some other schmuck to marry her. I can cut her loose as long as I pay for the kids. I've got no problem with that but her final payment will be a big one. It will be worth it to be rid of her but by the time we've done the paperwork and paid the lawyers ..." His words trailed away.

Once more he cast his eyes over the canola crop. Ethan looked up. It was a warm day for September. He was hot standing still in his riding gear. He wasn't sure if they needed heat or rain at this stage. Whatever it was he hoped it worked out for his brother.

"We'd better keep going," he said.

They both climbed back on the bike and Ethan drove along the track. Finally they passed the assorted sheds and he rolled to a stop at the house gate. Blake disentangled himself from the bike and leaned on the fence as he took off his helmet. Ethan unhooked the backpack.

"Want to come in for some lunch?" Blake asked. His face was grey now.

"Sure." Ethan wasn't hungry but any excuse to help get his obstinate brother settled was worth following up.

They went slowly up the path. Pookie appeared and began to weave between Blake's legs.

"Hello, buddy. Have you missed me?"

He bent to pat the cat and lurched forward.

Ethan grabbed his good arm.

"Whoa," he said. "How about we get you inside?"

Blake allowed him to take his weight.

"Boots," Blake said.

Ethan lowered his brother onto the chair near the door and helped him get his boots off then removed his own. The chair was a new addition, as was removing boots. After Lucy left Blake had never bothered.

Once more Ethan took Blake's arm and they squeezed through the back door and into the kitchen. Ethan pulled out a chair from the table and watched as Blake lowered himself onto it. The bike journey had taken its toll.

"There should be some baked beans in the cupboard," Blake rasped.

Ethan went to the pantry cupboard. He tugged open the door.

Blake let out a low whistle. At the same time Ethan caught a glimpse of something toppling towards him. He threw himself sideways, covered his head and crouched against the wall. There was a thud as something fell on the floor beside him. Ethan's heart pounded in his chest. The memory of his first vehicle recovery mission in Afghanistan engulfed him. It was as if he was there. He smelt the stench of burnt flesh.

"Hey, bro. It's only a tin of fruit. It didn't hit you, did it?"

Blake's voice came to him as though along a tunnel.

Ethan sucked in a breath and let it out slowly. He willed his hands to drop to his sides. As he reached for the tin he could see the tremor in his hand.

"Ethan?" Blake's voice was loud this time, urgent.

"I'm okay," Ethan said.

He straightened up, put the tin of fruit back in the cupboard and took out a tin of baked beans. Damn it, where had that reaction come from? It was a long time since he'd had one of those flashbacks. During his last deployment he'd had to recover several vehicles outside the wire. Even though there were Grunts providing security, it was not always enough to deflect an object. Sometimes it was just a rock thrown by kids, but it could also be some kind of homemade explosive.

He got busy heating the beans and making toast with bread he dug out of the freezer. Gradually his heart rate returned to normal and his hands regained their strength. Blake didn't say anything more to him, instead he made a fuss of Pookie who was happily purring in his lap.

Once the food was on the table, Ethan sat down. He cut Blake's toast into manageable bites for a one-handed man and watched as he began to eat. Ethan had no appetite for the bright orange beans in their sloppy sauce.

"Aren't you going to eat?" Blake said through a mouthful.

Ethan put a piece of soggy toast in his mouth and chewed it round and round. He had been hungry half an hour ago. This past week hadn't been a good one. He'd had trouble sleeping and bad dreams when he did. This episode was the first waking one he'd had in a while.

"You still having those flashbacks?" Blake's question pierced the silence between them.

Blake was a good mate but he hadn't been there. The thing was too hard to explain. Ethan would rather forget that part of his life and start a new one. His time in the army was over. He'd spent some time before his discharge with the psych. Ethan knew the drill and he knew he'd do okay. He was lucky, there were no physical scars. It was different inside his head though, where a smell or a noise could bring it all flooding back. Blake had spent enough time with him since his return from his last tour to know he still carried those memories.

"Not often."

"What does the quack say?"

"Haven't seen him in a while."

Blake opened his mouth to speak then shook his head. "Guess neither of us take kindly to interference."

His mobile rang. He took it from his shirt pocket and looked at the screen.

"Speaking of which, it's Barb. My escape must have been discovered."

"You'd better answer or she'll be over here."

Blake swiped the screen and put it to his ear.

Ethan cleared away the plates. He tipped his half-eaten portion into the bin and rinsed the dishes while Blake placated their mother.

"Ethan's here. I promise I'll take it easy." His tone was soothing. "Talk to you tomorrow."

"I could come back tonight after I've done this houseboat job," Ethan said as Blake put the phone down.

"It's a two-hour round trip."

"What will you eat?"

"There are more tins in the cupboard and leftovers in the freezer. Besides, I only have to last till tomorrow afternoon." He paused. "Jenny's taken some leave. She's coming to stay for a while."

"I can see she's already been here." In spite of the can that overbalanced, Ethan had noticed the inside of Blake's pantry cupboard was orderly and the benchtops had been cleared of clutter.

"You'll like Jenny."

Ethan pulled his lips into a smile. He'd heard that before. He glanced at the clock on the wall.

"Damn, look at the time. I've got to get back home."

"Who is this woman you're helping out? Is she single?"

Ethan snatched up his helmet.

"A mate's sister." He gave Blake a glare as he reached the door. "I've no idea of her marital status and I'm not interested."

He turned his back on his brother's raised eyebrows and bolted for his bike.

CHAPTER
10

Savannah was pacing anxiously when she heard the approach of a vehicle. She glanced at the time on the microwave. It was two-thirty. She knew Ethan wasn't back yet. She'd been listening for the return of his bike ever since he'd left.

She took a deep breath and stepped out onto the back verandah. A vehicle was pulled up in the drive. She could see four heads through the windows. A man unfolded his tall frame from the driver's side and leaned over the roof.

"You must be Savannah," he said.

She paused, surprised he knew her name.

"And you're the Warners?"

"And friends." He tapped the bonnet of his car. "I'm Fred. My wife Jan and I have been regular customers of Jaxon's. He told us when we booked that you'd be here when we came this time."

Once more Savannah hesitated. It was quite clear now Jaxon's trip was no spur of the moment event as he'd intimated to her. He must have been planning it for months.

Another car pulled in.

"That's the rest of our party of eight." Fred waved to the car behind his. "I assume it's everything as usual? We'll head down and unload then I'll come back to do the paperwork." He gave her a charming smile. "Will you be giving us the instructions, Savannah?"

"Yes … well no."

"We know what to do of course, but I know the rules must be followed."

"I have someone to show you," she said. "Ethan. He'll be here soon."

Savannah hoped that was correct. She didn't want to hold these people up if they were experienced and regular customers. In fact it seemed silly to step them through the rigmarole Ethan had shown her this morning.

"We'll start unloading, Pete," Fred called to the man driving the second car. "Back up and follow me."

The driver lifted a hand in acknowledgement and reversed his vehicle.

"I'll bring the keys," Savannah said.

By the time she reached the boat, Fred and three other men were already trooping up the gangplank hefting boxes and eskies. She smiled at the women standing to one side, chatting and laughing like old friends. They all looked to be around sixty, hair in various shades of blonde, jewellery dangling from necks and arms, figures trim. She could always pick the ones who worked out.

The same couldn't be said for their partners. Ahead of her the four men were all on the front of the boat. Fred was tall and a solid build but the other three sported rounded bellies pushing against their designer polo shirts. He was giving directions about where to put the eskies. One of the men saluted and they all chuckled. She felt a pang of envy for their friendship and the excitement of their holiday.

"Excuse me."

Savannah turned around. The women had bags in each hand and were lined up to follow the path to the boat. She stepped to one side to let them pass.

"They're our keys?"

She spun back. Fred was standing below her holding out his hand. A smile lit his face.

She hesitated wondering if she was supposed to go on board, do a final check.

"The old girl's safe with us." Fred's smile grew wider. "We've got a couple of virgins with us but we'll show them the ropes." He let out a loud guffawing laugh, took the keys that dangled from Savannah's outstretched hand and turned back to guide the first of the women across the gangplank.

Savannah frowned at him. What kind of party was this?

"Two of our friends have never been on a houseboat before." Jan was the last in the line and had stopped beside Savannah. "It's Fred's little joke."

"Come on, old girl," Fred called. "The sooner we've got everything aboard, the sooner we can pop those champagne corks for you ladies."

Savannah felt an inward shudder. Jan was either used to his patronising tone or oblivious. She took the hand he offered and stepped along the gangplank onto the boat. Fred gave her a pat on the bottom as she passed.

Savannah turned away. Gross, she thought as she trudged back across the lawn to the shack. Fred was a sleaze. She'd keep out of the way while they got organised. Hopefully Ethan would be back any minute.

She stood inside the shack and watched the loading of the boat through the sliding glass door. Once the clock on the microwave reached three o'clock she began to pace. A knock at the back door startled her.

"Savannah?"

Fred's singsong voice made her stiffen. She drew in a breath and went to the door.

"Hello again." Fred beamed at her as she pushed open the screen. "We're all ready to go. I'm assuming it's okay to park our cars in the area behind the shed as usual?"

"Yes." Savannah remembered that from Jaxon's notes.

"We'll do that and hopefully Ethan will be with us soon." Fred's smile got wider but his lips barely parted when he spoke. "We'd like to get going so we can find a spot to camp before dark."

"I'm sure he will be."

She watched through the screen as Fred and Pete drove their cars past the shack and tucked them in alongside Jaxon's big shed, out of sight from the road. As they were walking back the sound of a motorbike grew louder.

"Please be Ethan."

The bike roared into view and eased to a stop beside the two men. Jasper gave two quick barks from his side of the fence.

"Yes," she breathed.

She hesitated. Should she introduce them? They appeared to be doing that for themselves. Ethan had removed his helmet and was shaking their hands. Fred and Pete disappeared down the track with Ethan following. None of them had so much as glanced in her direction.

Savannah felt awkward. Should she go and watch what Ethan did? She walked back through the shack to the front windows. Ethan was already on board and Fred and Pete were untying the ropes.

There was a lot of activity on the deck of the houseboat. The ropes were wound up and the gangplank was pulled in. One of the men was signalling from the back. With a blast of its horn, *Tawarri* backed out into the river. Savannah kept watching as they manoeuvred around out in the middle, just like Ethan had done with her on board this morning. Then the houseboat was gliding back towards the bank again. Ethan appeared on deck and as the boat gently nudged the bank he climbed over the front rail and jumped to land.

There was another blast of *Tawarri*'s horn. Ethan lifted his arm in a wave and made his way back up the bank. Savannah hurried out to meet him.

"There you are," Ethan said. "I thought you must have been on board when I got here. Sorry I was a bit late."

"No problem." Savannah's anxiety had disappeared now that the customers were safely on their way.

"They're good to go. You shouldn't have any worries with them, barring the unforeseen of course. Several of them have driven houseboats before."

"Fred said he'd been a regular customer of Jaxon's."

"He was a bit full of himself but a couple of the other guys appeared to be sensible."

"That's good at least."

Jasper gave a series of barks.

"Coming, buddy," Ethan called in the direction of his yard. He picked up his helmet. "I'd better get home. He'll be keen for a walk."

"Oh." Savannah wasn't looking forward to another long period alone after the activity of people setting off on the houseboat. She was used to living on her own but it was different in the city. Out here it was so quiet.

A loud bang echoed from behind them.

Savannah's heart thumped. She spun and peered at the bush beyond Jaxon's shed.

"That sounded like a gun," she yelped.

"Know a bit about guns, do you?" Ethan looked at her. One eyebrow was raised and a small smile twitched on his lips.

"Well no," she said. "But what else could it be?"

"It probably was a gunshot. It'll be Gnasher taking a pot shot at something."

"Who's Gnasher?"

"Lives over the road in the bush."

"And he has a gun?"

"Several I think, but he's harmless."

"Harmless!"

"He's probably having a shot at a rabbit."

Savannah stared towards the distant bush. Was this the neighbour Jaxon had tried to warn her about? Perhaps Ethan wasn't the one to be wary of after all.

"You don't need to worry," Ethan said. "His property is fenced and he rarely leaves it."

Savannah looked back at this man she hardly knew. She'd been determined to keep him at arm's length and yet he was her only real connection here on this stretch of the river.

"Thanks," she said. "And thanks again for today."

"When does the next boat go out?"

"Not until Friday. The other three are all going out that afternoon for the weekend."

"I'll make sure I'm around on Friday."

That was four days away.

"Would you like to eat with me tonight?" she blurted. "A thank you for your help."

"No need. I told Jaxon I'd do what I could."

"Sounds like you were expecting me to know more about the boats though?"

"Maybe. Jaxon didn't exactly spell it out."

"Let me make it up to you with dinner."

"Thanks but I'm going to get an early night."

"I'm sorry," she said, oddly disappointed. "My brother hasn't been up-front with either of us."

"Water under the bridge. Look, I really should go. I'll see you on Friday."

She stepped back as he started his bike. He gave a nod of his head and rode away. She lifted her hand in a half wave. She listened as the sound of his bike faded then grew louder again as he entered his own yard. The bike stopped and Jasper gave several excited barks. She couldn't hear what Ethan said in response but she could hear the cheerful tone of his voice.

She sighed and went back inside. What had she been thinking in asking him to eat with her? She'd made herself seem desperate. She opened the fridge. Not much in there. She closed the door and glanced around. Her eyes stopped at the papers on the table.

She snatched up the pages and let out a groan through clenched teeth. Fred hadn't signed the paperwork or paid the rest of the deposit. She'd been so relieved when Ethan had finally turned up and Fred had been keen to get underway. They'd all forgotten the paperwork.

Savannah paced the room, tapping the papers against her other hand. There was little she could do now. She'd have to make sure she sorted it all out when they came back. She decided to do a work-out to clear her mind. She followed it up with a pot of tea and made herself something to eat from the meagre offerings in the fridge. Just as well Ethan hadn't taken up her offer. She'd have to go into town for more supplies tomorrow.

She watched television for a few hours but she was still restless and not feeling the least bit tired. The sun had long gone down and the outside temperature with it. She dragged on a jumper and took one of Jaxon's beers from the fridge. It was the last one. She'd have to buy more of those tomorrow as well.

Savannah flicked off the television. Instantly she heard the heavy thud of Ethan's music from next door. She popped the top off the beer and let herself out the sliding door onto the front verandah where she settled into a chair. Ethan's "early" must be different from hers, it was well after nine. The music was much louder outside, so close to the shared fence, but she was tired of being cooped up inside. Hopefully he'd kill the noise soon.

It was a beautiful cloudless night. There was just the sliver of a moon and a million twinkling stars in the sky. Not a sight she took in very often. She relaxed and sipped on her beer. Her eyes adjusted to the light and she stood up and wandered towards the bank. The deep throb of a motor sounded somewhere in the distance then faded away.

During the day to her left she could see quite a long stretch of river. She knew if she followed the water in that direction she'd come to Riverboat Point. To her right the land jutted out and the river disappeared around a bend not very far along from the shack. She walked across the lawn and the drive then picked her way through the small shrubs to the fence.

Jaxon's note about the neighbours made even less sense to her now that she knew about this Gnasher bloke who lived across the road. She'd seen no sign of him. She wondered who else might be considered neighbours.

Ethan and Jaxon's shacks were quite close but over this side of the property in daylight all she could see was trees. She knew there was a house in there somewhere because she'd seen a gate and a road leading in, but how close it was she had no idea. Did anyone live in it or was it a holiday place?

She peered into the darkness. Some trees were darker than others and gaps appeared as shades of grey. Her eyes caught the flash of a light. She stood still, watching the spot. Had she imagined it? A quick flash appeared again, not very bright and impossible to tell how far away it was. Perhaps there was a house and people in it. A house light could be revealed as branches moved in the breeze. She caught a quick glimpse again. She listened. No sound, not even the wind. There was no movement to disturb the trees. It could be that the light was moving – maybe a torch or a vehicle.

She watched but the light didn't reappear. Perhaps tomorrow she'd go next door and introduce herself. Find out who these other neighbours were. She turned around and caught her foot on a branch, jarring her leg. She let out a yelp.

Jasper barked in response. She stood still a moment looking at the ground in front of her, checking for any more obstacles. Then she realised what no sound meant. Ethan had turned off his music. She'd been so intent on peering at her possible neighbours she hadn't noticed.

Ethan leaned forward in his chair. He'd heard Savannah swear from somewhere down below his house. The noise had been followed by a quick bark from Jasper.

"Steady, mate," he murmured.

They both sat still, listening. Finally Ethan heard the front door of the shack slide and then back again. Savannah must have been outside walking around. He could just make out the glow from her lounge light and then it faded.

He felt bad now about turning down her dinner invitation. She probably didn't like the solitary lifestyle after living in the city. Ethan relished it. Tonight he'd wanted time alone. He was determined to get his life back on an even keel and making small talk with Savannah would have been too hard.

He eased back in his chair and took another slurp of tea. He hated the taste of it but he was willing to try chamomile again rather than resorting to sleeping tablets. He knew his stress levels had been rising; broken sleep didn't help. He'd been drinking too much, trying to drown out the memories with alcohol and loud music.

Before Blake's accident, he'd been doing really well. He'd said goodbye to the army, moved into his patch of paradise and begun the process of life after deployment. He'd done some part-time work at the garage in Burra. It was a bit of a drive but he did it easily on his bike. He'd been able to help Jaxon with the houseboats even though he had reservations about their proximity to his patch of the river.

But lately things were different and he didn't know why. He had felt the telltale signs getting worse: the tension that built in his chest for no apparent reason and then today that uncontrollable reaction to the can falling from Blake's cupboard. Something had triggered the stress. The psychiatrist had told him he might not always know why.

Ethan knew he couldn't blame Mal for his restlessness, but being with his father had unsettled him. They were opposites. Mal could never accept a son of his had taken up arms, especially in a war he considered Australia should never have been a part of.

Ethan couldn't begin to explain all the good that had been done amongst the evil. Mal wouldn't want to know about the new roads that were once barely passable tracks, the young girls happily attending school classes previously denied them, or the strengthening Afghan army working to help their citizens in need. Amid poverty and extreme hardship Ethan knew the Australian presence had made a difference.

There were people like his parents who thought the forces shouldn't have been involved. It was easy to sit back in the comfort of Australia and make those choices. In some ways coming home had been the hardest part for him. Most of the other blokes had wives or girlfriends or parents looking forward to their return.

They had been busting to hand back their gear, get through decompression with its medical checks and paperwork, and get home.

Taking time to debrief was necessary. A lot had been learnt since Vietnam days when soldiers flew out of the pressure cooker of a combat zone and were home to their families in twenty-four hours. They were expected to pick up where they'd left off and forget about a war that had changed them forever. He and Gnasher had talked about the differences several times. Ethan didn't want to end up like the Viet vet, trapped between reality and the scenes from war that still played over in the old man's head despite the distance of time.

Ethan had tried to reassure Savannah but he himself wasn't convinced it was a rabbit Gnasher saw through the sights of his gun. It could just as easily be an imagined Viet Cong soldier.

Ethan thought about the shot they'd heard and his own situation. Funny how something as simple as a can rolling out of a cupboard could evoke such a strong reaction while a gunshot didn't faze him. The brain worked in strange ways.

He looked up at the starry night and thanked whichever lucky star was his that he'd done two tours and come home physically in one piece at least. There had been several close calls. He swallowed the last of his tea.

"Bed calls, Jasper," he said.

The next morning he woke feeling refreshed. Maybe it was the chamomile tea – who would know – but for the first night in a few, he'd slept well.

He let Jasper out for his morning constitutional and busied himself making breakfast. Jasper was back quickly, a soft paw at the door asking to be let in.

"Bit chilly out there this morning, mate?"

The golden light of the sun, still below the horizon, was softly illuminating the trees but there was no warmth in it yet. Ethan ruffled Jasper's ears, the fur cold under his warm hands.

"Let's get you some food."

Jasper gave a low growl and stared towards the back door.

Ethan listened. He heard the scrape of a footstep then Savannah appeared on the other side of the glass. That she was there at this hour of the morning was strange enough but it was what she was holding that brought a smile to his lips. He opened the door.

"Good morning," he said and his grin broadened. "I don't recall asking for home delivery."

Savannah didn't smile back. She shivered and clutched the large pack of toilet rolls close to her chest.

"I'm very sorry but I need to ask for your help again," she said.

"Come in."

She hesitated, glancing at Jasper beside him.

"Drop," he said.

Savannah stepped just inside the door. He slid it shut behind her.

"Toilet blocked?" He raised an eyebrow.

"No," she said. "I've had a call from the people on *Tawarri*. They're nearly out of toilet paper and there's no extra in the cupboards."

This time Ethan raised both eyebrows.

"They're camped at Old Man's Landing, which they said I can get to by vehicle. Fred said it wasn't far but I've no idea how to get there."

"It's a good spot. Not far."

"I wondered if you could direct me?"

Wearing loose clothes, her shape was hidden. They made her look thin, and with her short-cropped hair she appeared waif-like, but he knew she was no weakling. She studied him with eyes that were alert, piercing.

"Or better still, could you come with me and show me the way?" she said.

Ethan scratched his forehead. He had planned to get back to Blake's place early. He wanted to check on his brother before he started work on the machinery.

"I'm sorry," she said. "I don't like imposing on you all the time. I hope this will be the last thing for a while."

Her tone was brusque. He knew she didn't like asking. Ethan made up his mind.

"It won't take long if we go by boat."

"Boat?"

"By road it's a long trip, in the tinnie about fifteen minutes."

"You mean that little tin thing tied up by the houseboats?"

"That's Jaxon's. Mine's a bit bigger."

Her forehead crinkled and her fingers dug into the paper rolls. "I ... I haven't ever been in a small boat like that."

"Best way to be on the river."

"Are you sure you couldn't just direct me in the car?"

"No time." He reached past her and slid the door open. "You'll need a coat. Meet me out the front of my place in ten minutes."

She opened her mouth then closed it again.

"Okay," she said.

She gave him one last questioning look then stepped outside.

"See you in ten," he called after her as she went down the stairs.

Back inside he hurried through his morning jobs, chomping toast and gulping coffee each time he passed the kitchen bench. It was the second time Savannah had interrupted his morning breakfast ritual but this time he didn't mind. He had an excuse to go for a quick trip on the river. Even though there'd be no fishing at least he'd be out on the water again. He pulled on his coat and a thick beanie.

"You'll have to stay here, mate," he said to Jasper who waited at the door. "By the look of it I don't think our Ms Smith would cope with you in the boat as well."

Savannah was waiting for him. She wore Jaxon's hi-vis coat over her clothes and her own version of a beanie on her head. The huge packet of toilet rolls was still clutched firmly to her chest.

"Let's go," he said and led the way down the path to where he kept his tinnie. The earlier golden glow had gone, leaving a pale blue sky littered with wispy grey clouds. There was no mist on the river this morning.

"This is a much better set-up than Jaxon's," she said as they walked the boards below the retaining wall to the small mooring where Ethan tied his boat. "Why doesn't he do this?"

"Money, I'd be guessing. There was a flood a few years back before both of us bought here. It washed away the bank. The people I bought from had built the jetty but there were no houseboats when Jaxon bought his place."

Ethan took the toilet paper from her and stashed it under the seat. He held out his hand. "Step into the middle of the boat and sit on the front seat."

She looked from him to the boat then took his hand. She moved awkwardly and the boat wobbled but her balance was good. She moved easily to the seat on her own. He undid the rope, climbed in and started the motor.

They coasted out to the middle of the river. Savannah faced him from the other end of the boat. She glanced from side to side taking in the scenery. He picked up speed. She gripped the side of the boat.

"Beautiful time of the day on the river," he called over the noise of the motor.

She gave him a small grin in response and turned her eyes back to the passing scene.

The water was like glass. The tinnie sliced through it. The noise of their progress echoed around them. Waterbirds sat on partly submerged branches, swooped around the banks or floated on the river, busy with their morning tasks. The crisp air burned his cheeks and made his nose run. He inhaled the fresh smell and savoured the taste of the river on his lips. This is where he loved to be.

They saw no other boats as they followed the twists and bends of the river. They passed a few places where houses and shacks lined the banks then came to high cliffs lining one side. Ethan couldn't stop himself sweeping them with a searching look. The only danger from up there might be a tree branch toppling to the river but it was hard to break the habits learned in a war zone.

As they rounded the sharp bend a large sandbar stuck out into the river opposite the cliffs and the houseboat came into view.

"There it is," he called.

Savannah twisted on her seat to look. Ethan eased back on the throttle and turned the bow towards the bigger boat, then cut the motor so they gently nudged up against the swim deck at the back of the houseboat.

Fred came out of the back door as Ethan reached to hold onto the handrail. The older man was wearing a purple polo shirt over black and purple tartan shorts. A black and purple cap was jammed on top of his head. He looked more like he should be stepping onto the golf course than manning a houseboat.

"Ahoy, there," Fred called.

A grin stretched his face but there was something about his eyes. Ethan didn't like the man.

Savannah leaned forward and tugged the toilet paper rolls out from under the seat.

"Here you are," she said and lifted the packet onto the platform.

"I'd invite you in for coffee," Fred said, "but there are a few sore heads." He jerked his thumb over his shoulder and lowered his voice. "A couple of the ladies can't hold their drink like they used to."

"Thanks but we'd have to say no anyway."

Savannah's tone was crisp. Perhaps she didn't like Fred either.

"Ethan kindly offered to run me out here but he has to go to work."

Fred bent to pick up the toilet paper. "Well, we couldn't do without the necessities. There was no cling wrap or foil either. Luckily one of the ladies threw in her own. Jaxon usually provides it. He's always run a tight ship." He gave Savannah a patronising look and turned away to go back onto the boat deck.

She squared her shoulders. Ethan could see she was going to stand.

"Don't," he said. He put up one hand and held tight to the swim deck with the other.

Fred twisted round to look at them. Savannah stayed on her seat glaring up at him.

"We didn't finalise the paperwork before you left," she said. "Jaxon wouldn't have let that slip either."

"Don't worry about it." Fred's stretched smile was back in place. "Jaxon knows we're trustworthy. See you on the weekend."

Ethan let go of the rail and they drifted away from the houseboat. He started the outboard and from the corner of his eye he saw Fred lift a hand in a lazy wave. Ethan turned their nose for home. In front of him Savannah remained rigidly staring over his shoulder. No doubt Fred and the houseboat were firmly in her sights. Neither of them had returned Fred's wave.

Once they were round the bend, Savannah glanced back at Ethan.

"What paperwork?" he asked.

She drew in a quick breath through her nose.

"He didn't sign the hire agreement."

"At least you've got his money."

"Not all of it. I didn't get the bond off him either."

Ethan raised his eyebrows but didn't say any more. Her face was set in a grim look but the multi-coloured beanie gave her a comical air. Ethan could tell she was beating herself up about it. He decided it was best not to say anything. He shifted his gaze to the river ahead. They travelled the rest of the way in silence.

CHAPTER

12

The moment the boat touched the tiny jetty, Savannah prepared to get out.

"Thanks for taking me," she said.

"No problem."

She didn't give him time to make any further conversation. She moved away along the jetty, clambered around the slippery bank to Jaxon's side of the fence and hightailed it back to the shack.

She was cross with herself about the toilet rolls. Ethan had suggested she do one more check and she hadn't. Jaxon had said the boats were ready to go. Worse than that, she was embarrassed about letting Fred take the boat without finalising the paperwork and paying the bond. Ethan hadn't said anything but she'd seen the rise of his eyebrows and the twinkle in his eye. He must think her a right fool and useless to boot.

She knew nothing about boats, from the proper stocking of them to driving them. At this rate Jaxon wouldn't have a business left to come home to and they'd both end up homeless.

Back inside the shack she paced the floor.

"Damn it, Jaxon," she growled at the empty room. "Somehow I've got to make this work."

She looked out the sliding door towards the three houseboats. From now on she'd be more focused. She would give each of them a thorough check. That at least was something she felt capable of doing and she'd start right now.

She took the three sets of keys and the page listing what should be on board each one and let herself out the back door. Over the fence she heard Ethan's bike start and roar away. He'd done her another favour but she didn't want to think about him beyond that.

She marched down to the bank, stepped carefully along the path and put the gangplank up to the first boat. On board she opened every cupboard and inspected every piece of furniture. This one was called *Our Destiny* and it was shipshape so far as she could tell. Plenty of toilet paper stashed in each bathroom cupboard as well as the toiletries supplied.

Jaxon had a huge supply of everything in a shipping container inside the shed. She'd had to take three keys to get into the shed to get the toilet paper. In the half dark of early morning she'd fumbled around with the padlock. It held a chain that connected the front sliding door of the shed to the side entrance door. Once she got that undone she needed another key to unlock the side door and then another key to open the door he'd made in the shipping container.

There was quite a bit of electrical equipment on the shelves along one wall of the massive shed. One bay was taken up with Jaxon's ute and that was full of tools. There was also a battered squat-looking bike with four wheels. He no doubt wanted to leave everything secure while he was away but it seemed like a lot of locking up. Savannah had decided she wasn't going to bother with the padlock. She'd left it with the chain inside the shed.

She climbed up onto the sundeck. Everything was dusty and leaves scattered the deck. That would have to be cleaned before the boat went out. She wondered if *Tawarri* had been the same. Too late to worry about it now.

She moved on to the next boat and then the third. They were fully equipped as well. There was cling wrap, foil and paper towel in each kitchen. It must have just been an oversight that *Tawarri* didn't have the extras. The only thing was the sundecks. All of them needed cleaning. There'd be little point going over them now though. She'd have to do it the day before they were due to go out.

Her stomach grumbled. Fred's phone call had woken her from a deep sleep. She'd thrown on clothes and set out on her mission to get the toilet paper to him without stopping for breakfast. The few supplies she'd bought on her trip to town were low or gone. She had plenty of time and nothing else to do but get back in the car and head into Riverboat Point.

Savannah turned left out of the driveway onto the dirt road. Then she stopped and reversed until she was level with Jaxon's elaborate letterbox. She hadn't ever looked inside. It was dirty and full of cobwebs. He must get mail even if it was only junk. She wondered where it was delivered.

Back in her car she drove slowly, peering left and right. Not far from Jaxon's gate on the opposite side of the road was a rough driveway littered with white rocks. There was a gate in the wire fence with a tree at either side. A sign hung on the gate stating Private Property, Keep Out. Savannah braked and peered past the gate. The track on the other side disappeared from sight into the bush beyond. It didn't look like many vehicles drove along it. She assumed that was the entrance to Gnasher's property.

She wondered how Gnasher lived. How did he get his groceries? What if he took sick? Who would know? She looked again at the sign and remembered the gunshot. He obviously didn't encourage visitors.

She drove on, looking to the left this time. She had meant to ask Ethan if he knew who lived over Jaxon's other side fence. After a while she came to a gate. It was a fancy white iron gate like you'd see on a house yard in the city. Once again the sign wasn't friendly. Bold black letters on a white sign declared, Private Property, Trespassers Prosecuted, and underneath, Beware Dog. Savannah didn't like the idea of going in there to find out who the owners were.

So what did Jaxon's note about the neighbours mean? None of them encouraged contact so there appeared little for her to worry about. Even Ethan was aloof in spite of the help he'd given her. The whole area wasn't conducive to neighbourly relations. Savannah shrugged her shoulders against the shiver that prickled down her back. The perfect place for anyone who was antisocial or not wanting to be noticed. Maybe it was just that all Jaxon's neighbours weren't the friendly type and he'd been warning her to keep away. But then he'd known she'd have to ask Ethan for help.

She slapped the steering wheel with the flat of her hand. Maybe that was it. He knew it was unlikely she'd have contact with Gnasher or whoever lived over the other fence but she'd have to work with Ethan. Jaxon had thought it necessary to warn her. But why? What could there possibly be about Ethan she needed to watch out for? She shook her head and kept driving.

When she reached the T-junction she stopped. Old Man's Landing Road went right towards the main road and left towards she knew not what – the river? Fred had moored *Tawarri* at Old Man's Landing. Perhaps this road would take her there. Ethan had said it was quicker to go by boat but she decided to check it out for herself. Savannah turned left. She had nothing to do and she might as well see where this road led.

The dirt road twisted and turned but gradually took her north. If she'd remembered the name of it this morning she could have driven herself here and not asked Ethan for help. As she rounded the next bend, a tyre hit a pothole and the car thumped below her. She eased back on her speed. The road ahead was uneven and dotted with holes. By the time she reached the next bend she was crawling from one deep rut or well-worn hole to another and her hip was beginning to ache from the jarring.

Finally the road ended in a huge clearing. Permapine railings defined the area between parking space and trees. In a gap, a sign pointed through the trees to Old Man's Landing. Savannah pulled up close to the sign and got out of her car. She stretched and bent her body, twisted from side to side and rolled her shoulders. The last few kilometres had been extremely rough going. She wondered about the ability of her little car to make it through such a rough road but she was here now. Ethan had been right about the time. It was almost a half an hour since she'd left the shack.

She turned a full three-sixty degrees. Without the sign pointing to the river she would have no idea she was anywhere near water. The road led to this clearing but all around her was bush made up of straggly taller tress and assorted smaller bushes. They were sparse enough to walk between but the random growth made it impossible to see very far ahead.

She set off along the dirt path. After five minutes she stopped and listened. A bird called. The trees rustled in a gentle breeze but there was no other sound. The sun went behind a cloud. Savannah shivered. She wasn't cold but there were goosebumps on her arms. The isolation pressed around her like a shroud. She had no idea how much further it was to the river or even if this path was really going there. She turned and went back the way she'd come. A surge of panic pushed her on until she burst through into the clearing.

She got back in her car and locked the door before she turned the key. Her heart skipped when the engine was slow to respond. Imagine being stuck out here. The rumble of the motor was reassuring. She took a deep breath and turned her car in a wide circle to face the track out.

A four-wheel drive entered the clearing, drove on past her and pulled up in the parking area. Savannah looked back to see its doors fly open and three children pile out, pushing each other and laughing. The sun came out again. How different the place seemed now. What a coward she'd been not to follow the path all the way to Old Man's Landing. It was the isolation that had overwhelmed her. How did people stand this kind of life?

CHAPTER
13

Savannah pulled up in front of the supermarket, not sure where she could get a snack. There were no cafés that she'd noticed.

"Hello, you're still in town," Faye greeted her brightly when she entered the shop.

"Just out of town actually," Savannah replied. "I'm looking after my brother's place."

Faye leaned closer. "You're not Jaxon's sister?"

"I am."

"Savannah?"

She was startled to hear the woman shriek her name. Faye reached across the counter and grasped her hand.

"Welcome to Riverboat Point," she said. "I'm so sorry I didn't realise you were Jaxon's sister when you came in before."

Savannah stared at Faye. "How did you –"

Faye cut her off. "Jaxon asked me to look out for you. He told me you'd be coming to take care of the boats and to make you welcome." She reached over with her other hand, patted Savannah's and let it go. "He said you had long black hair but I can see a likeness to him now that I look at you properly."

Once again it hit home to Savannah how Jaxon must have planned all this. He'd been confident she would come.

"What can I help you with today?" Faye asked.

"I've got a list of groceries but I wondered if there was anywhere to get lunch?"

"We only have the reheated pies and pasties here." Faye nodded towards a pie warmer behind her. She leaned close again. "They're not much chop really but the fishermen like something hot when they come in to buy bait. The tea room's the best spot. Everything's homemade there."

"I haven't noticed it."

"Riverboat Point's best kept secret." Faye gave a huge smile. "Old Nell Jones and her husband Bob love to cook. They live in an old house on the street behind the pub. It used to be a shop once so they use the front room to serve food. There's a sign on the gate says Nell and Bob's Tea Room. You can't miss it."

Savannah put a hand to her stomach as it rumbled in anticipation.

"Sounds like you could do with a feed," Faye said and chuckled.

"Do they serve coffee?" Savannah asked.

"Only the instant kind. Bernie at the pub makes good coffee but only on weekends until the tourist season cranks up. Not worth running his machine at this time of the year. You'll enjoy Nell's tea. She brews it in a pot and serves it in china teacups."

"Sounds good," Savannah said.

"Give me your list. I'll get your shopping together while you eat."

"I don't want to bother you."

"No bother," Faye said. "I'm not busy today and Jamie can help."

Savannah pulled her list from her pocket. It felt odd to hand it over. Helpers had done her shopping when she'd first come home from rehab. She hadn't liked it then. Along with the personal washing and the cleaning it was an invasion of her privacy.

"Off you go." Faye shooed her towards the door.

As Savannah stepped outside Faye called after her.

"Tell Nell you're Jaxon's sister. He was a regular customer there."

Savannah got back in her car and set off for the tea room. Faye's conversation played over in her head reminding Savannah how little she knew about her brother. They'd been close when they were young but high school had changed so many things. She'd lost her little brother among the carnage that was her life back then. As soon as school was finished she'd left home. After their parents' death she spent so long in hospital and rehab. Jaxon had only been seventeen then. She hadn't given any thought to how he must have struggled. He'd gone to live with the family of a close friend so that he could finish year twelve. By the time Savannah had been able to manage on her own he'd finished school and taken up an apprenticeship with an electrician, another family friend.

She pulled up in front of the tea room and pushed her sense of guilt about her relationship with her brother away. Food, she needed food. A pebbled path wound through a tidy cottage garden to the front door. She wondered whether to go straight in or knock but when she reached the door there was a sign declaring, 'Tea room open, do come in'.

She pushed open the door and a bell tinkled over her head. A couple seated at one of the four tables looked up at her with curious eyes. She shut the door with another tinkle of the bell. They went back to their food. Savannah's runners squeaked on the polished wood floor.

"Hello, young lady." A man with snowy white hair and a face full of wrinkles stood in the doorway opposite. "Have you come for lunch?"

"Yes, please." Savannah salivated as the smell of baking food reached her.

"I'm Bob. Welcome to our tea room. Take a seat wherever you like."

She looked around and chose a table.

"We've got some of Nell's pasties just out of the oven," Bob said, "or there's quiche or vegetable soup."

"Oh." Savannah had thought there'd be a menu.

"Or you can have all three if you're hungry." Bob chuckled.

"A pasty please." She didn't normally eat pastry but the smell coming from the kitchen was irresistible.

"Something to drink?"

"Could I have a pot of tea?"

"Coming right up."

Bob left and Savannah glanced around. There was a lace curtain at the small window, tablecloths on all the tables and a small vase of flowers in the centre of each. It reminded her of childhood visits to her grandparents.

The chair she'd chosen placed her with her back to the couple. The room wasn't very big and their proximity made her uncomfortable. In the city she enjoyed Asian food and was often in places where she would be jammed up close to other customers, but here it felt an invasion of privacy, hers and theirs.

"Where is she?"

Savannah looked up as a woman bustled through from the house. She was small and round with softer wrinkles than Bob's but the same snowy white hair. A colourful apron with a bib covered her clothes. Her husband was close behind her.

"We've just had a call from Faye." The older woman's eyes spar-kled. "She tells me you're Jaxon's sister."

Savannah stood up, conscious she was the centre of attention.

"Yes," she said. "I'm Savannah."

"It's so lovely to meet you, Savannah. I'm Nell."

"And you know me already," Bob chirped beside her.

"Jaxon told us to keep an eye out for you but you're not how he described."

"He hasn't seen me for a while," Savannah said. "I've given up on the long dark hair phase."

Savannah flicked a look at the seated couple who were watching the exchange with interest. The woman had a piercing look, her companion's was brooding.

"You must call in often," Nell said. "Jaxon did. We loved to see him, didn't we, Bob?"

Bob nodded and smiled.

"We'd better feed the young lady, Nell," he said. "She looks hungry."

"Of course," Nell said. "You make yourself comfortable and we'll be right back with your lunch."

No sooner had they bustled out than the woman seated at the other table spoke.

"Hope you don't mind but we couldn't help overhearing," she said. "You're Jaxon's sister?"

"Yes," Savannah said. Had the whole town been expecting her?

"We're Belinda and Ashton Palmer." The woman rose and came across to her table. Gold bangles jangled on her arms and several gold chains hung around her tanned neck. "We're your sometimes neighbours." The skin around her mouth stretched in a tight smile and her brow remained smooth.

Savannah knew that look. Belinda had used botox and yet she'd be only a few years older than Savannah. Ashton nodded at her from his seat. His lips lifted in a half smile before he went back to his food.

"Nice to meet you," Savannah said.

"We're usually only here for the odd weekend," Belinda said, "but we're staying for a week or so this time. We must catch up."

"Yes," Savannah said remembering the signs on the Palmers' gate.

"Are you busy this afternoon? I could pop over. It'd be nice to have some female company." She glanced towards Ashton who was intent on his food. "Gets very lonely out there by the river."

"I'll be home," Savannah said. She felt relieved she wouldn't have to negotiate the Palmers' gate and dog.

"Great. Do you drink sparkling?"

"Yes," Savannah said. She didn't add not much and not usually during the day.

"I'll bring a bottle."

Bob returned with a tray loaded with food and a teapot in a knitted cosy.

"You enjoy your lunch," Belinda said. "Ash and I will be on our way soon. I'll see you this afternoon. We've left the money on the table, Bob."

"Thank you, Belinda. See you next time."

Bob set some cutlery in front of Savannah then a plate with a pasty covered in golden flaky pastry. Savannah pursed her lips as saliva shot into her mouth. He followed it with a pot of homemade tomato sauce, a teacup on a saucer and the teapot.

"We thought you might like this," he said with a big smile and placed a plate with two cream-filled cupcakes next to the teacup.

Savannah couldn't imagine how she'd fit one of them in let alone two, but they looked delicious and she didn't want to spoil Bob's hospitality.

"Thank you," she said.

"Bye," Belinda waved as she and Ashton left.

Savannah turned. Belinda swept her with a penetrating look then briskly turned away.

"Now this is on the house," Bob said once the door shut behind the couple.

"Oh, no, I couldn't ..."

Bob put up his hand. "Nell and I insist. It's our welcome to Riverboat Point gift. Enjoy," he said.

By the time Savannah arrived back at the supermarket her stomach felt fit to burst. She had managed to eat all the food Bob and Nell had put in front of her. It had been delicious but eating two cream cakes on top of the pasty had been too much.

There were several people lined up at the supermarket checkout and a man behind the counter was serving them. Savannah glanced around but couldn't see Faye. She decided to wait. Once more she scanned the noticeboard. Jaxon's notice was still there. There were a couple of people offering to babysit, another to do housework, a houseboat for sale, an appeal for an old caravan to be used as a spare room and several other requests or offers. Her gaze stopped at the note from someone called Mandy who was trying to get a few locals together to keep fit. 'Can't do it on my own,' she'd written.

"Hello, Savannah."

She turned at the sound of Faye's shrill voice.

"You found the tea rooms okay?"

"Yes." Savannah was pretty sure Faye already knew that since she'd phoned to check up.

"Nice lunch?"

"Yes."

"I've got your groceries packed up," Faye said. She waved her hand towards a box and bags on the shelf behind the counter. A bunch of flowers, their stems in a plastic bag, sat on top of the box. "The flowers are from us."

"There's no need."

"We don't get many new people here." The man had finished with the customers and had joined in the conversation. "Jaxon's been a great addition to our community. His family are most welcome."

"This is my husband, Charlie," Faye said.

"Nice to meet you, Savannah." He shook her hand warmly and she stuttered a response. She would never have picked him as Faye's husband. He appeared so much older.

"You too," she said feeling bad about her earlier churlishness.

"Jaxon's done a lot for the community and his business is going from strength to strength."

Charlie looked at her as if he expected her to say something.

"You don't know how long he's going to be away, do you?" Faye filled in the space.

"No." Savannah looked from one to the other.

"He's always been so reliable," Charlie said. "We hadn't realised this trip away was going to be longer than a week."

"He said he'd help with the upgrade of the community hall," Faye said.

"That can wait but –" Charlie started.

"He's been coaching our Jamie at tennis," Faye cut in.

"Tennis?" They'd played as kids. She didn't know Jaxon still played.

"Jamie doesn't have a lot of friends," Charlie said.

"He has … special needs," Faye said softly. "He enjoyed having a hit with Jaxon."

"I'm very sorry," Savannah said. "I don't know how long he plans to be away but I'm sure he'll be back soon. He won't want to leave me in charge for long." She smiled. She'd spoken with a conviction she didn't feel.

"Oh well, say hello from us when you speak to him next." Charlie turned to pick up her box. "I can help you to the car."

"I've thought of a few more things I need."

"Just bring them over," Faye said. "I'll add them to your tally."

Savannah sped off to find cheese, dip and crackers. If Belinda was going to bring champagne they would need something to go with it even though she didn't feel the slightest bit hungry now.

What a crazy morning it had been. From her embarrassment at her poor management skills to her panic at being alone at Old Man's Landing to being overwhelmed by friendly people here in town. To add to the mix was her confusion over Jaxon. If he was so well liked and his business was booming why would he up and leave on an extended holiday? Charlie had said to say hello. She'd say more than that when she got the chance.

Savannah paused, her hand hovering over a packet of water crackers. What if something had happened to him? Instantly she dismissed the thought. He'd been way too well organised for someone who'd met with an accident. He'd meant to go away. It was the why that had her puzzled.

CHAPTER
14

Ethan looked at his watch. It was already mid-afternoon and he was in need of the parts he'd ordered yesterday. He wiped his hands down the sides of his jeans. He was filthy from head to toe. Today's jobs had been particularly messy. He'd had trouble with the bolt in the header's oil sump and when it had finally come loose so had the pool of oil. Most of it dropped onto him.

The smell of it reminded him of Afghanistan and the workshop in Tarin Kot during his first deployment. One night towards the end of a sixteen-hour shift, the team had been working to get a light-armoured vehicle ready to go back out on patrol. They'd had a particularly busy time with several long shifts in a row. The fatigue had started to play tricks with his brain and he had borne the brunt of the oil spill. By the time he was able to get to the shower the dark liquid had seeped into every nook and cranny. His bloodied knuckles had stung as he'd tried to scrub away the oil and the smell had stayed with him for days.

Today was the same but to a lesser degree. He had oil soaked in patches on his clothes and a blood-encrusted little finger on his right hand from when his spanner had slipped. At least he could take a break. In Tarin Kot there were no breaks until the job was done and the workshop clean. The pressure wasn't quite the same here, not till harvest at least.

He wasn't ready to move on to the next job and there was little he could do to the header until he picked up the parts. He'd have to take Blake's ute again and leave his bike here.

"Hello?"

Ethan spun at the sound of a female voice.

A woman stood before him. She wore jeans and a windcheater. Her long fair hair was pulled back in a ponytail. Her eyes looked clear and bright. She didn't wear make-up.

"I'm Jenny," she said and thrust out her hand.

Ethan looked down at his own grimy hands then held them up.

"Nice to meet you," he said. "No offence if I don't shake your hand."

She smiled. It was an easy, warm smile.

"I'm happy with that," she said.

"You just arrived?"

"A while ago. I'm glad to see Blake's looking better than the last time I saw him in hospital."

"Barb's been playing mother."

"I've brought lasagne with me. Blake and I wondered if you'd like to eat with us."

Ethan looked down at his filthy clothes. Tiredness seeped through him and the last thing he felt like tonight was playing gooseberry with his brother and his new girlfriend. "Thanks, but I'm a bit of a mess. Think I'll take an early mark and go home."

She put her head to one side. "I make a pretty good lasagne."

"Another time I'll take you up on it."

"Okay, well at least call in for a coffee. Blake wants to see you before you go."

"I need to borrow his ute anyway. I'll be down in a while."

Jenny nodded and turned away to walk back to the house.

Ethan cleaned up the shed. He'd had to do nearly a day's work to sort it all out when he started and he liked to keep it that way. Especially while Blake was out of action to mess it up again. He used the degreaser on his hands then made his way past the sheds and down the track to the house. He pulled off his boots and let himself in via the outside laundry door to wash his hands with hot soapy water. They still didn't come clean.

He looked down at his clothes. Blake never cared about dirt but Ethan wasn't sure how things were situated with Jenny in residence. He knocked at the back door.

Jenny opened it immediately.

"Since when do you knock at the door?" Blake called from behind her.

"I'm pretty dirty," Ethan said to Jenny.

"You can have Blake's grotty chair," she said. "He doesn't need it at the moment."

Jenny held the door for him to step through then went to the kettle.

"Coffee?" she asked.

"Tea please."

"I'll have coffee," Blake said. "I've slept half the day away."

Ethan studied his brother. He still had rings around his eyes and the bruise on his cheek was like a rainbow but the rest of his face showed a better colour. He'd had a shave and his hair was still damp.

"Jenny's just given me a bath," Blake said.

Ethan held up his hands. "Stop right there," he said.

"He's too broken for anything more than a wash," Jenny said as she placed cups in front of them. "I'm going outside for a while. I've nearly tamed that side garden." She kissed Blake on the lips.

He gripped her tightly with his good arm and kissed her back.

She eased herself away, picked up some gloves from the bench and let herself out the door.

"Don't be too long," Blake called after her. "I'm not totally broken."

Ethan's heart sank. He recognised the puppy dog look on his brother's face. He hoped this Jenny didn't turn out to be another of his mistakes.

"She's a good woman," Blake said, still watching the door Jenny had exited through.

"She seems nice."

Blake turned back to look at him. "I know what you're thinking."

"Do you?" Ethan raised an eyebrow.

"You're just like Barb. She thinks Jenny will be a dud like the others, but Jenny's different."

"I'm sure she is." Ethan blew on his tea and took a slurp. "I was actually thinking about the harvester," he said to change the subject. "I've ordered some new parts. Should be in town tomorrow and I need a few other things. Can I leave my bike here and take your ute?"

"Of course. You don't have to ask."

"Don't want to leave you stuck without a vehicle."

"Bit of trouble driving at the moment. My leg's giving me curry and my arm's not much better. I'm not supposed to move it much."

Ethan looked at the bent shape under Blake's fresh shirt.

"You made a bit of a mess of it this time," he said.

"Jenny says I'm lucky."

"You always have been. How many times have you come off that bike and not done too much damage?"

"She's a nurse. She reckons if it had been a smidge deeper with the burns and grazes on my leg I would be looking at skin grafts."

"Perhaps you'll take her advice then and take it easy until you heal."

"Maybe."

Blake's face had taken on a sheepish look. Maybe Jenny would be good for him. Who knew?

"I can keep things ticking over here," Ethan said.

"Mal's got shearers next week. He'll need help."

"He won't want me there."

"He's got the neighbour's daughter coming over to help but he'll need another pair of hands."

"All he has to do is ask."

"Or you could offer." Blake stood up. "Damn it, Ethan, you two are as pig-headed as each other."

"You know he doesn't like me being around."

"That's not true." Blake hobbled to the bench then back to the table. He thumped it with the hand of his good arm. "How can I sit around the house when there's work to be done?"

"Okay, okay, take it easy. I'll ring Mal tonight."

Blake locked his gaze on Ethan. "You'll have to be diplomatic."

"I said I'd talk to him, all right? Sit down. I don't want that nurse coming back in here telling me I'm upsetting you."

Blake's face broke into a grin and he eased himself back onto his chair. "Did I tell you she's a good woman?"

"You might have mentioned it." Ethan stood up. "I'm off. I'll see you tomorrow."

"You can tell me about your chat with Mal."

"Sure," Ethan said through tight lips. It was the last thing he wanted to do but he'd do it for Blake's sake.

"Maybe you should take a leaf out of my book," Blake said. "Have a shave and wash those long dark locks. You look like a wild man."

"I've been busy." Ethan turned his back on his brother. Before Jenny appeared in his life it was often Blake who let his personal habits go. Except for the longer hair, Ethan usually kept a neat appearance, another thing he could credit to his army training.

Jenny looked up from the garden as he made his way to the shed where Blake kept his ute. He raised his hand in farewell. Perhaps Blake was right about her. She did come across as a nice person and she was obviously concerned for him. Blake might have found the right woman at last.

Only problem was Ethan was starting to get busy helping everyone else and he wasn't any closer to finding himself some work. The garage in Burra hadn't needed him for a while although that would probably change once harvest started.

Then there was Savannah to sort out as well. He'd have to get a list from her of when the boats were going out over the next few weeks. He couldn't be in two places at once. Perhaps he should try Jaxon again, get him to come home a bit earlier. He'd been a bit vague about his return date.

Ethan backed the ute out of the shed and turned onto the track to the front gate. Suddenly his simple life was looking complicated. He could feel the tension pressing in his chest but he was determined he wasn't going to go backwards like he had last week. The late afternoon sun was warm through the back window of the ute. He turned the radio on. "Losing My Religion" was playing. He upped the volume, wound down the window and belted out the familiar song.

CHAPTER
15

Jasper gave a couple of sharp barks. Savannah stood up from the table on the front verandah. He sounded close. Could he have got out of the yard Ethan left him in?

The sound of an engine reached her ears. She looked at her phone. It was after four. She'd given up on Belinda and made herself a pot of tea. She was enjoying being on her own now that she'd had people contact in town. It didn't seem so isolated when you knew there was a community not so far away.

The vehicle came closer. Jasper barked again. Whoever it was had pulled up in her driveway. Savannah made her way along the front of the shack to the carport. A door slammed. A car had pulled in behind hers and was now reversing out again.

"Hello," a female voice called.

Belinda. Savannah's heart sank. She'd been enjoying her tea on the verandah and had lost her earlier interest in being sociable with the neighbours.

"Sorry I'm late. Ash wanted help with some gardening. He'll come back for me later."

Savannah recalled the neatly groomed Ashton. Her first impression hadn't pegged him as the gardening type. Nor Belinda for that matter.

Belinda smiled and held up a bottle of sparkling in each hand. "I've brought supplies."

Savannah's sinking feeling hit the bottom of her stomach. It looked like Belinda was planning to stay quite a while. She'd changed into casual jeans. Her white shirt was a vivid contrast to her deep tan which was complemented by the apricot loose-knit jumper draped across her shoulders. Her neatly brushed blonde hair sat perfectly in a classic bob just above her shoulders with not a strand out of place.

"Come round to the front." Savannah hoped her own smile looked genuine, thankful at least that she still wore her new jeans and the only decent shirt she'd brought with her. "It's nice on the verandah."

"Wow," Belinda stopped in front of the glass doors. "Jax has certainly made some changes. This used to be a couple of small windows and an old wooden door. Now it's nearly all glass."

Savannah slid open the door. "I'll get some glasses."

"And the view from here ... it's lovely."

Savannah turned back. The late afternoon sun still cast a golden light on this side of the river. The other side was full of dappled shadows and the water looked inky. She was growing used to its different moods.

"The trees still give you a little privacy from your boats but Jaxon has certainly cleaned up this yard," Belinda said. "You could barely see the river at all from here when he first came."

She walked up and down looking in the direction of the boats.

"Did you see much of my brother?"

Belinda stopped her pacing and turned round.

"We're not here often and Jaxon was busy but we caught up from time to time."

Her smile was tight and once again Savannah wondered why someone would inject herself with poison to smooth out a few wrinkles at an age when it shouldn't be necessary.

"Let's get this drink."

Belinda followed Savannah inside and put the second bottle in the fridge. Savannah rummaged in the cupboard for glasses. There were a couple with stems at the back.

"Oh, is this lovely platter for us?"

"Yes," Savannah said. Glad now that she'd put together some cheese and vegetables on a plate. "I'll add the crackers."

"You've even got flowers."

"Faye from the supermarket gave them to me."

"You're lucky, I don't think she gives much away. Runs a tight shop. Still, I guess she has to out here. Wouldn't be a lot of business." Belinda turned her back to the flowers. Her piercing gaze swept the room.

"It's more than the flowers. I can see there's been a woman's touch in here. Jaxon was always tidy but dust and must ..." She flapped a hand in front of her nose. "It didn't worry him. I think it's a boy thing. When we come to our place next door the first thing I do is throw open all the windows. Let in that lovely river air. Ash thinks I'm mad."

"Do you live in the city?"

"Yes, but it's always so nice to be here. I wish we came up more often." Belinda waved the bottle and turned on her heel. "Let's have this drink."

Out on the verandah she popped the cork. Savannah picked up the packet of crackers and followed, feeling like she was the guest instead of the host. The glasses were soon filled. Belinda picked one up and gave it to Savannah then lifted the other to toast.

"Here's to new friends," she said.

Their glasses clinked together.

"Yes," Savannah said. She watched Belinda take a couple of mouthfuls before trying it herself.

"That's very nice," she said.

"It's a nice Adelaide Hills sparkling." Belinda turned the bottle so the label faced Savannah. "I buy it by the case load."

"Shall I put it in the fridge?"

"It's not that hot out here now," Belinda said. "Besides, the top's off. We'll just have to drink it." She took another mouthful.

Savannah sipped hers then put it down. It was delicious. The bubbles exploded in her mouth. She'd have to be careful or they'd soon be exploding in her legs. It didn't take much to make her wobbly.

She offered Belinda the platter.

"Thanks," she said and took a tiny sliver of cheese and a carrot stick.

Savannah did the same. They both sat down.

"So, you've come from Adelaide to look after Jaxon's houseboats. Aren't you a kind sister?"

"I had some time up my sleeve." No need to mention she'd lost her job and Jaxon had got her here under false pretences.

"Here's to little brothers." Belinda raised her glass again and took a swig. "They always need our help, don't they?"

Savannah smiled and took another sip of the bubbly. Jaxon had only asked for her help as a guarantor, which she was now regretting, and then this help while he was away. Not much really considering they'd lost both their parents at a young age. Still, she'd never asked him for anything. She'd learnt to stand on her own two feet well before her parents' death.

"Have you seen any movies lately?" Belinda cut into her thoughts.

They chatted on, comparing movies and music they enjoyed until somehow the topic came back to Jaxon and the houseboats.

"Does he plan to be away long?"

Belinda's tight smile was still imprinted on her face. Savannah felt skewered by her sharp look.

"We're staying for a while ourselves," Belinda said. "We could have dinner together."

"He hasn't decided on a return date yet," Savannah said. She didn't want people to know he had coerced her here and that she didn't know his plans. "It's been a bit of a sharp learning curve for me. I don't know much about boats."

"Ash is good with boats. He's got a couple. We both helped Jaxon get started."

Savannah watched as Belinda refilled her own glass and topped up Savannah's.

"How do you mean helped?"

"I helped clean but don't ask me what Ash did. Something to do with pumping out the sewerage tanks and refilling fuel tanks."

Savannah averted her eyes and took another sip of the sparkling to hide her surprise. Belinda's fingernails were immaculately groomed and she had rings on nearly every finger. It was hard to imagine her cleaning anything let alone someone else's mess.

"I hope you don't mind me saying but I don't think Jaxon was really sure where to start when he first took on the boats," Belinda said. "At least I know about cleaning. I can't abide dust and grime."

Savannah found herself glancing around the verandah. She'd swept it and brushed cobwebs from the rafters but she wouldn't want to subject it to close scrutiny. Normally she wouldn't give a damn what someone else thought about her housekeeping skills but she found herself wanting to impress her new friend. She took a bigger mouthful of sparkling and Belinda filled both their glasses again.

"Only one boat out at the moment?" Belinda stood up and walked to the edge of the verandah.

"Yes." Savannah cut herself a chunk of cheese and took two crackers from the plate. The sparkling was making her hungry in spite of her big lunch. "The other three all go out on Friday."

"And you're doing it all by yourself? That's amazing."

"Ethan is helping me."

"Ethan? Is he the guy from next door?" Belinda came back to her chair.

"Yes, without Jaxon here there's no-one qualified to show the customers how to drive the houseboats."

"And yet he went away." Belinda played with her glass and gave Savannah a sideways glance.

"I guess he knew Ethan would help. He's done it before."

"What's he like?"

"Ethan?" Savannah paused. How would she describe him?

"We've had our place several years but we're not here regularly. We haven't met him yet. I heard he's a bit solitary."

"Perhaps."

"Word is he's done service in Afghanistan and doesn't like people."

Savannah put her head to one side. It felt pleasantly fuzzy. "He does come across as someone who prefers his own company," she said. "Not that he's alone."

"No?"

"He has a dog."

"Now that I can understand. Ash has his great lump of a guard dog. Ugly thing but a great animal."

"Jasper's huge."

"Have you come across Gnasher out the back?"

"Not exactly."

"You wouldn't want to. Shoot you as soon as look at you. I caught him trying to climb our fence once. Crazy old guy. What with him and this Ethan we're surrounded by loony war vets."

Savannah sat back in her chair and thought about that. Ethan did run hot and cold but she wasn't sure he should be labelled a loony.

"You have a lovely figure."

She was startled by Belinda's change of topic.

"You're shapely with it too," she said. "Are those boobs real? I hate mine. I'm thinking I'll go to Thailand next year for a holiday and have a boob job while I'm there."

"No surgery." Savannah looked down and wished the same could be said for the rest of her. She couldn't stand the sight of her damaged naked body but she knew in clothes her figure looked good.

"I find I have to skip meals to keep the weight off," Belinda said. "How do you keep so trim?"

"Exercise."

Belinda groaned. "I joined a gym once but I'd come home unable to do a thing for days. The trainer was ex-army. Another loony."

Savannah chuckled. The bubbles had warmed her body. She felt relaxed. "Why did you join?"

Belinda drained her glass and laughed. "Ash said I'd put on a bit of weight. I liked the idea of those big balls and maybe a bike or a treadmill but Mr Fitness Freak had us pumping iron, hanging off walls and skipping like maniacs. He was always preening in front of the mirror and flexing his muscles. I like a good male body but there was nothing to like about him. I hated the gym. Easier to cut back on the food." She picked up the bottle and peered at it. "Empty. Shall I get the other one?"

Before Savannah could answer Belinda let herself inside the shack. It was a pity she had obviously signed up at the wrong gym or the wrong class. There were plenty of fun ways to work off a few kilos and keep fit. Savannah was testament to that. She looked up as her visitor popped the top of the second bottle and quickly held it over her glass as froth erupted from the neck.

"Ooops!" Belinda cackled.

Savannah watched her refill both glasses. She knew she shouldn't have anymore but she was enjoying the company. She'd had a couple of close friends before her accident but in the long months of rehab they'd lost touch. In hindsight she knew it was more to do with her mood swings and periods of silence than their lack of care. Finally they'd just stopped visiting. Now she was finding it pleasant to have some female company, especially out here.

"My last boss sounds a bit like your gym instructor," she said. "He was always strutting around barking orders and acting like he was God's gift to women."

"Is there a man in your life, Savannah?"

"No," she said firmly.

"I can't believe a gorgeous woman like you doesn't have a string of men chasing after her."

"I could show you a few simple routines to keep fit," Savannah said, keen to change the subject. "I was a … am a fitness instructor."

"I really think I've gone off the idea of gyms."

"You can do these exercises at home. You don't need equipment."

"Really?"

"You should look after your inner core if you do nothing else. It's so important for women to keep all our internals working well."

"I'm not keen." Belinda cackled again and took another mouthful of sparkling.

"Come on." Savannah stood up and clutched the table as her legs wobbled beneath her. Her head was light but she felt no pain. "They're easy." She turned her chair around, lowered her hands to the seat and did some tricep dips. "These are good for your arms."

"If you say so." Belinda stayed seated.

Savannah went round and dragged her up.

"Come on. Push-ups next."

"Oh no, fitness freak alert!"

Savannah dropped Belinda's arm. "I'm not a freak," she said sharply then put her hand to her mouth. Where had that come from?

"Show me then." Once more Belinda let out her chortling laugh. She appeared not to have noticed Savannah's abruptness.

Savannah lowered herself to the ground and did some small pulsing push-ups.

"Looks okay." Belinda carefully lowered her glass to the concrete and then herself. She stretched out flat.

"You'll get your clothes dirty. Just your hands and your toes on the ground." Savannah demonstrated again then looked across as Belinda attempted it.

"Your hands aren't quite right."

Savannah eased to her feet and put a hand out to steady herself. She really had drunk too many bubbles.

"I feel like a beached whale," Belinda groaned.

"You don't look like one. Here." Savannah bent over and showed Belinda how to place her hands. The earth tilted and she tumbled to the floor, partly on top of Belinda. The glass toppled over and the sparkling frothed across the concrete. They both shrieked with laughter.

"Savannah?"

She looked up. Ethan was standing at the end of the verandah bathed in the golden glow of the setting sun. His damp hair was swept back from his clean-shaven face. He wore a t-shirt that high-lighted the muscles of his chest and arms, and from her eye level, a pair of jeans that also hugged him well.

"Hello, Ethan." Savannah scrambled to her feet and helped Belinda up.

"Sorry," he said backing away. "I didn't know you had a visitor."

"So you're the elusive Ethan." Belinda brushed herself off and held out her hand. "I'm Belinda, or Bel as my friends call me." She leaned in close to him. "We're neighbours."

Savannah could see the surprise on his face.

"I met Belinda in town today. She lives on the other side of this place."

"I see." Ethan's expression was unreadable.

"We're usually only here for weekends and don't see many peo-ple," Belinda said. "Ash likes the solitude but I enjoy some company from time to time." She turned back to Savannah. "It's been fun but I really should get home. Ash will want something for dinner. I'll ring him to pick me up."

"I'd offer but I don't think I should be driving," Savannah said.

Belinda pulled a mobile from her hip pocket. "Ash will come."

"I can take you."

They both turned back to Ethan.

"I've only got the farm ute but –"

"You could take my car," Savannah blurted.

"Aren't you both so kind." Belinda's face was pulled in her cus-tomary tight smile. "Thank you."

"I'll get the keys." Savannah took a deep breath and concentrated on walking steadily. Her legs felt like rubber.

By the time she came back out Belinda had her arm through Ethan's and was chatting animatedly about football. So much for her writing him off as a loony. She looked like she was his best friend and who'd have thought she'd be a football fan?

"Here you are." Savannah held out the keys and Ethan extricated his arm to take them.

Belinda gave Savannah a hug. "Thank you for a lovely afternoon. We must do it again before Ash and I head back to the city."

"Yes." Savannah nodded.

Ethan led the way to the car. Savannah lifted her hand in a wave as they backed out. She shivered. The night air was suddenly cold. She went back to collect the glasses and the platter. Two empty bottles sat on the concrete beside the table, a silent testament to her overindulgence. There was already a sour taste in her mouth and her head was fuzzy. She knew she would pay for this afternoon's frivolity.

CHAPTER
16

"What a great girl Savannah is." Belinda let out a chortling laugh. "We've had the best time."

Ethan flicked his look between the side and rear-view mirror as he turned the car to face out. He had no idea what she and Savannah had been doing when he'd arrived but it was obvious they'd been drinking a while.

"It looked that way."

"You sound disapproving."

Ethan was surprised by her forthright response.

"I didn't mean it like that," he said. If he was honest, he had felt disappointed to find Belinda and Savannah carrying on like a couple of schoolgirls. When he'd arrived home from the farm he'd taken a good look at himself in the mirror. Blake had been right. He was a mess. He'd got to work and prepared a curry, green chicken this time, and made an effort to clean himself up. Then he'd decided he should make amends after his knockback of Savannah's dinner invitation and ask her over to his place. He hadn't expected Belinda to be there.

"Savannah was telling me what a great help you've been to her." The inflexion in Belinda's voice made it sound more like a question than a statement. He glanced across the dimly lit car interior.

"Jaxon asked me to give her a hand."

"Ash and I haven't seen him for ages. Is he away for long?"

"I don't know when he'll be back." Ethan kept his eyes on the road ahead, looking for the gate into Belinda's property.

"Houseboats are a big job for someone with no experience. Ash and I helped Jaxon out in the early days."

"Did you?"

"We're not up here on a regular basis but we lent him a hand when we could."

Ethan slowed the car and turned the nose towards the gate to Belinda's property. He stopped. The gate was shut. Up close he realised it was new. A length of chain with a padlock dangled around one side.

"We were a bit sceptical at first," Belinda said. "It's a way out of town and we didn't think people would bother coming out here when there's already a houseboat business operating from River-boat Point."

"Jaxon's been busy enough."

"How do you find it with houseboats coming and going?"

He turned to look at her. In the dim light, her eyes bored into him, her lips curled into a half smile revealing bright white teeth and the gold around her bronzed neck gleamed. She was a good-looking woman.

"I can't say I was keen on the idea. I like my quiet patch of the river without too many comings and goings."

She leaned closer. "Just how Ash and I feel."

Ethan opened his door. "I'll get the gate."

"Don't worry," she said. "I'll walk from here. The dog will only go mad if a strange car comes in."

Ethan looked back at the gate with its warning sign. "What kind of dog?" he asked.

"Ash has a Rottweiler, Brutus. Here he comes now."

Ethan looked past the gate where the headlights picked out a dark shape approaching. He heard the barking above the noise of the idling engine.

Belinda opened her door and leant out.

"Be quiet, Brutus," she commanded. "It's only me."

The dog stopped just short of the gate and quieted.

"Sit," she bellowed then turned back to Ethan.

"Thank you for driving me." Her voice was sugary. She leaned closer. The smell of her sweet perfume wafted around him. "Perhaps next time we could go to your place – where it's quieter. Savannah was teaching me pulse push-ups. Maybe you already know how to do them?"

She raised an eyebrow, rested a hand on his thigh and pressed her lips to his cheek. It was no peck on the cheek, more a lingering caress.

He eased away. "Not so quiet at my place either, I'm afraid." He tried to keep his tone light. "I have Jasper."

"Is he as good-looking as you?" Belinda's face was still close to his. Short of getting out of the car he could hardly back off any further.

"In a doggy kind of way." Ethan attempted a chuckle. "Jasper's a great woolly German Shepherd."

She sat back. Her lips curved up in a meaningful smile.

"I'll have to remember that when I come to visit then."

She turned away from him to slide out of the car. At the door she leant down.

"Thanks again, Ethan." His name came out as a soft whisper.

"No problem."

She closed the door. The smile he'd been holding back spread across his face. He waited for her to open the gate and close it again. She hooked the loose chain together and snapped the padlock shut, then gave a wave as she set off along the track.

Ethan reversed out and turned back the way he'd come. He let out a long slow whistle. He was well aware of what Belinda had been offering. Once he might have taken up the offer but that was another part of his life he'd vowed to change. No more one-night stands. Anyway there was this Ash she kept talking about. Maybe the relationship wasn't close but Ethan wasn't one to cut another man's lunch.

He pulled Savannah's car in under the carport, switched off the engine and put his head back. The smell of Belinda's perfume lingered. He could still feel the pressure of her lips where she'd kissed his cheek. It was no simple thankyou kiss. She had made him an invitation.

Just another part of the evening that had thrown him off balance. For a brief moment earlier he'd been embarrassed when he'd come across the pair of them on the verandah. He assumed Belinda had been truthful when she said Savannah had been teaching her how to do push-ups. It was certainly a more palatable explanation than what had crossed his mind.

He got out of the car. Perhaps Savannah would still want to eat. The only sign of food had been a cheese platter. He'd seen a totally different Savannah tonight, sprawled across Belinda on the floor, her head tossed back, laughing, eyes sparkling. He'd thought her a good-looker right from the start but tonight he'd seen something else. It was probably the alcohol but she'd appeared relaxed, happy. Then he had another thought. Maybe it was the female company she preferred.

The back of the shack was in darkness so he went round to the front, where the light from inside illuminated the verandah. No harm in inviting her over for a meal. He was only trying to be friendly with Jaxon's sister, not take her to bed.

He stopped at the door. Savannah was inside at the table, her head in her arms. He slid the glass open.

"Hello, just returning your keys."

He jangled them up and down but she didn't respond.

"Savannah?"

He stepped inside. On the table in front of her were a glass of water and a packet of painkillers. He couldn't help smiling. Little Miss "I can do everything" couldn't hold her drink.

He put a hand on her shoulder and gave her a gentle shake.

"Savannah, you should go to bed."

Her head lurched up and she looked at him through one bleary eye.

"Ow!" She rubbed her neck. "Ethan?"

He put a hand under her elbow. "Come on."

"Where are we going?" She frowned at him and pushed herself up from the table.

He put an arm around her waist to steady her. "You're going to bed."

She tensed and tried to push him away.

"It's okay," he said.

"Oh," she wailed. "No it's not." She pulled out of his hold and made a dash for the toilet.

He went to the doorway and looked out at the moonlight on the river while Savannah emptied the contents of her stomach. Finally the sound of her vomiting ceased, the toilet flushed and water ran in the bathroom.

"Ethan?"

He turned at her feeble bleat.

"Oh no," she said. "You are here. I hoped I'd imagined you."

"Just dropped your keys back." He pointed to the table.

"Thanks."

Her face was ashen under her blonde hair. There was a vulnerability about her that he'd noticed when she'd come asking for his help with the hot water. He'd only seen a brief glimpse then, now she looked totally exposed. She swayed.

He took a step towards her. "Will you be all right?"

"Yes." She groaned. "I'm never drinking champagne again."

He grinned. "You should go to bed. Do you need help?"

"No ... thanks ... I can manage."

"Goodnight."

He let himself out the door and made his way back to the side fence where he'd climbed over. He and Jaxon talked about putting in a gate between their yards. Perhaps when he came back.

Jasper barked at him from the top of the stairs.

"Looks like it's still just you and me, mate," Ethan said.

He pressed play on the dock and dished up a serve of curry. He sat at his table with his back to the room and took a mouthful. His image was reflected back at him in the glass from the window as he ate. Beyond was blackness. A strange feeling swept over him. It surprised him to realise it was loneliness. He missed Jaxon being next door. They'd caught up at least once a week.

The other realisation was his need for female company. Over and over in his mind he could see Belinda and Savannah laughing together, smell Belinda's perfume, feel the warmth of Savannah's body as he'd tried to help her up. It was all very well to say no more one-night stands but he wasn't a monk.

He pushed away the remains of his meal and strode to the fridge. Jasper lifted his head. Ethan bent to ruffle his fur then crossed to the window to look out at the river glittering in the moonlight. Still he couldn't clear his head of Belinda's face so close to his nor the sparkle of Savannah's smile or the shape of her body as she'd lain spread-eagled on the ground.

"Damn, damn, damn!"

Ethan strode back to the bench and turned the music up. Metallica blasted from the speakers. He took the top from his beer. He was restless again tonight but for a totally different reason.

CHAPTER
17

Savannah stumbled to the kitchen and flicked on the kettle. It was her third attempt to get up and start the day. Trouble was it was nearly two o'clock. At this rate she might as well stay in bed and start again tomorrow.

She'd woken twice in the night and brought up anything that remained inside her. The last time it had caused her such pain she'd stayed on the toilet floor in a miserable state until she'd been strong enough to crawl back to bed.

Around nine o'clock she'd tried to get up but her head hurt so much she'd lowered it to the pillow and pulled the covers over her. She'd tried again at eleven with no success but at least the water she kept sipping had stayed down. Now she still felt terrible. Her body ached – her insides from the throwing up and her arms and legs from lying on the cold floor. At least the pain in her head had eased to a dull ache and she felt like food.

She took some bread from the pantry to make toast while she brewed a pot of tea. Once it was ready she took it to the dining table and sat down. Her tablets and glass were still there from last night and perched beside them were the car keys.

"Oh no," she groaned and put her head in her hands.

Ethan's concerned face reappeared in her scrambled brain. He had been there to see her lack of ability to manage her alcohol. She searched her memory for recollections of the previous night when he'd returned from dropping Belinda home. How bad had she been? She remembered him helping her to her feet and then ...

"Oh no," she groaned again. He'd been there when she'd thrown up. What else had she done? What must he think?

She took a small bite of toast. Then again what did she care? He obviously drank heavily sometimes. She recalled the morning he'd smelled like a stale brewery. But that only meant he'd had a big night. He could probably hold his drink, unlike her.

Savannah pressed her hands to her cheeks. Her jaw rested on her thumbs. She stared into her cup of tea. She was not a big drinker. Never had much opportunity in her teens, then came her fitness work and then the accident. There'd been too many pills in those years. She did like a beer from time to time and the odd glass of wine or sparkling.

She flopped her hands and head to the table. She'd enjoyed Belinda's company but just the thought of bubbles made her stomach churn. Thankfully she hadn't made a fool of herself in front of her new acquaintance. Only Ethan had witnessed her disastrous state.

She sat up again and ate more of her toast. No point wallowing in self-pity. It got you nowhere. She'd learned that the hard way. On the bright side it had been a bit of fun trying to show Belinda some exercises. Savannah wasn't sure if Belinda really wasn't much good at exercise routines or if she'd deliberately foiled Savannah's attempts to help her.

Whatever the reason, it had been worth the surprise on Ethan's face when he'd found them sprawled on the verandah. Not that she'd spent too long looking at his face. She had to admit she liked well-toned male bodies, even if she only checked them out from afar. And last night Ethan was the perfect advertisement, his buff body encased in snug-fitting clothes and his hair still damp.

Her stomach did a small flip and this time it wasn't because of her alcohol binge.

"Damn it, girl," she muttered to herself. "He's out of bounds."

Anyway, after last night he'd probably think her a fool. She drank the rest of her tea and carried her dishes to the sink. Time to do some work. It would clear her head of the alcohol haze and any thoughts of Ethan.

She went to the cupboard under the carport where she'd discovered Jaxon stored all kinds of cleaning equipment for the houseboats. It was stocked with every kind of cleaning product and explained why there'd been so little in the house. No need to have two supplies. She took as much as she could carry and set off down the path to the river. The sundecks of each of the three remaining boats needed a going over. That would keep her busy for some time.

The late afternoon sun was warm and the sky was filling with heavy grey clouds that trapped the balmy air. *River Magic* was the last of the three boats and by the time she stepped on board Savannah had worked up a sweat.

She climbed the steps to the sundeck with less enthusiasm than when she'd started. As she ascended to a point above the floor level of the deck she paused. Each of the boats had an outdoor table of some description and at least eight chairs. *River Magic* was no different, except in its case the heavy chairs were stackable and the last time she'd been up here they were in two stacks at the side of the deck. Now one of them was standing alone in the front right corner.

Savannah took the last few steps, put down her cleaning equipment and gazed around. Nothing else was different. There were no other items of furniture on this boat to be out of place. The deck was dusty and littered with leaves like the other two had been. Apart from the chair, all looked as it should.

She crossed the deck and stood near the chair. The back of it was slightly lower than the protective glass that ran across the front of the deck. She looked up and goosebumps prickled between her shoulder blades in spite of the warm afternoon. From here she could see to the glassed front of Jaxon's shack and nearly the full length of the verandah including the nook with the outdoor furniture.

She lowered herself to the chair. Anyone sitting here would be hard to see behind the darkened glass. She looked ahead. And they would have a clear view of Jaxon's shack. Goosebumps prickled down her back again. Who would have sat here? Who would have access?

She looked around. The closest house was Ethan's. The tall trees along their shared fence line only allowed glimpses of it. Obviously whoever had sat in this chair was watching Jaxon's place not Ethan's. And the only person she could think of was Ethan.

A gust of wind swirled along the river. It ruffled the water and stirred the branches of the trees. A shudder coursed right through Savannah this time. She stood up and carried the chair to the stack. She wasn't mistaken. The last time she'd been on this deck all the chairs had been stacked.

The wind grew stronger. The boat creaked beneath her. Birds swung across the water and circled the trees. A leaf blew in and dropped at her feet beside two others. She blinked as an eddy of air carried more leaves and dust this time. Anger surged through her and she let fly with some choice words. Her afternoon's work was about to be undone.

She snatched up the broom and dusters. At the top of the steps she turned for one last look towards the shack. Why would Ethan sit up here and watch? Perhaps he was some kind of pervert. She didn't like the thought of it but he could be moody and aloof. The friendliness might be just an act to woo her into a false sense of security. Whatever his reason, she couldn't think of anything that was reassuring.

She let herself off the boat, slid its gangplank into place and made her way up the path. By the time she reached the carport the sky was covered with grey clouds and she was battling the wind. She stowed the cleaning equipment in the cupboard, certain now she had wasted her time. Dirt and debris swirled through the air.

There was a crash and a clink from the front verandah. She hurried around to find the two empty wine bottles had fallen. The sound of Jaxon's landline phone startled her. It was the first call she'd had for days. She stepped inside, slid the glass firmly shut behind her and snatched up the phone.

"Hello?"

"Is that J&S Houseboats?" The female voice was young.

"Yes, I'm sorry I should have said." Savannah still didn't have her head around this business.

"My name is Tara. My friend is getting married and we'd like to celebrate with a girls' weekend."

Savannah hesitated. That was code for a hens' weekend. Did Jaxon allow that kind of booking?

"We'd like to hire a houseboat," Tara continued.

Savannah flipped opened the black diary. Jaxon had left everything up to her and a booking was a booking.

"What date were you looking at?"

This time it was Tara who paused.

"And how many nights?" Savannah added.

"We were hoping for two."

Savannah checked Jaxon's list of rates. "Three is the minimum," she said.

There was another pause. "Do you have anything for next weekend?" Tara asked.

Savannah stopped flipping the diary pages forward.

"I know it's short notice," Tara babbled. "We've tried a few places with no luck. We're just desperate to organise something special for our friend. She wasn't going to do anything. She's recovering from major surgery. We never thought she'd make it to the wedding but she's recovering well. We think she needs some pampering before her big day."

Savannah knew what it was like to go through gruelling times. She turned the diary to the dates Tara wanted, just over a week away. There were two boats available although one of them was out until the Friday, which would leave her little time to get it ready. She hadn't experienced it yet but she was beginning to understand there was a lot to do when a boat came back. *Our Destiny* was the only option but it was the smallest of the boats. It could only sleep six, *Tawarri* eight and the other two were ten-berth boats.

"How many people?"

"Six of us."

"I'm assuming you want Friday to Sunday?" she said.

"Yes." Tara gave a tiny squeak. "Do you have a boat available?"

Once more Savannah hesitated. So long as Tara and her friends paid, what difference did it make what their reason for hiring was?

"Two of you would have to share a sofa bed."

"That'd be fine." Tara's excited voice squealed in Savannah's ear. "So you can book us in?"

"Yes, if you pay the deposit today."

"Credit card ready," Tara said.

Savannah went through the details with her. By the time they'd finished she was full of admiration for what Tara and her friends were doing for their friend, the bride. Savannah couldn't help remembering her own long painful recovery and wondering if it might have been speeded up or at least made more bearable if she'd had that kind of support. Still, it was no use speculating about what could have been. She'd pushed her friends away instead of accepting their help.

"There's just one more thing."

Tara's voice snapped her out of her self-pity.

"None of us can drive a houseboat. Is it okay if we just stay moored at the bank?"

Savannah had no idea. She quickly thought back through all the notes Jaxon had left her. There was nothing she could recall about having to leave the bank.

"Of course," she said.

When she hung up she became aware of the sound of the wind again. It was buffeting the shack and there was an occasional clatter on the tin roof as leaves and debris were flung about.

She left the office and went to stand in front of the sliding door. Thick clouds covered the sky. Evening had come early. She flicked on the light.

Small waves, stirred by the wind, disturbed the normally calm surface of the river. Dirt and leaves swirled past and large raindrops began to splatter the concrete floor of the verandah. She cast a look over the houseboats. All her hard work would definitely be undone. She would have to clean them again before they went out on Friday.

The rain became heavier, striking the roof. Savannah's gaze stopped at the upper deck of the last houseboat. She pictured herself up there, sitting in the chair behind the smoky glass. Whoever sat there would be almost invisible and would have a clear view, right into the lounge where she stood. She shivered and closed the blinds on the gloomy evening.

It had to be Ethan who'd sat there. It was the only explanation. But why? And if not Ethan then who? That troubled her more than thinking it might be her neighbour.

CHAPTER
18

Ethan glanced at Gnasher's gate. Jasper was spending a lot of time there sniffing. Finally he lifted his leg then moved on, nose to the ground. Something had caught his attention, perhaps a fox had been through this morning. The wind and rain of last night would have washed away any previous scents. Ethan tossed a broken branch from the road to the bush on the side. The wind had scattered debris everywhere.

He moved his shoulders up and down and rubbed his hands together against the cold. It had been a while since he'd visited the old war vet. He'd try to get over there on the weekend. Trouble was there were no quick visits when it came to Gnasher. He liked to talk and Ethan's time was filling up with jobs. Once he got back he had to ring his father. Blake had berated him yesterday for not doing it already. Who knew how much help Mal would need with the shearing? Ethan could feel the tension building inside him. Working with Mal was similar to the pressure of working in a war zone. It felt like he was preparing for a trip outside the wire.

He pushed the thought away and set off again. First he'd enjoy his morning walk then he'd think about Mal. Jasper was up ahead on the other side of the road now, following the fence line that led to Belinda's gate. Once again the dog stopped, sniffed around and lifted his leg. It was going to be a slow walk at this rate. Ethan urged Jasper forward.

They made it as far as the fancy white gates before Jasper stopped again. Ethan went closer. The new gates had appeared flimsy in the headlights but up close he could see they were far from that. The chain and padlock were also heavy duty, as was the wire fence that met the gates on both sides. This was not a mere marking of a boundary. It was designed to keep people out.

Ethan thought about the Rottweiler that had come to meet Belinda. Perhaps the fence had been built to keep him in. That would make a very expensive dog fence. Still, Belinda had given the impression she had money. He smiled now at the thought of her obvious proposition the other night. He got that a lot when he was in the army. A night out on The Strand in Townsville was always a good night for him with the ladies. It was reassuring to know he was still appealing without the uniform. Just a pity it was the wrong woman who'd noticed.

His thoughts strayed to Savannah and the suppleness of her body as he'd helped her up from the table. She hadn't spoken to him or acted in any way that gave a hint she might find him of interest other than to help her with the boats.

He rounded a bend in the road. Ahead of him Jasper gave three short barks. Ethan faltered a moment at the sight of his dog sitting at Savannah's feet. She had her hands clenched to her chest, her head pulled back, eyeballing the animal.

"Jasper, come," Ethan commanded.

The dog bounded back to him.

"You should have that dog on a lead." Savannah put her hands to her hips, glaring at him.

Ethan couldn't help his sweeping gaze of her body. She wore a singlet top that stretched firmly over her curves and an equally snug pair of three-quarter gym pants. A jumper was tied around her waist. He raised his gaze to the dark patches made by moisture over her breasts. She'd been working hard.

"Are you able to control your dog?"

She was watching him. How long had he been staring at her? He reached down to pat Jasper's head.

"He's only young." As opposed to Ethan, who felt ancient some days. "He was just saying hello."

"Well now that he has, I'll be on my way."

"How are you feeling today?" He smiled.

"I'm fine, thanks." Her chin lifted and her eyes narrowed.

"That's good." Ethan wanted to say more but she didn't look like she wanted to chat.

"How did you know I'd be here?"

Her tone was accusing.

"I didn't." Ethan shrugged his shoulders, perplexed by her hostility.

She moved forward. As she drew level with him she studied him closely. Jasper crept a few steps towards her.

"Stay," Ethan snapped.

Savannah paused.

"I meant the dog," he said.

"Of course you did." She glared at him a moment longer then jogged away. The jog turned into a run and she disappeared around the bend.

"That went well, Jasper." Ethan scratched his head. "I get the feeling our neighbour wasn't pleased to see us this morning." He squatted down and grasped Jasper's jowls in his hands. "Let's face it, she's never pleased to see you but I thought I was at least on friendly terms." He ruffled the dog's head and stood up.

"Let's go."

Why was he even trying? He'd vowed to distance himself from Jaxon's sister, only helping when he had to. It had come as a surprise to him to realise he wanted to know more about her. She wasn't the imposition he'd first imagined.

Dinner last night with Blake and Jenny had really brought his feelings to the fore. Watching his brother so obviously in love had stirred a yearning in him. Ethan wanted that closeness with a woman, something more permanent. It would come as a shock to many that Ethan Daly wanted to settle down. The blokes in Townsville would laugh if they knew. He glanced around as if one of them might suddenly appear but the road was empty – only him and Jasper.

In Afghanistan he'd been confronted by how cheap life could be. Even more so on his second tour when he'd been out among the villages. It had been a shock. It had changed him. Once he was safely back on base in Australia, army life hadn't been the same. He'd yearned for a place of his own and some peace. He'd found that to a certain extent but now he wanted more. It had taken last night's dinner with Blake and Jenny to make him realise he needed someone to share it with.

Savannah was different from many of the women he'd known. She was good-looking in an understated way. She could stand on her own two feet. She asked for his help only when it was something she couldn't do herself. If it was something she could learn and do herself she did, and yet he'd seen the hint of a vulnerable side she tried to hide. She kept fit, seemed to prefer her own company, although she'd obviously been enjoying herself with Belinda, and she wasn't much of a drinker if the other night was anything to go on. She was a puzzle. It piqued his curiosity.

He stopped and called Jasper.

"Time to head home, mate. I've got work to do."

The thought of ringing Mal was a growing tension in his chest. He had to get it over and done with. Besides, there was a glimmer of hope to follow. Soon Savannah would need his help again with the houseboats. He'd have to think up a way that might ease him past the barriers she threw up. He was determined to get to know her better.

Ethan came out of the shed at the sound of a vehicle. Jenny's car rolled to a stop beside him and Blake lowered the passenger side window.

"Didn't hear you arrive today," he said.

Ethan leaned down and nodded a hello in Jenny's direction.

"I had a few things to do at home first," he said.

"Like ringing Mal?"

"I rang him this morning."

"I know." Blake grinned. "He's been on to me since."

"Checking up on me?'

"He usually phones me every other day."

Ethan straightened up. A ripple of envy swept over him. It was wasted energy.

"Mal doesn't want me there," he said.

"Of course he does. He needs help. He's just not good at asking for it."

"Where are you two off to?" Ethan changed the subject.

"Jenny's taking me to look at the crops. Going to see if any damage was done with that storm last night."

Jenny leaned across to look at Ethan. "Want to come with us?"

"Why not?" He climbed into the back seat. "Thanks again for the meal last night, Jenny."

"My pleasure. You'll have to join us again before I leave."

"You going soon?" Ethan asked.

"Early next week. I have to get back to work."

Ethan saw her glance at Blake but he was looking out his side window.

"Everything go all right getting that part in the header?"

"Nearly finished," Ethan said. "I'll have the header back together by this afternoon and that's the last of it. You'll be good to go."

"Blake's lucky to have your help," Jenny said.

"Yes." Ethan reached forward and patted his big brother's head. "Yes, he is."

"Won't be much longer and I'll be able to manage on my own again."

Blake spoke gruffly and once more Ethan saw Jenny glance his way. This time she had a wry smile on her face.

"Go left after this gate," Blake said.

The air was certainly tense between them this morning. Perhaps a lovers' tiff, Ethan thought. They'd been happy in each other's arms when he'd left them last night.

"Doesn't look like you got much rain," he said.

"Stuff-all. It's the wind I'm worried about. It got pretty wild during the night."

"Same my way."

They drove on in silence until they crested a hill and the canola crop stretched out in front of them.

"Wow," Jenny said. "I guess it's not farming terminology but that looks pretty."

"Wait a couple more weeks," Blake said. "This will be a sea of yellow."

"I'll have to come back and check it out."

Ethan watched as they looked at each other.

"Yes, you will," Blake said with a grin.

He opened his door and got out, making his way into the crop.

"You never wanted to be a farmer?" Jenny asked. She was looking ahead at Blake inspecting his crop.

"Not really. I enjoyed the freedom of growing up on the farm but I was always tinkering with the machines rather than working with the animals. Dad and Blake bought this property when Blake married." Ethan stopped talking. He hadn't meant to raise the issue of Blake's marriage.

"Blake loves this place," Jenny said. "He tells me he nearly lost it with the divorce."

Ethan remained silent. He didn't know how much his brother had told Jenny about his business matters. He wasn't going to be the one to fill in any information Blake may have omitted.

"Sad that a marriage fails," Jenny went on. "Especially when there are children, but I'd never thought about the extra implications for someone like a farmer. He could have lost everything."

"He could have."

Jenny twisted in her seat to look at him. "I hope you don't mind me asking but where do you fit into all this? You don't live on the property."

"I'm only helping out. I enjoy working with machines."

"But not with animals?"

Jenny was studying him with genuine interest.

"It's just that Blake said the same." She glanced away to where Blake was still inspecting his canola. "He seems to love growing things but he has a special dislike for sheep."

"It's nothing sinister. Neither of us are serial animal killers." Ethan grinned. "Our parents love working with animals and their property isn't suited to growing crops. Blake's land is. He can graze their sheep here from time to time. It works out well for all of them."

"He's asked me to come and live here." She turned back. Her eyes were filled with apprehension.

"You don't want to?" Ethan was worried Blake was moving too fast.

"We hit it off really well from the start. It's not Blake I doubt. It's me – living here."

"Too isolated?"

"Not really but I love my work."

"There's a hospital in Burra."

"I'm a trauma nurse."

Ethan held her gaze. "Adrenalin junkie."

"You understand."

Ethan nodded. He imagined it was similar to working in a war zone, thinking on your feet, alert for every possibility, never knowing what might come your way.

"How do you cope being here after Afghanistan? Life must be so different."

"Now I get my kicks from landing a fish for my dinner."

He grinned. She didn't. He looked away to see his brother heading back towards the car.

"It's an adjustment," Ethan said. "But I've only got myself to worry about."

There was silence for a moment.

"I don't want it to end up spoiling things between us," Jenny said in a quiet voice.

Ethan was at a loss. He was the last person to dish out relationship advice.

"You two seem very suited," he said lamely. "Blake's a lucky guy."

Blake climbed back into the front seat.

"Why is Blake a lucky guy?" he asked.

"Having your own personal trauma nurse," Ethan said. "You're an accident waiting to happen."

Blake's face lost its grin. He looked at Jenny. "We're a good match in so many ways. We want the same things."

Ethan watched Jenny glance from Blake then back to the windscreen.

"Food," she said. "All this fresh air has made me hungry."

"Good idea," Ethan said and rubbed his hands together. Anything to change the subject.

Jenny turned the car for home. Blake didn't say anything. He stared from his side window long after the canola crop was lost from sight.

Back at the shed they invited Ethan for lunch. He declined. They needed some space and he didn't want to be the go-between.

"I'll finish the header then I'm going home," he said. "I've got a bit of catching up to do before I help Mal with the shearing."

"We might come for a visit over the weekend," Blake said. "Show Jenny the river before she goes back to the city."

"Sure. Why don't we make it Saturday night? I'll cook a curry."

"I love curry," Jenny said.

Blake rolled his eyes.

"I'll tone it down for you," Ethan said.

He reached in the window and poked Blake's good shoulder before the car moved away. Hopefully by Saturday night they'd have cleared the air and sorted out their differences.

His thoughts strayed to Savannah. Perhaps she'd come and eat with them. She might feel more inclined to accept his invitation if she knew others were going to be there. Or not.

Ethan turned his attention to the header. Machines made sense to him. Family complications and puzzling next-door neighbours faded from his thoughts.

CHAPTER

19

Savannah stepped under the shower. She closed her eyes and turned her face up to the warm water. It was Friday and this afternoon she had three houseboats going out. That meant she had to face Ethan again. She'd made a fool of herself drinking too much the night Belinda had come over. She'd hoped she wouldn't see Ethan again until today and by then it would be forgotten. But no, she'd seen him on the road on her morning run and he hadn't forgotten. He'd made a point of asking her how she was feeling with that smirk on his face.

She pressed her palms against the cold tiles.

"Damn you, Ethan Daly," she muttered.

Right now she'd prefer not see him again but she needed his help. Not only did she have three boats going out today but *Tawarri* was due back tomorrow and she could tell from Jaxon's list there were things that needed doing she didn't understand. It was so frustrating to depend on Ethan.

She bent forward and sent the water cascading over her lower back and down her legs. At least she physically felt better. When she'd come across Ethan it had been her first run since she'd arrived and she'd needed it. She'd been exercising daily but running had given her a good aerobic workout. Everything ached but not in a bad way. This morning she'd run again before she'd gone into Riverboat Point.

She turned the green and white crusted taps to off as tightly as she could. The water from the showerhead slowed to a trickle. Jaxon had spent money on doing up the shack along with the electrical work but he hadn't brought the plumbing into line with the twenty-first century. At least the water had stayed hot since her first day here.

She rubbed herself vigorously with the towel. Somehow she kept getting back to Ethan. No matter how hard she tried to push him out of her head he kept infiltrating her thoughts.

Then there was that stare of his. She shivered and wrapped the towel tightly around her. He'd looked her up and down as if her clothes weren't there. She'd had that look from men in the gym. They were usually the type who thought they were God's gift. She would often stare them down but in Ethan's case it made her think of the seat on the deck of the houseboat. Was he the peeping Tom? If it was him it made her feel sad rather than exposed.

Once she was dressed, Savannah flicked through the pile of envelopes Faye had given her. She left one aside before she stacked them on Jaxon's desk. Mostly junk mail but this one was handwritten and addressed to J&S Houseboats. She opened it. There was a cheque inside and a note. It was a deposit for a booking. She marked it off in the black book and tidied it all away again except for the cheque. She picked it up and went back to the kitchen where she sat it on the table propped against the ornamental motorbike.

Her trip to Riverboat Point this morning was meant to be quick. She'd bought food for the weekend. While she was at the shop Faye had appeared with the bundle of mail. Turned out Jaxon's fancy pushbike letterbox at the gate was just for show. There was no mail delivery. All mail was held at the store.

She looked at the cheque again. What had Jaxon's notes said about banking? She didn't recall a bank anywhere in the town. That would be her next task but for now she wanted lunch. There were three groups coming in a couple of hours to take out the remaining houseboats. This time she would be ready with paperwork. She wasn't going to make the same mistake she had with Fred.

"Hello?"

Savannah looked towards the sliding doors and pulled her face into a smile.

Belinda was waving at her through the glass. Savannah crossed to open the door. At least Belinda didn't have any bottles in her hands.

"I'm just on my way home from town." Belinda's eyes sparkled. "Ash is off fishing. What are you doing this afternoon?"

"Those three houseboats are going out. I'll be busy." Savannah was relieved she had a real excuse.

"Oh, that's too bad," Belinda said. The smile left her face.

Savannah hesitated. "Maybe this evening?"

"Ash has invited a friend. He'll expect me to cook."

Savannah wondered about their relationship. The way Belinda spoke about her husband it seemed she did things more out of duty than love.

"Perhaps tomorrow?" Belinda looked hopeful. "We're going home on Sunday."

Savannah felt a tinge of regret. She'd hoped to spend some more time with Belinda – without the drinking. "I've got a boat coming in during the day. What about we catch up for dinner?"

"That would be good. I'll come to you." Belinda's voice became animated. "I'll bring the drinks."

"Oh." It wasn't quite what Savannah had expected although it was a relief to know she wouldn't have to run the gauntlet of getting past their dog. "Sure. Anything you or Ash don't like?"

"Don't worry about Ash. He's not good company at the moment. I'm sure he'll make his own plans. I eat anything." Belinda patted her stomach. "Just not huge amounts. I'll come over about six. We can have a drink on your verandah before it gets dark. Such a nice view."

Belinda turned and stood staring ahead. Savannah followed her gaze to the moored houseboats.

"They're all going out you said?"

"Yes," Savannah replied. Belinda took a lot of interest in the houseboats.

"It'll be nice for you to have the place to yourself. It must seem a bit busy when all the boats are moored out front. Ash and I only have glimpses of the river from our place. He loves the seclusion of it. Sometimes it's as if we're all alone in the world."

Savannah looked at the three houseboats and tried to imagine the front of Jaxon's place without them. It would have been that way when he bought it. She just didn't remember taking a lot of notice at the time.

"Give me the city any day," she said.

"Me too," Belinda replied. She turned to Savannah. "I'll get out of your hair. See you tomorrow."

"Yes," Savannah said and gave Belinda a wave as she walked away and round the side of the house. Belinda was entertaining. The dinner was something to look forward to at least.

Savannah took out her phone and checked the time. She could still fit in a bite to eat before the customers arrived. She just hoped Ethan would remember.

After she'd come back from town, she'd cleaned the outside of the three boats again. They'd been covered in dirt and leaves after the storm. Once that was completed to her satisfaction she'd gone through the insides. She was confident now that all was in readiness for the afternoon departures. The groups were staggered. The first would be there at three but the other two were later, one at five and one at six.

She thought about the work when the boats came back. There was sewerage to empty and tanks to be refuelled. Ethan had offered to help her with that. Then there was the cleaning. Each boat had to be gone over in detail and restocked ready for its next trip. That alone would take her all day. At least the returns were staggered. Two boats were due back on Monday morning and the third on Tuesday. *River Magic* would go out again the day after its return and the rest were booked for the following weekend. Savannah didn't know how Jaxon managed everything and worked as an electrician.

She ate some lunch then brought all the paperwork from the office and set it out in groups on the dining table. There was still more than an hour before she expected the first group to arrive. She decided she'd step through her exercise routine. Her aches and pains had been minimal the last few days. She wanted to keep it that way.

Three o'clock approached and she was back standing beside the paperwork on the table. She'd looked at it several times already but she cast another glance over it. A knock at the back door startled her. She hadn't heard a vehicle.

"Hello," Ethan said as she opened the door. "Thought I'd get here early this time."

"No customers yet," Savannah said. She stood in the doorway. Now what? She thought. Ethan waited.

"Would you like to come in?" she said.

"Thanks." He followed her into the living area and stopped in front of the dining table. "I see you're on top of the paperwork this time."

"I hope so." Savannah straightened the three piles.

"I reckon that's what caught Jaxon out in the early days."

"Really?" She turned to study Ethan. There was no teasing grin, just a soft curve of his lips and warm sparkle in his eyes.

"I don't think he had much idea at the start but he was a quick learner," Ethan said. "After the first couple of boats went out he didn't ever mention problems again."

"Could something have gone really wrong and that's why he ran off?" she asked. Savannah watched Ethan straighten and the smile slip from his face. She was sure he had to know more about her brother's disappearance than he was letting on.

"I don't think he ran off."

"But why leave if he was getting his business working well?"

"He just wanted a holiday."

"Perhaps something had gone wrong," Savannah persisted.

"Not that I know of. He had the odd dodgy customer but he usually had a laugh about their antics. With his electrical work and the houseboats he was happy as a pig in mud."

Savannah kept her gaze on Ethan.

"And he ups and takes a holiday?"

Ethan turned away from her to the view through the glass. "It had nothing to do with the electrical work or the boats."

"But there was something?"

Savannah stepped closer. Ethan turned and looked her steadily in the eye.

"If there was, he didn't confide in me. My only instructions were to watch out for your arrival and help where I could."

His dark brown eyes were mesmerising. Savannah wanted to believe him. Her trust in her fellow human beings had been sorely tested on several occasions. It had left her hurt and cynical. She didn't find it easy to make friends. And Jaxon's vague warning hadn't helped.

The sound of a vehicle broke the silence between them.

"That might be the group for your first boat," Ethan said. "I'll see if I can lend a hand with the loading while you get the paperwork sorted."

Savannah trailed behind him out the door. A group of young men were climbing out of the first of two cars in the driveway. She took a deep breath and went to find out which one was Tom Barclay, the person who'd made the booking.

Tom was already shaking Ethan's hand thinking he was Jaxon and Savannah his partner. She put him straight but each new lot of customers who arrived made the same assumption and she couldn't be bothered explaining. She and Ethan were working together well by then. She gave out the basic instructions with the dos and don'ts, got the papers signed and took their money. Ethan helped them load and took them out for their driving instructions.

One thing each group had said was they'd had trouble finding J&S Houseboats because of the lack of signage. Their various GPSs had been little help and it had only been the mud map Jaxon had emailed them with their receipts that had helped them find the place. She'd need to do something about that.

As the last boat headed back into the bank to let Ethan off she went down to meet him. The sun was low in the sky. The group on board *River Magic* wouldn't be able to travel far before they had to find a place to moor for the night.

She waved at the toot of their horn then followed Ethan up the path.

"Thanks very much," she said once they reached the carport.

He stopped to look at her.

"This is taking up a lot of your time," she said. "Jaxon will have to pay you when he gets back."

Ethan stared at her. She felt like his eyes would swallow her.

"I don't mind helping a mate," he said.

Savannah wasn't sure if he meant her or Jaxon. She felt an odd tingle of excitement at the thought it might be her.

"It's very generous of you," she said and forced herself to look away. "*Tawarri* gets in tomorrow. I'll need help then too."

"I'll be here all day. There'll be fuel needed and the sewerage to pump out."

Once again Savannah knew she was totally reliant on his help. She felt irritated at her lack of knowledge yet eager to spend more time with Ethan.

"You're a quick learner, like Jaxon. Except for the turnarounds you'll be doing most of the jobs yourself soon."

Savannah found herself enjoying the confidence he placed in her.

Ethan's eyes sparkled again.

"My brother and his girlfriend are coming over for curry tomorrow night," he said. "Why don't you join us? We can toast your first full week in business."

Savannah was about to say she'd love to when she remembered Belinda was coming over.

"I can't," she said.

"Don't like curry?" One of his eyebrows raised in a quirky look.

"I love curry," she said, "but I've already asked Belinda over."

"Bring her too," he said. "There will be plenty."

Savannah thought a moment then said yes. She didn't think Belinda would mind going to Ethan's. She was happy to have company.

"Can I bring something?"

"No," he said. "Just yourselves." He turned to walk away and then stopped and looked back at her. "Maybe some sparkling. I don't keep any of that."

She opened her mouth but he was already striding away. One thing she wouldn't be taking was sparkling. From now on she was strictly a beer girl. Belinda could have any she brought to herself.

CHAPTER
20

At ten-thirty the next morning Savannah was pacing the floor. *Tawarri* should have been back by ten. She was sure Fred was playing on her lack of knowledge of the business. She wasn't planning on letting him get away with it.

She stopped in front of the sliding door, let herself out and walked down to the river's edge. She peered left and right. A small boat was making its way along the river but there was no sign of the houseboat. She turned and followed the drive to the gate. The only sounds were birdcalls and the odd rustle of leaves.

She peered at the thick bush on Belinda's side of the fence. It didn't look as if anyone would live in that property, just as it didn't across the road on Gnasher's block. She hadn't seen Ethan on her run this morning or heard a bark from Jasper. She stood perfectly still and listened. Not a human sound to be heard. The rest of the world could be dead for all she knew. She was totally alone. At least she would have Belinda's company later and Ethan's at dinner tonight. She found herself looking forward to it.

She glanced again at the fence that divided the properties. It didn't look strong enough to stand up in the wind let alone keep that dog of Ash's in. What was to stop it coming over here and attacking her? Savannah peered at the bush expecting to see a large mouth full of teeth at any moment. A few metres in she noticed another fence. It was newer and higher, like the one that followed the roadside boundary of the Palmers' property. That was why the dog couldn't come her way. For some reason they'd built their fence just inside their property. Maybe Jaxon or the previous owners hadn't wanted the cost of a new fence but even so, if the Palmers were going to the trouble of putting up a new fence surely they'd want it to follow their boundary.

A distant droning sound made her look up. She spotted a small plane a long way off. So there were other humans out there somewhere. She pursed her lips. None of them was Fred and his friends.

Savannah went back to the shed and let herself in. She gathered the linen and toiletries that would be needed for *Tawarri*. There was a box on a homemade trolley. She assumed Jaxon used it to transport the gear to the boats. She stacked as much as she could inside it and towed it back to the verandah. Still no sign of a boat. She decided to brew herself a tea.

Tawarri pulled back into its space at eleven-thirty. Savannah was ropable. She ignored Fred's cheery wave as he tied one of the mooring ropes to the tree.

"You're very late," she said as he came up the path to meet her.

There were dark bags under his eyes and his skin was sallow but he still had the same patronising look on his face.

"Jaxon never worries too much about the time we return," he said.

Savannah drew a deep breath in through her nose.

"Your booking conditions clearly indicate the return time is to be negotiated. This boat has to go out again this afternoon." It didn't but Savannah wasn't going to let the smarmy Fred get off so easily. "I've little time to get it ready."

"It wasn't in the best condition when we got it."

"What do you mean?"

"You already know about the missing toilet paper and cling wrap. There were other things. Just minor but not up to Jaxon's usual standard." Fred grinned broadly and patted her shoulder. "We understand you're just learning though. We managed."

Savannah resisted the urge to slap his hand away. From the corner of her eye she could see movement from the boat as the others began to unload.

"We've saved you some cleaning time," he continued before she could get a word in. "The ladies have gone over the boat from top to bottom. Better than when we took it out."

"You didn't pay the hire fee before you left and I'd still like the bond money," Savannah cut in before he could gush any more.

"Little point to the bond now," Fred said. He threw out his arms. "We're back safe and sound."

"Fuel costs."

"That won't be much. We didn't end up going far." He winked at her. "Turned into a real party boat. We were having too much fun to sight-see."

Savannah forced herself not to cringe away from him.

"Money please," she said.

"Didn't we pay that before we left?" Fred's wife had come up the path carrying an armload of boxes. "I collected everyone's share and put it in your wallet, Fred. We certainly haven't been anywhere to spend it."

"I didn't realise, pet." He gave Jan a pat on her bottom. "I'll take care of it."

She smiled at Savannah and went on up the path.

"There's the hire fee and an extra two hundred." Fred held out a wad of fifty dollar notes. "Should more than cover the fuel."

Savannah felt exposed but she counted it carefully where she stood.

"I'll get you a receipt."

"No need," he said with a smug grin.

People were trudging around them, loaded with bags, boxes and containers. Their chat lacked the exuberance it had at their departure. Savannah didn't think the women looked quite so glamorous and perky as they had before they left. One of the women in particular looked terrible. The man beside her had his arm around her.

"Just ridiculous to go so far," she complained as they passed Savannah.

"This was much better than our last trip, don't you think?" Fred said to the pair.

The man gave him a nod but the woman glared.

Fred was oblivious.

"Let's get everything stacked up here." He waved to a point at the top of the path. "Pete and I will bring the cars down."

The two men set off up the path. Savannah noticed the woman continued to glare after them. Not a happy camper. None of the rest of them was smiling except for Jan.

With the money gripped tightly in her hand, Savannah made her way back to the shack. She'd write the receipt regardless of Fred's casual response. She had no idea of fuel costs but she hoped the bit of extra money would cover it. She was annoyed at her mismanagement of this first hiring and Fred's smug attitude only made her feel it more.

Inside she stashed the money in an envelope. She still had to work out what to do with cash and cheques. She tidied up all the papers relating to Fred's hire and wrote a receipt. The sound of cars moving outside drew her to the door. Fred's party were loaded up and both cars were moving away by the time she reached the end of the verandah.

She made a half-hearted attempt to wave the paper she was clutching. A dust trail billowed behind the vehicles then they were through the gate and gone. Savannah listened until the sounds of their engines faded away. Fred hadn't waited for the receipt. Good riddance to him. She turned and made her way to the boat.

The deck was tidy and at first glance, the living area was too. The sink and the stovetop sparkled in the sunshine slanting through the windows and the benchtops were clear. She made her way down the passageway opening bedroom doors and glancing in bathrooms. The bottom of her runners squelched. They stuck to the linoleum floor with each step she took. The floor was still wet. Inside the bedrooms, the carpets looked okay but the bedding spilled onto the floor. The beds had to be stripped anyway but she thought they could have been left pulled up. The bathroom tiles were wet and in one bathroom, empty soap packets and assorted toiletry containers littered the basin. Already Fred's boast about the tidiness of their clean-up had been proven to be a lie. The gall of the man to insinuate the boat had gone out in this state.

The door of the last bathroom was jammed and she had to push hard to open it. She looked down at the soggy towel that was wedged below it then the smell hit her. She clapped a hand over her mouth and nose but it was too late to keep out the mingled stench of vomit and faeces. The floor was awash with yellow chunky liquid and the toilet splattered with brown from the seat to the base. There was a gaping hole in the wall where the toilet roll holder should have been.

Savannah stepped back quickly and pulled the door shut on the putrid mess. Her cup of tea gurgled in her stomach. She gagged and made a dash for the back door. On the swim deck she placed her hands on the rails and sucked in deep breaths of fresh air.

Damn Fred and his superior attitude. He was nothing but a liar and a cheat. She thumped the railing and winced as it jarred her arm. A couple of birds paddling on the river, took off in fright as she yelled a string of abuse to the departed Fred and his crew.

CHAPTER
21

Ethan stopped. He peered to the left and the right of the track. It was too quiet.

"Cooee," he called. "Incoming."

He stood still and listened again. There was a small thud to his left which meant Gnasher was on his right but he took the bait and turned. There was a rustle of leaves behind him and strong arms grabbed him.

"You're getting soft, Digger," a voice hissed in his ear.

The smell of unwashed clothes and body odour assaulted his nostrils. Ethan shrugged away from the arms that held him.

"Bloody hell, Gnasher," he said as he stepped back. "When did you wash last?"

"I was just heading to the river. Heard you coming a mile off." Gnasher grinned, revealing the gaps where he'd lost teeth. "Thought I'd stay and put you through your paces."

"You stink, mate." Ethan smiled back at the old bloke.

"I've been a bit crook."

Ethan studied Gnasher. That usually meant he'd been on a bender. He might look like he was homeless but he was particular with his personal hygiene. There was a three-day growth on his normally clean-shaven face. Apart from the stink he looked well enough.

"Rotten guts," Gnasher said. "I've come good now. Must have been something I ate."

"Why are you going to the river to wash?"

"Pump's not working."

"How about I take a look at it?"

"Sure."

Gnasher retrieved a backpack he'd stashed when he'd been stalking Ethan and made off along the track. Ethan followed, thankful there was a gentle southwesterly to keep the smell away from him.

They stepped into the clearing where Gnasher had his living quarters. It was basic, a caravan inside a large shed that was open along the front. The camp was a contrast of basic living and modern technology. There were rabbit skins hanging from a wire near the old Holden that Gnasher sometimes drove into town to do odd jobs for people. Once or twice a year he drove it to Adelaide to see his daughter Cheryl and grandchildren.

The publican from Riverboat Point delivered beer every fortnight and once a month Charlie from the supermarket delivered his food supplies and mail. Gnasher was happy with his life. As happy as he could be. Ethan knew he still suffered from the terrors. They'd compared war stories on a couple of occasions. Enough so they understood each other. Different generations, different wars, but the same nightmares.

"You've got a TV," Ethan said.

He strolled across to inspect the large flat screen set up by the couch in the corner behind the car.

"I want to watch the footy grand final."

"You could have come to my place."

"I decided it was time. Cheryl's given me a pile of those old *Carry On* movies. They're always good for a laugh. I'll put the kettle on."

Gnasher dropped his pack on a chair at the small table and made his way to the back of the shed where he had a kitchen set up: benches, shelves, microwave, oven and even the kitchen sink. The floor of the shed was concrete but he had all the mod cons he wanted. Anything he needed he built. He'd been a carpenter by trade and a handyman until the drinking had stopped him from holding down a job.

Ethan wandered over to the couch. The TV had a DVD recorder attached. It was an impressive set-up.

"You joining the twenty-first century?" To Ethan's knowledge Gnasher had never had a television. The few times he came over to watch some footy, he'd go outside if the news was on or the ads were too crazy. The idiot box, as he called it, made him jumpy.

"You might need to make this end of the place more weatherproof," Ethan said.

The shed had large tarpaulins that could be rolled down to enclose the space. Gnasher usually only had them down during the coldest months, preferring his home to be open to the bush. He used the van for sleeping and warmth when it was too cold to be outside.

"We'll see," Gnasher said over his shoulder.

Ethan made his way around the side of the shed, past the bins and drums where Gnasher put his rubbish. There were always more empty beer bottles and cans than anything else but he kept it all tidy. At the back of the shed was the lean-to Gnasher had built. It housed a laundry, toilet, shower and bathtub. Beside that was the rainwater tank. The tank had a tap to give access to drinking water if Gnasher needed it but the pump fed water to everything else.

Ethan lifted the box that covered the pump. The motor was old and the last time he'd tinkered with it he'd warned Gnasher he'd need a new one before long. That had been a few months ago, so the pump had done well but Ethan could see it had had it now.

He went back to the shed.

"Pump's stuffed, mate," he said. "You'll need a new one."

"Thought so."

Gnasher put two mugs of black tea on the table and sat down. Ethan followed suit.

"A trip to town, or would you like me to order one for you?"

"Na, thanks mate. I need to do a couple of jobs. Looks like I'll be going in sooner than I thought, that's all."

"I reckon you should clean up first or Faye won't let you in her shop."

"You don't think she'll like my brand of aftershave?"

"You're welcome to use my shower."

"You're a good bloke for a grease monkey."

They lapsed into silence, the tea still too hot to drink.

"You been getting a few bunnies?" Ethan nodded towards the skins.

"I was getting low on meat."

"My mother used to fricassee it. Can't say I'm that keen on it."

"Nothing like fried rabbit," Gnasher said. "I was raised on it."

They both took slurps of tea.

"I'd have baked a cake if I'd known you were coming," Gnasher said. "You after something?"

"Just a social call. Haven't seen you for a while."

"Here I am."

"You watch the game last night?" Ethan asked.

"No." Gnasher got up and walked to the edge of the concrete, looking out across the cleared land towards the bush.

"You missed a good one. Cats won but only by a point. It could have gone either way right down to the last few seconds."

"You didn't bring your dog."

Gnasher came back to the table. His hand trembled as he lifted his mug to his mouth.

"Already took him for a walk this morning." Truth was Ethan didn't like Jasper sniffing about on Gnasher's land. He had all kinds of snares set up from trip-wires to rabbit traps not too far from the track.

Gnasher's eyes darkened.

"I wouldn't do him any harm."

"I know that," Ethan said. "But he's still young. Not always well mannered. Wouldn't want him lifting a leg in your kitchen again."

Gnasher's frown turned to a smile.

"Young fellas, you never know what they might get up to."

Ethan stood up and drained the last of his cup.

"You good to go?" he said. "Bring your washing as well if you like. Might be a while before you get your new pump."

Gnasher picked up a plastic washing basket.

"Good idea," he said. "I'm down to my last pair of jocks."

Gnasher ended up staying a couple of hours. Ethan made lunch which they ate out on the deck, Gnasher in a pair of boxers while the rest of his clothes dried. He'd shaved, which along with his number two haircut, gave him a tidy appearance.

"This is good, thanks," Gnasher said and he took another mouthful of soup.

"Just leftover chicken and veg."

Ethan hadn't known what to feed the old bloke. If he'd been crook he may not have had any alcohol for a day or so which would explain the shakes. His stomach was probably in need of something wholesome. Ethan always enjoyed soup when he was getting over a wog. He'd dug around in his freezer and found a couple of serves.

"That bloke next door got himself a woman?" Gnasher nodded in the direction of Jaxon's shack.

"His sister. She's taking care of the place while Jaxon's away."

"Those bloody tourist boats. I thought they'd be history by now."

Gnasher gripped his hands together tightly and pressed them to the table. Below, Ethan could see the old bloke's feet tapping on the deck.

"I bought my block because it was isolated and on a dead-end road."

"I wasn't keen either but it hasn't been too bad. They come, get on the houseboat and go off on the river for several days. Not too much disruption to the peace."

"So this woman any good?"

Gnasher ate some more soup. Ethan looked over his shoulder. Through a gap in the trees he could see Savannah on the sundeck of the boat that must have come in while he'd been over the road.

"Savannah's a hard worker."

"Yeah, but is she a looker?"

Ethan turned back to his soup.

"Haven't paid much attention. She seems nice."

"Seems nice?" Gnasher thumped the table. "You are alive, aren't you, Dig? Even from this distance with my eyes I can see she's got a decent pair of knockers."

Ethan took another mouthful of soup. There were lots of things he and Gnasher had talked about but women wasn't one of them.

"Could be handy having her right next door. Specially if she's only here for the short term. A holiday fling with no complications."

"Shut up, Gnasher."

Jasper rose to his feet. Ethan glared at the old man. His gutter talk made Savannah sound like a tramp. She wasn't like that.

Gnasher held Ethan's glare then suddenly his face crinkled in a smile and he winked. He stood up.

"Thanks for your hospitality, mate. Beautiful day. I reckon my clothes will be dry by now."

Ethan felt ashamed of his outburst. What did it matter what Gnasher said about Savannah? She couldn't hear him and Ethan didn't care. That's what he told himself.

"You're welcome anytime, mate," Ethan said. "If you want to use the laundry or the bathroom till you get your pump, go for it. If I'm not here I'll leave the place open."

"You're a good bloke," Gnasher said. He gripped Ethan's hand in a firm shake. "Be seein' ya."

Ethan saw Gnasher out the door and watched as he plodded down the steps to the clothes line. Sometimes he felt sad after spending time with Gnasher and today was one of those times. It bothered Ethan that the old Viet vet lived such an isolated existence and drank so much. Ethan knew he couldn't change Gnasher's lifestyle. It was more that he feared he was seeing himself in the future. Ethan lived an isolated life too. He wasn't close to his family, except for Blake. He'd fought in a war that wasn't well supported by the Australian public and there were times when the demons drove him to drink too much.

He went back to his kitchen to start his curry. He enjoyed cooking. He was glad Savannah had accepted his invitation. Once the curry was cooking he'd head over to give her a hand. The thought of it lifted his sombre mood.

CHAPTER

22

Ethan went down to *Tawarri* and stepped on board.

"Hello?" he called.

There was no answer. He stuck his head inside the living area of the boat. A strong smell of disinfectant greeted him. He called again. Still no answer from Savannah. He walked the full way round the outside and climbed a few of the steps to check the sundeck. She was nowhere to be seen. Perhaps she'd finished and was waiting for him up at the house.

He retraced his steps and followed the path until he reached the sliding door. Music was playing and through the glass he could see Savannah. She had her back to him and she was exercising in time to the music. He watched her a moment. Her body moved in perfect symmetry. No sign of the stiffness she sometimes had when she walked. He tapped on the glass. She spun around and slid open the door.

"How's the clean-up going?" he asked.

"Terrible," she said. She ran her fingers through her wet hair. "I had to have a shower. The boat was filthy. I can't believe people could leave it in such a state."

"Really? Didn't they clean it?"

Savannah was wearing a singlet top. It was hard for him to keep his gaze away from the great shape of her breasts under the tightly stretched fabric.

"Most of it wasn't too bad I suppose but one bathroom was putrid." She shuddered. "Wall-to-wall poop and vomit. It makes me gag just to think about it." She put her hands to her nose. "I wore gloves but I don't feel as if I'll ever get rid of the smell."

"Can't smell anything from here," Ethan said with a grin. "I stuck my head in the front room of the boat. It smelled fresh to me."

"I've used a whole bottle of disinfectant. That smarmy Fred," Savannah growled and her chest swelled.

"Charge him a cleaning fee." Ethan tried to keep his gaze on her face.

"I would if I thought I had any chance of getting it. He only gave me a small amount of the bond and some of that will cover the fuel cost. It's just lucky the boat's Jaxon's. He'll have to take the loss."

"I guess it's a learning curve."

"Learning curve isn't what I'd call it."

Savannah planted her hands on her hips. The fabric stretched even tighter across her breasts.

"I've written a big note to Jaxon. Fred won't ever be allowed to book with J&S Houseboats again. Well, not if I've got anything to do with it."

Ethan dragged his gaze away to the verandah.

"I'll go and shift the fuel truck," he said.

"You didn't bring Jasper?"

He looked back at her, keeping his gaze locked to hers.

"Thought he might get in the way."

"Oh, okay. I don't mind if he comes over here."

"He's okay. He's got the whole yard to roam in. Do you know where the keys are?"

"Keys?"

"For the fuel truck."

"Oh, yes. They're in the cupboard where Jaxon keeps all his keys. I'll get them."

She hurried off to a side room. Ethan turned his back on the shack and looked at the river. He took slow steady breaths. There was something about Savannah. She was getting under his skin. And that exercise outfit pushed buttons he wasn't sure he wanted pushed.

"Here you are."

He turned back. She was holding out a set of keys.

"The key for the septic tank truck is on there as well."

"Thanks."

"I'll be right with you."

Ethan moved away quickly. He was sure his thoughts were written all over his face.

By the time he'd shifted the truck closer to the houseboat she was waiting for him. She'd changed into jeans and a loose-fitting t-shirt. Her hair fluffed around her face giving her a softer look than when she spiked it. He couldn't help but like what he saw.

He jumped down from the truck almost on top of her. She smelt good too.

"How am I ever going to drive that?" she said.

"I can teach you."

"Don't I need a licence?"

"This is private property. You can do what you like."

"I'm still not sure I can drive that," she said waving a hand towards the truck.

"You can drive a manual car. It's not too much different."

"How did you know my car's a man ...?" Her puzzled expression changed to a smile. "Of course. I'd forgotten you drove Belinda home in my car. Thanks for doing that."

"No probs." Ethan pulled on the heavy-duty gloves and unhooked the hose. "Let's see how much fuel Fred and his crew used."

"Not much according to Fred."

The gauge clicked over and over in a constant rhythm for quite some time. He could see Savannah could barely keep her anger contained by the time he'd finished filling the tanks.

"That's way more than he said. Bloody Fred. The money he left won't cover that and the extra cleaning and the damage."

"What damage?"

The boat appeared in good shape from the brief look Ethan had given it.

"The vomit bathroom has had the toilet roll holder pulled from the wall."

"I'll take a look at it."

"Would you? I've no idea how to fix it but it can't stay how it is with a gaping hole in the wall. I was thinking I'd have to patch it with paper and tape."

"That might be all I can do." He grinned at her and they went on board.

"It will require a carpenter," Ethan said. He stood up from his squatting position by the hole. "Might have to be paper and tape until then. Let's move on to the septic pumping, shall we?"

She clamped her lips together and followed him.

Ethan had to give her credit. She wasn't afraid to give things a go even though she often had no idea which way was up. While the septic was pumping out they moved on to swap the gas bottles. Ethan vaguely recalled Jaxon rolling them down the hill from the cage by his shed where they were stored but how had he got them to the back of the houseboat? Ethan had never taken any notice.

He stood next to Savannah on the bank with the gas bottle between them. They both stared at the boat. The bottles that needed swapping were at the back and the side decks were narrow.

"Would he have used the little boat?" Savannah asked.

"Maybe, but then you've still got to get it out of that and up onto the deck."

Ethan looked at the gas bottle. It should float by itself. All they would have to do was steer it.

"We can float it along the side of the houseboat then pull it up onto the back," he said. "It'd be easier than trying to manage it in the tinnie. We just need some rope."

"Plenty in Jaxon's shed."

He followed her to the shed and selected a rope that would do the job. Once he'd secured the bottle, he pushed it out into the water while Savannah held the two ends from the side deck of the houseboat. When the bottle was afloat he joined her on the boat and they edged it all the way to the back of the boat. He hauled it up onto the swim deck and together they manoeuvred it into place. Then it was just a matter of doing the reverse procedure with the empty bottle.

By the time they'd finished Ethan noticed Savannah was favouring her left leg. There was no way she could do this by herself. She was going to need help and Ethan had a busy week coming up with the shearing. He was beginning to wonder if Jaxon had really thought his plans through properly. Even without the physical problem that was giving her bother from time to time, she wouldn't have been able to swap the gas bottles alone.

"I can manage now," Savannah said when Ethan had parked the trucks back in their places. "Although I'm not sure what happens with that septic truck. I think someone comes out to empty it if I call them. I'll have to read Jaxon's notes again. There's so much to remember. I really appreciate your help. I don't know how anyone can do all that on their own." She had a puzzled look on her face. "How did Jaxon manage it?"

Ethan thought one man on his own could do it but it would take a while. He wasn't going to have that conversation with Savannah.

"I didn't help much, I know that."

He smiled and the worry on her face softened. Her hair moved in the breeze. The blue of her eyes was highlighted by the blue of her t-shirt and her pink lips looked … kissable.

Ethan stepped back.

"I'll be off then," he said. "There's a bit more prep to do for our meal."

"Of course. I hope I haven't kept you too long."

He shook his head.

"See you later," he said and took off back to his place before he drooled.

He went up the stairs two at a time, Jasper plodding faithfully behind him.

Ethan had enjoyed the afternoon with Savannah. She'd shown no sign of her prickly side. They worked together well, just like they had when they'd sent the three houseboats on their way.

The delicious smell of curry wafted around him as he opened the door. He hummed to himself and set to work on the final meal preparations.

CHAPTER
23

Savannah went outside as soon as she heard the vehicle. She hoped Belinda would be happy to eat at Ethan's. She hadn't wanted to admit it to herself but she'd missed Ethan as soon as he'd left. Preparing the houseboat had been hard work but he had made it bearable.

"Hello," she called as Belinda's car rolled to a stop.

Belinda popped out from the driver's side waving her bottle of sparkling.

"Ethan's invited us next door for curry if you'd like to go."

Belinda's eyes lit up. "Sounds like fun. Shall I drive us?"

It seemed silly driving out of one driveway and straight into the next but Savannah was happy to save her leg. There was another car already outside Ethan's place as they pulled in.

Belinda went ahead of Savannah up the stairs. Ethan greeted them and Belinda planted a kiss on both his cheeks.

"Hello again," Savannah said then fell silent as she noticed the other two people in the room watching her.

Ethan waved them over.

"This is my brother Blake and his friend Jenny," Ethan said. He turned back. "And these are my neighbours, Savannah and Belinda."

They all shook hands and said hello.

"You're just next door?" Jenny said.

"I am," Savannah said. "It's my brother's place and Belinda lives on the other side of us."

"Let's pop the bubbles," Belinda said. "Who else would like some? Savannah?"

"I've brought beer," Savannah said quickly and pulled a sixpack from the plastic shopping bag she was carrying. "There's some cheese and crackers in there as well." She handed the bag to Ethan.

"You didn't have to but thank you," he said.

The smile he gave her made her stomach tingle. She turned away.

"I'll have a glass of bubbles," Jenny said. "That'll do me. I'm the des tonight."

"Des?" Belinda looked blank.

"Designated driver," Blake said.

"Oh," Belinda said.

Savannah was glad she'd asked the question. She hadn't understood the des reference either.

"I still can't drive with this crook arm so Jenny has to drive regardless," Blake said.

"You have to rest that leg as well," Jenny said. "It's not healing as quick as I'd like."

"You want some bubbles to lift your spirits, Blake?" Belinda asked. "Bubbles make everything better."

Savannah stared hard at Belinda. Had she winked at Blake?

"I'm a beer man but I'm on so many tablets I rattle at the moment."

"I think you could have one tonight." Jenny smiled at him. "Nurse's orders."

"Are you a nurse, Jenny?" Belinda poured the sparkling into two glasses Ethan had put out for her, talking as she filled them. "I always thought I'd do nursing. All those dreamy doctors on tap. Then I realised I'd have to deal with blood and stick needles in people and it put me right off." She gave Jenny a glass and raised her own. "Cheers everyone."

Savannah, Blake and Ethan raised their bottles. Just for a moment there was silence again as everyone took a drink.

"This is a great spot, Ethan," Jenny said. "Look at the colours in that sunset."

Belinda spun around. "You have a much better view of the river than we do," she said. She crossed to the sliding doors leading to the deck. "We're a bit obscured by trees."

"You could remove some," Blake said.

"Ashton prefers the trees," Belinda said.

Savannah watched as her neighbour's eyes narrowed and her lips pursed. A steely look crossed her face. For a moment she looked sombre and then the tight smile returned. Perhaps she was under her husband's thumb.

"Take your drinks out there," Ethan said, "before it gets too cool."

"So what did you do, Blake, to get yourself into such a bust-up?"

Belinda put her arm through Blake's and guided him outside. Jenny trailed along behind with a slight smile on her face.

"Can I help?" Savannah asked Ethan.

"Not a lot left to do. I've just got the rice to cook and we're good to go."

"It smells divine."

"I've toned it down a little for Blake. He's not a huge curry fan."

"I love it."

Savannah glanced around. The room was not at all what she'd expected. It was a large rectangle with the kitchen taking up one end, a dining table close to the glass that made up the side facing the river and assorted armchairs and a couch took up the rest of the space. The floor was covered in large white tiles with a swirl of grey through them. There was a brightly coloured rug under the dining table and one large abstract painting on the end wall. Everything looked modern, almost minimalist. She assumed the bedrooms and bathroom were through the door off the lounge area.

She looked back across the long bench. Ethan had his back to her, checking the rice. Belinda's playful tones drifted in from outside, punctuated by Blake's deeper voice and the occasional chuckle from Jenny.

"Thanks again for your help today," Savannah said. "I don't know how Jaxon does all those things on his own let alone how he thought I might have been able to pull it off. I don't know how I'm going to manage the other three when they come back."

"I've been thinking about that," Ethan said. "When are you expecting them?"

"The two big ones will be back late tomorrow afternoon. I gather most of the people on board have to be at work on Monday. The smaller boat won't be back until Tuesday morning."

"I've got to help with shearing next week but I could do the two boats that come in tomorrow as soon as they get in."

"That's very good of you but they don't have to go out again till Friday."

"It's going to be a busy week. Blake can't do much so I'll be at the farm from dawn till dark."

Savannah felt her spirits dip. It didn't sound like she'd see much of Ethan over the next week.

"I'll have to be back early on Friday if there are boats to go out," he said.

"Actually, one of them is to go out first thing in the morning. The people will arrive Thursday night ready to set off early the next day."

"Okay," Ethan said. He scratched at his cheek. "I'll see them off before I go to the farm. Who knows, by Friday I might not be needed out there anyway. The shearing should be nearly finished by then."

"I'm sorry," she said.

"It's not your fault."

"Nor yours." Savannah felt her annoyance at Jaxon resurfacing. "My brother's going to owe us both big time when he gets back."

Blake hobbled back through the door.

"How's that food going?"

"Ready now," Ethan said and took the pot of boiling rice from the stove.

"I think I'm allowed one more beer," Blake said.

"I'll get it." Savannah took a bottle from Ethan's fridge. She was surprised to see how tidy its shelves were. Lots of containers and jars labelled and stacked neatly.

"Where do you want us to sit?" Blake asked.

"Anywhere you like, big bro."

Savannah took the beer to Blake.

"How's the houseboat business going?" he asked.

"Busy." She watched as Ethan began to serve the meal. "I'm grateful to your brother for all his help. I've learnt a lot in the last few days."

"It's getting cold out there," Jenny said as she stepped back inside. Belinda was right behind her.

Ethan brought the bottle of sparkling to the table and a bottle of red.

"Will you join us now, Savvie?" Belinda waggled the bottle.

"No thanks, I'll stick with my beer."

"Jenny?"

"I've had my quota."

"Looks like I'll have to drink the rest myself," Belinda said and poured herself another glass.

She sat next to Savannah on one side of the table, Jenny and Blake sat opposite. The table was set and a variety of condiments were laid out in the middle. Ethan brought over a pot of rice then the steaming plates of curry and took his place at the head of the table.

"Okay if the wounded bloke has a medicinal red?" Ethan looked past Blake to Jenny.

"Just a small one shouldn't hurt."

"I am here you know." Blake looked from Jenny to Ethan with a smile on his face.

"Anyone else?" Ethan lifted the bottle.

The other two women declined and so did Savannah. She was enjoying herself and two beers were her limit.

They all began eating and complimenting Ethan on his cooking.

"A man who can cook." Belinda draped a hand over his arm. "Where have you been hiding?"

Savannah felt uncomfortable at her friend's obvious flirting, first with Blake and now with Ethan. Still, if Ash wasn't much fun maybe this was how she enjoyed herself.

"It's very good, Ethan," Jenny said. "What do you put in it?"

"This one's beef, of course. I like to start from scratch with all the basic ingredients."

"I usually resort to a jar," Jenny said.

"So do I," Belinda added. "It's too much like hard work otherwise. What other talents do you have, Ethan?"

"He can half ride a bike." Blake grinned at his brother.

"At least I can stay on it."

"No guts no glory."

"Does Jenny know what a health risk you are?" Ethan chuckled.

"I've got the idea." Jenny gave Blake a gentle nudge.

"Well at least you've got your own personal nurse, Blake," Belinda said, refilling her glass. She took a big mouthful.

"What do you do besides holiday here, Belinda?" Ethan asked.

"Call me Bel." She leaned closer to him. "All my friends do."

"So, Bel, when you're not here what do you get up to?" Blake's eyes sparkled with mischief.

"Since my mother died I've become my father's housekeeper, secretary, nursemaid … I'm the family gopher mostly. It keeps me busy. That's why I enjoy coming to the river so much. I can relax and have fun, make new friends."

Savannah studied Belinda as she lifted her glass and downed the rest of its contents. It had sounded as if Belinda was bossed around by all the members of her family. No wonder she liked to let her hair down when she was out.

Ethan refilled Belinda's glass.

"My favourite occupation is fishing," he said. "I'm happy to sit for hours on my own catching a fish for my dinner."

Belinda began questioning him about fishing. Savannah and Jenny cleared the plates then brought the cheese platter to the table. Belinda was the centre of attention between Blake and Ethan. She was flirting outrageously and they seemed to take it in their stride. Savannah wondered what Jenny thought about it but she kept chatting to Savannah as if oblivious of the woman dallying with her boyfriend.

Finally Belinda paused. She tipped the last of the bottle into her glass then turned back to Ethan.

"So, you ride bikes. Are they the big ones that throb between your legs?"

She drew out the word throb. Blake burst out laughing. Savannah saw Ethan grin. She looked down at the table. Belinda was really going too far. What would Ashton think if he was here? Savannah was guessing Belinda only misbehaved when she was out alone.

"You're a dreadful woman, Bel," Ethan chuckled and stood up. "Anyone for another drink?"

"We should go," Jenny said. "We've got a long drive ahead of us. I'd better get this poor invalid home to bed."

"Yes ma'am," Blake replied with a twinkle in his eye.

Savannah stood up. She felt like the party gooseberry.

"I must go too."

"Aw, Savvie." Belinda gripped her hand. "The party's just getting started."

"I've had a big day," Savannah said. The tone in her voice reminded her of her teenage days when she'd made constant excuses to avoid the parties of so-called friends.

"I'll drive you." Belinda wobbled to her feet.

"No, it's only next door," Savannah said. She wouldn't have gone with Belinda even if she had been ready to leave. Savannah took no risks in cars no matter that it was such a short distance.

"Thanks, Ethan." Jenny kissed him on the cheek.

"See you bright and early Monday, bro." Blake gave Ethan a playful slap on the back and Savannah saw him wink.

Ethan turned back to Savannah.

"Are you sure you won't stay for a red?"

He had an odd look on his face, was it pleading? She wasn't sure. He was obviously having fun with Bel, as she called herself. It wouldn't matter if Savannah left.

"No, but thank you for the meal and for your help today."

She turned to go.

"Wait," Ethan said. "Take the rest of your beers."

"Keep them," Savannah said.

"No, please, you should take them." He hurried to the fridge and returned with the remains of her sixpack, which he pressed into her arms.

"Thanks," she said.

Belinda looped one arm through Ethan's and waved a glass of red with the other.

"I'll catch you next time we're up, Savvie. Hopefully next weekend."

The fake smile left Savannah's face as soon as she turned her back. She pounded down the stairs. Next weekend! By then Jaxon had better be back and she could get herself out of here and off to Adelaide where she belonged.

Married or not, Belinda was after Ethan and he wasn't exactly knocking back her advances. Savannah had seen the wink Blake had given his brother before he left. She bit her lip to stop the hot tears that were forming in her eyes. It had been so long since a man had paid her attention. She'd mistakenly thought Ethan might genuinely be interested in her.

"You bloody fool, Savannah," she hissed.

Jasper gave a small whine as she reached the ground. She stumbled past Belinda's car and along the drive into the darkness. The cold night air calmed her a little but she couldn't stop the tears that rolled down her cheeks.

CHAPTER
24

Savannah drove past Nell and Bob's Tea Room but there was a closed sign on the gate. Up the hill she noticed several cars outside a little church. Half the population of Riverboat Point could be there.

She went back to the main street and pulled up by the pub. The front door was open and she could see people inside. They were keen for a Sunday morning. Faye had said the pub made coffee on weekends. Perhaps that's what they were drinking. Savannah decided to give it a go.

The two men propped on stools at the bar stopped their conversation and looked her up and down. One of them had no hair and not many teeth. He let out a low whistle and the other bloke, who had not much more hair but a lot more teeth, grinned.

"Hello," they said in unison.

"Hello," she replied and strode to the bar. She could feel the two sets of eyes watching her.

"You visiting town?" one of the men asked.

"Yes," Savannah replied.

"Better than what we usually see at the Riverboat Hotel on a Sunday morning," the other one said then chortled loudly.

A man with a thatch of red hair and a handlebar moustache walked through a doorway behind the bar.

"What can I get you this fine morning?" he asked Savannah. The moustache moved up and down as he spoke.

"Faye at the supermarket said you make good coffee."

"Sure do."

"Coffee!" The toothless guy nearly choked on his beer.

"Ignore Alf," the barman said. "He only drinks beer. Used to even clean his teeth in it."

"That's why he hasn't got many left." Alf's mate laughed.

Savannah wasn't sure whether or not to believe them.

"Can I have a cafe latte, double shot, please?" she asked.

"Coming right up. The wife has just made a batch of banana muffins. Would you like one with your coffee?"

"Sounds good," Savannah said.

"Cream with it?"

"No thanks."

"Muffins," Alf mumbled. "We never get offered muffins."

"You don't drink coffee," the barman said. He sent a shot of steam from the coffee machine. "I'm Bernie," he said to Savannah. "You just passing through or staying?"

"Staying," Savannah said. "I'm looking after my brother Jaxon's place."

"Ah! That's why Faye would be looking out for you. Jaxon's a favourite of hers."

"Jaxon's a good young bloke," Alf spoke over the sound of the coffee machine. "Helped me out once or twice."

He got off his stool and came towards Savannah with his hand held out.

"I'm Alf and this is me mate, Foss. Very pleased to meet you."

Foss gave her a one-fingered salute. Alf gripped her hand with his then wrapped his other hand around hers and shook it vigorously.

"Anna, did you say?"

"Savannah."

"Welcome, Savannah."

He bestowed an even bigger smile on her, gave her hand a final pat and went back to his beer.

Bernie put the coffee and muffin on the bar in front of her.

"You're welcome to sit here or the beer garden has a nice view of the river."

"Thanks," Savannah said. She handed over her money and gave Alf and Foss a wave. "Nice to meet you. Think I'll take my coffee out to the sunshine."

"No worries," Alf said. "And don't forget, anything you need just let me know. If I'm not here Bernie knows where to find me."

Savannah took her coffee and muffin through the door to the outside area jammed between the wall of the hotel and the building next door. There were hanging plants to give the garden effect and street frontage that looked towards the river. She took a seat in the sun and settled back to enjoy her coffee.

She hadn't slept well last night. She'd tossed and turned until the early hours and then slipped into a deep sleep and had weird dreams. She was looking for Jaxon and every time she thought she'd found him it would be Ethan and Belinda instead. Finally she discovered them in bed together. She woke in a sweat with bedclothes tangled around her and a terrible sad feeling in the pit of her stomach.

Once she was up she couldn't resist peeking next door. Belinda's car was gone. All was quiet. No sign of man or dog. Savannah assumed Ethan had slept in. She went for a long run and then, with nothing else to do, she'd decided to drive into Riverboat Point for a coffee.

The sun was warm on her back, the coffee was good and the muffin deliciously soft. She leaned back and closed her eyes. After such a restless night she felt she could almost doze off. If only she could get thoughts of Ethan and Belinda out of her head.

"Excuse me."

Savannah's eyes flew open and she sat up.

"Sorry, I didn't mean to give you a fright."

A woman of about her age stood beside her. She was wearing black trackpants and a polo top that clung to her muffin-top bulges. A scarf around her forehead kept a mass of dark curls away from her face. She had a duster tucked in a back pocket and a dustpan and broom in her hand.

"I'm Mandy Sampson. Are you Savannah?"

"Yes."

"Bernie said you were out here. I clean the pub. Do you mind if I sit a moment?"

"No," Savannah said. Not too enthusiastically. She had been enjoying the sunshine and the peace.

Mandy sat in the chair opposite. Up close she appeared a little older than Savannah.

"I heard you're looking after Jaxon's place while he's away and that you're a fitness instructor."

Savannah looked around. There was no one but the two of them in the beer garden.

"How did you know all that?" she asked.

"This is a small town. Everyone knows your business. Even if you forget someone else will remind you." Mandy chuckled. "Before I was pregnant with my last baby they were running a tab in the front bar to guess its birth date, sex and weight. Wouldn't surprise me if someone was waiting outside our bedroom window as he was conceived."

Savannah leaned in, her mouth open.

Mandy gave her hand a quick pat.

"Just kidding, she said. "Faye at the supermarket told me you were in to fitness. I was hoping to come out and see you, then Bernie said you were here. It was meant to be."

Savannah tipped her head to one side and frowned. She couldn't remember telling Faye she was a fitness instructor.

"Meant to be?"

"I was hoping you might lead our group," Mandy said. "There's me and a few other local women who want to get into better shape. Three of us have young kids and a few others are older but not getting much exercise. We've formed a fitness group but it's the blind leading the blind. We manage a weekly walk but the exercises are a bit hit and miss. I've cut pictures from magazines but even so, we don't know if we're doing them properly. Would you be interested?"

"Interested?" Mandy had spoken so fast Savannah had lost her back at the "blind leading the blind" and she was still trying to figure out how Faye knew about her fitness work.

"In leading our group," Mandy said. "Being our instructor."

Savannah stared at the beaming young woman across the table. Her chocolate brown eyes were shining. She was almost buzzing with excitement.

"You want me to be your fitness instructor?"

"Yes."

Savannah opened and closed her mouth. She pursed her lips and shook her head. She'd left all that behind her. She would have to look for work again when Jaxon came back but fitness instructor was not going to be on her list of possible jobs.

"None of us has much money," Mandy said, "but we'd be happy to pay you a small fee."

"I haven't done anything like that for years."

"You look in good shape."

"Well, I work out myself but –"

"We meet twice a week," Mandy cut in. "Eleven o'clock at the little hall next to the church. Whoever can get there comes. Sometimes there're only two of us and the most is seven. You'd make eight. We're not much good at keeping fit but we're good company."

"I've got the houseboats to take care of."

"I know that's busy. I've done some cleaning for Jaxon in the past when he's been busy with electrical work."

"You have?" Savannah stored that little piece of information away. Cleaning *Tawarri* had been a huge job. She'd wondered how she would manage if there'd been a much tighter turnaround.

"Just think about it. Everyone needs some time out and keeping fit together is a fun way of doing it."

Savannah thought of the classes she'd run before the accident. Instructing had been her life. But her life had changed irreparably. She believed there was no going back. Then she thought of Belinda and their impromptu exercise session on the verandah.

"I haven't instructed for years," Savannah said.

"Surely it's like riding a bike? I'll give you my number."

Mandy pulled a pad and pen from her top pocket.

Savannah watched her write on the paper then rip it from the pad.

"When Jaxon returns I'll be going back to Adelaide."

"I realise that. Even if you came a few times just to give us some pointers it would be such a help."

Savannah took the page Mandy pushed towards her.

"I'll think about it."

"Thank you." Mandy stood up. "I'd better get back to work. I do hope you can join us. We meet Tuesdays and Thursdays."

"I'll check the calendar."

"Nice to meet you," Mandy said. She hurried off, picked up a bucket she'd left by the door and went on into the bar.

Savannah studied the name and number on the little page. Now that she thought about it the name seemed familiar. Where had she seen it before? Puzzled, she pushed the paper into her wallet. Even more puzzling was Faye knowing her background. Perhaps Jaxon had told her about Savannah's past, but why would he do that? Unless it was Belinda. She was the talkative type. Maybe she'd told Faye about their little fitness attempt on the verandah.

What had Mandy said about small towns? Everyone knows your business. It certainly seemed as if everyone knew much more about Savannah than she knew about them. It was not a comfortable thought.

CHAPTER
25

Our Destiny was back by nine-thirty and the four people were unpacked and gone by ten. Savannah wandered down to where all four boats were tied up at the bank. She'd spent most of Monday cleaning the two that had come in on Sunday night. *Tawarri* was shipshape again except for the hole in the bathroom wall, so she had a couple of days to clean the last boat before its next booking. Ethan had promised to call in tonight or tomorrow night to do all the bits she needed help with.

She went on board to do a quick check. After her experience with Fred's group she was never sure what she'd find. She opened up the rooms and peered into cupboards. At first glance all looked tidy enough. The bathrooms were clean, that was a plus, and there were no holes in any walls that she could see. She pulled the sheets off the beds and made a pile in the middle of the floor with the towels on top.

She stood hands on hips looking around then lowered herself to the couch in the living area. This boat was different from the others. It only had two bedrooms along one side and a living area that ran across the front and down the other side. Being the last boat to tie up, it was close to Ethan's boundary. She could see his tinnie at the little jetty and the start of the path up to his house, glimpses of which were visible through the trees.

She wondered again what had happened between him and Belinda the other night. The good-looking party girls always got the guys but Belinda already had her man, so why did she need to make a play for another? The thought of the two of them together burned inside Savannah. By the time Ethan had come over on Sunday to help with the boats she'd been miserable with jealousy. She'd barely said more than a few words to him.

She stretched her left leg out and lifted it up and down. The ache travelled up into her hip. She'd been haphazard with her exercise regime since she'd come to the river. There was a lot of work involved in cleaning and preparing the houseboats. It was a long time since she'd done as much physical labour as she was doing now. The most exercise she got with her previous job had been avoiding the hands of her lecherous boss.

After the accident the doctors had said her level of recovery would depend on how much effort she put in. Savannah had put in more than 100 per cent and exercise had become her friend. Right now she didn't feel like dragging herself back up the bank to put herself through the paces.

Although she'd been upset at Belinda's behaviour, Savannah felt glum knowing her only female neighbour had gone back to Adelaide. Ethan said he'd be away all week helping his parents. She assumed Gnasher was still around but that thought didn't comfort her. She wondered about him. Did he roam around shooting at anything that moved or did he really just shoot the odd rabbit? Regardless, she kept to the opposite side of the road on her runs in case the old guy took a pot shot at her.

She stared out at the river drifting by. Why was it she had never felt the slightest bit lonely living by herself in the city and yet out here she felt it keenly?

She took out her phone. No messages, no missed calls. No-one but Jaxon cared if she lived or died, and apparently even he had given up on her. It was only ten-thirty on Tuesday morning and a long lonely week loomed ahead.

Tuesday morning! Savannah sat up. Mandy's smiling face jumped into her head. The exercise group met at eleven on Tuesdays. A few days ago it had been the last thing Savannah felt like doing, but now the idea almost appealed to her. She wrapped the bundle of linen in one sheet and threw it over her shoulder. Jaxon had left instructions about a linen service she had to connect with in town. She locked up the boat and made her way back to the shack. As she went she had a sudden idea of where she'd seen Mandy's name before.

Voices echoed from the little hall. There were only two cars out the front but from the noise there had to be several people inside. Savannah stuck her head in the door. Four women in assorted versions of exercise attire stood in a huddle chatting excitedly. There was a pram beside one of them and a couple of toddlers played with toys on a mat in the back corner.

Savannah turned at the sound of footsteps crunching behind her.

"You came," Mandy's voice squeaked with excitement. "I'm so glad. The others will be thrilled as well. Come on in."

Savannah followed her into the hall. The old building had seen better days. The paint was flaking on the walls and a couple of windows were cracked, but the wooden floor felt solid enough under her feet. She put her bag of gym equipment and her foam roller at her feet.

"Hi, everyone," Mandy called.

The group stopped talking and turned to say hello.

"Savannah's here. Isn't that great? Now we'll have some proper exercises."

The four women were effusive in their welcome. As the last one turned to face her, Savannah could see from the bulge of her belly that she was pregnant. She found herself mentally adapting exercises and they hadn't even begun.

"Do you mind if we play music?" the pregnant one asked.

Had she said her name was Rosie? They'd all spoken at once.

"Music is good," Savannah said.

"Crank it up, Rosie," Mandy said.

"Not too loud," one of the older women said.

"Oh come on, Bet. We need it loud enough to hide the sound of our creaking bones," her companion said and poked her in the ribs.

Rosie's choice of music floated around the hall and the women all looked expectantly at Savannah.

"Let's make a circle and do some stretches," she said.

"Stretches," Bet said. "Now there's a good idea."

The others chuckled. Savannah looked at Mandy who'd taken the spot on her left.

"I made up our sessions from ideas I found in a magazine. They didn't mention stretches. You set us straight."

Savannah breathed in a deep breath to steady her nerves.

All five women did the same.

Oh dear, she thought. All eyes waited for her next move.

"Turn your head to the right, ladies," she said. "Hold it there, now back to the left."

After each stretch the next one popped into her head and the women dutifully followed her lead. She'd panicked on the drive into town worrying she wouldn't remember. It was one thing to follow your own exercise routine, quite another to lead a group, all eyes on you waiting for your next instruction. The women were like sponges, absorbing everything she said and trying their best.

The toddlers came and climbed on Mandy and Rosie as soon as they lay on their mats. Savannah got them going with some leg raises and sit-ups alongside their mothers. She brought out her weights, stretch straps and foam roller to add interest to the routines but mostly she stuck to exercises that didn't need equipment. An hour went by in a flash.

"That was great," Rosie said.

"I can tell I'll be sore tomorrow," Bet said.

"Do a few stretches," Savannah said. "Keep yourself limbered up."

"Will you come again on Thursday?" Mandy asked.

Once again all the women stared at her.

"Why not?" she said. "It's been fun."

"See you then," Rosie said. "I've got a doctor's appointment. Can you lock up, Mandy?"

"Sure."

The other women left as Savannah packed up her gear.

"That really was a great work-out," Mandy said. "Thanks, Savannah."

"My pleasure," she said and found that she meant it.

"I hope you're happy with two dollars each." Mandy pressed a bag of coins into Savannah's hand.

"Oh … no, you didn't have to …"

"Of course we did. The others are more than happy to pay. It's not much."

"It's plenty." Savannah felt terrible taking their money. "I haven't led a class for years. I'm a bit rusty."

"You were great," Mandy said. "And I can't wait till Thursday."

"You've done some cleaning for my brother, haven't you?"

"A while back now. Things were a bit quiet before he left."

"I saw your name on his list of contacts. Would you still be interested?"

"Sure. He usually wanted me after I'd finished at the pub. Do you need help?"

"Not yet. I really don't know how much longer I'll be here. It's just nice to know there's help if I need it."

"You've got my number," Mandy said.

Savannah loaded her gear into her car and waved as Mandy drove away. Now what? She wasn't ready to go back to the quietness of the shack yet. Then she remembered the linen in the boot. She drove to the supermarket. There were a few items she needed to buy and she could ask after Jaxon's mail.

Faye was talking to an old bloke at the counter. Savannah remembered him from her first trip to the supermarket. She grabbed her few things and was back at the counter quickly. The two of them kept talking.

"I thought things were on the up, Terry," Faye said. "The new chap at the garage – what's his name, Mark something? He seems very nice."

"He's not much of a mechanic. He had a tractor in pieces and he didn't seem to know which bit went where when I was in there."

"Whose tractor?"

"Warners'."

"It's probably a hundred years old," Faye chuckled.

"He's bitten off more than he can chew, I reckon. He's plenty to keep him busy with tyres and petrol and the like. Not enough time to work on vehicles."

"It certainly won't be any good if we can't get our cars serviced," Faye said. "Let's give him time to settle in. Anyway Terry, I'd better get on."

"I don't know who's going to work on my old car now that Bert's left," Terry said. He picked up his biscuits and paper, gave Faye a nod and made his way out of the shop.

"How are you today?" Faye asked as she scanned Savannah's items.

"Fine thanks. I've got a boot load of linen. Jaxon left instructions to bring it here for collection."

"That's right. The fellow comes through twice a week. Takes the linen from Captain's Houseboats as well. Drive round to the shed at the side, Jamie will unload it for you."

"It seems a waste. I could wash all this stuff myself."

Faye chortled. "Not if you want your sheets to stay white."

"Oh?"

"River water will turn them brown." Faye stacked her shopping. "I hear you've been taking a fitness class."

Savannah gave her a sideways look.

"Bet called in on her way home." Faye gave a chuckle. "She was hobbling a bit but very pleased with herself. Good on you. Mandy's been trying to get a fitness group going for ages. They're all delighted you've taken it on."

"They'll have to be quick learners," Savannah said. "As soon as Jaxon returns I'll have to go back to the city."

"That's a shame. You're fitting in so well here."

Savannah picked up her groceries and the newspaper.

"I'll see you Thursday if not before," Faye said.

"Thursday?"

"For your next fitness class. I'm going to come along."

Savannah grinned. Mandy was certainly right about everyone knowing your business.

CHAPTER
26

Dust hung in the air filled with the noise of bleating sheep. Ethan brushed at the flies that hovered under the brim of his Akubra and adjusted his sunglasses. The mob he'd brought down the track from the nearby paddock lifted their heads at the sound of other sheep and quickened their steps. They gave him no grief going through the gate. When the last one was through he moved his bike forward and stopped next to the opening. Hundreds of sheep packed the holding pens. He closed the gate and rode around to the other side of the shearing shed. It was time for afternoon smoko.

Not that he was in a hurry for it. After their initial job allocation meeting yesterday morning he'd managed to avoid his father. It was for the best. Mal was tetchy at shearing time and Ethan felt as taut as the newly strung fence. Sleep had eluded him for the last two nights. He could function without it but it was the why that bothered him.

He'd been up at five-thirty to take Jasper for a walk, had a quick breakfast and set off to be at his parents' farm for a seven-thirty start. The shearers were just checking their shears as he'd arrived. His job was to bring in the sheep and return them to their paddocks after they'd been shorn. Luckily Blake's accident had happened at the end of mustering. The sheep were in the paddocks close to the shearing shed. All Ethan had to do was bring the next mob up as they were needed. It had taken him half the day yesterday to get back into the swing of it. He hadn't helped with shearing for a long time.

Inside the shed were three shearers, a wool classer, two rouseabouts and Mal who was in charge of packing the wool, weighing it and labelling it. When Ethan wasn't shifting sheep he was general dogsbody. He could do any of the jobs in the shed except the shearing and classing.

He pulled alongside Jenny's car. One of his father's dogs was resting nearby. It lifted its head, eager for a pat. He obliged then climbed over the rail of the yard to where Blake was working alongside Jenny. She was squirting the cuts on the newly shorn sheep to prevent infection and he was administering the lice spray. Then, between the two of them, they painted the station brand on the rump of each sheep. Jenny had got the hang of it very quickly. It was something Blake could do without moving about too much, although Ethan wondered how much longer he would last.

It was a warm day with hardly a cloud in the sky. By the end of it the shearers would be glad of a shower and the hot meal Barb would prepare for them before they tumbled into bed in their quarters a short distance from the shed. The other helpers all lived within driving distance. Ethan could have stayed with Blake or even his parents but he had Jasper back at home. He had plenty of space under the house but he needed exercise and company.

The sound of the shearing had stopped. Everyone inside the shed would be eating. Ethan waited for Jenny and Blake to finish the last few sheep. Jenny climbed the fence with ease, Blake took the long way round to use the gate. They headed for the side door of the shearing shed, where Barb's afternoon smoko would be set out in boxes beside the urn and the mugs.

"What do you think of shearing, Jenny?" Ethan asked.

They walked slowly, waiting for Blake to catch up. His brother's injured leg was slowing him up considerably.

"I had no idea of the work involved."

"Bit different from trauma nursing."

"Yes, but just as demanding." Jenny leaned closer. "Blake's had enough but he won't admit it. He's been standing for two days. Apart from being exhausted I'm sure his injuries will be giving him pain."

"He won't listen to me."

"Nor me."

"What are you two whispering about?"

Blake had caught up with them as they stopped at the end of the shed to wash their hands. Sixties music played in the background. The shearers' choice of radio station was the only music in the shed.

"I was warning Jenny about how pig-headed you are," Ethan said.

Jenny turned and flicked some water from her hands at Blake.

"And I was saying I'd already worked that out."

Barb came out of the shed. Her old floppy hat was as faded as her once rich brown hair. She had a smile for the three of them. Barb had mellowed. Ethan was comfortable around his mother these days.

"There you are," she said. "Don't want you to miss out on my jelly cakes."

"You're kidding," Jenny groaned. "Are they pink?"

"Of course." Barb threw an arm around Jenny and drew her inside. They looked an odd couple: Jenny tall and lean in tight-fitting shirt and jeans, Barb short and solid in her trademark loose shirt and beads. "You two'd better hurry up," she called over her shoulder. "They'll all be gone."

"We'll be right there," Blake answered but he put a restraining hand on Ethan's arm. Once the women were out of sight he leaned against the wall of the shed and pushed back his hat.

"Jenny's going back to Adelaide tomorrow."

Ethan studied his brother's pale face. His fringe was wet with sweat and although the bruise on his cheek had faded there were dark shadows under his eyes.

"Do you think you can hold the fort tomorrow if I don't get here till lunchtime?" Blake asked.

"Maybe."

Ethan wasn't sure how. He hadn't perfected being in two places at once. So long as he and one of the other rouseabouts worked things out between them, they'd manage.

"Jenny's not leaving until mid-morning," Blake said. "I'd like to see her off."

"Okay I'll do it, but I have conditions."

Blake's eyes darkened.

"You sleep in tomorrow and take it easy."

Blake opened his mouth to speak but Ethan put up his hand and wagged a finger at his brother. "And you stay the rest of the week with Barb and Mal."

Blake groaned.

"You're doing too much, bro. If you don't look after yourself you'll end up back in hospital."

"Jenny's been nagging you, hasn't she?"

"Jenny strikes me as a sensible woman and not the type to nag at all."

"I asked her to marry me."

Blake's quiet voice was enough for Ethan to know his brother wasn't joking.

"I see."

Blake pulled himself up straight. "No, you don't. You don't get it at all. You're happy living the playboy life but I'm not. As much as my ex-wife was a bitch I liked being married. It's not just the sex."

Ethan raised an eyebrow but Blake went on.

"It's about companionship and enjoying the same things. It's having someone to laugh with in the good times and someone prepared to share your troubles at the end of the day."

Blake stopped. He was staring off into the distance but Ethan got the feeling it wasn't the yard full of sheep he was looking at.

"Fair enough," Ethan said.

"Jenny's the one." Blake looked him in the face. "I know it."

"But she doesn't think so?"

"She says she loves me but she loves her job too."

"She's a nurse. I'm sure the local hospital would snap her up."

"She's a trauma nurse. There's little opportunity for that here."

Ethan had already been through this with Jenny, just as Blake had obviously done as well. He tried to lighten the mood.

"What? You'd keep her busy by yourself without all the other accidents that go on around this part of the country."

Ethan's attempt at humour didn't take the frown from his brother's face.

"It's not a joke, Ethan. We want to be together but we can't see how."

Ethan didn't think the pain etched in his brother's face was just from his physical injuries. It made him think of Savannah. She'd been quiet when he'd gone over on Sunday evening to help her with the two returned houseboats. She'd favoured her left leg more than he'd noticed her do before but she didn't complain. He wondered what had happened to cause that limp. An old injury she'd said. Perhaps she'd been in pain. Her tetchy side had been out in full force. She'd grumbled something about going back to Adelaide and to hell with Jaxon. It had hit Ethan then that he didn't want her to go. He could relate to Blake's predicament.

"You'll find a way to sort it out," Ethan said.

"It's easy for you to say. You and your one-night stands."

"I don't do that anymore."

"You're kidding me. What about you and Bel on Saturday night?"

"She's harmless."

"You reckon? I thought you were in for a big night there."

"With Belinda? You're joking?"

"No, but it was a shame about the other one. What was her name? Savannah? She was a much better looker. Pretty quiet though. Not really your type."

"Only four left," Barb called from the door of the shed.

Blake waved. "We'll be right there."

Ethan gave his brother a horrified look. If he thought Ethan was bedding Belinda maybe Savannah had the same thought. That might explain her sudden departure from dinner when he'd badly wanted her to stay. He'd hardly had a chance to talk to her that night. And maybe that's why she'd been so prickly on Sunday.

"Belinda's married," he said.

"She sure didn't act like it."

Ethan shook his head. He'd invited Savannah for dinner to get to know her better. He wasn't the slightest bit interested in Belinda.

"You're wrong about me, Blake," he said. "I do get it. You and Jenny make a good pair. Hell, even Mal and Barb do in their own way. I want that too."

And as he said it, Ethan had an idea about managing the next day without Blake.

"When I've got the last lot of sheep in for the day I'll take over in the yard," he said. "You and Jenny can head off early. And don't worry about tomorrow morning. We'll manage," he said.

Blake gave him a funny look.

"Boys!" Barb's shout was a replay from their childhood.

"Coming, Barb," they chorused.

CHAPTER

27

The sun was still below the horizon when Ethan returned from his short walk with Jasper. He gave the dog some breakfast then took the stairs two at a time. Once again he'd had a restless night and yet he had a spring in his step. When he'd got home last night he'd called in on Savannah. She had agreed to come with him to the farm today. It had taken a lot of talking. He'd had to hint at the "owing him a favour" card, which he hadn't liked doing. If anyone owed him for helping out with the houseboats it was Jaxon.

Savannah had been reluctant at first, assuring him she didn't know one end of a sheep from the other but she'd finally given in. Ethan had seen how quickly she picked up the business of running the houseboats. He was confident she'd get the hang of helping in the shearing shed just as quickly. He liked the idea of working with her.

He flew around his kitchen taking bites of toast as he went. The slow cooker had been put to lots of use this last week. This time he dropped some lamb shanks on top of onion, garlic and carrots, plugged in a few bits of rosemary then covered it all with beef broth. He tipped in some red wine for good measure and turned the cooker to low. It was only fair that he could offer Savannah a meal when they got home, and tonight it would be just the two of them.

Car lights shone in his driveway. Jasper barked. Ethan tossed down the last of his coffee and flicked off the house lights. Savannah had agreed to take her car rather than be passenger on the back of his bike. He'd been looking forward to her sitting up close behind him all the way to the farm but the car would be good. At least they'd be able to have a conversation.

"See ya, mate," he said as he passed Jasper's enclosure. "I'll have some nice bones for you tonight."

He opened the passenger door and folded himself into the seat.

"Good morning," he said.

Savannah nodded. "You can push that seat right back," she said.

He fiddled around with the lever making room for his legs while she backed out of the driveway.

"Take us up to the main road and turn left," he said.

Once more she nodded and they set off. Light was slowly filling the sky. He could see only a few scattered clouds.

"It should be a fine day," Ethan said.

Again the nod.

They passed Belinda's gate and he was reminded of the dinner he'd hosted the other night.

"I guess the Palmers have gone back to Adelaide by now," he said.

"I guess."

It was going to be a long drive to the farm at this rate. He glanced across at Savannah. Her hands gripped the steering wheel tightly and her shoulders were hunched forward, every bit of her focused on the driving. He wondered if she always drove like that or was it having him in the car that made her so tense?

That reminded him of his pills. He hadn't taken them in the rush this morning. He'd missed before. One day wouldn't hurt.

Savannah stopped the car at the edge of the main road and leaned forward in her seat. Across the road the signpost seemed to have her attention.

"Worried you won't find your way back?" he asked.

"No," she glanced at him. "Jaxon said there was a J&S Houseboats sign on this post and back at the T-junction. I keep forgetting to have a good look. If the sign had fallen off it might still be on the ground."

"It shouldn't fall off. Those signs are bolted on," Ethan said as Savannah edged the car out onto the bitumen. "I remember them. They were blue with white writing." He twisted around to have another look. "They're both gone, did you say?"

"Yes."

"That's odd," he said. "Maybe a happy customer souvenired them."

"Maybe."

Once more Savannah was focused on the road ahead. They travelled in silence. The road stretched out before them. It was so different sitting in a car rather than moulded to his bike. He watched out the windscreen as the thicker scrub gradually gave way to saltbush and lower vegetation.

"It's very desolate out here."

Ethan turned his head from the scenery to look at Savannah. Her shoulders were back and colour had returned to her knuckles. She appeared a little more relaxed. Perhaps she was getting used to having a passenger.

"Station country," he said. "A long way between neighbours."

"This is where you grew up?"

"We're not there yet. About another thirty klicks."

"Why did you leave?"

She glanced his way then back to the road.

"Sorry, none of my business," she said. "It's just that I can't imagine living out here. I thought Jaxon's place was the back of beyond."

"There are plenty more isolated properties than my parents' place. They're only just off this highway and ten minutes from town."

"And your brother's farm is close, you said?"

"As the crow flies. They share a boundary but it's almost easier to go out onto the highway than to drive over the hills. It's fine on a bike or if you're not in a hurry."

She went quiet for a while.

"Explain to me again what you want me to do," she said.

"You'll be spraying the cuts on shorn sheep to prevent infection."

Savannah kept her eyes on the road but he could see her knuckles going white again.

"You'll have a bottle with a pump and spray nozzle." He could see her forehead furrow. "Have you ever seen anyone spraying weeds in the garden?"

She flicked him a questioning look.

"It's a plastic bottle you hold in one hand connected with a tube to a spray nozzle. You just have to squirt the cuts. It's not hard."

"Where will you be?"

"Most of the time I'll be working beside you. The sheep have to be sprayed for lice and branded. From time to time I'll have to bring in more sheep. One of the others will come out and take over my job. It will be a bit of a juggle but it should work. Blake will be back by this afternoon."

They travelled on in silence. Ethan kept his eye on the range of hills growing steadily larger ahead of them.

"Not much further now," he said. "There's a drum and a sign at the entrance."

The sound of the engine changed slightly as Savannah eased back on the accelerator.

"It's coming up on your left."

She slowed the car to a crawl as she turned from the bitumen onto the dirt track. Ethan couldn't help glancing in the side mirror expecting to see another vehicle bearing down on them but the road was empty behind them.

"Drive past the house yard. The shearing shed's a bit further along on your right."

They passed the house just as Ethan's father let himself out the back gate.

"If you stop a moment I'll introduce you to Mal, my father."

Savannah did as he asked. Mal walked towards them. Ethan wound down his window.

"Was hoping you'd be back," Mal said.

Good morning to you too, Ethan thought.

"Why wouldn't I be?" he said instead.

"Your brother's deserted us."

"Only for the morning."

"He should have said he wasn't up to it. I would have got someone else to help. Too late now."

"This is Savannah. She's going to lend us a hand."

Mal bent and peered through the open window. Ethan was suddenly anxious. He didn't want his father scaring Savannah. She was already edgy.

"Good morning, Mr Daly," Savannah said.

Her tone was firm. It reminded Ethan of when she'd first arrived and had called him Mr Daly.

"Morning," Mal said, glaring at her. "You from Riverboat Point?"

"Next door to Ethan."

"You done much sheep work?"

"Savannah's a quick learner," Ethan cut in. "We'd better head to the shed. Catch you over there." He waved Savannah on.

"Your father isn't what I expected," she said as they moved off.

"In what way?"

"The ponytail, the loose shirt, the leather necklace. He looks like he's stepped out of the seventies."

"Wait till you meet Mum. She lives in cheesecloth and is very fond of beads." Ethan pointed to a row of straggly gums. "Park over there."

She stopped the car where he'd indicated and they both got out. He pushed his hat to his head, she tugged on a cap. Short bits of hair poked out underneath. She twisted her head from side to side and rolled her shoulders several times.

"This way."

He started to walk towards the yards. She didn't follow. He turned back.

She was staring at the yards. He tried to imagine them as she was seeing them. Old rails coated with strands of wool, empty chemical containers stashed in a corner, the bare ground littered with manure and tufts of wool, no roof overhead. A bit different from her city work environment.

"Coming?"

A flicker of concern crossed her face as she met his gaze. She pulled her shoulders back and glanced at the yards again.

"Show me what you want me to do."

He nodded and set off before she had the chance to see the smile creep across his face. Today should prove very interesting.

CHAPTER
28

The sun was hot on the back of her neck. Savannah turned up the collar of her polo top. She'd discarded her jumper shortly after she'd started work. The morning sun had heated the air quickly and although she wasn't moving around that much, she was warm.

So far the sunny day was the only positive she'd encountered. The pong of sheep with the dust stirred up by their hooves hung in the air and mingled with the pungent odour of the spray and the sharp smell of the branding ink. The stench was so strong she felt like she was bathing in it. Little black flies crawled over her at every opportunity.

"Ready for the next lot?"

Savannah lifted her head to look at the woman next to her. Pam was the wife of one of the shearers. She travelled with her husband and worked as a rouseabout when needed. She worked in the shed and came outside when Ethan was off getting more sheep, like he was now. Pam was very efficient. She sprayed the sheep for lice and painted a brand on their rump in less time than it took Savannah to spray their cuts.

Savannah had worried when she'd first seen the garish red lines in various spots on the sheep, such a sharp contrast to the shorn white bodies. Ethan had assured her the cuts were superficial and the spray was to guard against infection. After that she'd felt at least she was being useful.

She squirted the last two sheep.

"Done," she said.

She watched as Pam opened the gate at the end of the long skinny area that looked like a passage between yards.

"Out you go," Pam called. Her weathered hands gave the leaders a tap on their rumps.

Savannah clapped her hands to urge the rest forward. She didn't like touching them.

She lurched back as a sheepdog came from nowhere, leapt nimbly onto the rails, crossed the backs of the sheep she'd just sprayed and dropped to the other side. It was enough to urge the last stragglers forward and into the next yard.

That was another thing she didn't like. There were two dogs. When they weren't working they flopped down in whatever bit of shade they could find. Without warning they could appear and work the sheep. It made her nervous. At least there was only one here at the moment. The other was off with Ethan.

"You're doing well for someone new on the job," Pam said. "It's not rocket science but I've worked with a few who had no idea." She took a swig from her water bottle. "You live with Ethan?"

"No." Savannah was surprised at the strength of her reply. "I live next door. Not permanently. Just visiting. Ethan's helped me with some jobs for my brother so I'm returning the favour."

"Oh, I thought he was sweet on you," Pam ducked her head. "My mistake, sorry." She busied herself with the pot of branding ink.

Savannah reached down for her own water bottle stashed against the post beside her and took several large gulps of water. If Pam thought she was Ethan's girlfriend she wondered what the others thought. Maybe his parents had that idea too. Savannah rolled the idea around in her head. What did it matter what they thought? After today she was unlikely to see any of them again.

She pictured Ethan as he'd looked this morning. The headlights had illuminated him as he'd strolled towards her car. He'd been wearing a brown jacket against the chill of the pre-dawn air. Underneath was a faded blue shirt that stretched across his broad chest and tucked neatly into his jeans. When he climbed in beside her she'd noticed his clean-shaven face. His skin looked so smooth. Such a contrast to his unruly hair. She tried to imagine him in uniform. Soldiers had to have short hair, didn't they? As soon as he'd shut the door she'd smelled him. What was it about the slight hint of aftershave and scent of fresh male body that had her stomach doing flips?

"How are you managing?"

Savannah spun to see Mal studying her from the yard behind. He was tall like Ethan but that's where the similarities ended.

"Fine thanks."

She hoped her voice carried more confidence than she felt. Somehow she got the impression it was important for her to do well, for Ethan's sake. She wiped the back of her hand across her mouth and put the bottle down by her feet.

"You doing okay, Pam?"

"No probs. We're a good team here." Pam's face split in a wide grin and Savannah felt pleased at the older woman's commendation.

"It'll be smoko soon," Mal said. "You'll be able to take a break."

"No probs," Pam said. She moved away to do something with the ink bucket.

Mal lifted his hat and scratched his head. "It's a long day out here."

"I'm good so far." Savannah stared at him.

He held her gaze a moment. Savannah thought he wanted to say more. Instead he pushed his hat back firmly and pulled a notepad from his top pocket. He opened the gate in front of him and as the sheep filed into the next holding yard, he counted them. She hadn't realised that's what he'd been doing the first time she'd watched him. Ethan had explained it to her.

From her position behind Mal, Savannah tried to count as the sheep pushed through, sometimes two or three at a time. She lost the number quickly.

Mal jotted in his book, closed the gate and opened the one that led to the yard where she and Pam worked on the sheep. He whistled and the dog jumped into the yard with him. The sheep raced forward and were soon ready for their spray and brand.

Savannah gritted her teeth, picked up the spray unit and began squirting sheep again. She didn't look back but she sensed Mal was watching her. She concentrated on the job at hand, determined to appear efficient.

Finally Mal whistled. Out of the corner of her eye she saw the dog rise from its position in the empty yard and leap over the rails. She glanced behind her. Mal had gone.

"How's it going?"

She spun the other way at the sound of Ethan's voice.

"I didn't realise you were back."

"Next mob are ready to go," he said. "I can take over again here, Pam. You go and get smoko. They'll want you in the shed as soon as the break's over."

Pam handed over her gear. Savannah realised the motor that had been running all morning had stopped.

"Don't take too long." Pam grinned at her. "You've earned some of Barb's cakes."

Savannah smiled back. She hadn't spoken to Pam much but they'd worked side by side well enough. In spite of that she was relieved to have Ethan back. Strange to admit it but she felt more at ease when he was working with her. Perhaps because she didn't have to pretend she knew what she was doing.

Once they'd done the last of the yarded sheep Savannah followed Ethan to the small room tacked on the side of the shed. Outside was an old concrete trough with a block of soap. A towel hung from a nail. They both washed their hands. His brushed hers as he handed over the towel. His touch sent a tingle up her arm.

"Ready?"

His smile sent her already alert body into a higher state of awareness. Relieved that he had his back to her, she followed him into the shed.

"Barb, this is Savannah," he said to the only other woman there besides Pam.

"Hello, Savannah." Barb wrapped her in a warm hug.

"Pleased to meet you," she said, glad she had the excuse of the welcome for the huge smile that split her face at the sight before her.

Ethan had been right. His mother was dressed in an embroidered cheesecloth shirt worn over the top of loose-fitting pants. Her fading brown hair flowed over her shoulders. Several strands of colourful beads hung around her neck and a long pair of earrings dangled from her ears. The pair of workboots she wore on her feet were the odd things out.

"Sorry I didn't come over and say hello earlier," Barb said.

Her face lit up with a warm smile. This was where Ethan got his good looks from.

"I've been flat out with the food today. My oven decided to play up this morning." She waved her hands about as she spoke. "I had trouble milking the cow, nearly lost the whole bucket. Then I found the pig in my vegie patch. Mal needs to fix his pen. Luckily the damn pig hadn't done much damage before I found him or he might have become dinner earlier than expected."

"Oh," Savannah said lamely.

"Tea or coffee?" Ethan asked, unfazed by his mother's diatribe.

"Tea please."

"Have you met everyone else?" Barb asked.

Savannah flicked a look around the end of the shed where the men were resting on old chairs and bags finishing their morning tea.

"Yes," she said. "This morning."

No sooner had she spoken than some of the men moved off, gathering their belongings as they went.

"Piece of cake?" Barb asked. She held out a flat tin with chunky slices of dark chocolate cake.

"Oh, wow." Savannah reached in and took a slice. "Thanks."

Ethan took a piece and started eating.

"Anything else you want?" Barb asked.

"No, thank you," Savannah said through a mouthful of cake. "This is delicious."

Ethan shook his head.

The others in the shed began to take up their positions again talking among themselves as they went. Barb started packing up. Across the concrete floor opposite them Mal sat studying his notepad. He didn't raise his eyes. Ethan stood eating his cake. His mother bustled on one side of him packing away food and his father sat on his other side studying his notepad. Talk about awkward.

Music played in the background. Sheep shuffled and the shearing crew prepared to start again.

"How much longer will shearing take?" Savannah asked Ethan.

"About two more days."

"And Blake will be okay to come back?"

"He'll be here this afternoon. You can relax a bit then. Have a look around at the shearing in progress."

The motor purred to life as the shearers began their work.

"So long as she doesn't get in anyone's way." Mal had stood up and was watching them.

Savannah felt every bit the nuisance he had intended to make her feel. She was grateful Ethan was the only witness. "I'll get back outside then."

Behind her she heard Barb's warning tone as she spoke her husband's name followed by Ethan's outburst.

"Bloody hell, Mal, talk about making someone feel welcome."

Savannah kept walking. The voices faded. She clenched her hands. Damn the old bugger. He had something up his nose.

Footsteps crunched behind her.

"I'm sorry about my father," Ethan said.

"Don't worry about it."

"If it wasn't for Blake we'd be in the car heading for home right now."

Savannah turned. Anger burned in Ethan's eyes. It was him she felt sorry for, not herself. Her parents had died some time ago but when they were alive she had no doubt they loved her. Ethan's relationship with his parents was very different.

"I can look after myself, Ethan," she said.

He took a step towards her. The fire had left his eyes. His face relaxed as he bent towards her.

"Ethan ..."

Her words were lost in his kiss. His arms gripped her shoulders and pulled her close. Then, just as suddenly he let her go.

"I'm sorry," he said.

"I'm not." Her brain was telling her she was stupid but her insides were on fire. His lips had been warm and soft and tasted like chocolate.

"When we get home, will you come for dinner?" he asked. "Just the two of us this time?"

"Okay."

She'd replied before she had time to think about it. Once more her brain was sending her warnings that her body was ignoring.

"I've got to mix some more spray," he said.

He smiled and for a moment she thought he was going to kiss her again. He turned quickly and strode away.

She put her fingers to her tingling lips. It was a long time since she'd been kissed like that. In fact, had she ever been kissed like that?

CHAPTER
29

Savannah stared at the river beyond the houseboats. The thick cloud cover meant there wasn't a lot of moon or star light and yet she was sure she'd seen a light. From Ethan's deck she had a good view through the trees.

There it was. She turned more to the right but it was gone again. It reminded her of the night she'd seen the light in the distance over the Palmers' fence. Perhaps she should ask Ethan to take a look.

She took a step. Jasper stood in the doorway watching her.

Savannah sucked in a breath. She stood perfectly still. Her heart thumped in her chest. Why did dogs have this effect on her? Perhaps something had happened in her childhood but there was no-one to ask anymore.

"Ethan," she called. "Can you come out here?"

She heard a cupboard close in the kitchen then his footsteps across the floor. Jasper came outside with him.

"What's up?"

"I thought I saw a light." She pointed. "Out there."

"On the river? Could have been a boat."

"I didn't hear anything."

They both watched for a moment but the light didn't appear again.

"Could have been someone kayaking," Ethan said and turned on his heel. "Food's ready."

Savannah was quick to follow him in case Jasper blocked her path again.

"Have a seat," Ethan said. "I'll just put Jasper to bed."

She took her jumper from her shoulders and hung it over the back of her chair. The dog followed his master outside. She listened to the clatter of claws and the thud of Ethan's shoes on the wooden steps as they went down. From the river there was the distant sound of a motor, something bigger than the tinnies and speedboats that often went up and down.

She fiddled with the bamboo placemat. They were going to be alone. It had been just the two of them driving home in the car but that had been different. She'd been full of questions about everything she'd seen and done today and there was no way he could kiss her while she was driving.

What had that been about anyway? Was Ethan the type that played any available woman? She hadn't thought so and yet there had been Belinda at their last dinner. What had gone on there?

He burst through the door. She jumped. The placemat slithered from her fingers and fell to the floor. He gave her a funny smile. She ducked down to retrieve the mat. By the time she was upright he was in the kitchen serving the meal.

"That smells divine," she said.

"Lamb shanks." He crossed the room carrying two plates. "Would you like a beer or a glass of red?"

"I didn't bring anything."

"My shout."

"Red please." It seemed the right thing to choose but it brought an instant vision of Belinda, her arm through Ethan's, clutching a glass of red in her other hand.

He poured two glasses, turned on some music and sat opposite her.

"Tuck in," he said.

Savannah hadn't felt hungry but her mouth watered and she took an eager mouthful.

"Mmm! That's good."

"Glad you like it."

"I can't believe how much I've eaten today."

"All that fresh air and exercise."

"I enjoyed it," Savannah said. "I'd be happy to help again. Are you sure Blake will be okay?"

"He only put in a few hours this afternoon and Barb will make sure he gets a good rest tonight. He should be fine."

They were silent for a few minutes while they ate.

"Your mum's a good cook," Savannah said. "Is that where you get it from?"

"Maybe. I've only taught myself since I left the army."

"Sick of army food?"

"They fed us well. Too well really. Some blokes don't know how to look after themselves when they leave. I didn't want that to be me. I eat a lot of fish here but I haven't had time to catch any lately. I don't have a very wide repertoire. If it can go in the slow cooker or I can fry it in a pan, I can manage."

Savannah took another mouthful. What did she say next? She'd never been good at small talk.

"Jaxon said you used to be a fitness instructor."

She lifted her head. Ethan was studying her across the table. His brown eyes were dark pools in the soft light.

"Yes."

She hadn't realised there was only one light on in the kitchen and the light over the table didn't seem as bright. There must be a dimmer switch but she hadn't noticed him use it. Music played softly in the background. She gripped her knife and fork tighter and kept eating. What was she doing here?

"I've got a small gym set up in my spare room," Ethan said.

"I don't use much equipment these days."

"You like to run?"

"When I can. It's good cardio."

"You can't flex cardio." He grinned at her.

She looked down. That grin made her stomach flip. She studied his deep green shirt. They'd both gone home for a shower before dinner. He'd changed his farm shirt for a t-shirt that hugged the muscles of his arms and accentuated his well-toned chest.

"It's a joke."

She dragged her gaze from his body back to his face. He was looking past her. It was dark outside so she knew he would only be able to see his own reflection in the glass.

"What is?"

"In the FOB there's a lot of waiting." He was still focused on something behind her.

"FOB?"

"Everything revolves around the gym."

"Ethan?"

He was somewhere else. Savannah recognised the look. She'd experienced it herself often enough, reliving a past event while the real world receded.

"Ethan," she said gently. She reached across the table and placed her hand on his.

He lowered his gaze at her touch then looked directly into her eyes. She saw the pain before the recognition.

"Sorry." He rolled his shoulders and continued eating. They ate the rest of their meal in silence.

Finally he reached for her plate. "Finished?"

"Yes, thank you. That was delicious."

He took the dishes to the kitchen. He kept himself busy scraping plates and stacking the dishwasher.

She was curious. There was a hidden side to Ethan. Perhaps something to do with the army.

"What's FOB?" she asked.

He stopped wiping the bench and looked at her. It was hard to gauge his expression across the room in the dim light.

"Forward operating base."

Something about the way he said it chilled her.

"I'm sorry I can't offer any dessert," he said.

"I don't need it."

"Have another wine."

"It's late." She stood up and took her jumper from the back of the chair. "Thanks again for a fantastic meal."

He crossed the space between them in an instant.

"Sav, please don't go yet."

Her stomach flipped at his use of her nickname. It sounded so intimate coming from him.

"I'm sorry about before," he said. "I don't know why I was suddenly on another planet." He shrugged his shoulders. "It has nothing to do with you. I didn't mean to put you off."

"You didn't," she said.

He took her hand and locked his eyes on hers.

"Stay a little longer," he said.

She tried to ignore the effect his touch was having on her body.

"It's been a long day."

"I know."

He drew her closer.

"I ..."

Her words were lost by his mouth on hers. His lips were warm and soft, his tongue gently probing. His arms wrapped around her, pressing their bodies together. A tingle started in the pit of her stomach and spread with a warming sensation that made her toes curl. The jumper slid from her fingers as she reached around him. She could feel the firmness of his back beneath the softness of his shirt. At the same time she was aware of the sensuous feel of his hands moving over her.

She eased her lips from his. Was this how it had been with Belinda? She looked into his eyes. Could she trust this man? He leaned forward and they were kissing again. Their bodies locked together. She melted in his arms. He dragged his lips from hers and kissed her neck.

"Savannah," he groaned in her ear.

Suddenly she was aware of the music and Meatloaf's gravelly *I would do anything for love.* How many times had she worked out to that music, punching the bag? She pulled away from Ethan. *But I won't do that.* The words were loud in her ears. She wasn't going to give herself to this man, not any man, not again.

"I really do have to go," she said.

She bent to pick up her jumper. He reached a hand towards her. "Why?"

His eyes were pleading.

"We can catch up tomorrow."

"I'll be at the farm all day," he said.

"I'll cook you dinner." The words were out of her mouth before she had time to think about them.

His face lit up and he reached for her again.

She turned and fled. She knew if he touched her one more time her resolve would be totally undone. Her heart pounded in time with her feet on the wooden steps. She was a teenager again. Awkward and embarrassed and yet …

She stopped at the spot where she'd climbed the fence between the two properties and looked up at his house. The dim light glowed from the living area windows but there was no sign of Ethan. She shivered. The warmth she had felt in his arms was gone. She climbed the fence and hurried into the shack.

CHAPTER
30

"Watch it!" Mal yelled.

Ethan ducked out of the way as his father urged a mob of shorn sheep through the gate.

"If you've got nothing to do, Pam could use a hand clearing the boards."

Mal turned on his heel and walked back towards the shearing shed. Ethan followed. He'd been daydreaming again and yet he felt a ripple of tension through his body. All day he'd had trouble keeping thoughts of Savannah out of his head. Last night she'd melted into his arms, returned his kisses and then run away. He'd felt her quick departure like a blow to his chest. Had he moved too fast? Did she regret kissing him? Surely not if she'd offered to cook dinner. It created another opportunity for them to be together.

Savannah was an enigma. She was a striking woman yet oblivious of her good looks. She had an injury of some kind but she enjoyed exercise. In spite of her city background she had adapted to the isolation of the river. He didn't know what to make of her other than he felt the need to be with her. Not as someone just to take to his bed, although he wouldn't deny he'd relish that, but someone to spend time with in other ways. He felt relaxed when he was with Savannah.

So relaxed he'd drifted off for a moment when they'd talked about exercise. The old joke, "you can't flex cardio" had taken him back to the FOB and the gym they created to pass the time between trips beyond the wire. Lumps of concrete became weights. They kept fit, trying to outdo each other and forget for a while where they were. Most blokes took up smoking to help pass the time. He'd managed to avoid it. He'd chewed gum until his jaw ached and played patience with the earphones of his iPod jammed in his ears.

Ethan rubbed at his chest. What was he meant to be doing? His hands tingled.

"Ethan!" He jumped. Mal's shout brought him back to the shed.

"Bloody hell, man. Pam's going under. Do you want to be here or not?"

Not, Ethan thought. He glared at his father. Mal held his look. Pam moved around Ethan to reach the edges of the fleece on the table. He was aware of Chas, the wool classer, continuing his methodical inspection of the fleece.

Ethan spun and strode along the boards behind the shearers.

"I'm here because you need help, old man," he breathed. Sheep were annoying bloody animals. He wouldn't work with them by choice. Give him an engine any day. He picked up a fleece, carried it to the sorting table and threw it out. The wool billowed in the air then settled on the table where he proceeded to pull off the dirty tufts. Chas, looking like a chef in his back apron, inspected the fleece without looking up. Pam took up the broom to sweep away the scattered clumps around their feet.

Ethan could sense Mal in the background. It gave him some sat-isfaction to know that as much as he didn't really want to be here, for Mal it must be even more irksome to have the black sheep of the family working in his shed. The neighbour's daughter was here as well but with Blake being injured and another local lad off at boarding school, Mal needed all the help he could get.

Ethan ducked his head and looked behind. His father was busy inking their label on a full bale. He gave Ethan no more thought than he'd give anyone who worked for him – possibly less. Ethan couldn't help wondering if things might have turned out differently had he not joined the army. Probably not. There were cracks in their relationship long before that. The army was the last straw. Mal and even Barb had cut him off back then. His own parents.

The late afternoon sun slanted through the dusty louvre win-dows. Ethan kept working. Not long till smoko then only a few hours and he could head on home for whatever Savannah was cooking for dinner. Not that he cared. He just wanted to be with her. He was curious to see where it would lead. Did she feel the same way about him?

"Ethan!"

He took a deep breath to still the rage that simmered in his belly. Across the table Pam gave him a sympathetic look. He glanced over to his father who was standing beside the off-cut bins beckoning him.

"Here," Mal called.

At least he hadn't whistled. Although the farm dogs were prob-ably held in higher esteem than the younger son. Ethan crossed to his father.

"You put that last lot of wool in the wrong bin."

Mal jabbed a finger towards the wire cages they used to store any low-grade wool that didn't go in the bales.

Ethan shook his head and the rage burned deeper. There was little difference between the contents of the bins.

"Keep your shirt on," he said.

"What do you mean, keep my shirt on?"

"It doesn't matter in the scheme of things." Ethan clenched his hands at his sides, it was only a bit of wool, not life and death.

"And what scheme would that be? The one according to Ethan Daly, who doesn't give a damn about what happens here?"

Ethan opened his mouth and the rage surged up like vomit from inside him. He yelled at his father, spewing forth a tirade of abuse. Nothing he said made sense but the anger drove him on.

Blake's voice came to him as if through a tunnel.

"Take it easy, mate. Calm down."

Ethan looked around. He was outside squatting with his back against the tin of the shed. When had he come outside? Blake was beside him, bent over, concern on his face.

"What's going on?"

Barb hurried towards them. The car door left open behind her.

"You're lucky you missed your son using language that wouldn't be heard in the gutter." Mal had come outside.

"Leave it," Blake murmured.

Ethan felt the gentle pressure of his brother's hand on his shoulder. He gripped his head in his hands. What had he said?

"Are you sick?" Barb squatted in front of him, her face close to his.

"I'm all right," Ethan rasped. The words echoed in his head.

Barb used her sleeve to wipe his forehead.

"You don't look all right," she said.

"I'm fine, Barb. Don't fuss."

"There's work to be done." Mal turned on his heel and went back inside the shed.

"For goodness sake, Mal." Barb looked back at Ethan. "What happened?"

"It was my fault." Ethan tried to get up but nausea swept over him. Perspiration formed on his forehead again.

"You're as white as a ghost," Barb said.

Ethan's stomach gurgled and saliva squirted into his mouth. He leant to the side and spat. He wiped his mouth with the back of his hand and noticed the tremble in his fingers.

"This is no good." Barb stood up. "I'll unpack the food from the car then you're coming home with me."

"I can't." Ethan's words were overridden by Barb's.

"Blake, stay with him while I set up smoko."

Ethan stared after her.

"I want to go home," he said.

"This is one time I agree with Barb," Blake replied. "You need to rest before you get on your bike."

"I'll be all right."

"I've never seen you like that, mate." Blake slid down the corrugated iron and sat on the ground stretching his legs out carefully in front of him. "I know Mal can be frustrating –"

"Frustrating's one word for it," Ethan cut him off.

Barb bustled past carrying an armload of plastic boxes. She cast a concerned look over Ethan then went on into the shed.

"The dogs get better treatment than I do," Ethan muttered and suddenly he felt sorry for himself. He'd been a good son in his teenage years, served his country in a war zone twice and where had it all ended up? In the dirt beside a bloody shearing shed.

Maybe he should see the psych again. He'd been managing so well. This outburst had come from left field. Perhaps he'd never be able to survive without the tablets.

Ethan sat forward. "Damn!"

"What's the matter?" Blake asked.

"Nothing," Ethan said but he was trying to remember what he'd done this morning. Had he taken the tablet? Perhaps not. He struggled to his feet. "I've got to go home."

"No you're not." Barb was back. "You're coming home with me until I'm satisfied you're okay."

Ethan drew himself up.

"No need to carry on," she said. "I won't take no for an answer. You're coming back to the house for a rest where I can keep an eye on you."

Blake gave him a wry smile. Only a week ago he'd been caught up in Barb's Florence Nightingale attempts. No doubt it was amusing for him to see them both snaffled up in care again.

"Just go with it, mate," he said. He used his good arm to brace himself as he got back to his feet. "A rest won't hurt you."

"Look who's talking," Barb said. "You two are grown men and yet when it comes to your health you're like little boys." She hooked her arm through Ethan's. "Can you make it to the car? Blake, take his other arm."

"I can walk," Ethan said. He was aware of the eyes from the shed watching him.

Barb drove him to the house without speaking. Once she switched off the engine she turned in her seat and studied him.

"You look like crap, Ethan."

"Thanks, Mum."

He put his head back against the seat. He knew she was right.

"After you left the army you were gaunt but you filled out a bit, looked more relaxed," Barb said. "I thought that place on the river was just what you needed."

"It is."

"We haven't seen you in ages. You look like you haven't slept."

"I've had a few late nights. I'll be fine." I just need to remember to take the tablets, he thought. If he'd missed a couple of days that would explain the jittery feelings. Withdrawal wasn't good.

"Stay here tonight. It will be good to have both my boys home."

Overwhelming tiredness swept over him. He didn't think he'd be able to stay on his bike long enough to get home.

"I'll rest here a while but I can't stay the night. I have to get home to Jasper."

Barb pursed her lips but she said no more. They both got out of the car and went inside. His old room was just the same. The motorbike quilt, the posters on the wall, the dirt bike trophies on the chest of drawers, its vivid blue paint patched with every sticker he'd ever received.

Ethan sighed and fell onto the bed. He was very tired. Even so, something else nagged him. There was another reason he had to go home. He couldn't remember why. He rolled over and let himself sink into the depths of sleep.

CHAPTER
31

Savannah put down the phone. She'd just taken another house-boat booking. It was for February next year. That was so far away. She felt sad to think she wouldn't be around then and yet worried that she might be. Jaxon's disappearance weighed heavily on her. What if something had happened to him? Ethan seemed sure he was definitely on holiday but maybe Ethan had something to do with Jaxon's disappearance.

She slapped her hands to her thighs in frustration. She'd been over and over this before. Ethan said Jaxon would return when he was ready. She had to trust that was correct.

She picked up her gym bag and took out the towel. This morning Mandy and the other women had welcomed her to their Thursday morning fitness session like a long-lost friend. Faye had been there. The exercises had gone well and they all said they'd be back next Tuesday. But would she? Jaxon might suddenly turn up. How long could this living an alternative life go on for?

And what was she going to do about Ethan? Last night had rekindled a part of her she thought was gone forever. But could she trust her judgement when it came to men? She'd made a fool of herself before. Who was to say this was any different?

Savannah groaned and put her hands to her head.

"Stop this."

She needed to keep busy. She put the bottles of sparkling in her fridge with the chocolates and the flowers in a jar with a ribbon around it. She'd bought them for Tara's group. All four houseboats were booked for the weekend. She took the four sets of keys and set off to check the boats. She hoped Ethan had remembered there was a hire going out first thing tomorrow. The customers were arriving tonight, sleeping on board *River Magic*, ready for an early start. There were two other boats going out tomorrow afternoon and then Tara's group who would be on board *Our Destiny* and staying put for the weekend. Savannah hoped she hadn't made a mistake allowing them to do that. A group living at the bottom of the garden all weekend was quite different from one staying overnight for an early getaway. Hopefully the women would be a sensible bunch and they'd like the extras she was putting in for them.

She checked the boats over then checked again. She'd patched the hole in *Tawarri*'s bathroom wall as Ethan had suggested. It was only cardboard and tape but it would have to do until she could find someone to fix it properly. It didn't look too bad but she'd have to explain to the group not to touch it.

"Bloody Fred," she hissed.

She closed the door on the bathroom and took a deep breath. Everything was ready to go. All that was needed was the customers.

She left the boats and went back to kitchen. She could chop all the ingredients for the stir fry. Dinner with Ethan was something to look forward to. She hummed as she sliced the chicken, chopped the capsicum and garlic and trimmed the beans. She put them in dishes in the fridge. All she'd have left to do was cook it. She wasn't sure how hot Ethan liked his food. The curry he'd made last weekend had been mild but he said that was to accommodate Blake's taste. She deseeded some chillies, sliced them and put them aside. That was a decision for later.

She wandered around the living area, straightened a chair, flicked a dead fly from the windowsill, checked the mouse trap in the pantry. She took out her phone. It was only four o'clock. Ethan wouldn't be home for hours yet and she wasn't expecting the group hiring *River Magic* until dark. She needed to do something. She picked up her gym bag and took it into the bedroom.

A jog, that's what she'd do. Burn off her nervous energy. She set off down the driveway and turned out onto the road. The sky was overcast, making the afternoon dull. She kept to the left side of the road. Not that she'd ever seen any vehicles along here other than customers but she felt more comfortable keeping as far as possible from Gnasher's fence line as she could. She didn't want him to mistake her for a rabbit.

Above the sound of her feet crunching on the dirt road she thought she heard a vehicle. She slowed to a stop and listened. A bird chirped, something rustled in a bush on Gnasher's side of the road. Up ahead was the gate to his property but no sign of a car. She set off again.

In front of her the road swept gradually to the left. Once she rounded the bend there was a long straight stretch and the Palmers' gate. Belinda was closing it. On the outside of the gate facing the road was their car.

Belinda looked up as Savannah approached. Her face lit up in a smile.

"Hello, Savvie." She waved. "You're still being energetic."

"Hi Belinda." Savannah stopped by the car. Ash studied her with his dark grey eyes from the driver's seat. "Hello," she said.

He nodded.

"We're just heading into town. We were going to call in on our way back," Belinda gushed. "We only arrived at lunchtime. We're staying around for a few days, thought we could catch up for a meal. Are you home tomorrow night?"

"Yes."

"That'd be great. Around seven?"

"For dinner?" Savannah hadn't realised she was meant to cook the meal.

"Yes. Perhaps you could invite Ethan. Ash would like to come too, wouldn't you?"

"Yeah, sure," he said with a smile that didn't reach his eyes.

"The four of us. It'll be great fun. It's so kind of you, Savvie."

Savannah ran her fingers through her hair. How had Belinda done that?

"We'll bring the drinks. You could raid your red supply, Ashton. I know Ethan likes a drop of that."

Belinda winked at Savannah.

"I don't know what Ethan's plans are but I can ask," Savannah said.

"If not it will be a cosy threesome."

Belinda air-kissed her cheeks.

"We'll let you go. Don't want to hold up your fitness routine. See you tomorrow night." She waggled her fingers at Savannah and set her jewellery jangling. "We're so lucky to have such great neighbours. Except for him across the road." Belinda nodded towards Gnasher's property. "Still, only one loony out of three neighbours isn't too bad. In Adelaide we're surrounded by crazy people, aren't we Ash?"

"Not exactly crazy," Ash said in a quiet voice. "Just not friendly."

"That's why we love coming here so much." Belinda hurried round to the passenger side of the car. "Thanks again for inviting us," she said and ducked into the car.

"See you tomorrow," Ash said. He gave her a brooding look, lifted his fingers in a tiny wave and pulled out onto the road. A cloud of dust hung in the air behind the car as it moved away. She put her hands to her hips. Talk about being railroaded. She would like to have been invited to their place. She was curious about their holiday house.

"Next time," she murmured and set off in the direction their car had gone.

Savannah wasn't sure whether she wanted Ethan to be available for dinner tomorrow night or not. It would be nice to have him there for Ash to talk to but she couldn't imagine how she would feel watching Belinda try to come on to Ethan like she had the other night. Perhaps with Ash present she'd be more circumspect.

Savannah followed the twists and turns of the road for quite a way before she turned and retraced her steps. She was deep in thought. How would Ethan react to guests? How would this hens' weekend go? What to give the Palmers for dinner? Before she knew it she was passing their gate again. Around the next bend she passed Gnasher's.

Up ahead, Jaxon's letterbox came into sight and then a bit further on from that she saw movement. She slowed her steps and then stopped. Puffing she put her hands to her hips and peered ahead. It was a man. He was almost naked except for a pair of shorts and some kind of weird hat on his head. And he was carrying something over his shoulder, a sack or a bag, it was hard to tell.

The man walked as if he was watching out for something. His head turned from side to side, then he paused as if he was listening.

There wasn't a lot of vegetation near Savannah but she edged off the road and crouched behind a bush. Just as she did the man stopped and turned around. He looked back down the road but still he was too far away for her to make out his features. She wondered if he could see her. She felt silly, as if she was playing a kids' game of hide and seek. The man walked on and turned into Ethan's place without looking back.

Now what should she do? Ethan wasn't home. The man could be planning to steal something, although he was dressed rather oddly for a thief. Savannah jogged on to Jaxon's gate. She heard Jasper bark. She stopped and listened. No more noise from Jasper. Perhaps the man had given him something to eat to keep him quiet or even poisoned him.

She ran down Jaxon's driveway and across to the small garden shed. She peered around the corner. Nothing. She listened. No sounds other than the usual birds and insects. She stepped around the shed, watching where she placed her feet. There was a metre between her and Ethan's fence.

She was relieved to see Jasper inside his yard. He stood rigidly still, watching her.

"Hello, Jasper," she whispered.

He turned his head slightly and twitched his ears.

Savannah backtracked and went inside. She had some ham in the fridge. Perhaps Jasper would take it and not bark. She wanted to see what the old man was up to without Jasper giving her away.

Ham in hand she went back across the yard and climbed the fence. Jasper came forward and pressed his nose to the wire of his enclosure. It was quite spacious really. Almost the whole area under the house was enclosed. There was a dog house, a bed, a bucket of water and a bowl for food, all kitted out for a guard dog.

"It's only me, Jasper," she said with more bravado than she felt.

She moved her hand along the wire and slipped the ham through. Jasper was on it in a flash. Savannah hurried up the stairs on silent feet. When she reached the back landing, she was level with the sliding doors that led to the main living area. She paused. What should she do now? She looked at the door. The screen was closed but the glass was open. Further along there was a gas water heater box on the wall and it was humming.

Savannah slid the door open. She checked left and right. Nobody there. The door to the rest of the house beyond the living area was open and she could hear water running. She looked around Ethan's living area. It was neat and tidy.

There was a thud from the other end of the house. The sound of the water had stopped. Savannah backed towards the sliding door. Her heart was thumping in her chest. It was stupid of her to come up here alone. She should ring the police. She turned to bolt.

"Gedday."

Savannah couldn't stop the yelp that erupted from her mouth. She twisted her head back over her shoulder. There was the man she'd seen on the road.

Jasper barked and then kept it up.

"Shaddup!" the man bellowed.

Savannah flinched at the sound and Jasper went silent.

"Bad enough you yelling at me without the bloody dog joining in." The man grinned. He was still in the shorts but minus the hat. His hair was wet. A towel hung around his neck, not covering much of his hairy chest and large belly. "You looking for Digger?"

"Digger?" All kinds of wild thoughts ran through Savannah's head.

"Ethan."

"No … I …" Savannah rethought her answer. "Yes."

The man studied her a moment with an amused look as if he could read her mind.

"He's not here."

"Oh, that's okay. I'll come back later."

She edged back a tiny step. The man knew Ethan and she had come to the conclusion that he wasn't robbing the place. It was none of her business. She wanted to get home.

"You must be Ethan's neighbour. The sister." He crossed the gap between them in a flash. "I'm Gnasher. Live over the back. Just using Ethan's shower till my pump gets fixed."

Savannah looked from his face to the hand he offered. She took it and her hand was squeezed in a firm grip. Up close she could see his arms and legs had good muscle tone. He wasn't the flabby guy she'd first assumed.

"I'm Savannah," she said, relieved to know he was Ethan's friend but nervous to meet the guy who took pot shots at things.

"I've seen you about," he said. "Recognised you."

"Seen me?"

"Down by those boats." He jerked his head in the direction of the river. "And jogging past my place."

He glanced in the direction of her chest. Savannah was suddenly aware of her skimpy running outfit. She took a step backwards.

"Can I make you a cuppa?" he asked.

"Oh no, thank you."

"Ethan wouldn't mind." Gnasher filled the kettle and got out a cup. He obviously knew his way around Ethan's kitchen.

"I have to get back."

Savannah slid the screen door shut between her and Gnasher.

"Nice to meet you," he said.

"You too."

Gnasher chuckled. She turned and for the second day in a row she ran down Ethan's stairs, this time with the sound of Gnasher's laughter ringing in her ears.

CHAPTER

32

The warm water soaked her hair, pounded on her shoulders and ran in rivulets over her body. Savannah closed her eyes and turned her face to the water. She never backed away from confrontation but Gnasher had spun her out. She wondered if he'd still be there when Ethan came home and whether he'd tell him about her blundering visit.

She turned off the water and reached for a towel. Goosebumps sent a shiver through her even though she'd just stepped out of a warm shower. Ethan's kisses, the feel of his body pressed against hers – Savannah rubbed her hair vigorously with the towel. They would have dinner together again tonight. He'd be around some of tomorrow to send off the houseboats. Where was this heading?

Savannah wrapped the towel around herself and tucked the corner in with force. She was crazy to fall for him. She'd been determined not to. She'd have to go back to the city when Jaxon returned. Then again, maybe she needed some uncommitted romance to put some zing in her life. Perhaps that was all Ethan wanted too. She had no idea of his past relationships. A guy like him would have to be sought after. What did he see in her? Was she just convenient, the girl next door, only here for a while?

That was the kind of talk she wasn't supposed to allow and yet with her past it was hard not to. As a very overweight teenager she'd been set up by the one boy she'd looked up to. He'd made her feel like she was special. He'd kissed her and then, when she became the butt of his friends' jokes, he'd dropped her like a hot potato. Years later, after she lost weight, there'd been several men she'd met through the gym but they'd been nothing more than a casual fling. For some of them she'd simply been another gym conquest: master the equipment and the instructor, then move on.

She thought back on those days before the accident. In hindsight she knew she'd got what she'd asked for. She'd been flattered good-looking men found her new body desirable. She'd been suckered a few times, thinking they wanted more than a quick fling. Her trust dissolved and before she knew it she was calling a few dinners, a movie and some sex, a relationship. Whatever it was, she'd thought she was happy. Then came the accident. Her life was two pieces: the time before the accident and the time after.

In her bedroom she slipped into jeans and a long-sleeved t-shirt. The shirt was a teal blue. She pulled the sheet off the mirror and gave herself a long hard look. With clothes on there was no indication of the mangled body underneath. She ran her fingers through her hair and swept it to the sides of her face. It was too long now to spike. It flopped slightly forward on one side and covered the scar at her hairline.

She peered at her eyes. She hadn't worn make-up since the accident. Maybe it was time to try some mascara and colour for her lips again. Where did one get things like that in Riverboat Point?

"Hello?"

Savannah jumped at the sound of a male voice.

There was a loud knock at her back door.

"Hello?" he called again.

"Coming," Savannah replied.

She looked at the clock on the microwave as she passed. Five-thirty. She hadn't heard a car but assumed the guy was here for the Thursday-night houseboat booking.

She took the keys and went outside. There were just the four of them. The others wouldn't arrive until after dark but once again they were worried about finding the place without signage. Savannah had an idea for that. Too late to help this group but she really must do something about replacing the missing signs tomorrow. By the time they'd done their paperwork and unloaded it was dark. She left the light on outside the big shed as an extra beacon for those still to arrive.

She glanced over towards Ethan's place. No lights on there but she hadn't expected him to be home yet. She went inside and fiddled around, setting the table and tidying up her running gear. She put the television on. Once again she had nothing to do.

It was a still night and warm. She had the sliding door open and the sound of voices greeting each other carried up from the river. The rest of the group must have arrived. A short time later their music blared, accompanied by the odd voice, male and female, raised in laughter. She hoped they wouldn't be planning a late night if they were going to get away early tomorrow.

She flicked channels then turned off the television. The time on her phone reminded her that Ethan should have been back by now. Maybe with all the noise she hadn't heard his bike. She went outside to check again. Still no lights at his house.

She took a beer from the fridge, turned off the lights and sat out on the front verandah. The sounds of the group on the houseboat were much clearer out here. She could make out different voices – a couple of deep male voices and one higher pitched, a giggly woman and one with a singsong voice. They were laughing and talking, totally oblivious of her sitting alone on the verandah. She felt a pang of envy. How good would it be to have a group of close friends to spend a weekend on a houseboat with?

She curled her right leg up under her and stretched the left out in front. It didn't have the flexibility of the right. A bit of pain nagged high in her thigh but it wasn't bad. She took another swig of beer and massaged the muscles at the top of her leg.

The crunch of footsteps sounded from the driveway. Her heart leapt. Ethan was back. She hobbled to her feet and went to meet him. As she reached the carport a female giggled. Savannah stopped; in the light from the shed and the half-moon she saw two people approaching.

"Hello," the man called. "Are we heading in the right direction? Our friends are on a houseboat."

"I can hear them," the woman said.

"Keep following the path down," Savannah said. "Be careful when you reach the bank, it could be slippery."

"Thanks," he said.

"Goodnight," she called.

Savannah went back to her chair and listened to the excited sounds of the group greeting the newcomers. By the time she was on her second beer the night had cooled a little. She threw a jumper over her shoulders and resumed her seat on the verandah.

The crew on the houseboat were in full party mode now. The music was louder and the voices more raucous. Perhaps she should have said something about the noise level if they were staying the night. Bit late now. She didn't want to be the party pooper. Besides, there was no-one else around for a long way, she was the only one who could hear them.

She glanced at her phone and was shocked to see it was nearly nine o'clock. Where was Ethan? Had they worked late or had he met with an accident? Anxiety needled in her chest. He'd been so sure he'd be back for dinner. She couldn't imagine he would stand her up. Where was he? She got up and paced the verandah for a while. She took another beer from the fridge and the small cheese platter she'd prepared earlier and set them on the outside table.

Jasper barked once.

Savannah listened. Could he hear Ethan returning? She moved off the verandah to the side fence. Jasper gave a series of sharp barks. She stayed perfectly still, listening. Jasper stopped barking. She heard the scrape of his claws on concrete. He gave a final throaty woof and went silent.

Savannah continued to listen but all she could hear was the noise from the houseboat behind her. A shiver prickled down her back. She went inside, got a blanket and wrapped herself in it. Outside again she sat on one chair and dragged another close for her feet. At least she could hear people. Even if she wasn't actually with them, it was better than shutting herself up inside, alone.

She shook her head as she wriggled into a better position on the chair. Who'd have thought she'd be in this situation? In her last job her smart-arse boss had called her Solo. She'd lived alone and managed very well without people. She sighed then yawned. She put her hands to her face and allowed her eyes to close. It wasn't the most comfortable position. Even so, she could almost go to sleep — if she wasn't so worried about Ethan.

A loud bang echoed through the air. Women shrieked. Jasper barked wildly. Savannah lurched up. Her feet hit the ground. She tried to move forward but she got caught in the blanket. She put a hand to the verandah pole to stop herself from falling. A sharp jab shot down her leg. She sucked in a breath.

The music stopped and there was a babble of voices. Had the bang come from the boat? It was hard to tell. Perhaps something had exploded. Savannah threw off the rug, shrugged into her jumper and flicked on the outside lights. She made her way down to the boat where several dark figures moved on the deck and on the bank.

"Is everyone all right?" she called.

"What was that?" Sam, who'd paid the deposit, came up the path towards her.

"I don't know," she said.

"It was a gunshot." Another guy came up behind Sam.

"Come on, Paul," Sam said.

"Surely not a gunshot," Savannah said. She glanced around, her thoughts going straight to Gnasher.

"I know a gunshot when I hear one," Paul persisted. "Who would be out here shooting?"

Worried murmurs came from the women on the deck.

"There's an old bloke over the road," Savannah said. "He shoots rabbits sometimes but he wouldn't come near here." She hoped she sounded convincing.

Paul snorted. "There'd be no bloody rabbit left. That was a high-powered rifle. It would blow a rabbit to pieces."

The worried voices grew louder.

Savannah held up her hands. "Look," she said, "I'm sure it's a misunderstanding. Maybe the sound echoed along the river."

Paul shook his head.

"I think it's time we all went to bed," Sam said.

"Good idea," Savannah said. "You want to set off early in the morning. Ethan will be here to get you away."

"Come on, Paul." Sam put his arm around his mate's shoulders. "We'll have a nightcap then turn in. Back inside everyone, it's fine."

Savannah watched them go, grateful for Sam's good sense. She had no idea what she would have done with a boatload of hysterical people. She made her way back to the shack. All the outside lights blazed but the inside was in darkness. Jasper had stopped barking. Everything was suddenly very quiet. She took her things inside, locked the doors and closed the blinds. She put the television on, turned it down low and settled onto the couch with the blanket.

"Where are you, Ethan?" she murmured. He would have known what to do.

CHAPTER

33

Ethan was up as the early morning sun spread a pale golden glow in the eastern sky. His first thought was Savannah. What must she think? He'd said he'd be home for dinner last night and he hadn't turned up.

He glanced once more towards Savannah's place. It was unlikely she'd appreciate a visitor at this early hour. He took Jasper for a walk instead. He felt bad in many ways but most of all he hated letting her down. What a mess he'd made of yesterday.

He'd fallen asleep so easily in his old bed at the farm then several hours later he'd snapped awake. Savannah's dinner was the first thing that came into his head. His parents' house was in darkness. Everyone was asleep. He gathered his things and walked down to the shearing shed, guided by the moonlight. The ride home took forever. He knew he'd be too late but a small part of him hoped Savannah had left a light on, a sign that she'd waited. But her place was in darkness.

Ethan hadn't bothered to turn on any lights when he got in. Jasper had followed him up the stairs and flopped straight on his mat. Ethan went to his pill packet, swallowed one down then pulled off his boots and jacket and discarded the rest of his clothes as he made his way to his bedroom. He'd fallen into his bed and amazingly had gone back to sleep.

Now as he watched Jasper trotting along the road for home he remembered something else. Savannah had a houseboat going out first thing this morning. He quickened his pace.

As they approached his drive Jasper barked and ran ahead. No doubt a bird or a rabbit had attracted his attention. Ethan followed. He couldn't stop the smile at the sight of Savannah halfway up his stairs with Jasper eagerly wagging his tail at her from below.

"Hello," he called and saw the relief on her face. "He really wouldn't hurt you, you know."

"I know," Savannah replied croakily.

"Jasper, come!" he commanded.

"I'm sorry …"

"I'm glad …"

They spoke at once.

"Why are you glad?" He took the stairs two at a time to reach her. She swept hair away from her eyes.

"You're home," she said.

He stopped on the step below her and looked straight into her eyes.

"You need my help?"

Her eyes widened.

"I was expecting you for dinner."

"Of course." He took her hands in his. "I'm sorry about last night. A bit went on at the farm and I … well, I didn't get back here until midnight."

"Is everything all right there?"

"Yes, for now. I'm not going back today. I'm at your beck and call."

"You might wish you hadn't said that."

Ethan was relieved to see her lips curve up in a smile. He leaned forward and kissed her. She gave a little gasp then returned his kiss. He reached around her and pulled her close.

"Hello?"

Jasper barked at the male voice. Savannah jerked back.

"That'll be Sam," she whispered and peered around Ethan.

Her face was flushed a rosy pink. He leaned closer.

"Who's Sam and why are we whispering?"

"The guy from the houseboat," she said as she slipped past him. "Coming," she called.

At the bottom of the stairs she looked back at him. Her eyes sparkled.

"I need your help now," she said softly. "They'll want to get away."

"I'll be right there," he said. "Just let me change my shirt."

She gave a short nod and headed for the fence. Must make that gate, he thought as he bounded up the stairs.

Ethan watched Sam at the wheel.

"You're a natural," he said.

"I've driven a few boats before," Sam said.

"He's being modest," his friend said.

"I've never driven a houseboat before," Sam said. "They respond differently."

"You look like you've got it under control," Ethan said.

"Paul and I will probably take turns for a while. Till these free-loaders get the hang of it."

The other three blokes standing nearby made various comments about Sam being in charge. They were a friendly bunch. No sign of the ladies at this early hour though.

"I was ready to let go the ropes last night."

Ethan looked back at Paul.

"Someone took a pot shot at us."

"It wasn't at us, Paul." Sam raised his eyebrows.

"What do you mean?" Ethan asked.

"Your girlfriend didn't seem too concerned," Paul said. "Reckoned it was some guy shooting rabbits but I know guns and that was a high-powered rifle fired close by."

"A rifle?" Ethan thought of Gnasher straight away. Surely he wouldn't be shooting anywhere near Jaxon's place.

"We don't know what it was," Sam said. He tapped the wheel. "Have you got the gist of this, Paul?"

"I reckon," Paul said. "Between the two of us we should be right."

"Take us back to the bank and I'll jump off," Ethan said.

He watched as Sam headed to the bank. Savannah was standing on the lawn, waiting.

"Enjoy your holiday," Ethan said to the group and let himself out onto the front deck. He waited for the boat to gently nudge the bank then he leapt over the railing. The motors rumbled in reverse, the horn tooted and the houseboat slid out into the flow of the river.

"One down, three to go," Savannah said. "Well, only two really, the third boat is staying put."

"Cancellation?"

"No."

She gave him a nervous grin.

"They asked if they could stay here. It's six women on a hens' weekend."

Ethan felt his eyebrows rise.

"It's your business," he said. He put his arm around her. "I know it doesn't make up for standing you up last night but how about I make us breakfast? And I will make dinner tonight as well."

Savannah stopped. He turned to face her.

"I really am sorry," he said.

"That's okay." She gritted her teeth. "Dinner might be a bit tricky."

"Why?"

"Belinda and Ash are coming over."

"Oh." Ethan couldn't help the disappointment in his voice. He really wanted to spend time with Savannah – alone.

"She kind of invited herself really." Savannah watched him closely. "She asked after you. Hoped you could join us."

He held her gaze. He so wanted to kiss those pink lips of hers.

"Ethan?"

He scratched his forehead and concentrated on what she'd been saying. "Sure, why not? What time?"

"Seven o'clock."

"I'd like to meet Ashton. See what kind of a man is married to such a flirt."

"I like her."

"So do I, but you have to admit she behaves like a tart."

Savannah raised her eyebrows.

"You weren't in the car the night I drove her home. She all but propositioned me."

"She certainly likes to enjoy herself. It will be interesting to see what she's like when Ash is around."

"What are we having for dinner?"

"I've got a chicken stir fry I didn't use last night," she said.

He groaned. "I'm sorry."

"You've said it already." She took his hand and pulled him forward. "I will hold you to breakfast though. Then I've got another job I need help with."

She brushed her lips over his. Before he could respond she broke away and ran across the lawn.

"I'll be your way in five," she called over her shoulder.

It was a beautiful morning, perfect for breakfast on the deck. Ethan made scrambled eggs. He carried it outside to where Savannah sat quietly watching the river, Jasper not far from her feet.

"You've got a new friend," Ethan said nodding towards the dog.

"I thought he was guarding me." She gave Jasper a wary look.

"He probably is." Ethan chuckled. "But in a friendly way."

"This looks good," she said and started on the scrambled eggs.

Somewhere under the house a drum expanded in the warming air. Savannah jumped at the noise.

"Only a drum," he said but it reminded him of the conversation with Sam and Paul on the houseboat. "I hear there was a problem last night."

"Problem?" Savannah looked at him blankly.

"The guy on the houseboat said they heard a gunshot."

"Oh yes. I'd forgotten. I was on the front verandah of the shack. It sounded like it came from close by. It echoed so it was hard to tell." She paused. "Do you think it could have been Gnasher?"

"I doubt it." Ethan was quick to defend his friend but the thought had crossed his mind. "He wouldn't be over here."

"He was yesterday. He used your shower."

"Keeping an eye on my place, are you?" He grinned. Anyone else he'd be annoyed but he liked the idea of Savannah watching his back.

She drew herself up. "I saw some guy disappearing into your driveway. He was acting weird. Thought I'd better check it out. I should have just rung the police."

"I'm glad you didn't. Gnasher's a friend. His water pump's had it. He's using my place until he gets a new one."

"That's what he said."

"You spoke?"

"We introduced ourselves," she said vaguely. "He called you Digger."

Ethan chuckled. "It's army slang. He likes to call me that because he was a sergeant. He doesn't mean any harm."

"I'll have to take your word on that."

"I know he can act a bit odd at times but he's a recluse. Not used to being around people much. I can't imagine he'd come over here at night and fire his gun."

"There was a fair bit of noise coming from the houseboat and it was a still night."

He looked from her to the river. He didn't want to believe Gnasher would be so stupid as to fire a gun near people. Besides, he only had a twenty-two, and from what Savannah and Paul had said, the sound was very loud.

"I'll call in on him today. See what he knows."

His mobile rang. Ethan glanced at the screen. It was the farm number, probably Barb.

"Sorry," he said. "I have to take this."

"Just remember you're at my beck and call." Savannah's lips twitched.

He grinned and pressed the screen of his phone.

"Meet me at the big shed when you're ready," she whispered.

He nodded.

"Hello," he said into the phone.

"Just wanted to make sure you were all right." His mother's voice crackled back

"I am." He walked to the end of the deck. "I'm sorry about yesterday."

"I do care what happens to you, Ethan."

He sucked in a breath. Those few words had nearly undone him. Behind him he could hear the sounds of Savannah clearing the table.

"I'm sorry about my outburst yesterday," he said.

"You are getting professional care aren't you, Ethan?"

"Yes."

"Blake said you were seeing a doctor."

"Yes."

"It's your father who's hurting."

That snapped him back to reality.

"Perhaps he should seek some help. I can recommend a good counsellor."

"Sarcasm won't help, Ethan." Her voice had a hard edge to it.

"I don't know what will then."

She was silent a moment. "I'd like to see your place."

"You're welcome anytime."

"Perhaps in a few weeks."

Or perhaps never. She wouldn't come without Mal and Ethan was sure his father wouldn't be coming to visit anytime soon.

"I'm assuming you don't need me out there today?"

"They'll be finished before lunch. They can manage."

"Good. Well, I've got some work to do here."

"I'll let you go."

They said their goodbyes. Ethan stared at the silent phone in his hand.

Jasper padded up behind him and nudged his leg. Ethan looked down at the deep kind eyes of his mate. He ruffled the dog's ears.

"No point in looking back, is there, Jasper?"

He thought of Savannah and the mischievous look she'd given him.

"We've got better things to do."

CHAPTER
34

"Sav?"

She looked up at Ethan's call.

"I'm around the back."

Behind Jaxon's shed there was an assortment of junk, from pipe to bits of bike to sheets of iron. She'd been rummaging through it while she waited for Ethan. He stuck his head around the corner.

"What's happening?" he asked.

"I need some signs to direct people here. I thought we might be able to make something from some of this junk."

Ethan strolled up to her. Jasper was with him. Savannah watched the dog sniff through the junk pile.

"I haven't found anything useful yet," she said.

"I've got a better idea," Ethan said. "I've got some offcuts of timber I used to make Jasper's kennel. It's already painted blue. All we have to do is paint the words on it. If we use white paint it will have that rustic look that people seem so keen on."

"Brilliant idea." Savannah beamed. "I think I saw paint in the shed."

"I'll go and pick out some suitable pieces."

She went back to Jaxon's shed with a spring in her step. Inside on the shelves there was a box of paint. She pulled out a tin of white. Brushes might be a problem. She hummed to herself as she searched.

Her worry about Ethan had vanished. She'd even been able to joke about Belinda without feeling wary. She accepted Ethan's assurance he wasn't interested and she got distinct pleasure from knowing he was keen on her. She'd thought he was going to kiss her again this morning. Their conversation had been about Belinda and Ashton but his look was for her. She hadn't been able to resist kissing him before she'd dashed back to the shack.

Now he was helping her as promised. Just the two of them. Jasper padded into the shed. He looked at her and flopped down on the floor. Ethan followed him in with two large blue planks.

"Just the three of us," Savannah said.

Ethan dropped the planks and looked at her sideways.

"I thought you were getting paint."

"I have." She lifted the tin. "No luck with brushes yet."

Ethan held up two thin brushes. "These should do it."

They bent over the wood deciding how the words should be laid out. Savannah found a thick pencil and drew the letters on the wood while Ethan stirred the paint. Then they took one brush each and filled in the outlines. He asked her about her life in Adelaide. She steered the conversation back to him.

"What do you do when you're not at the farm?"

"Fish."

"All day every day?"

"It doesn't exactly pay the bills but I'm fairly cost neutral." Ethan stopped painting to inspect what he'd done so far. "I was working part-time as a mechanic in Burra but the guy hasn't needed me for a while. He probably will once harvest gets in full swing."

"How far is Burra?"

"Just the other side of my parents' property."

"That's a bit of a drive."

"Takes no time on a bike," he said with a grin.

A shudder went through her.

He put a hand on her shoulder. "I'm joking. I stick to the speed limit."

"I was in a car accident once," she said. "I was asleep in the back seat so I don't know what happened. They told me there was a bike involved. Evidently there wasn't much of the rider left to identify."

He kept his eyes focused on hers. She could see there was no longer any laughter there.

"That must have been a terrible time," he said. "Accidents happen but I do my best to take care of myself. I value life too much to throw it away that easily."

They stood a metre apart, the boards on trestles between them. The bright sunny day had receded.

Damn, Savannah thought. Why had she blabbed about the accident?

"How will these signs stand up?" she asked. It was best to keep the conversation away from personal stuff.

"I've got two stakes. I'll nail them to the back of the signs and we can knock them into the ground."

He started painting again. She did the same. The scraping of their brushes and Jasper's soft snores were the only sounds in the shed. The conversation had dried up. Trust her to take the shine out of the day.

"You need to take more care with your paint, Ms Smith."

Savannah frowned as he reached across and dabbed some white paint on the letter she was working on. She looked up. The sparkle was back in his eyes.

"Is that so, Mr Daly?" She raised her eyebrows at his roughly painted letters and dabbed several spots. "People in glass houses shouldn't splash paint."

"Why not?"

She opened her mouth in horror as he dabbed some on her cheek.

"That matches the other one now."

She lifted her brush but he jumped away. She pranced around the trestles, her brush raised in the air.

Ethan put up his hands, the paintbrush still clutched in the fingers of one.

"No, not the paint treatment," he yelped.

Jasper leapt between them and turned to face Savannah. He gave a low growl.

She stood still and lowered her brush.

"Easy mate," Ethan said and ruffled the dog's ears. "We're only playing."

Savannah kept her eyes on the dog. Her heart thumped in her chest.

"It's okay, Sav. Relax." Ethan's voice was gentle. "Say sorry, Jasper. You've frightened the lady."

"It's not his fault." Savannah's voice came out in a croak.

"I'll take him home for a while." Ethan gave the dog a pat. "Come, Jasper."

They left the shed. Savannah's shoulders relaxed. Damn it, she'd done it again. Each time she started to relax with Ethan she did something to upset the balance. She returned to her sign, determined to finish the painting. Once Ethan nailed on the posts she was sure she could knock them into the ground herself. He could do his own thing until later, when the boats went out.

"He's happy with a bone."

Savannah glanced at Ethan as he took up his brush.

"I'm sorry, Sav. I get that you're nervous of dogs. I shouldn't have brought him with me."

"I understand he's your friend. You've every right to bring him here." Savannah shrugged. "I don't even know why I'm scared of dogs. We never had one growing up."

"Jasper should have been protecting you. I was the one who attacked you with the paintbrush."

Ethan's head was bent over the sign. Savannah dabbed a bit of paint on his ear.

"He's not here to protect you now," she said.

Ethan moved like lightning. Before she could react he had trapped her hands in one of his. In the other he held the paintbrush above her nose.

"Ethan, no," she squealed.

"No noise or Jasper will be here in a flash." His lips curled in a grin.

"Are you trying to scare me?"

"No." His eyes darkened and he bent towards her. "I'm planning to kiss you."

Tingles went down her spine. His lips reached hers. They were warm, soft, insistent.

His arms wrapped around her and pulled her to him. The brush slid from her fingers. She melted against him and reached her arms up around his neck. She was lost. All her thoughts of being strong vanished. His hands roamed down her back, cupped her buttocks and pressed her to him leaving her in no doubt about his need for her.

His lips were all over her face and her neck, his hands were roaming. She closed her eyes and tipped back her head. The weight of him pushed her backwards. The trestle behind her moved and she fell, taking Ethan with her.

Savannah shrieked as her bottom hit the concrete with a thud and a sharp pain shot down her leg. Ethan had put his hand out and rolled away from her but he'd connected with the paint pot which fell and tipped white paint down her arm.

"Sav."

He was by her side, his face full of concern. He tried to pull her close. She tried to push him away. She was covered in paint, no need for both of them to be.

"Let me help," he said.

She pushed her clean hand to his chest. "I've got paint all over me."

"Where are you hurt?"

"I'm not."

He scooped her up. She sucked in a breath as the pain jarred again. He held her close. She closed her eyes and inhaled his delicious male scent.

"What shall I do?"

Just hold me, she thought. She opened her eyes. He was staring at her in alarm.

"I'll be all right." She looked over his shoulder at the mess on the floor. "Which is more than can be said for our signs."

Paint had splattered across them spoiling some of the letters. Ethan lowered her carefully to the floor.

"I can fix them," he said. "It's you I'm worried about."

"My left leg isn't as strong as it used to be. It was mangled in the car crash. It doesn't manage tricky situations very well. It's taken a lot of work to be able to walk and run properly again, and sometimes it catches me out. Falls or sudden movement can cause pain."

"I thought I'd broken you."

"It'd take more than that to break me, soldier." She twisted her lips in a smile. There was no need to focus on her injuries.

"Is that so?"

Savannah held up her paint-covered hand.

"I'd better go and get cleaned up or I might stay like this."

"I'd love to come and help you," he said, "but if I don't clean up these signs they'll be no use."

She went to move away but he grabbed her clean hand and leaned in. His lips brushed hers.

"You keep running out on me."

He nuzzled her ear.

"Next time you won't escape," he murmured.

She shivered. If it wasn't for the paint setting on her skin she wouldn't be going anywhere. She took his chin in her hand and turned his face to hers.

"Careful what you wish for," she said.

She planted a kiss on his lips then strode away, as well as she could on her aching leg. At the doorway she stopped and looked back. He was watching her. Just as she turned he winked. She forced her body to keep moving in the direction of the shack. She needed a cold shower.

CHAPTER
35

Ethan managed to save the painted letters on the signs. Most of them had evaded the splashes of paint. He would outline the letters with a thick black texta once they'd dried. The signs would do until they could get the replacements for the signposts. He nailed the stakes to the back and stood them outside in the sun to dry. Back inside the shed, he did his best to clean up.

By the time he'd finished he was ready to eat again. He was surprised it was nearly midday. Savannah was expecting the next lot of customers mid-afternoon and he had to fit in a visit to Gnasher before then.

Outside the sunshine had vanished under grey clouds. He made his way to Savannah's back door. She called him inside before he could knock.

Her hair was still wet from her shower and she was in a snug-fitting t-shirt and trackpants. Not all the paint had come off, but not from want of trying by the look of her glowing skin.

"I've made sandwiches," she said. "I'd like to put those signs out before the next lot of customers get lost and complain."

He would love to take her in his arms and resume where they'd left off but she was right. There were jobs that had to be done. "How about we take the food with us and eat on the way?" he said. "I've got a couple of things I have to attend to before they get here."

Once more she drove him in her car. The sign on Jaxon's gate was clear enough. They planned to put one of the homemade signs at the T-junction and one at the turn-off from the main highway.

"Did you see that?" Savannah slowed the car to a crawl. "There's a horse in the Palmers' property."

He followed her pointing finger. In amongst some sparse trees was a bay-coloured horse.

"I didn't know they had a horse," Savannah said.

"It's not much of a horse from the look of it. Skin and bone."

"Why would they bring a horse out here?"

"Too big for their backyard in the city," he quipped.

Savannah raised her eyebrows at him and drove on.

It didn't take much effort to hammer in the signs. They'd had some good winter rain for a change and the soil was still soft enough to drive a stake into. Savannah was happy with the results. She gave him a quick hug after the second sign went in. It was risky. The chemistry between them was explosive. A sudden shower of rain sent them back to the car. Savannah drove them home.

"Can't see the horse now," she said.

"It's a big property. It could be anywhere in there."

"It would have cost a bit."

"The horse?"

"No, the property. All that river frontage. I know what Jaxon paid for his place and it's much smaller."

Ethan thought of his own property. He'd purchased it around the same time as Jaxon bought his.

"I think they've owned it for a long time," he said. "Could be there are parents involved in the ownership. I've never seen anyone there until now. There have been the odd signs that someone's about but nothing more. They've always kept to themselves and that suited me."

"Belinda said they helped Jaxon with the houseboats in the early days."

"They may have. I'm not always around."

Gnasher's gate was up ahead.

"Drop me here," Ethan said. "I'm going to check on Gnasher."

Savannah slowed the car to a stop.

"I'll be back by three," he said.

She raised her eyebrows at him again.

"Truly, I will," he said with a grin and shut the door. He could understand her scepticism. He'd been late for the first houseboat he'd had to take out and last night he'd missed her dinner altogether.

Gnasher's gate was padlocked. As usual Ethan climbed over and set off along the track. He pulled his hood over his head and hunched his shoulders against another light shower of rain. Right now he was more concerned about how to broach the subject of guns with Gnasher.

"Incoming," Ethan called as he approached Gnasher's shed. The rain had masked the sound of his footsteps but he was never sure if Gnasher would be in hiding having heard his approach. It was a game the old bloke liked to play from time to time.

Ethan heard a noise. He paused. It was the sound of snoring. Gnasher had rolled down the tarpaulin at the end of his shed where he kept his car. That was the direction the snoring was coming from. Ethan stepped around the tarp and stopped. In front of the car was the framework of a wall. That hadn't been there when he'd called in last. Through it he could see Gnasher's new TV. It was off. Gnasher was stretched out on the couch, surrounded by a sea of tinnies. He'd been on a bender.

Ethan went to the kitchen area. Gnasher's fridge was well stocked. He must have had a grocery delivery. Ethan took out bacon and eggs and set about cooking them. He was just serving them up when he heard Gnasher clamber to his feet, the tinnies clattering around him.

Ethan glanced over. Gnasher did a huge stretch, let out a long fart and scratched at his chest. Then he made his way to the kitchen.

"Morning, Dig," he said and sat at his table. "Good of you to cook me breakfast."

"It's afternoon," Ethan said. He put a plate piled high with thick toast, bacon, eggs and mushrooms in front of Gnasher. "This is lunch."

"Good on ya." Gnasher took a bite of toast. "You joining me?"

Ethan put his plate with one egg, a piece of bacon and toast on the table.

"I've eaten but there's always room for more."

"Met that neighbour of yours yesterday."

"Savannah?"

"She's a good-looker."

"She said she'd seen you."

"Nearly caught me in all my glory." Gnasher cackled. "I was coming out of your bathroom. Lucky I had my shorts on or she'd have got a real eye full."

Ethan smiled. He could understand why Savannah had seemed a little flustered by her meeting with Gnasher.

"That was in the afternoon?" he asked.

"Yeah," Gnasher said. "I came back here fresh as a daisy. I was gonna settle back, watch the footy ..."

He got a faraway look in his eye. For a moment he stared into the distance then he shook his head and shovelled in a forkful of egg and bacon. Ethan watched him chew then swallow.

"So you were here all night watching footy?"

"No."

Ethan waited. Surely Gnasher hadn't been drinking and using his gun. He knew better than that. But if he was on a bender who could be sure? Perhaps he had been the one to fire the shot. That's if a gunshot was what they'd all heard.

"I was here all night." Gnasher dropped his knife and fork to the plate with a clatter. "But not watching that bloody idiot of a machine." He jerked his thumb over his shoulder. "The rubbish they have on it. I turned it off, put on my music and had a few quiet beers." He nodded his head as a full stop.

"I thought you'd enjoy the footy." Ethan took a sip of his coffee.

"I would if they'd let me." Gnasher resumed eating.

"Who?"

"I don't know. The bloody people who run the television. It's all that other crap that comes on."

"The adverts?"

"Not just them. There's shorts from other shows. It's all crap!"

"You should have put your DVD on instead," Ethan said. "Watched one of them. No ads."

"Wasn't in the mood."

Gnasher wiped his plate clean with his last piece of toast. Then he sat back and burped.

"Thanks for that, mate." He smiled his gappy grin. "You're not a bad cook for a grease monkey."

Ethan gathered the plates.

"I'll clear up." Gnasher stayed where he was looking up at Ethan. Even though his eyes were red they looked sharp.

"Any word on the pump?" Ethan asked.

"No."

"You're welcome to keep using my place."

"I appreciate the offer."

"I'll leave you to it then."

"Thanks for lunch," Gnasher said.

Ethan nodded and stepped out into the grey afternoon. The rain had stopped but there was a chill in the air now. He jogged along the track to warm himself up. His visit to Gnasher hadn't gone quite how he'd planned. He'd wanted to check if Gnasher had been out firing his gun last night as much as to see how he was. Somehow Ethan felt as if Gnasher knew exactly why he'd been there. It gave him a queasy feeling. He didn't like to think Gnasher would be so stupid as to fire a gun near people.

Ethan glanced at his watch.

"Hell!"

It was three o'clock. He'd been at Gnasher's much longer than he'd intended. He turned his jog into a run. He was going to be late for Savannah again.

CHAPTER
36

Footsteps pounded down the driveway. Savannah was walking back from showing her latest customers the parking space beside the shed. She turned and couldn't help the smile that spread across her face. Ethan was jogging towards her, concern written all over his face.

"Don't panic," she said. "Only one group ready to go and they've just finished getting organised."

He came to a standstill beside her, puffing gently.

"Sorry," he said. "I ended up cooking Gnasher a meal."

"That was kind of you."

A car turned in at the gate.

"That's probably the next lot," she said.

"I'll see to the others."

"They're on *Tawarri*. I've explained about the hole in the wall."

He nodded and set off towards the river. Savannah greeted the next lot of customers.

The next hour was filled with helping the clients and doing the paperwork. Now they stood on Savannah's front verandah sheltering from another shower of rain.

"What's next, boss?" Ethan said.

"I'm going to make sure I've got everything ready for tonight's meal. It's come in cold so I thought I'd bake a dessert. The next group will get here just before Belinda and Ash are due."

"This is the group of women?"

"Yes."

"So you won't need me?"

"Well." Savannah linked her arm through his. "I've been thinking. Do you own a suit?"

"I think this is the point where I'm supposed to get worried."

"Hear me out. If you don't like the idea I won't press you."

He spun to face her and wrapped his arms around her.

"Press me all you like."

His eyes had that deep dark look again and it was all Savannah could do to concentrate. She eased out of his arms.

"Let's discuss it over a coffee."

He gave a small groan but followed her inside.

Damn having the Palmers over for dinner tonight, Savannah thought. She was as anxious as Ethan to see where this was heading.

Just on six o'clock car lights shone in the darkening driveway. Savannah went to the end of the verandah and opened her umbrella. It was a big multi-striped thing. Another find in Jaxon's shed.

Two cars pulled up. The passenger window of the first lowered and the driver leaned across.

"Savannah?"

"Yes."

"I'm Tara and this is the bride-to-be, Emily."

"Welcome to J&S Houseboats," Savannah said.

"Thanks for helping us out," Tara said.

"It's very good of you," Emily said. "I think."

Savannah stared as Tara began to laugh.

"It wasn't until we turned into your driveway that Em discovered what we were up to. The other girls are in the car behind."

"I knew you were up to something," Em said. "But you could have been taking me to a strip joint for all I knew."

"Way out here?" Tara laughed again.

"You never know," Emily said.

"No, you don't," Savannah said and winked at Tara.

Her face lit up again. What a bright bubbly person she was. Emily was lucky to have such a good friend to go to all this trouble. Savannah hoped they'd enjoy the extras she'd organised.

"Drive down a bit further," she said. "I'll help you load your gear onto the boat. Then I'll show you where to park your cars."

"Em's still recovering from an operation so she has to sit while we do the work."

"Fair enough," Savannah said. "Follow me."

She lifted her umbrella and walked ahead of the cars to the point where they could unload. Ethan had wedged some wood into several spots on the path where the slope was steep. It would help the women step more evenly to the boat. He'd come up with the suggestion while they discussed her plans for Tara's group over coffee. He'd liked her ideas and the steps had been his contribution.

"Be careful," Savannah cautioned. "The path down is slippery."

"Hang on, Em," Tara called as she rushed around to her friend's side. "Take my arm."

Savannah could see Emily was moving very cautiously. She offered her arm.

"Take mine too," she said.

They made their way slowly down the path with Savannah holding the umbrella up to keep the drizzly rain off them.

The rest of the women followed. Tara introduced them once everyone was aboard.

"Look at the gorgeous flowers," Emily said from her position on the couch. Tara sat next to her.

"A welcome gift for the bride-to-be," Savannah said.

The women were all excitedly checking the houseboat and its layout.

"The towels are folded into heart shapes and they've got chocolates in them," someone called from a bedroom and the other three rushed to have a look.

"You've been busy," Tara said.

"The internet," Savannah said. "You can find out how to do anything."

Everyone pitched in to bring their bags and supplies aboard. None of them seemed like princesses. Savannah had a good feeling about the women and she was glad she'd planned a few extras for them.

"Bring your cars back up to the shed," she said.

Tara and one of the other women followed her out. Savannah collected the umbrella from the deck. The rain had stopped for the moment.

"Thanks for this," Tara said. "We really appreciate you having us at such short notice and not expecting us to go off cruising."

"My pleasure."

"Emily needs some spoiling and your extra touches were very thoughtful."

"It's not over yet."

Savannah studied Tara in the light from her car. She hoped her next idea would go down okay.

"Once you're settled I've got someone lined up to serve you some bubbly. It's a bit cool for the deck unfortunately, but he can serve them inside."

"He!" Tara giggled. "You wicked woman."

"He's not a stripper," Savannah said quickly. She hoped she wasn't getting Ethan into anything too tricky.

"Oh well," Tara said. "We'll take whatever you've got. It will be better than me serving the drinks."

"We'll be down in about ten minutes."

Savannah jogged back to the shack. She didn't own many dresses or skirts. The only decent clothes she'd brought with her were her new jeans and the blue top she'd worn last night. They would have to do. She was sure the women would only have eyes for Ethan flashed up in his suit rather than her anyway.

There was a tap on her back door.

"Come in," she called.

Ethan was right on time. He stepped through the door. Her heart skipped a beat.

"What happened to the suit?" she stammered.

"I thought hens would prefer this look better. Don't you like it?"

"Like it!"

Her knees trembled. She shook her head. He was wearing a pair of blue jeans, dark brown belt and a white Bonds singlet. Even though they covered his body they left little to the imagination. His unruly hair framed his deep brown eyes and his face bore a shadow of stubble.

"I could put this on if you think it'd be better." He held a green and white checked shirt at arm's length and slowly turned three-sixty degrees. He could have stepped from the pages of a magazine.

"That's not fair," she groaned.

He made a move towards her.

"Stop," she cried. "We've got to serve the drinks. Belinda and Ash will be here in about twenty minutes for dinner."

"At your service, ma'am."

"Can you get the bottles from the fridge? I'll carry the cheese platter."

He stood tall and gave a salute.

She placed her hands firmly on either side of the board but they still trembled.

"Hell and snakes," she muttered as she led the way to the houseboat. It was an old saying of her mother's and it seemed appropriate for the situation.

First she was going to have to watch as he served drinks to a group of women on a hens' weekend then act the perfect hostess while they entertained the Palmers for dinner, when all she wanted to do was throw herself into his arms. At least he could put his shirt back on for that or Belinda may not be able to resist, even with Ash there.

The front light lit up the deck of the houseboat. She must remember to explain to Tara about generators and things or they'd have no power by morning. Savannah could see all the women milling around inside.

"You ready, soldier?" she said over her shoulder.

"Yes, ma'am."

She smirked as the bottles clinked together.

Tara slid the door open and Savannah stepped into the room carrying her platter.

"Good evening, ladies," she said. "Welcome aboard *Our Destiny*. I hope you've got your champagne glasses ready. Tonight we've got a special waiter for you. Please welcome Ethan."

There were squeals of delight, clapping and a wolf whistle as Ethan stepped through the door. He popped the first bottle accompanied by more shrieks and began filling glasses. Savannah worked her way towards Tara offering the platter as she went.

"Where did you find the hunk?" Tara asked.

"He's my neighbour."

"Lucky you, girlfriend," Tara said and dug Savannah with her elbow.

"I need to show you how everything works before I go, and we can't stay long. We've got friends coming for dinner."

"Let's do it now," Tara said.

Savannah put the platter down on the bench.

She jumped as Tara gave a piercing whistle.

"Listen up, ladies," Tara said. "I'm about to get the ins and outs of how this boat operates. We're not going anywhere but there are a few things to learn. You enjoy Ethan's company 'cause he can't stay long but he's out of bounds. He belongs to Savannah."

Savannah opened her mouth and closed it again. There were murmurs of "lucky girl". Ethan met her gaze across the room. He was smirking at her.

CHAPTER
37

Ethan's hands were on her as soon as they stepped back inside the shack. They stumbled into the kitchen and he backed her to the bench. Their mouths were locked and their bodies pressed together. His hand slid between them, under her shirt and inside her bra.

Savannah groaned and pulled her head away from his lips. He tasted so good.

"We have to stop," she said. "They'll be here any minute."

"Can't we turn off the lights? Pretend we're not here?" Ethan nibbled her ear. "We could hide at my place."

That's when she noticed the lipstick on his cheek and his neck.

"You've got lipstick all over you."

"You wicked woman."

"I don't wear lipstick."

He grinned. "Some of those hens were very fond with their farewells."

"You'd better go clean it off." She tapped his bottom as he turned. "And put your shirt on."

"Yes, ma'am," he said.

Savannah watched his bum as he walked away then turned her attention to the food. Behind her there was a tap on the glass of the sliding door. She spun to see Belinda and Ashton standing outside. Belinda was waving her usual bottle of bubbly.

Savannah took a deep breath, swept some hair from her eyes and crossed the room. Ten seconds earlier and they would have seen Ethan almost undressing her.

"Hello," she called loudly. Both for their benefit outside the glass and for Ethan's in the bathroom.

She welcomed them inside. Belinda looked dressed to kill. She was wearing a vivid red, longline polo top over a short brightly patterned stretch skirt and red leggings. A black wrap hung around her shoulders. She reminded Savannah of Cruella de Vil in *101 Dalmations*. Savannah felt pale in comparison. Ash looked cool in a brown leather jacket and blue jeans.

"Where's that gorgeous neighbour of yours?" Belinda's eyes swept the room with a piercing gaze.

"Ethan's —"

"Here." He walked across the room to them. "Hello, Belinda."

He leant forward as she kissed both his cheeks. His shirt hung open so the singlet was visible.

You call that putting a shirt on, Savannah thought. What was he thinking?

Belinda handed Savannah her bottle.

Ash was holding another bottle of bubbles and a bottle of red. "Have you two met?" Savannah asked. "Ethan, this is Ash, or do you prefer Ashton?"

"Either is good," he said.

"Let me take those bottles." Ethan held out his hands. "I'm your drinks waiter for tonight. I've been getting a bit of practice. Would you like a red now or a beer?"

"Beer would be good, thanks," Ash replied.

"I'll go straight to the bubbles," Belinda said.

Ethan followed Savannah to the kitchen bench for the glasses and popped the top on the sparkling.

"Bubbles for you, Sav?" he asked with a wicked look on his face.

"I'll stick to beer thanks," she said.

He winked at her then turned back to deliver a glass of sparkling to Belinda and a beer to Ashton. He was really enjoying himself. Savannah tried to concentrate on her stir fry.

"I told Ash what a nice little shack this is. Jaxon has made some great improvements."

Belinda surveyed the room again. Savannah tried not to notice her conversation was nearly exclusively with Ethan. The stir fry demanded her attention.

"Can I help?"

Ash's proximity surprised her. He'd come into the kitchen nook without her noticing.

"All good."

She stretched her face into a smile. Although he looked interested she didn't get the feeling it was genuine.

"I hope you like stir fry?"

"Anything would be better than Belinda's cooking," he said.

Savannah's eyes widened.

"I heard that," Belinda said. "You don't deserve me."

"Do you like to cook, Belinda?" Ethan asked.

"Not really."

Ash gave a soft snort. He perused Savannah's food and strolled back to the cheese board. He was an odd guy. Still, it was an odd relationship, she thought.

"Almost ready," she called. "If you'd like to take a seat I'll bring it over."

Ethan came over to help her. His shoulder rubbed against hers as he picked up a plate. She glanced at him. He winked. He'd done it deliberately. How was she going to get through this dinner?

"It's a huge serving," Belinda said as Ethan put a plate in front of her. "You know me, Savannah, you won't be offended if I don't eat it all?"

Once again the soft snort from Ash. What was with him?

"No, just eat whatever you feel like," Savannah said.

Not that she'd served a huge amount for Belinda. She'd had to stretch what was originally intended for two. The men got the biggest serves.

"Who's for the red?" Ethan brought the bottle to the table. They all had a glass except for Belinda who stuck to her sparkling.

"This is delicious, Savannah," Belinda said.

"Save room for dessert. It's a cool night so I've made a baked lemon pudding."

"Oh!" Belinda groaned. "You're doing your best to torture me. I love anything citrus."

"I'm sure a small amount won't hurt that figure of yours," Ethan said.

Savannah glanced at him. He was deliberately flirting with Belinda. She ignored them and turned her attention to Ash.

"So what is it that you do, Ash?" she said. "When you're not visiting the river."

He turned his steel-grey eyes on her. His look was cold and yet amused. Savannah felt a shiver run down her spine.

"A bit of this and that."

"Ash runs the family business," Belinda cut in.

"Bel exaggerates. I'm in charge of some."

"What does it entail?" Ethan asked.

"Imports mainly."

"We get to travel." Belinda gave a smug smile as if she knew something Savannah didn't. "And having access to the river house is a bonus."

Savannah watched the gold jewellery flash on Belinda's arms as she pecked at her meal. She was still none the wiser about the Palmers' business and life beyond the little snippets they gave away.

"How long have you had your place here?" she asked.

"A few years now," Belinda replied.

"Which part of Adelaide do you live in?" Savannah persisted.

"Eastern suburbs," Belinda said then turned back to Ethan. "It's funny we haven't met before now. We got to know Jaxon as soon as he bought the place."

"It's a good part of the river here," Ethan said. "You've been up a bit lately."

"Yes, while business is quiet we make the most of it."

Ethan looked at Ash. "Do you fish?"

"No."

Savannah flicked a look at Belinda who only had eyes for Ethan. Hadn't she said Ashton was fishing last week?

"You do go fishing sometimes," Belinda said quickly giving Ash a sharp look. "You just don't catch any fish." She turned back to Ethan. "The only animal Ashton is interested in is Brutus," she said. "And horses. The kind you bet money on."

"We saw you had a horse next door," Savannah said.

"Yes," Ash replied.

"He's not ours," Belinda said at the same time.

"We're looking after him for friends," Ash said.

"Poor thing," Belinda said. "He's on his last legs, that's why he's here."

Savannah looked from one to the other. Ash was staring at Belinda with that cold look of his.

"When he dies we have plenty of space to bury him," he said.

"Our friends have got nowhere," Belinda prattled on, oblivious to Ash's glare. "They'd have to pay to have him disposed of. It's so sad."

Savannah was horrified but she kept her mouth shut. Fancy giving your friends a horse so they could bury it for you when it died.

"You'd need a pretty big hole for a horse."

Savannah gaped at Ethan. Trust him to think of the practical details.

"Ash has one of those digger things."

"It's a small bobcat, Bel, not a digger thing."

"Everyone finished?" Ethan began to collect the plates.

"Yes. That was very nice, thank you, Savannah." Ash sounded like a child who'd been urged to use his manners. He was a cold fish. For the life of her Savannah couldn't see anything between him and Belinda. No hint of a spark or connection that would convey their intimacy.

"I'd better check on dessert." She stood up and her arm bumped Ethan's. Immediately she felt warm again. She wondered how long the Palmers would stay.

"We noticed a houseboat down at the bank with lights on as we came in," Belinda said.

"Yes," Savannah said. "There's a group on board but they're staying put for the weekend."

"That's odd, isn't it?" Ash said.

"They wanted the houseboat experience but not the travel." Savannah didn't want to mention it was a hens' weekend. She imagined Ash wouldn't approve.

"Perhaps we could hire a houseboat one day," Belinda said. "It's something we've never done."

"Perhaps," Ash said.

Don't be too enthusiastic, Savannah thought as she set out plates of steaming pudding.

"Oh!" Belinda groaned. "This is divine. How lucky are we? Two neighbours who can cook." She ran a finger down Ethan's arm.

Savannah had to stop herself rolling her eyes. They all tucked into the pudding.

"Have you travelled much, Bel?" Ethan asked.

"Usually once a year we go somewhere," Belinda said.

Savannah was startled by something touching her leg. She looked across at Ethan who sat opposite. He was turned to Belinda but it was his foot sliding up and down her calf. She gritted her teeth and tucked her legs under the chair. He wasn't making this dinner any easier.

"How long are you here, Ash?" she asked.

"Depends on the horse."

"Oh."

"Let's open the other bottle of bubbles," Belinda said.

"It's late, Belinda." Ash stood up. "Time to go."

Belinda didn't complain. She got dutifully to her feet. Savannah was glad they were leaving.

The minute the sliding door slid shut on them, she closed the blinds. Before she could turn Ethan wrapped his arms around her. She leaned into him as he nibbled her neck.

"I thought they'd never leave," he murmured.

They both jumped at a tap on the glass. Ethan pulled up the blinds. Belinda was waving at them from the other side.

Savannah slid open the door.

"I left my wrap," Belinda said.

Savannah looked back at the table. The wrap was draped over a chair.

Ethan reached it in two strides and offered it to Belinda.

"Thank you." She hovered at the door. "Look, I just wanted to apologise for my brother. Ashton can be a bit cool sometimes."

Savannah glanced at Ethan. His eyes were as wide as hers.

"He's not as social as me," Belinda said.

A car horn tooted.

"Let's catch up again soon." She winked at Ethan. "Thanks again," she called over her shoulder as she strode away.

Savannah slammed the door shut. "Omigod," she said but her voice was swallowed up by a spluttering noise behind her. Ethan clutched his stomach and then burst forth with a loud guffawing laugh. She stared at him a moment then began to laugh herself.

"What a crack-up," he gasped. "They're brother and sister not husband and wife."

"I can't believe we didn't see that."

"You were the one who told me they were married."

"Does that change anything for you?"

"What do you mean?"

"It makes Belinda available."

He laughed. "I'm about as interested in her as you are in Ashton."

"He creeps me out."

Savannah shuddered for a different reason as Ethan pulled her close again and kissed her. She responded to his lips, his tongue, his touch. Please don't let there be any more interruptions, she thought as he shuffled her backwards to her bedroom.

She let go of him long enough to pull his shirt from his shoulders.

He tugged hers over her head and undid her bra with one hand.

Light spilled into the room from the lounge. She kicked the door shut with her heel.

"I can't see you," he whispered.

"I like the dark."

He cupped her breasts. "You've got a beautiful body. I want to see it." He nibbled her ear.

"I've been mangled, Ethan." She pulled his singlet from his jeans and slid her hands up his stomach. "It's not a pretty sight."

"Okay," he said. "Dark it is ... this time."

She was grateful he didn't force the issue. She wasn't ready to expose her ugly body but she wanted to be with him.

He undid her jeans. She gasped as his hands slid lower.

"I'll just have to feel my way," he said.

"Go right ahead," she whispered as they tumbled onto her bed.

CHAPTER
38

Sunlight streamed around the bedroom curtains as Savannah struggled to open her eyes. She put one hand behind her head and flung the other out in a long stretch. Beside her the bed was empty. She sat up. Where was Ethan? She picked up her phone. It was almost nine o'clock. She grinned and flopped back onto the pillows. They had been awake late into the night.

There was a clink of a glass from the kitchen and the sound of water running. He was still here. Savannah sighed and closed her eyes.

She flung them open again at a sound from the doorway. Ethan stood looking at her. His buff body still naked, flawless, reminded her of her own shortcomings. She drew the sheet over her.

"Don't worry about covering up on my account," he said. "I've checked out those scars already."

"While I was sleeping?"

"Best time."

"Pervert." She threw a pillow at him.

He caught it and sat on the bed beside her. His deep brown eyes studied her carefully.

"You've got a beautiful body, Sav. Those scars are part of who you are. Don't let them define you. Life's too short." He traced his finger gently across the scar on her forehead.

She shivered at his touch and something in her heart let go. He was right. She'd been hiding the scars for so long it had become part of her being.

He lay down beside her and took her hand.

"I have to be honest with you."

Uh-oh, she thought. Here it comes. There's always a but.

"I've got my own demons."

She twisted her head. He was looking up at the ceiling. His expression was serious. What was he going to tell her? She waited and finally he turned to her and spoke.

"Have we got plans for today?"

"No."

"No customers or dinner parties I don't know about?"

"No." Where was this going?

"I've been thinking about those women on the boat."

"Have you?" It wasn't what she'd been expecting him to say. She relaxed, rolled over and pulled him to her. "I'll have to rectify that." She didn't care that it was daylight and the sheet had slipped away. Savannah pushed the doubt from her head. There'd be time to talk later.

Hunger finally drove them from the bedroom. Savannah made tomato and cheese toasties. Ethan made tea for her and coffee for him. Outside the sun sparkled on the water. The grey clouds from yesterday were all gone, leaving behind a few scattered puffs of white in the blue sky. They sat among the debris of last night's dinner, Ethan in boxers and she in her jumper and knickers.

"It looks like it will be a good day," she said. "No rain."

"Which brings me back to the women on the boat."

She grinned at him. "Are you testing me?"

"You can drag me back to bed later, you wanton woman."

"Is that so?" She raised her eyebrows.

He winked. "Hear me out."

"Go ahead."

"I'm assuming none of them is confident to take the houseboat out?"

"I guess so."

"How about we offer to take them for an afternoon cruise?"

"Would you do that?" Savannah jumped up and threw her arms around his neck. "What a lovely idea. I'm sure they'd think it was terrific."

"I'll help you clean up then I'd better head home. Feed Jasper, have a shower. Then we can go and ask them."

"Don't worry about the dishes. You get over to Jasper. He'll be wondering where you are."

Ethan gave her a quick kiss.

"I told him I probably wouldn't be home for the night."

"Confident, weren't you?" She grinned and kissed him back. His smooth bare skin felt wonderful under her fingers. "You'd better get dressed, soldier. Don't want those women to see more of you than they already have."

"I'm going out the back door." He went into the bedroom and came back with his jeans and boots on. "Back soon," he said.

Savannah showered and remade the bed. Then she began to clear the table. She hummed as she carried the glasses to the sink, thinking of Ethan. She shrugged her shoulders at the thought of his touch. She was having trouble concentrating on anything else.

Behind her a phone went off. It wasn't her ringtone.

She went to the table. In among the plates and cups Ethan's phone rang and vibrated. She picked it up.

"What the ...?" she mumbled. Jaxon's name was on the screen.

She pressed answer and put the phone to her ear.

"Hello?"

The phone beeped. She looked at the screen. The call had ended. She pressed the number to recall. It went straight to Jaxon's message bank. She put the phone back on the table and went to check her own. No missed calls from anyone let alone Jaxon.

What was he up to? Why would he try to ring Ethan and not her? She was sitting at the table staring at her screen, willing it to ring when Ethan returned.

"What's up?" he said.

"Jaxon rang on your phone."

She nodded at it beside her on the table. He strolled over and picked it up.

"Did you answer it?"

"Yes."

"What did he say?"

"Nothing. He hung up."

"Perhaps it dropped out." He slipped the phone into his pocket. "He'll try again, I guess."

"Has he been in touch with you since he left?"

"Only once."

"You didn't tell me."

"I didn't know you then." Ethan shrugged his shoulders. "I'd forgotten about it."

"I'm worried. What if something's happened to him?"

"He wouldn't be ringing."

"What if someone else had his phone?"

"Why would they be ringing me?"

Ethan bent over her and wrapped his arms around her neck.

"Don't worry about him. I'm sure he's fine. He'll turn up one day and tell us all about his fantastic holiday."

Once more she didn't know whether to be angry or worried, but Ethan was probably right. Jaxon would turn up when he was ready. She wanted him to come home but then there'd be no reason for her to stay. Where would that leave her and Ethan?

"Come on," he said. "Let's go and see if these ladies want a ride."

A couple of hours later Ethan backed *Our Destiny* out into the river. The toot of the horn brought delighted squeals from the women who were all excited at the prospect of actually going somewhere.

"Left or right, bride-to-be?" he asked.

Emily was seated beside him on a chair with Tara standing on her other side. Their friends were out on the deck.

"I don't know," she wailed. "Which is best?"

"They're both good. How about we go half an hour downstream then come back and go half an hour upstream?"

"That's a great idea," Tara said.

Savannah was just inside the door, watching on. Ethan was full of good ideas. He could be so practical and sensible. The more she got to know him the more she found to like about him.

"This really is very kind of you." Tara turned to Savannah. "Both of you. I'm sure you've got better things to do with your Saturday afternoon than take a boatload of crazy women on a ride."

"It's good to get out on the river," Ethan said. "I haven't been out for a while and we had a free afternoon." He twisted sideways and winked at Savannah.

As if she wasn't drooling over him enough, that wink set off another fizz in the pit of her stomach. She felt even more attracted to him after his attentive care of Emily. She'd had some kind of major stomach operation and had to be very careful. He'd been the one to get the chair for her. He'd made sure she was seated and comfortable and had a small glass of bubbles at hand to toast the journey.

Savannah watched as he spun the wheel and pushed the throttle. He was wearing the same green checked shirt he'd worn yesterday but this time it was done up and tucked into his jeans. Not that it mattered. She knew every bit of what was under those clothes.

"We're off," Tara said and clinked her glass against Emily's as the boat moved forward.

Savannah moved to stand beside Ethan. He reached around and pulled her close.

"You haven't been this way on the river either, Sav."

"No."

"You'll get to see Riverboat Point from a different view."

"Don't you go out on the river much?" Emily asked.

"I've only been here a couple of weeks. This is my brother's business. Ethan and I are helping out while he's away."

"There's the town," Ethan said.

Savannah stared as the jetty and buildings came into view. They'd hardly been anytime on the water.

"It takes so long in the car."

"That's why I often use my tinnie if I only want a few things," Ethan said. "Much quicker by boat."

"What a quaint little town," Tara said. "We didn't see much in the dark last night."

"I was too busy wondering where on earth you were taking me." Emily chuckled.

"It's a friendly place," Savannah said. She peered at the buildings as they passed. They looked different from this perspective and Tara was right, quaint was a good word. Up close the cracks in the pub wall and the fading paint on the supermarket roof were clearly visible but from here it was picturesque.

They cruised on down the river until Ethan thought it time to turn back.

One of the girls out on the front deck dug a bottle from the esky and refilled glasses. She poked her head in the door.

"Time for top-ups," she said.

"I'll be in that, Sandy," Tara said.

Sandy brought the bottle to Tara and Emily. "How are you enjoying this, Em?" she asked as she poured.

"Loving it. You girls look settled in out there with your jeans rolled up and your feet resting on the rails."

"There's room for more chairs. Why don't you and Tara come out?"

Emily looked from Tara to Savannah.

"Would you like to sit outside?" Tara asked.

"Don't stay in on my account," Savannah said. "I'll keep the captain company."

"Go on, Emily," Ethan said. "One more taste of the wind through your hair and freedom before you get married." He gave her one of his heart-melting winks.

"I'm game," she said.

Savannah and Tara took an arm each and guided Emily out the door while Sandy put out more chairs. When everyone was settled Savannah came back inside.

"Coffee, captain?"

"That'd be good. Thanks."

She made them both a cup and sat next to him on the chair Emily had vacated.

"No wonder people enjoy doing this," she said. "It's very relaxing."

Ethan was staring off to the other side. She followed his gaze. A sandbank jutted into the river and beyond it was a guy in a tinnie with a fishing rod.

"You like fishing?" she asked.

"I'd rate it my number one pastime. Not much point being on the river if you can't fish."

"So this kind of holiday doesn't appeal?"

He turned back to her. "Depends on the company," he said. "It's not something I've ever done."

They passed Riverboat Point again and then they were back to where they started.

"I'm going up on the sundeck," Savannah said. "I want to have a sticky at the Palmers' place from up there."

"Go for it," Ethan said.

Savannah went outside and followed the deck around to the back. She took the steps up and just made it to the top as they drew level with the Palmers' house. It was set well back from the water and partly obscured by trees. From river level it would be hard to see. The house was two storey, all glass and angles. A bit further on there was a small jetty with a large speedboat and a tinnie tied up beside it. The speedboat was black, a sleek mean-looking machine. Must have cost someone a packet. Then something else caught her eye. Further back in the bush she could see a bobcat moving about. It was too far away to see who was driving but she assumed it was Ash. Surely the horse hadn't died already.

She went back to Ethan.

"Looks like Ash is digging a hole. Do you think the poor horse has died?"

"Maybe, or maybe he's just being prepared if he knows it's going to happen soon."

"Don't you think it's awful?"

"Animals get old and die just like people, Sav. What do you think happens to dead horses?"

She pursed her lips. There he was being Mr Practical again. She leaned in against him.

"I feel sorry for the horse."

"I know you do." He kissed the top of her head. "Just think, the horse gets to spend its last days looking at this view instead of being in a stable somewhere."

"Mm." She sighed. It surely was a nice outlook and the Palmers had a big stretch of it. She settled back to watch the scenery go by. Every so often the raised voices and laughter of the women out the front drifted back to them.

"I recognise that spot," she said pointing off to the right.

"Old Man's Landing," Ethan said. "Time to turn around."

CHAPTER
39

Ethan moved his lips from her face to her neck.

Savannah stirred. Her nose twitched.

He traced his fingers between her breasts and gently caressed them.

"Are you awake?" he murmured in her ear.

She rolled towards him. "I am now."

"Want to go fishing?"

"Maybe." Her lips curled into a smile and she reached for him.

He slapped her on the bum and jumped out of bed.

"Come on then, get up."

She opened her eyes. "It's still dark. What time is it?"

"By the time we're ready it will be daylight." He kissed her. "Rug up. It'll be cold on the river."

She curled into a ball and pulled the blanket over her head.

"Meet me down at my jetty in ten minutes if you want fish for dinner."

She groaned. He grinned and let himself out. Savannah had cooked him dinner two nights in a row. Tonight he planned to cook her fish. He didn't mind if she came with him or not. She probably needed some space and he was okay with that.

"Hello, mate," Ethan said as Jasper barked a greeting. "Sorry I wasn't home again last night."

Ethan tapped his chest and the dog jumped up.

"You miss me?" He grabbed the fur on Jasper's face, gave him a playful shake then let him go. Jasper barked, sniffed Ethan's feet then hurried off down the drive.

Ethan bounded up the stairs. He boiled the kettle and made coffee in a thermos then threw together some sandwiches. He didn't know if Savannah would come with him but he wanted to be prepared.

The sky was lighting with a pale golden glow by the time he made his way down the path to his boat. He was pleased to see a shape huddled on the jetty.

"You're coming fishing?"

Sav turned to him, her face darkened by the hoodie pulled over her head. He caught a glimpse of her beanie underneath.

"I'm coming in the boat with you. I don't know about fishing."

He helped her into the tinnie, loaded his gear and they were away. He headed upriver. There were no signs of life on board *Our Destiny* as they passed. The ladies had enjoyed a late night. Ethan had heard their laughter and voices long after Savannah had fallen asleep in his arms.

They headed on past the Palmers'. No sign of anyone about there either. Ethan continued on to his favourite spot then cut the engine and let the boat drift. He baited the hook and cast. Savannah sat crunched into a huddle, her hands jammed between her legs. The air was crisp but not freezing.

"There's coffee in the thermos," Ethan said. "That'll warm you up."

Savannah poured them one each then wrapped her hands around her cup.

He grinned at her. "Best part of the day."

"For fish."

Ethan's reel whizzed. He put down his mug. "Yes, for fish," he said.

It only took him twenty minutes to put four good-sized callop in his bucket. Savannah admired each one reluctantly.

"Wait till you eat them." Ethan smacked his lips. "They're fleshy, not fatty and they're sweet. You'll love them."

"I look forward to it."

"We can go home now."

"Really?"

"That's enough for a couple of meals."

He started the engine and turned the tinnie for home. The river was flat; they were the only ones making waves. Along the banks the trees and cliffs were mirrored in the water. The sky was turning a brighter blue with every minute. He could see Savannah taking it all in. He hoped she'd like it enough, and him, to want to stay on after Jaxon returned. Jaxon's plan had been to get his sister to take a river change for a while. He'd been worried about her. Said she was lost in the city. The Savannah Ethan had got to know might have had her problems in the past but she seemed to know what she wanted and went for it. He was happy about that.

"What are you grinning at?"

He shifted his gaze to her and sucked in a deep breath.

"The scenery. It's spectacular."

She watched him closely as he tied the tinnie up to the jetty.

He helped her out.

"Coffee?" she asked, rubbing her hands together.

"Make it at my place. I'll clean the fish."

Jasper came bounding down to meet them. Savannah gave the dog a wide berth. Ethan picked up his gear and the bucket of fish and made his way to the fish sink by his shed.

She returned with steaming mugs of coffee and watched him as he worked. Jasper took up his usual position nearby.

"Is there anything you're not good at?" she asked.

He looked at her a moment. He could say long-term relationships but so far this one had lasted more than one night.

"Can't think of anything," he said instead.

"And you're so modest." She flicked a leaf at him.

"What's today's plan?"

"I'd like to say sleep but there's little chance of that. Once Tara's group heads off I'll have to clean their boat and get it ready to go out again."

"I can help with that."

"I'll have three boats coming in tomorrow and two have to go out again the next day. I can't expect you to be here to help every time."

Jasper leapt to his feet and ran towards the drive, barking as he went.

"Looks like we've got visitors."

Ethan handed Savannah the fish on a plate.

"Would you take these up to the fridge for me? There's cling wrap in the bottom drawer."

Savannah hooked her fingers through the handles of the mugs and took the plate in the other hand.

Ethan rubbed his hands together under the tap. He looked up as Blake's ute rolled past the shed and came to a stop. Blake raised his hand in a wave from the passenger side.

Ethan strolled over to meet him, glancing over the cab of the ute as the driver got out. He was surprised to see it was Barb. Jasper stopped barking and sniffed at her feet and legs.

"Sit, Jasper," Ethan said. "Is everything all right?"

"We're on a Sunday drive," Blake said with a silly grin.

Ethan raised an eyebrow. "An early one." They would have left the farm about the time he and Savannah were on the river catching the fish.

"I wanted to come." Barb reached up and pulled his face to her for a kiss. Her lips were warm on his cheek. "You smell like fish." She looked around. "It's terrible you're not even an hour away and I haven't seen your place. It looks like you've settled in well here."

"You've been fishing?" Blake said.

"Yes. Took Savannah out for her first trip."

"That's nice," Barb said. Blake rolled his eyes behind her.

"Come on up." Ethan gestured to the stairs. He didn't know what to make of this visit.

Savannah appeared at the top of the stairs.

"I'll leave you to catch up," she said once they'd exchanged greetings.

"Oh don't go," Barb said. "I've brought cake." She slapped her thigh. "Bother, I left it in the ute."

Blake groaned. "Now you tell me."

"I'll get the cake," Ethan said.

Blake was still moving gingerly. Extra trips up and down stairs wouldn't help.

He was out on the deck waiting when Ethan returned with the cake.

"Sorry about the surprise visit," he said in a low voice. "Barb only decided late last night she was coming. Mal's gone to Adelaide with the wool. I left you a message."

Ethan patted his pocket. His phone must be at Savannah's place again.

"Doesn't matter," he said. "It's always good to see you."

"Bit rude to call on a single guy this early."

"Any earlier and I wouldn't have been home." Ethan grinned at his brother. "I was out fishing."

"What are you two whispering about out there?" Barb called. "Kettle's boiled."

They sat on the deck. The day had warmed up, the conversation was general, Ethan felt relaxed. Savannah had to leave to deal with the houseboat. He invited her back for lunch.

"You'll stay too, won't you?" He looked at Barb and Blake. "There's plenty of fish."

"But that was going to be your dinner," Barb said.

"Doesn't matter. I'll find something else."

"I'll bring a tossed salad back with me," Savannah said.

"And my phone please."

She gave him a smile and left.

"We have to head off straight after," Blake said. "I'm going back to my place this arvo."

"You're looking a lot better," Ethan said.

"I am. I've worked out how to do just about everything with one arm and it's not giving me much pain now. It's the burn on my leg that still gives me grief. Jenny's coming back in a few days. Just a quick visit."

Ethan had wanted to ask about her but didn't want to broach the subject with Barb there.

"It's good she's coming back so soon," he said.

"Can't live without me."

Barb gave a soft snort.

"Savannah's a nice girl," she said.

"You two look pretty cosy." Blake grinned.

"We're getting on all right," Ethan said. He gathered the cups. "Want to see the rest of my place, Barb?"

By the time he was waving them off Ethan was totally relaxed. He couldn't remember the last time he'd felt so easy in his mother's company. It took him back to happier times.

They went inside and Savannah started cleaning up in the kitchen. He took her hand and led her to the couch.

"Come and sit for a while."

"I have to get back and start cleaning," she groaned.

He sat down and drew her onto his lap.

"I'll come with you. Let's just sit a minute."

She snuggled into him.

"Just for a minute," she sighed.

It was quiet. Ethan's eyes closed.

"I like your mum."

He flicked them open again. "That's good."

Savannah tipped her head to look at him.

"You don't see much of your parents, do you?"

"No."

"They don't live that far away."

"We don't see eye to eye on things."

"I didn't notice that today. Lunch was good fun. Blake's a funny guy."

"Mal wasn't there."

Savannah rested her head against his chest again. She traced her fingers up and down his arm.

"Can I ask why you don't get on?"

"It's old news."

She looked up at him again. Her gaze locked on his.

"Do you want to tell me about it?"

Ethan adjusted her weight on his legs. Did he?

"Sorry," she said. "I'm being nosy."

"It's simple really. I'm the black sheep of the family. Blake's been the compliant farm boy, happy to stay on the land."

"And your parents?"

"Can't believe they had a son who would take up arms. They marched against the Vietnam War in their younger days."

"And that's it?"

"That's enough. Mum and Dad have never forgiven me for joining the army. Being sent to Afghanistan was the last straw."

"Why did you?"

"I was posted. When the army says go, you go."

"No." She reached up and ran a finger around his jaw. "I meant what made you join the army?"

"I knew I wasn't going to be a farmer. I liked working with my hands but with machines. I wasn't much of an academic. The army trained me to be a mechanic and I was of use to my country as well."

"And your parents couldn't accept that?"

"They thought I'd done it to spite them." Ethan thought about that a moment. "Maybe some small part of me did. Anyway, they couldn't cope with a son who joined the army and, even worse, went off to a war they didn't believe in – twice. They wiped their hands of me."

"Your mum came to see you today."

Savannah's eyes were round with concern. A little frown wrinkled her brow.

"Barb's been different since I returned from Afghanistan the second time."

"There's been a lot of publicity about war – Gallipoli, remembering the sacrifice. So many have lost their lives. Maybe she's realised she's lucky to still have you. She doesn't want to lose her son."

Ethan thought about that. Perhaps Savannah was right. There was something in the way she spoke that made him think she wasn't just thinking about him and his parents.

"You said you'd been in an accident," he said. "Did you lose someone close to you?"

She lowered her head and rested it against his chest. Perhaps he'd pushed too far but he'd just told his family story. He knew little of hers except Jaxon was her brother.

He rubbed his hand in a circle over hers and waited.

"My parents," she murmured.

He stopped circling and gripped her hand. "I'm sorry. That's terrible for you." It explained a few things though – her determination, her strength and her willingness to help Jaxon out. He imagined for her it would have been sink or swim. He was glad she'd chosen to swim. "Jaxon hasn't ever said anything. You must find it very hard."

"I miss them but it won't bring them back. I just wish I knew what Jaxon was up to. He can be a pain but he's my only family now." She sat up. "I'd better get stuck into the cleaning. I know we had the fish for lunch but you still owe me dinner."

"I'll think of something," he said.

She climbed off his lap.

"The hens' group were sad you weren't there to see them off," she said. A twitch played at the corner of her mouth. "They said to say thank you for looking after them so well."

"It was your good business sense."

"Rubbish." She grinned. "They were all perving over your body." She bent and kissed him. "Save that body for me," she said. "That will be my dessert."

Ethan stayed where he was, listening to her footsteps recede down the stairs. He'd opened up to her but not about everything. Now he was torn between his promise to Jaxon and his desire to be honest with Savannah. He picked up his phone. Jaxon had tried to ring and probably hung up when Savannah answered. Ethan selected his number. They really needed to talk.

CHAPTER

40

Savannah paced up and down listening to Mandy's message bank.

"Hi, it's Savannah," she said as soon as she heard the beep. "I'm hoping you might be free to help me clean the houseboats today. Can you return my call? Thanks."

She should have called Mandy yesterday. Ethan had helped her with *Our Destiny* and she'd forgotten about ringing Mandy. He'd cooked burgers for dinner at her place and they'd had an early night. Goosebumps tingled down her arms. They'd gone to bed early but it had been quite a while before they'd slept.

Reality had hit early this morning. Ethan took a call from the garage in Burra. They had a big job on and needed his help. He'd set off almost immediately. At least he couldn't take her fishing again like he'd suggested the night before. Although he'd also offered to teach her how to operate the tinnie and she liked the idea of that. Taking a short run to Riverboat Point was appealing.

Savannah stopped pacing and looked at her phone, willing it to ring. She'd been sure she'd be able to get Mandy to help her. She'd tried to catch her a couple of times with no luck. The other three boats were due any moment. She'd have to tackle them on her own and hope Ethan would be back early enough to help with the fuel and septic.

She hung out a load of washing while she waited. Jasper lay, head resting on his paws, watching her through the fence.

"Pity you can't help me with the cleaning," she said.

He lifted his head, tipped it to one side, then lowered it back again.

She went back inside. Through the sliding door she caught a glimpse of *River Magic* gliding towards the bank.

"Now it starts," she muttered. She felt tired and she hadn't even begun.

Sam and his group were full of excitement. They'd had a wonderful time and wanted to book another trip as soon as they could all agree on a date. They were still unloading when *Tawarri* berthed beside them. The air was full of the voices of happy campers. All Savannah could think of was the work she needed to do.

Her phone rang. Her heart lifted at the sight of Mandy's name on the screen.

"I can help," Mandy said. "Would you like me to come out now?"

"Yes please."

Savannah tucked her phone back in her jeans pocket. She walked with more of a spring in her step now that she knew help was on its way. Just after the last car turned out of the drive, Mandy turned in.

"Am I glad to see you," Savannah said.

Mandy moved briskly. She wore a navy polo top and trackpants this time and her runners. Once more her wayward curls were held back from her face by a brightly coloured scarf. She looked like a woman on a mission.

"Where do you want me to start?"

"Can you strip the beds and start cleaning *River Magic*? I'll carry down the clean linen and fill the trolley with the toiletries."

"The quad bike makes it easier."

"Quad bike?"

"Jaxon used to have one."

"Is that the thing in the shed?"

"Maybe. Do you want me to take a look?"

"Sure."

They walked up to the shed. Mandy chatted happily, full of enthusiasm for the next fitness session. Savannah opened the shed.

"That's it," Mandy said pointing to the four-wheeled machine beside Jaxon's ute. "You can put small things in the tray on the front." She looked around. "There should be a trailer somewhere."

She poked around behind Jaxon's ute.

"Here it is."

She started the bike and hooked the little trailer on the back. Then she slid the front door of the shed partly open.

"We just load up and take it all down in one go." Mandy raised her voice above the sound of the motor reverberating inside the shed.

Savannah was gobsmacked. She'd made many trips back and forth with things for the boats. This would make it much easier.

"I don't know how to drive it," she said.

"Hop on the back," Mandy said.

Savannah hesitated. Mandy patted a piece of wood perched on top of the guards above the back wheels.

"Put your butt on there and watch over my shoulder," she called.

Mandy took them for a drive around the yard then made Savannah get in the driver's seat. They went around the clothes line in a kangaroo-hopping fashion in fits of laughter. Jasper barked. Savannah was sure they were yelps of encouragement. Finally, she managed to go a distance without jerking.

"You've got it," Mandy said. "I'll get started on the boats."

Savannah wasn't sure she'd mastered the controls but she managed to make it back to the shed without too many jerks. She loaded up everything she needed and drove carefully down the slope, stopping as close to the path as she could.

She looked up and down the river. There were a couple of speedboats going in opposite directions and a huge houseboat passing by but no sign of *Riverboat*. After her episode with Fred she'd learned to lay down the rules firmly with the customers. The group on board *Riverboat* were mainly young blokes. She'd made it perfectly clear the return time was ten o'clock and it was nearly midday. She hoped she wasn't going to have a repeat of the Fred experience. *Riverboat* was booked to go out again tomorrow afternoon. She didn't want any delays.

The sound of a car drew her back up the drive. Belinda waved as she got out.

"Hello," she called.

Savannah gritted her teeth behind her smile. She had so much to do.

"Fancy a drink this afternoon?" Belinda asked.

"Not sure I'll have time."

Belinda pouted. "Ash is going back to the city overnight. I'll be all alone but someone has to stay because of the horse."

Savannah relented. "Come over about four. I'll take a short break when you get here."

Belinda gave her a tight smile. "That's perfect. Ash won't leave till then anyway."

"How is the horse?"

"Still hanging in there, poor thing. One of us has to stay on the property. We can't leave it on its own but the vet doesn't think it will last much longer."

Savannah recalled the bobcat. She shrugged her shoulders to hide her shudder.

"I'd better get back to it."

"It's a big job all this houseboat business, isn't it," Belinda said looking towards the river.

"I'm lucky Mandy's come out to help me today and Ethan's been fantastic."

"Yes, considering." Belinda patted her arm and winked. "It must be your charm that's got him helping."

"Considering what?"

"He doesn't like houseboats."

Savannah frowned.

"He was telling me that first night we met," Belinda prattled on. "He doesn't like the idea of the houseboats being here. Says it spoils the peace and tranquillity of the river."

"He prefers to fish," Savannah said but Belinda's words rang true. They sounded like something Ethan would say.

"Look, we should exchange phone numbers," Belinda said. "That way we can just call each other to make arrangements. I meant to ask you the other night."

"Good idea."

They swapped numbers and Belinda was getting in her car as Mandy came up the path.

"Hello, Mandy," Belinda gushed.

"You two know each other?" Savannah said.

"We've met in town," Mandy said.

"You clean the pub, don't you?" Belinda said.

Mandy nodded. There was no sign of her usual bright smile.

Belinda shut the car door. Mandy stared at her.

"I'm so grateful Mandy's come out to help me with the boats," Savannah rushed to fill the silence.

"The mop head's had it," Mandy said turning her back on Belinda. "I'm hoping Jaxon's still got some replacements in the shed."

She went on past them.

"You know I'd be happy to help out when you're stuck," Belinda said. "You don't have to call in others when I'm right next door."

"Thanks." Savannah tried to imagine her well-heeled neighbour cleaning up the mess left behind on Fred's boat. She just couldn't see it.

"See you later." Belinda waved a hand, flashing bright nail polish, as she backed out.

Mandy came to stand beside Savannah, a new mop head in her hand.

"You two seem chummy," she said.

"Belinda's been very kind."

Mandy was staring after the retreating vehicle. Lines creased her brow.

"Don't you like her?" Savannah asked.

"Just something about her. She and that brother of hers come into town and flash money around but they keep to themselves. I don't trust them." Mandy shrugged her shoulders. "Not my type, I guess."

Savannah looked along the empty driveway to the gate. She frowned. Belinda was a bit of a square peg in a round hole in a town like Riverboat Point. She could be gushy at times. It probably came over a bit strong for some of the locals.

"Your sheet and towel supplies are getting low," Mandy said.

Belinda was forgotten in an instant. "I took a pile into town …" Savannah pursed her lips trying to remember. "That was last Tuesday." Where had the time gone?

"They pick up and drop off Tuesdays and Fridays. They're pretty quick with their turnaround. Could be some waiting for you already. If not it should be there tomorrow. And this is the last mop head. You'll go through them pretty quickly."

"I'd better start a list."

"Jaxon kept a book and noted things like that down so he could keep ahead. He would leave it out for me if he wasn't here so I could jot down anything I noticed."

"He has a few notebooks in his desk drawer. I'll go and get one of those."

"He's left you in the lurch a bit, hasn't he?"

"I've surprised myself how quickly I've picked it up."

"Funny he didn't stay and show you the ropes before he left."

Savannah knew why he hadn't done that. She was sure he knew she would never have agreed to stay had he been here and told her he was going away.

"How's his holiday going anyway?" Mandy asked as they headed back to the boats.

"Fine."

"Do you have a date you're expecting him back?"

"Not yet."

"It's just that he offered to do some work on the community hall. A few of the locals are pitching in but it's come to a bit of a standstill now till he does his bit. It will be a better space for our fitness group. We'll even have somewhere to store equipment once it's finished."

"I'm sorry. I don't know how much longer he'll be away."

"There's a fundraiser coming up for Red Cross. We were hoping to use the hall. Still, as I told them, when people volunteer their time you have to accept when they give it."

The phone rang as they passed the house.

"I'll be back with you in a minute," Savannah said and ducked inside to answer it. She could start a list while she was there.

As she picked up she noticed the message light flashing. She peered at it surprised to see there'd been three missed calls.

"Hello, J&S House –"

"At last," a young male voice cut in before she could finish. "It's Tim. I'm on your houseboat. We've broken down."

CHAPTER

41

Savannah's heart skipped a beat. A million thoughts went through her head. How was she going to get help? What kind of help did they need? The boat had to be ready to go again tomorrow. Perhaps someone was hurt. She took a deep calming breath. First things first.

"Is everyone all right?" she asked.

"Fine."

Tick.

"Where are you?"

"We camped at Old Man's Landing last night and we didn't get far from there."

Tick.

"What's broken?"

"The boat's got power but we can't steer it."

End of ticks. Savannah had no idea what to do about that.

"We're making slow progress. One of the lads is a farm boy. Bit of a bush mechanic. He reckons the steering cable's snapped. There're two of them down the back using their feet to steer."

"Is that safe?"

"He reckons it's okay but the girls are getting jittery."

Savannah didn't blame them. She didn't like the sound of it even though she had no idea what they were doing. What to do? What to do?

Her first thought was Ethan but she didn't have his number. They hadn't needed to phone each other. She had the tinnie but no idea how to start the thing and what good would she be if she could?

"We'd be happy to keep ambling along like we are," Tim said. "But a few of the group have to get back by mid-afternoon."

Savannah thought about the trip she'd been on with Ethan. Then she remembered Ash's big speedboat.

"Is there a place where you could moor the houseboat?"

"Plenty of spots along this stretch."

"See if you can do that. I've got a friend with a boat. Perhaps we can ferry you all back here."

"That'd be great."

"Let's swap mobile numbers and I'll let you know as soon as I've got it organised."

Savannah ended the call and selected Belinda's number.

"Hi, Savvie. That was quick. You ready for a drink already?"

"No," she said. "I've got a problem and I was hoping Ash could help, if he hasn't left."

"Of course, if he can. What's the problem?"

Savannah explained. She hated asking but she didn't have any other ideas. At least if the boat was safely tied up and she could get the people off, she could deal with the rest later. She could hear a muffled conversation then Belinda was back.

"He'll come and pick you up in about ten minutes," she said.

Savannah ran down to tell Mandy what was happening.

"Good of him to help out," Mandy said begrudgingly. "That boat of his will be too big to get close to the bank. You'll have to wait at the swim deck of the houseboat."

Savannah hadn't thought of that. When they came back and unloaded it would be the same. Tim and his mates would have to transfer everything to the swim deck of *Tawarri* then carry their gear back to land from there. It was going to be a laborious process but she didn't know what else to do.

The deep throb of a large motor drew her attention upriver. Around the bend came the sleek black boat. Savannah watched its approach and gave Ash a small wave as he eased back on the throttle and let his boat glide up to the deck of *Tawarri*. Mandy helped her aboard and Ash turned the boat in a tight U before Savannah had a chance to sit. She looked back at Mandy staring at them from the houseboat.

"They're just upriver you think?" Ash called over his shoulder.

"Yes," she shouted.

He didn't look quite so Mr Cool today. He hadn't shaved and his eyes looked bleary as if he'd only recently woken up.

The boat surged forward at a faster rate. Wind whistled past Savannah. She snuggled back into the comfy seat behind him and ran her hands over the soft smooth covering. Surely it wasn't leather. In front of Ash's legs was a small door. There was a big covered space in the pointy front of the boat but she hadn't realised it was a cabin. At least that might mean more room for luggage.

She looked up as they passed his jetty. Harder to see the house from this level. They went on around the bend and further up the river. It was the same journey she'd made with Ethan in his tinnie and in the houseboat. It was much quicker in Ash's boat.

"Is that them?" Ash pointed ahead.

Savannah stood up and hung on to the seat in front. There was a houseboat moored near a sandy bank, *Riverboat* painted on its side.

"That's the one," she said.

Once more Ash cut back the engine and let his sleek boat glide through the water to the back of the houseboat. He tied his boat securely to the deck.

"We're so pleased to see you," called one of the girls.

"Sorry you've had trouble," Savannah said. "I hope your holiday was good."

"Up till this morning it was lovely."

Tim and his mates started handing down luggage.

"Shall we put some in the cabin?" Savannah asked Ash.

"No," Ash snapped. He pulled a smile that looked more like a grimace. "There's not much room in there. We'll have to do the best we can with the space out here."

They loaded up the three who had to leave first and their luggage. Ash turned the boat and they retraced the journey to *Tawarri*. Once they were off Ash went back for the next lot alone, it meant more space in the boat and Savannah could keep working while she waited for them to return.

Ash undid the ropes as soon as the last group were unloaded.

"Thanks for your help. I really appreciate it," Savannah called.

He nodded and locked his gaze with hers. She willed herself not to shiver. His eyes looked cold, like a snake's.

"Good to have neighbours you can rely on," he said. "Belinda said she'll catch you later." He lifted his hand in a wave and roared away.

"That wasn't quite the ending to our holiday we'd planned."

Savannah tore her gaze from the retreating boat and looked at Tim standing on the deck behind her. He'd been in the last group to be ferried back.

"I'm sorry," Savannah said. "I'll have to organise some kind of discount for your trouble."

"Don't bother," he said. "We had a great time. You've never seen anything so funny as two blokes steering a houseboat with their feet."

"At least you had someone practical on board who knew what to do."

"That's Angus."

He turned and called to the tall bloke in the checked shirt chatting to those remaining from their group.

"Hello, Angus," Savannah said. She had to tip her head back to look up at him he was so tall. "Tim says you're a mechanic."

"Not really, but I like to tinker. All that's wrong with your boat is the steering cable. It's snapped for some reason."

"Sounds bad."

"Not really," he said again. "If I'd had the right gear I could have tweaked it to get us back. Shouldn't be too hard to fix."

"Where would I get one from?"

"I don't know around here." Angus scratched the back of his neck. "I'm not familiar with this area. Try the garage."

"Thanks for being so good about it," she said.

"No problem for most of us. We've got a bit more time up our sleeves," Tim said. "Just the three who had to get back for work were a bit worried."

"All added to the adventure." Angus grinned.

She waved them off then hurried to the septic truck. She was getting used to shifting it back and forth. She still did a lot of gear crunching but she only had to move it a short distance. When she finished that she lined up the fuel truck.

"The boats are all clean inside and out," Mandy said.

Savannah looked up from the gauge on the fuel truck. She was refilling the last of the three houseboats.

"Thanks."

Mandy watched her as she stopped the fuel flow and recorded the amount in her phone.

"You really have embraced the whole job," Mandy said.

"Ethan taught me how to do this, otherwise I'd have to be getting him to do it all the time. The only thing I can't do by myself is replace the gas bottles," she said.

"Can I help with that?"

"You've done enough already. I'm so glad you could come out. Ethan will help when he gets home."

"You've mentioned his name a few times today. I've seen him around town but haven't spoken with him. What's he like?"

"Nice guy," Savannah said. Tired as she felt she couldn't keep the smile from her face.

Mandy grinned back. "Nice, hey? Nice and handy too, living right next door."

"He's been very kind. If it had been just up to me, Jaxon's houseboat business would have been sunk by now."

"I'd better head off," Mandy said. "It's nearly time to collect the kids from school. See you tomorrow."

"Tomorrow?"

"Fitness."

"Oh yes. I hope I can get there. Will depend on getting *Riverboat* repaired I guess."

"We'll muddle along if you can't make it but it's much more fun with you taking charge of our raggedy bunch."

"I'll try." Savannah walked with Mandy to her car. "I'll pay you as soon as I work out that side of things."

"Don't stress. It'll be a bonus when I get it."

Savannah waved Mandy off and immediately turned her thoughts to getting the houseboat fixed. If only she could ring Ethan. No point wasting time thinking about that.

She remembered the conversation she'd heard in the supermarket between Faye and Terry, the old bloke with the old car. There was a garage in Riverboat Point. Angus said it was easy. If she could get a replacement maybe Ethan could fix it when he got back. She dashed inside for her car keys.

There was no sign of anyone when Savannah pulled up outside the garage. Ethan had filled her car up from the tank at his parents' farm after her help with the shearing but she thought she may as well top up again while she was here. She was about to go inside and check what was going on when the gauge finally clicked over allowing the fuel to flow.

When she walked in to pay there was a bloke behind the counter talking on the phone.

"Not much I can do about it, mate," he was saying. "There's only one of me."

Savannah studied him. He looked about forty although it was hard to tell. He wore grease-covered overalls, had an unkempt beard and thick dark hair jammed under his stained brown cap.

"You're welcome to take your business elsewhere," he said and hung up. "Sorry about that."

Savannah handed over her card.

"Savings please," she said. "I'm Savannah Smith from J&S Houseboats just out of town."

He nodded. "Mark Turner."

"I'm hoping you can help me."

"I'm too busy to scratch myself but go ahead," he said.

"I've got my own mechanic. I just need a steering cable."

"For a houseboat?"

"Yes." Savannah felt a surge of hope until she saw him shake his head.

"I don't stock much of anything here. It's a marine shop you need. I can order one in for you."

"How long will that take?"

"If they've got one in stock I could have it here before the end of the week."

Savannah let out a sigh. She needed the boat to be ready tomorrow.

"There's no way to get it any quicker?" she asked.

"I could tell them it's urgent."

"Can you try? I've got a boat that needs fixing and it's booked to go out tomorrow afternoon."

Savannah gave him her details and left him to it.

At the supermarket she looked over the meat. She'd volunteered to cook dinner tonight. She picked up a pack of steak. With what she had lined up for Ethan she owed him a decent meal. Just for good measure she picked up some beer from the pub.

CHAPTER
42

Ethan climbed the fence from his yard to Jaxon's. Light shone from the kitchen window. It hadn't been the best of days. He was bone tired and looking forward to nothing more than some food and cuddling up to Savannah.

He let himself in the back door.

"Hello," Savannah called.

The air was filled with the smell and sounds of sizzling steak.

"Mmm," he said taking her in his arms and holding her close. He looked over her shoulder. "That smells good."

Savannah pushed him away to arm's length.

"You not so good," she said.

"I've showered and changed my clothes."

"You smell like a garage."

"My skin absorbs it. I've been up to my elbows in oil and grease several times today."

"Sit down," she said. "I'll bring you a beer."

There was an empty bottle of sparkling and two glasses on the end of the bench.

"Belinda been over?"

"Yes," Savannah groaned. "I relented and had one glass. She can sure tip it down though. She didn't leave until the bottle was empty."

"Went home to her hubby, did she?" He chuckled.

Savannah had her head in the fridge pulling things out. "I'm ignoring you," she said.

He gave her a playful tap on the bum.

"You can try," he said.

She stood up with a sixpack of beer in her hands. A smile played on her lips.

"Do you have to go back tomorrow?" she asked.

"No." He sat at the table. "Are you planning something?"

"It depends."

"On what?"

"I thought you might be needed at the garage."

"I won't get much work there anymore. They told me today they've decided to take on an apprentice."

"It was a fair bit of travel for you."

Savannah brought over two beers. He popped the tops and they touched them together. Ethan took a long drink from the bottle.

"It's work. I need some income. A week here and there at the farm isn't enough."

"The steak's ready," she said.

He watched her buzz about the kitchen. She was being very energetic.

"How was your day?" he asked.

"Busy," she said.

She put his plate in front of him. Beside the steak she'd served some potato bake. His mouth watered.

"Help yourself to salad," she said as she removed the cling wrap from the bowl.

"What have you been doing besides cooking for me?"

"Lots of things." Her reply was vague.

He took a mouthful of steak. It was pink and juicy. Just how he liked it. He ate a bit more with the creamy potatoes.

He looked across at Savannah. She'd only taken one bite of her steak and was studying him closely.

"I know that look," he said. "What are you planning?"

"I'm hoping you can help me," she said.

"You know I will. Weren't you able to get hold of Mandy?"

"Yes. All the cleaning's done and the refuelling et cetera. Only the gas bottles to swap."

"That won't take long."

"That's not the problem."

He put down his knife and fork. She fidgeted with hers.

"Spit it out," he said.

"The steering cable snapped on *Riverboat*. I had to get Ash to help me get the customers back here."

"Where's the boat now?"

"Just this side of Old Man's Landing. I've ordered a new cable but it might not be here for a few days. The boat has to go out tomorrow. I was hoping you could fix it for me."

"If it's just the steering cable I'm sure I can."

Savannah dropped her knife and fork and flew around the table into his arms.

He pushed back his chair to make room for her. Her body was warm and soft to his touch. His responded. He nibbled her ear.

"Let's get an early night," he murmured.

"Good idea." She eased herself up and gave him a wicked smile. "Finish your dinner first. You'll need all your energy."

She kissed him. He reached for her but she slipped away to her side of the table. He took another bite of steak. She did the same.

"You know if I was the paranoid type I'd think someone was trying to sabotage the houseboats."

He looked up. She was staring at him. A few wrinkles creased her brow.

"Steering cables break," he said.

"Two signs have disappeared."

"Souvenirs of a good time."

"Guns being fired."

"No-one's sure what they heard."

"No toilet paper."

He put his head to one side. "Could that possibly have been human error?"

"No!" She flicked a piece of lettuce at him. It didn't make it far across the table. "I'm sure that boat was fully stocked."

"Maybe Fred had a toilet paper fetish."

Savannah pulled a face. "Don't go there."

She plucked the lettuce leaf from the table and put it back on her plate.

"Then there was the chair," she said. Once more she was watching him closely.

"What chair?"

"When I hadn't been here very long one of the chairs on *River Magic*'s sundeck was positioned to look straight into this room."

She had an odd look on her face. He held her gaze, then the implication of her words hit him.

"You think I might have done that?"

"Did you?"

"Of course not." He was concerned. Surely she trusted him. "Sav, are you being serious about all this?"

"No and yes."

"There's a reasonable explanation for all of it."

"I know … except the chair."

"Those chairs get moved about all the time."

"But they'd all been together in stacks."

"Have you noticed anything different with the chairs since?"

"No."

He reached across the table and took her hand. "Forget about it, Sav."

The worry on her face softened.

"Now you'll think I'm crazy," she said.

"No, I don't. You've just been on a huge learning curve. There's been a lot of stuff for you to take in."

"I hadn't realised how much it would take." She pursed her lips. "What do you think about Belinda and Ashton?"

"Surely you don't think they clambered up onto a houseboat to watch through the window. They just come right in here whenever they want."

"No." Her cheeks turned pink. "I mean what do you think of them as people?"

"Why?"

"Mandy doesn't like them."

He scratched his head. All he wanted to do was take Savannah in his arms. "I don't think about them," he said reaching for her. "Let's get that early night. I'm going to ride to Adelaide first thing tomorrow, pick up a steering cable and I'll be back before lunch. I can replace it before your customers arrive."

"What about the one I ordered?"

"It won't hurt to have a spare."

"You'd do that for me?"

"No." He grinned. "For Jaxon. I've got something else in mind for you."

His phone rang. Jaxon's name showed on the screen. He held it to his side.

"Sorry," he mumbled. "I have to take this."

"Don't be long."

He gave her a half smile, let himself out the glass door and put the phone to his ear.

"How's it going, mate?" Jaxon's voice was chirpy.

"I've been trying to contact you."

"My sister answered your phone. I got a bit jumpy. Getting on okay you two?"

Ethan ignored him. "It's been long enough," he said.

"Everything going okay?"

"Most of the time."

"Is Sav enjoying herself?"

"I guess but it's too big a job for her," Ethan said. "You need to come home."

"I will soon."

The phone went quiet.

"Hello?"

Ethan peered at his phone. Jaxon had gone. He turned around. Savannah was watching him from the other side of the glass. In his haste to get outside he hadn't slid the door fully shut behind him. He wondered how much she'd heard. He slid the door open and stepped inside. Savannah stepped back, her eyes narrowed.

"That was my brother, wasn't it?"

"Yes," he said. He couldn't lie to her.

"He's okay?"

"Yes."

"Do you know where he is?"

"No."

"Would you tell me if you did?"

"Sav."

She held up a hand, palm facing him. "You've been lying to me."

"No I haven't."

"But he's been in touch with you and not me. Why?"

"It's complicated." He reached for her but she stepped away, pain etched on her face.

"Whatever scheme you and my brother have cooked up it ends here."

"I have no scheme, Sav. Jaxon asked me to help you when you needed it."

"And you thought you'd include taking me to bed."

An ache started deep in his chest. He shook his head.

"I think you'd better go," she said.

He wanted to take her in his arms, make her understand. He'd fallen in love with her. He hadn't planned to when he'd agreed to Jaxon's request to help his sister, it just happened. The steely resolve had returned to her face. He could see she was in no mood to listen.

He stepped outside. "I'll get the part and fix the boat for you."

She crossed to the door. "Not for me," she said. "For Jaxon, remember?" She slid the door shut and closed the blinds.

Ethan stood a moment staring at the glass. He'd blown it. He'd found the woman he thought he could spend his life with and now he'd lost her trust. Damn Jaxon and his secrets.

CHAPTER

43

Savannah sat slumped at the table, her hands wrapped around her mug of tea. She felt numb inside. The feeling took her back to the time after the accident when she'd finally been compos enough to be told her parents had both been killed in the crash, their funerals done. All she'd felt was emptiness, the same emptiness she felt now. She'd thought Ethan loved her like she loved him but it had all been a lie. Jaxon had put him up to it, she was sure. His poor lonely sister needed a man. She'd fallen for it.

She looked out at the grey morning. It matched her mood. Patches of mist clung to the edges of the river. It looked brooding and dull. She'd not slept well, aching for her loss of Ethan and broken by his deception. She'd been another conquest for him. An amusement while he helped her brother. Her life had a nasty habit of repeating itself.

She'd been awake when Ethan's bike had started up. He would be halfway to Adelaide. Once he came back it would be hard to avoid him. She still needed his help where the houseboats were concerned. Surely Jaxon would return now. All she had to do was keep things going for a bit longer then she could go back to her life in Adelaide.

She stared at the river. Somehow the thought of going back to the city held no appeal. She shrugged her shoulders. No point in self-pity. Experience had taught her the only person she could rely on was herself. She had the fitness class to look forward to this morning. The women there were good fun and appreciated her guidance. There were no hidden agendas.

That was still a way off. She got to her feet. A run was what she needed to clear her head.

She pulled on her running clothes. They were clammy with the cold but she'd soon warm up. She stretched, focused on the run and set off. Outside, the yard held pockets of mist and so did the road. It wasn't thick but was enough to change the features of the roadside. The pounding of her feet echoed in the still air.

A shot rang out and a high-pitched squeal. Savannah stopped and looked around. She was almost level with Gnasher's gate. There was another squeal. It sounded human. It pierced the air again. Savannah's heart went cold. It was the sound of a terrified woman.

She looked around again. What the hell was she going to do? She hadn't brought her phone and who would she call anyway? Ethan had gone, Ash had gone, the only people close by were Belinda and Gnasher ... and whoever was doing the squealing.

She climbed the fence and dropped to the other side. The mist was even thicker here. She followed the track, her heart pounding in her chest. Any minute she expected Gnasher to jump out from the mist waving his gun.

Every so often she stopped and listened. She heard no more shots or cries. She moved on. The bush ahead thinned and with it the mist. In front of her was a large shed. She took careful steps forward. Something moved in the shed. She froze. It was Gnasher. He stood looking down at a mound by his feet.

Savannah took a deep breath.

"Hello, Gnasher," she called just loud enough for him to hear her.

He turned and she walked slowly towards him. He had a few days' growth on his face, his cheeks and nose were ruddy and his eyes bloodshot. He frowned at her.

The mound at his feet whimpered. They both looked down. Savannah put a hand to her mouth. The mound was a woman. She was small with long dark hair and dark skin. Blood ran down her arm from a gaping wound.

Savannah looked from the bloodied cowering woman to Gnasher. Then she saw the rifle hanging from his hand.

"Gnasher!" she cried. "What have you done?"

The woman lifted her head at Savannah's voice. She started speaking excitedly in another language. Was it Chinese? Savannah couldn't understand her but she recognised the pleading tone.

"I didn't do anything." Gnasher shook his head. He had a puzzled look on his face. "She just came out of the fog."

"Help, please," the woman croaked.

Savannah understood that. She hurried over.

"What's happened to her?"

"I don't know." Gnasher lifted his arms in the air. The rifle went up with them.

The woman cried out again.

"I don't understand," Savannah said.

"Vietnamese," Gnasher said. "Sneaking into my camp. Thought she was bloody Viet Cong."

"You shot her?" Savannah gasped.

"Should have," he said and let his arms slump to his sides.

Savannah eyed the rifle. He laid it on the table, sunk into a chair and put his head in his hands. Gnasher didn't look in very good condition. Had the woman startled him and he'd fired? Where had she come from?

Savannah didn't know what to do. The woman had a jagged wound around the top of her arm, possibly from a bullet. Savannah had no idea what a bullet wound looked like but this one was a mess. At least the blood was congealing down her arm.

"Can you get up?" Savannah gestured with her hand.

The woman moaned as Savannah helped her. There was more blood on her legs and her dress was ripped.

"Get her out of here."

Savannah and the woman both jumped as Gnasher thumped the table with his fist. He picked up his rifle and stalked away into the bush.

Savannah put a careful arm around the woman and guided her along the track towards the gate. They made slow progress.

"I'll get you some help." She hoped her tone was reassuring. She wasn't sure the woman could understand her.

"My name is Sav." Savannah patted her chest. "Sav," she repeated when the woman looked at her.

She nodded. "Li," she said.

"Li?"

The woman nodded again.

"I'll get you some help, Li," Savannah said.

The gate was up ahead. Savannah knew it was padlocked. She hoped Li would be able to climb over. They rested against it for a moment. Savannah stared back along the track. The mist had cleared but the trees remained grey, their leaves dripping with moisture.

"Let's go," she said. She gestured with her hands showing they had to climb over.

Li nodded.

Savannah went first then reached back to help Li over. No sooner were they on the other side than a dog barked. Li cowered behind her. Savannah looked up the road in the direction of the sound. Ash came round the bend with a huge dog tugging him along. Their car moved slowly along behind. Savannah assumed it was Belinda at the wheel.

"Thank goodness." Savannah put a steadying hand on Li. Here was help when she needed it. They could put Li in Belinda's car and take her into town. Maybe there was someone there who could help.

The dog barked and pulled on its lead.

Behind her Li gave a small squeal.

"It's okay," Savannah said. "I don't like dogs either but this one's on a lead."

She waved at Ash. He waved back.

"I thought you were in Adelaide," she said as he got closer.

"Plans changed."

"I'm glad."

Belinda got out of the car. "What's happening?"

"I've found this poor woman at Gnasher's. Don't know what he's done to her."

Ashton gave Belinda a funny look. Almost a smirk. Belinda came closer. Li started babbling excitedly.

"Take Brutus away, Ashton," Belinda snapped. "Can't you see he's terrifying her?"

Ash patted the dog's head and tugged it away.

"Will you be okay?" he asked Belinda. He had an odd expression on his face. Even though he'd helped her yesterday Savannah still couldn't warm to him. He seemed to find poor Li's plight amusing.

"We'll be fine. Savvie and I can look after one tiny woman. Let's get her into the car," Belinda said. "We can take her back to my place and clean her up. If she needs more help we can call an ambulance."

Li tugged against her with a strength Savannah wouldn't have thought she could muster.

"It's okay," she soothed. "We're going to help you."

Belinda opened the back door of her car. "You get in with her, Savvie. She's obviously had a hard time of it, poor thing."

Li's eyes opened wide and she shook her head. They had difficulty getting her into the car. Belinda had to peel her fingers from the door frame. Savannah climbed in beside her and patted her hand gently. She looked so young.

The doors locked as the car picked up speed. Li slumped against her.

"How would she have got out here?" Savannah asked.

"Do you think Gnasher had her as his woman or something?"

"Surely not?" Savannah said. "Ethan goes over there regularly. He'd know about it."

Belinda gave her a knowing look in the rear-view mirror.

The full extent of Savannah's foolishness hit her. Ethan probably did know about it. He was mates with Gnasher. It was just another of the secrets he kept. Goodness knows what poor Li had endured.

Ash was waiting at the gate with the dog.

Li whimpered as they drove through.

"Shhh," Savannah soothed. "We'll soon have you safe."

She glanced back. Ash was shutting the gate behind them.

Belinda drove on. Thick bush lined this part of the track leading into the Palmers' house.

"How's the horse?" Savannah asked.

"It died last night."

"Oh." How sad, Savannah thought.

They came to a fork in the track. She caught a glimpse of the house straight ahead. Belinda took the turn to the right and slowed to a stop beside a large shed that was almost completely obscured by trees and bush.

She looked back at Savannah. "I hope you don't mind but she's a bit of a mess. We've got this shed set up quite comfortably for over-flow visitors. Let's clean her up here and see what needs to be done before we take her to the house."

Savannah thought it odd but that was Belinda. If the house was as fancy on the inside as it looked from the outside, Savannah could imagine she wouldn't want any blood spilt there.

Once again Li's strength surprised her and it was a struggle to get her out of the car. Finally they got her into the shed. It smelt stale inside. A mix of food and human scent, like someone had been liv-ing in it. Belinda flicked a switch and several strip lights flickered to life. The walls of the shed were lined and there were no windows. A large caravan filled the space opposite the door. The shed was big enough to hold three caravans. There were a couple of chairs, a mat on the floor and a battered cupboard with a sink at the back but otherwise the rest of the large space was empty.

"I'll be right back," Belinda said. She stepped outside and shut the door. It rattled as if it was being locked.

Savannah let go of Li's arm and tried the handle. The door wouldn't open. She pushed it but it wouldn't budge. It was solid and thick. Not like the door on Jaxon's shed that was just made of tin.

"Belinda?" she called.

Outside the sound of the car engine was very faint even though it was close. She pressed her ear to the door. The car noise faded away.

Li moaned. Savannah turned around. Li was looking at her and shaking her head. Tears flowed down her cheeks. What was going on? Savannah looked for the sliding doors she'd seen from the out-side. They were covered up by whatever it was that lined the walls.

It appeared the only way in or out of the shed was through this one side door and that was locked. She hit the door with her arm and instantly regretted it as pain stabbed. Savannah leant her head against the door and pressed her arm to her chest.

"If only we could understand each other," she said.

She turned around but Li wasn't there. Across the shed the caravan door hung open.

CHAPTER

44

Ethan glanced down the drive as he went past. Savannah's car wasn't there. He hadn't expected it to be. She had a fitness class in Riverboat Point. Either that or she'd packed up and gone back to Adelaide. He wouldn't blame her if she had, but she'd said it was in her best interest to keep the business going. He didn't think she'd leave until Jaxon returned.

He parked his bike and let Jasper out. Together they went upstairs and had something to eat. Downstairs again Ethan gathered up everything he thought he'd need to fix the houseboat and took it all down to his tinnie. Jasper followed him and pranced around as he loaded the boat.

"Okay, mate." He patted Jasper on the head. "You can come too."

Jasper jumped aboard and went to the front of the boat. It wasn't until Ethan was away from the jetty that the dog sat and lifted his face to the wind. Ethan turned the tinnie upriver. He had a good look at Jaxon's place as he went. Three houseboats were tied up to the bank. Hopefully it wouldn't take too much effort to fix the fourth and have it back.

Both the bigger boats were booked to leave this afternoon, otherwise they could have substituted *River Magic* for *Riverboat*. He had a good look at Ash's sleek high-powered boat as he passed. Lucky he'd been there to help Savannah. Ethan gave a wry smile. Knowing how she felt about Ash she would have loved that.

He motored on, following the twists and turns of the river. He passed a couple of other houseboats moving downriver and his favourite fishing spot where he'd taken Savannah. What a difference a few days made. They'd been so happy then.

Finally he saw *Riverboat* up ahead. He tied up to the swim deck and Jasper leapt out ahead of him, nose to the deck. Ethan inspected the damage. Whoever had told Savannah it was a broken steering cable was correct. It looked like a straightforward job. He set to work.

Even though he was focused on the task at hand he couldn't help but think of Savannah, just like he had half the night and all the way to Adelaide and back. He kept seeing the hurt look on her face. When he'd agreed to support Jaxon's holiday plans by helping out his sister if needed, he'd thought there'd be little to it. The last thing he'd expected was to fall in love with her. And once he did he'd never meant to hurt her. If only Jaxon had come back everything would have been okay.

Ethan flexed his fingers. Although Savannah wouldn't have been speaking to him, if she'd been at home he would have asked her to come and help. Jasper was good company but another pair of hands would have made the job quicker. He glanced at his watch. He hoped she'd be back by the time he returned with *Riverboat*. It would take the two of them to have the boat ready to go out at three.

Ethan searched the front of Jaxon's place as he manoeuvred the houseboat into its place on the bank. He cut the engine and jumped to land so he could tie up the ropes. Jasper gave an excited bark and followed him. Still Savannah didn't come.

He went back on board, put out the gangplank and picked up a bundle of sheets. At least the last group had stripped the beds and the boat looked like it had been given the once-over. It wouldn't be too hard to clean but they didn't have much time.

As he walked up the path he realised Savannah's car still wasn't under the carport. He dropped the bundle of sheets at the end of the verandah and went to the back door. It was locked. He knocked.

"Savannah?" he called.

Jasper barked.

Ethan bent to pat his head.

"Where is she, mate?"

He went back around the front. The blinds were up but the door was locked. He peered inside. There was a mug on the table and one of her jumpers draped over a chair. He hoped that meant she hadn't left for good.

He set to work getting *Riverboat* ready for the next lot of customers. The shed was open so he could get to the clean linen. There was just enough to kit out the boat. Maybe she'd realised stocks were low and had gone to collect some.

Just after three the first cars began to arrive but there was still no sign of Savannah. A small worm of worry turned inside him.

By the time he'd welcomed everyone, showed them the ropes, taken their money and put each boatload through their paces before waving them off, he was frantic with worry. It wasn't like her. No matter what she thought of him or how angry she was with Jaxon, he just couldn't see her walking out on the customers.

He took his tinnie back to the jetty then went all around Jaxon's place again. Perhaps Savannah's car had broken down somewhere between here and town. He got on his bike and set out to look for her. He slowed at Gnasher's gate then took off again. She wouldn't be in there. Not with her car anyway. He passed the Palmers' gate. If she'd finally had an invitation to Belinda's place she would have come home on time.

He kept going. Each time he rounded a bend he hoped to see her car on the side of the road ahead. When he reached town he pulled over at the first corner. Now what? he wondered.

Ethan perched on a stool at the front bar of the pub cradling a beer. He'd been to Riverboat Point twice today. The first time he'd called in to the garage, the supermarket and the tea room asking after Savannah. No-one had seen her. He'd ridden home again and paced back and forth for an hour before he decided he needed a drink. There was none left in his fridge and Savannah's place was locked up so he'd made the journey back to town.

"Howdy."

Ethan glanced sideways. An old bloke had come and perched on the stool next to his. Ethan scowled at him then looked back at his beer. He put it to his mouth and emptied the glass.

"My name's Terry. They tell me you're a bit of a mechanic."

"Do they?"

"Any good with old cars?"

"Maybe."

"That new bloke at the servo has no idea."

"Look, mate. I've got a bit on my plate at the moment. Maybe another day, hey?"

"Suit yourself, but I've got a car needs fixing and I'm willing to pay good money to have it done."

Terry flipped over a coaster and picked up a pen from the bar. He scribbled down a number and slid the coaster towards Ethan.

"That's my number."

Terry picked up his glass and moved to the other end of the bar.

Sad really, they were the only two in the pub at this hour but Ethan wasn't in the mood to talk. Savannah had disappeared. She obviously didn't want to be found. He'd blown his chance with her.

"Another?"

The barman lifted his empty glass.

"Yes." Ethan put his money on the counter.

The barman poured him a schooner and placed it in front of him.

"Thanks," Ethan said and stared at the glass.

More people came in. He heard their voices around him but he ignored them. A child cried. Someone bumped him. Ethan edged away.

"Hello."

He ignored the female voice beside him.

"You're Savannah's neighbour, aren't you?"

At the mention of Savannah's name Ethan looked at the speaker. She was a good-looking woman, fit with dark curly hair and a bright smile.

"Ethan, is it?" the woman asked. "I'm Mandy Sampson. I was out your way yesterday helping Savannah clean."

Ethan straightened up. "Have you seen her today?" he asked.

"No."

"Aren't you one of the fitness group?"

"Yes, but Savannah didn't show today. She said it would depend on what happened with the broken-down houseboat. I assumed she was still having trouble."

A child came and pushed between Mandy and Ethan.

"Mum," he whined. "Dad said I can't have a coke."

"I'll get you a lemon squash in a moment. Go back to Dad." She looked at Ethan. "I'd better order these drinks," she said. "Troops are getting restless."

He watched while the barman served her. He swallowed his pride.

"Savannah's not home. Her car's gone. She didn't give you any clues about anywhere else she might have been planning to go today?"

Mandy frowned. "No. She had two boats to see off this afternoon. Don't you help her with that?"

"Yes."

Mandy held his gaze. "Wasn't she there?"

"No, but it was probably just a misunderstanding. I'll sort it out when I get back."

A child yelped behind them.

"I'd better keep moving." She added some numbers underneath Terry's on the coaster. "Give me a call if you need." She tucked her wallet under her arm and gathered the four drinks in her hands. "See you later," she said and returned to her family.

Ethan shoved the coaster in his back pocket. Not quite the same as the phone numbers he'd collected in the old days. Not that he wanted those days back. He wanted Savannah. He tipped down the rest of his drink. It was time to go home. He'd try Gnasher on the way just in case he'd seen her, but it was a slim chance.

Ethan hurried out to his bike and hoped like hell Savannah would be at her place when he got there.

CHAPTER
45

Savannah sat on the edge of the bed looking at the thin waif of a girl lying under the filthy blanket. She was used to the smell now. When she'd first followed Li into the van she'd retched at the rancid smell of vomit and faeces. She'd thought the girl Li leant over was dead but she'd stirred at the sound of Li's voice.

Savannah had helped Li clean her up as best they could. Li called her Hung and Savannah assumed it was her name. Her body was emaciated but even so Savannah could tell she wasn't a child but a young woman. There was cold water and soap but the towels and bedding were filthy. Savannah stripped the bed and they lay Hung on the mattress and covered her with the best of the sheets and blankets.

Now Savannah turned her attention to Li. She wasn't doing much better than the girl in the bed. The wound ran jaggedly around the top of her arm in an arc for several centimetres. It gaped open and the skin around it was crusted with blood and turning purple.

Savannah pulled off her singlet top. It was the cleanest thing she had to put over the wound. She inspected the series of puncture marks in Li's leg. They looked red and inflamed. Savannah frowned.

"Is this a dog bite?"

Li stared at her with dull eyes.

Savannah tapped her fingers and thumb together imitating a bite. "Did a dog bite you?"

Li's eyes responded. "Yes." She nodded vigorously. "Dog."

"Brutus no doubt." Savannah shuddered at the thought of the great ugly dog sinking its fangs into Li.

None of this made any sense. Savannah tried desperately to think of a reasonable explanation. All she was left with was a headache and a bad feeling. Belinda and Ashton were not the people they'd led her to believe they were. Then another thought struck her.

"How did you get out of here?"

Li looked at her and shook her head.

Savannah made all kinds of gestures with her hands. "Outside." She pointed through the caravan door. "How did you get outside?"

Li struggled to her feet and hobbled to the caravan door. She pointed across the shed to the outside door.

"Ash," she said and waved her hand sideways.

Savannah looked from the door to her hand. "Open," she said. "Ash left the door open?"

Li gave a little nod and Savannah sank back on the bed.

"No doubt he won't do that again." She slapped her fist into her palm. "Jaxon and his great ideas."

She thought about the message he'd left about the neighbours and how she'd fretted over which neighbours she had to watch out for. She snorted. Turned out none of them was much chop. She let out a short mirthless laugh.

Li watched her closely from the end of the other bed.

Savannah stood up and went outside. The air was fresher in the shed. She rubbed her hands up and down her bare arms. She got down on her knees on the concrete floor and looked under the van. The toilet and shower pipes went down into the concrete. Back on her feet she walked all around the shed. It was fully lined. She picked up a chair and struck the wall with it. Some kind of plasterboard had been used and it was solid. Not a lot of sound would get out and there wasn't anyone close enough to hear it.

Perhaps Belinda intended to leave them here until they starved to death. Li and her friend weren't too good already. Savannah shuddered at the thought of the three of them dying slowly. She was strong and healthy. She would be the last.

She had no idea of the time but her stomach told her she'd missed lunch. Ethan would be back by now. Perhaps he'd come looking for her. She let out a sigh. Why would he after last night? Still, he might begin to wonder if her car was there but she wasn't. If he went inside he'd see all her things and her phone. She'd left that on the table. Surely he'd expect her to be there to see off the houseboats. She wondered if it was three o'clock yet. Her spirits lifted a moment then dropped again. Even if he did go looking he'd never expect her to be in a soundproof shed somewhere in the middle of the Palmers' property.

Savannah walked the perimeter of the shed again. If she was going to get out and get medical help for the two women, it was all up to her. She stopped in front of the sink. The tap stuck out of the wall above it. The sink and the cupboard below it looked like the old style that had been in Jaxon's kitchen before he did it up.

She stared at it a moment then pulled open the middle door. The pipes had to go somewhere. She was greeted by a musty smell. A few old dishcloths and a bottle of detergent lay on the bottom shelf.

The thick L-shaped pipe that led from the sink disappeared through the shed wall just above the base of the cupboard. The pipe wiggled when she shook it. There was a dark stain around the plasterboard and several cuts ranged out from the hole around it.

She didn't know how much time she had before Belinda came back or even if she was coming back at all. Whichever the case, Savannah wasn't going to sit around to wait and see. She grabbed hold of the pipe and shook it vigorously from side to side. Her arms ached with the effort but she kept going and was rewarded when the L section of the pipe broke off. A trickle of putrid brown water slopped onto the base of the cupboard.

She picked up the wooden chair again and smashed it on the ground. Two legs broke off. She was conscious of Li standing in the door of the caravan watching her. Savannah took one of the chair legs and wedged it into the gap around the pipe in the wall. She wrenched it up and down and the plasterboard cracked. She pulled chunks of the rotten board away. Behind it, shafts of daylight streamed through holes in the tin. It didn't take Savannah long to break away enough of the board to make a hole big enough for her to climb through.

"All I need to do is chew my way through the tin and I'll be out." She laughed. The sound she made was loud in her own ears.

Li bobbed down beside her and peered into the cupboard. She reached in with her good arm and felt around then she said something Savannah didn't understand and pointed.

Savannah got onto her hands and knees and tried to see what Li was pointing at. She stuck her head right in the cupboard. The tin around the pipe hole looked different from the tin above it. It looked like a patch, as if a square had been cut out of the shed and covered over with a separate piece.

Savannah dragged the mat over to the edge of the cupboard. She lay on her back and put her feet in the cupboard, testing the patched area. Then she brought her right leg up to her chest and kicked out with all the force she could muster. The tin popped out like a cap off a bottle. Savannah got back on her hands and knees. She'd made a hole big enough for her to squeeze through.

Li squatted beside her and looked fearfully into Savannah's eyes. "Dog," she said.

Savannah peered out through the gap. The light was gloomy. Perhaps it was late afternoon. She must have made a racket knocking that tin off but Brutus didn't appear. She hoped he was sleeping or tied up or even inside the house. Anywhere but near her.

Li got up and went back to the caravan.

"Dog," she said again.

Savannah was glad she wanted to stay. Their only hope was for Savannah to get away and get help. Li was in no shape to run and climb fences.

She gestured to Li. "I'll get help," she said.

Then, before her courage left her, she stuck her head through the gap.

The sharp metal edge of the tin dug into Savannah's arms and shins as she pulled herself through the hole. She clenched her teeth against the pain and struggled to her feet. The cool air raised goosebumps on her skin. A sports bra and running pants were not enough covering in the late afternoon. She felt a tickle on her leg and looked down to see blood running down to her socks from the grazes on her legs. Behind her she heard the cupboard shut.

"Good thinking, Li," she murmured. If anyone came to check it might take them a bit more time to realise she was missing.

Savannah took in her surroundings. She was standing in thick bush. There was no sign of Brutus. If Ash or Belinda were keeping an eye on the shed door they wouldn't see her. Savannah had no idea of her bearings. And she didn't know how much time she had. She couldn't stay still.

The track would lead her back to the gate but she would be exposed in the open. Shivers ran down her arms. She hugged herself. The scrapes on her arms stung under her fingers. It was time to get moving. She took a deep breath and edged along the shed wall to the side away from the door.

She peered around the corner. There was a general smattering of bush and trees between her and what she imagined would be the Palmers' other side fence. If she could get off their property and put a fence between her and Brutus she might be able to follow the fence line to the road.

She set off, moving from tree to tree, bush to bush in a stop–start fashion. Each time she reached a spot where she felt she had enough cover she paused and listened. At one point she heard a vehicle behind her. It sounded close enough to be on the property.

When it stopped she moved. Thicker bush blocked her way but she pushed through it. Branches scratched the bare skin of her arms and her midriff. Finally she burst into a clearing. Her hand flew to her mouth to smother her scream. On the ground, stretched out in front of her, lay the dead horse. It was a bag of bones and in spite of the cool air, flies buzzed all around it. Beyond the horse was a huge hole.

Savannah kept her hand over her mouth. She staggered around the hole, passed the mound of dirt that had come out of it and dropped into the safety of the trees on the other side. She squatted, bracing her back against a trunk and retched. There was nothing in her stomach to come up but a bit of spit. She licked her lips. She was so thirsty.

She couldn't get the picture of the horse out of her head. Then she remembered Ethan's practical message. Everything has to die eventually. She pushed herself up with the support of the tree. With what she knew about Ash and Belinda, the words no longer reassured her. She got the feeling with them death would be sooner rather than later.

Savannah took two deep breaths and started off again. Her shins were burning from the cuts of the tin and her left leg was beginning to jag with spears of pain. She stumbled. To her left she caught glimpses of the river. She paused to get her bearings. There was no sign of any boundary fence. A terrible thought registered. What if the Palmers' property went on and on? Perhaps it had been a mistake to head in the opposite direction to her car and her phone.

Behind her came the sound she'd hoped not to hear – a deep bark from Brutus. It was impossible to tell where or how far away he was but Savannah knew he would find her quickly if he was looking for her. Just as he had led Ash and Belinda to Li this morning.

The bark came again, closer this time. Savannah made a split-second decision. She turned towards the river and hoped like hell Brutus wouldn't follow her into the water.

Her steps were stilted now. Brutus barked again, closer. She forced herself to move faster. Sticks and thick grass hindered her. A branch whipped her face, another scraped across her stomach. She staggered past the last of the thinning trees to the muddy bank.

Savannah baulked at the huge expanse of water in front of her. She glanced at the trees behind. There was no going back. She took two steps forward, stopped and then fled into the river at another bark from Brutus. Much closer now. The water was freezing. The gasp caught in her throat. Under her runners the bottom felt soft. She waded out and tried to swim but the current took her. She was cold and her feet felt like lead inside her shoes.

A loud bark and a splash sounded behind her. She looked over her shoulder. Brutus propped on the edge of the river. He barked furiously.

Savannah ducked her head under the water. She held her breath for as long as she could then came up gasping for air. Her heart pounded in her chest. When she looked back Brutus was much further away. She let herself relax and go with the flow of the river. From her position on her back she saw Ash burst from the trees. She took a breath, twisted and ducked under the water again.

When she came up the next time, the jetty where his boats were tied up was between Ash and her. She trusted that meant he couldn't see her. She rolled onto her back again and let herself be carried along by the water. All the while she watched the bank expecting to see Belinda or Ash looking for her. She hoped Li and her friend were all right. If Savannah could just make it back to her place she could phone for help. Maybe Ethan would be there. How pleased would she be to see him right now?

Her face sank below the water and she came up spluttering. She reached down and worked at her shoes to get them off her feet. After several dips under water they came free. She gave a momentary thought to their cost then banished it. What did it matter? It was more than likely she'd disappear under the water with them, never to be found again. She could hardly feel her arms and legs and her body felt so heavy. Savannah closed her eyes. She was tired and very, very cold.

CHAPTER
46

Savannah crawled out of the water and lay sprawled on the sandy bank at the bottom of the path to Jaxon's shack. She dug her fingers in the sand, grateful to be there. She rolled onto her back and closed her eyes until shivers racked her body with such force they frightened her into action. She needed to warm up. She tried to stand but her legs wouldn't support her properly. She half crawled, half hobbled up the path.

At the end of the drive she tried to stand again. Her stomach convulsed and she retched. All she could taste was river water. She dragged herself across the lawn to the glass doors. They were locked.

She muttered a string of language through teeth clenched so hard together her jaw ached. She made her way around the house pausing a minute to stare blankly at the space under the carport where her car should have been. The shudders coursed through her body with such force they hurt. She struggled along the back verandah. The back door was locked as well. She huddled against it. She was sure she hadn't locked it when she'd gone out for her run this morning but that seemed so long ago. Maybe she had. Defeat threatened to engulf her. Then she pushed away from the door.

There was a spare key in the shed. Mustering her strength, she crossed the back lawn. She tripped and stumbled over the hose in the fading light. Jasper barked and she jumped in fright. She looked hopefully in the direction of Ethan's place but there was no bike and no lights. No help would arrive unless she called for it. She forced herself to keep moving.

She was so relieved when the shed door swung open. She dug her fingers into the hidey-hole. The key fell from her numb fingers. She picked it up and made her way back to the shack.

It took her several attempts to get the key in the lock but finally she was inside. She tugged the key out and latched the door behind her. She grabbed a towel to wrap around herself as she passed the bathroom on her way to get her phone. The dining table was empty except for a mug and Jaxon's stupid motorbike statue.

She tried to focus as she rubbed the towel vigorously all over her body. Where was her phone? She unlocked the sliding door and checked the outside table. No phone. Then she remembered Jaxon's landline. She didn't need a mobile to call for help. She stumbled back inside towards the office.

"I thought you'd end up back here if you didn't drown."

Savannah stopped. She thought her ears were playing tricks on her. She turned slowly. The towel slid to the floor and her heart skipped a beat. Belinda was standing just inside the door with something in her hand.

"Is that a ...?"

"Gun." Belinda waved the weapon in Savannah's direction. "Yes, it is."

It looked like a kid's plastic toy.

"I'm sorry it's come to this, Savvie, but you've caused me some grief today." Belinda's lips turned up in the tight smile that Savannah now knew was false.

"I can't let you spoil everything," she said. "That silly little bitch Li nearly did."

Savannah gripped the table for support. "You haven't … you haven't …" She stared at the gun.

"Killed her? No." Belinda gave a horrible cackle. "She and her friend are already not long for this world. I won't have to waste a bullet on them."

Savannah's brain went to fudge. She'd promised Li she'd help her and now she'd end up being no help at all.

"Whereas you, my dear friend, are way too fit." Belinda waved the gun slowly up and down. "You might need some help to disappear."

"We're friends, aren't we?" Savannah still couldn't believe this other side to Belinda was real.

Belinda gave a snort. "I had to get close to you. You were easier to take in than that brother of yours."

"Jaxon?" Savannah's heart leapt. Had Belinda killed him?

"If he'd just stuck to his electrical business – houseboats bring too many people. Our quiet patch of the river was getting far too busy. Ash started tinkering with the boats. We thought it might put Jaxon and his customers off but he got suspicious. Then gullible little you came along."

Her words stabbed at Savannah. She'd been taken in by Belinda. It was just like the pretty girls back at school who thought it would be fun to have a fat friend. She had thought they were her friends just like she'd believed Belinda to be, but they were cruel. Sucked in again, Savannah.

"There's a good view of your place from the top deck of those houseboats," Belinda went on. "I kept watch while Ash did whatever he could to sabotage the boats."

"You sat in the chair?"

"Did I leave one out? That was careless."

"The signs, and ..."

"The toilet paper." Belinda cackled. "I thought that one up. The steering cable was Ash. He's into the mechanics of boats. The gunshot wasn't one of his better ones. He thought people would blame Gnasher and get a bit hysterical."

Savannah gave a brief thought to her suspicions. It all fell into place now.

"Unfortunately Ethan came to your rescue," Belinda said, "but I was working on that."

Savannah gasped.

"What? You didn't think he fancied you, did you? You've got a nice set of boobs, Savvie, but you're no match for me. Ash was supposed to suck you in but he's never one to be charming. You've mucked it all up with your attempt at rescuing Li."

Savannah's head was spinning. Not only had Ethan used her but he'd been helping Belinda. She sagged against the table. They'd joked together about Belinda and Ash but the joke was on her. And he'd said he'd spoken to Jaxon but maybe it was an elaborate hoax. Her holiday at the river had turned into a bad fairytale. Everything she'd thought was real was fake. Jaxon's warning about the neighbours really did include them all.

"Gnasher and Li?" she asked.

"I wouldn't waste one of my girls on that stupid old man. Hopefully he was drunk enough he won't even remember he saw her. The girls are my imports. Brought into the country to please my clients." Belinda's eyes narrowed. "Trouble is those two bitches were too smart for their own good. Wouldn't do as they were told. Had to get rid of them." She waved the gun. "And now you. Lucky I got Ashton to dig such a big hole."

Savannah gaped at her.

"No-one's going to think to look for two illegal immigrants under a dead horse." Belinda's red lips curved up into a ghoulish smile. "Or for a nosy neighbour who leaves a note saying life's not worth living."

Although she was already chilled to the bone, a deeper shiver shuddered through Savannah. She flinched as Belinda made a sudden move to the right.

"Put this on." Belinda tossed her jumper at her.

It slipped through Savannah's fingers to the table. The fabric had felt warm against her skin. She couldn't resist picking it up and pulling it on. With the warmth she felt something turn inside her. Savannah had already come across more than her share of two-faced people. She'd been through too much in her life to lose it to this cow. She wasn't going to be the victim again.

Belinda took her phone from her jacket pocket.

In the gloom beyond the door, Savannah glimpsed a movement. She was surprised to see Jasper watching intently, his ears pricked. An idea began to form in her muddled brain.

"Ash will come once I call him," Belinda said. "Don't want you distracting him with your half-naked body. That's how Li got away. Bloody men. Always thinking with their –"

"No, no, no!" Savannah yelled with all her might. She snatched up the motorbike and threw it.

The statue hit Belinda on the shoulder and bounced against the glass. Jasper leapt through the open door with a growl and latched onto Belinda's hand. She screamed and the gun and the phone fell to the floor.

Savannah pushed them out of the way with her foot.

"Good job, Jasper," she said while frantically trying to think what to do next.

"Yes, good job, Jasper. Sit."

Belinda and Savannah both gaped at the apparition that stepped through the door.

"Gnasher?" Savannah croaked. He was dressed in khaki with bits of bush hanging off him. There were streaks of something black on his face and his funny floppy hat had more bush on it. In his hands he held a rifle.

"Looks like you don't need my help here," he said to Savannah.

"I'm glad to see you," she said. She was unsure of his mental state but he was clearly on her side for now.

Belinda edged to the door and Gnasher raised his rifle to her nose. "Sit down," he said. And she did.

Savannah felt a nudge at her fingers. Jasper sat at her feet among the broken pieces of Jaxon's statue. She looked down into the dog's deep, kind eyes. She squatted and threw her arms around his neck. He was warm and soft. Tears brimmed in her eyes. She'd been frightened of him all this time and it turned out he was her one true friend. She looked beyond him to Gnasher with his gun pointed at Belinda. Maybe she could count two friends on the river.

CHAPTER

47

Ethan slowed at Savannah's drive and relief flooded through him. Every light in the shack was on and Belinda's car was under the carport. Savannah must have been with Belinda all along. Her absence was probably to punish him for his duplicity and who could blame her.

He'd just call in to see her for himself, hand over the money for the houseboats and head off. He parked his bike under the carport and walked around to the front. As he drew level with the sliding doors he stopped. The blinds were pulled up and the scene inside was like some kind of bizarre tea party.

Savannah, Belinda and Gnasher were all sitting around the table. Savannah was wrapped in a thick blanket with that weird beanie on her head, clutching a mug. A gun and a phone sat on the table in front of her. Gnasher had dressed himself up as if he was on manoeuvres.

Jasper was at Savannah's feet but he rose as soon as he noticed Ethan through the glass. Savannah looked up, Gnasher turned and it was then that Ethan saw his rifle. It was pointed at Belinda. Her hands were tied to the back of the chair with a tie. Ethan recognised it. Jaxon had worn it to a fundraiser in Riverboat Point just before he'd left. Her feet were tied, one to each chair leg, with garbage bags.

Ethan slid the door open slowly. He didn't want to make any sudden moves that might upset Gnasher. Jasper came to meet him.

"Someone want to tell me what's going on here?"

"At last," Belinda gushed. "You've come to save me. These two have become quite delusional."

"Shuddup!" Gnasher snarled.

She pursed her lips and glowered at him.

Gnasher turned to Ethan. His eyes were focused and clear.

"Seems we've had some human traffickers in our midst," he said. "Scum of the earth." He looked like he was going to spit then thought better of it.

Ethan scratched his head. "Who?"

"Belinda here and that pasty-faced brother of hers. I've always thought they snuck about too much."

That was rich coming from Gnasher but Ethan let it go. He turned his attention to Savannah.

"Are you okay?"

"Yes," she said. "Although there's no longer any need to pretend that you care."

Her voice was as cold as steel. Surely she was taking her anger with him too far.

She looked exhausted huddled under the blanket, her fingers clenched around the cup.

Ethan could see it was empty.

"Mind if I make a coffee?" he asked.

Savannah stared into her empty cup.

"I'll have one too thanks, Digger," Gnasher said brightly. He was enjoying himself.

"I'd have one but I seem to be tied up." Belinda jigged her shoulders up and down.

"Shut up, scum," Gnasher said. He waved the rifle under her nose. Belinda glared back at him but remained silent.

Ethan moved slowly to the kitchen and boiled the kettle. He brought back a coffee for him and one for Gnasher.

He could see Savannah was shivering under the blanket.

"How about I make you another?" He reached for her cup.

She gripped it tightly then let him take it.

He brought back the steaming mug of tea and placed it in front of her beside the gun. Then he sat. Now there were four of them around the table. Ethan looked from Savannah to Gnasher.

"So, is someone going to fill me in?" he asked.

"I was on a bender last night. Woke up this morning to find a Vietnamese woman staring at me. She was dripping blood and yabbering. I thought she was VC come to get me. Fired a shot into the air to scare her off. Savannah here turns up and takes the girl away. I went bush, curled up under a tree and slept it off."

Savannah leaned towards him. "What made you come over here?"

"Once I'd had a bite to eat and my head cleared I realised I hadn't imagined it all. There were drops of blood on my kitchen floor. I was worried. If she was VC you might be in trouble." He shifted his rifle closer to Belinda again. "Turns out you were in a different kind of trouble. I was almost too late. Lucky Jasper was on to it."

"I was glad to see both of you," Savannah said.

"No VC here, mate," Ethan said.

"I know that." Gnasher looked him squarely in the eye.

"Why don't you put the rifle down for now? The prisoner's secure."

Gnasher nodded. He propped the rifle against his chair within easy reach.

Ethan bent down and ruffled the ears of his dog. Jasper lay stretched out between him and Savannah.

"What have you been up to, mate?"

"I saw him outside. I don't know what made him come but I was glad to see him." Savannah spoke softly. She was staring into her cup. "I remembered that day when we … when we were painting and he thought I was attacking you. He came to your rescue. I hoped he might do the same for me."

Ethan felt a surge of pride in his chest. "And he did."

She nodded but didn't look at him.

"Talk about soppy cosy neighbours," Belinda snapped. "You lot deserve each other."

"Shut up, Belinda." Ethan and Gnasher spoke in unison.

She turned her piercing stare on Ethan but said nothing.

He took a mouthful of coffee and studied Savannah. Her face was pale and her lips had a blue tinge. She still wouldn't look at him.

'Where did you take the girl, Sav?" he asked gently.

A look of horror crossed her face and she leapt to her feet. "Li," she said. "I should go and get her out."

"Out of where?"

"Belinda has her locked in a shed."

"Sit down, girlie," Gnasher said. "Ambos are on their way. Let them deal with it."

"But Ash —"

"Won't do anything unless he hears from Belinda," Gnasher said. "And you have her phone."

The blanket fell away from Savannah's legs. She was wearing a pair of three-quarter running pants and below that, on her shins were long red gashes. Her feet were bare.

"What happened to you, Sav?" Ethan asked.

She looked down at her legs as if she was puzzled to see them.

"Belinda had her locked in the shed with this Li and her friend," Gnasher said. "Savannah cut her way out and swam back here to get help."

"Stupid bitch," Belinda snarled. "You were so needy it was easy to suck you in. I read you like a book. Knew you'd come straight back here."

Savannah turned on Belinda. "You're the one tied up waiting for the police to arrive," she snapped. "You're going to pay big time for all the misery you've caused Li and the other women you've treated like bits of disposable rubbish." Savannah put her hands on the table and leant across at Belinda. "I hope they lock you up and throw away the key."

"You go, girlie," Gnasher cheered.

"Listen," Ethan said. He could hear the deep throb of a helicopter.

Alarm spread over Gnasher's face. He hunched his shoulders and picked up his rifle.

"Friendlies, Gnasher," Ethan said.

Then they heard the sirens and a boat on the river. A bright light swung along the bank below them.

"Help's here," Ethan said. Gnasher maintained his guard but Savannah's shoulders drooped and the blanket fell. There was mud on her pants and her jumper was undone. He could see her skin underneath it was muddy and her bra a murky brown. She must still be in the clothes she swam in. She started to shake.

"Sav, you need a warm shower," he said.

She picked up the blanket and wrapped it around herself again then she turned her determined look on him.

"Not till I know Li's safe," she said.

"At least take your wet clothes off."

She sat down and tugged off her running pants oblivious to the rest of them. She dropped them on the floor then wrapped the blanket tightly around herself again.

"Happy now?" she said.

Ethan could see she would take no more notice of him. Hopefully they'd learn soon enough of Li's fate.

The sirens grew louder and outside red and blue lights flashed off every surface. Gnasher swung his gaze from Belinda to the bright lights outside.

"All okay now, Gnasher mate," Ethan said. "Help has arrived."

CHAPTER
48

Savannah's heart hammered. She sat bolt upright. Light filtered in around the edges of the curtains. She'd been in a deep sleep but something had woken her. She listened. There was nothing more than the usual morning sounds of the river waking up to a new day. She lay back on the bed.

She wished she could write the last two days off as a bad dream but she couldn't. At least Li would be all right although there was concern about her friend. Hung's condition was critical.

The police had questioned Savannah then handed her over to the ambos. She'd been diagnosed with mild hypothermia and made to take a warm shower and put on dry clothes. She had Belinda to thank for the warm jumper and that, along with the blanket and the tea, had kept the worst of it at bay. Ethan's insistence she take off her wet running pants probably helped as well. She rolled over and pulled the pillow over her head. She didn't want to think about him.

The police had been so good. That first night, once everyone had left, they told her they'd have someone watching her house. They'd taken both Belinda and Ash into custody but it turned out they were already people of interest to the police along with their father and a few others. With a female police officer outside she'd finally crawled into bed in the early hours of the morning. She'd slept until the police had called to question her again. They'd found her car in another shed on the Palmers' property but she couldn't have it back for a few days yet. After that the visitors began arriving, carefully vetted at the gate by the police officer.

Mandy was first. Riverboat Point was abuzz with the news – everything from Savannah being whisked away to hospital in a helicopter to Belinda and Ash making amphetamines in their house. Mandy had come to sort out the fact from the fiction. She'd also whipped around the shack and given it a clean and brought fresh bread, milk and a homemade cake.

Next came Faye. She had flowers and a tray of Nell and Bob's pasties. They sent her their love. Savannah hoped she'd told the story well enough for the rumours to be replaced by the facts around town but she wasn't holding her breath.

Ethan called in as well. It was awkward between them. He didn't stop long. Just wanted to check she was okay. Jasper stayed on her front verandah for a couple of hours, sleeping in the sun.

Reporters tried to come onto the property but the police shut her front gate. There were helicopters buzzing overhead and extra boats out the front. Jaxon's phone kept ringing. She let it go to the answering machine. She kept the blinds half closed and stayed inside all day. When she flicked through the television channels she caught glimpses of the shack from the river and overhead shots. The smashing of a major people trafficking ring was big news. All Savannah felt was exhaustion. She was grateful when the sun went down last night. She'd taken Jaxon's phone off the hook, turned off her mobile and fallen into a deep sleep when her head touched the pillow.

Today she wasn't sure what to do. She hoped the reporters would have moved on to something new so she could go outside. She needed fresh air and she wanted to visit Gnasher, see how he was getting on.

The back door rattled. Savannah sat up again. It was locked but it meant someone was in her yard. Maybe Ethan? The door opened. Her heart raced. She knew it had been locked, she'd double checked all the doors and windows before she'd gone to bed.

She jumped out of bed and picked up her dumbbell.

"Sav," a familiar voice called. "Are you in there?"

She dropped the dumbbell onto the bed and stepped around the door.

"Jaxon!"

"I'm home." He held out his hands in a "ta-da" pose.

"You should never have left," she snapped.

She pulled a jumper over her pyjamas and pushed past him to the sink.

"I thought you'd be pleased to see me."

"I'm glad you're back," she said and flicked on the kettle. "But I'd rather not be seeing you."

"That's a bit harsh."

Savannah glared at him. He looked tanned and relaxed. His fair wavy hair had grown long, giving him a surfy appearance.

"Where have you been, Jaxon?"

"On holiday." He held his arms out wide again. "You managed the houseboats okay, didn't you?"

"Managed! What possessed you to set me up like that? I've had to put my life on hold to look after your business so you could play whatever game you were up to. I knew nothing about houseboats. Then there was Ethan. Getting your supposed friend to pretend to like your sister was a terrible idea. I could throttle you, Jaxon."

"Whoa, Sav, take it easy," he said when she finally paused for breath.

"Take it easy! Your bloody neighbours were running a people smuggling racket using next door as a halfway house." Savannah shoved a teabag into her mug and poured the hot water.

"Yeah. The police told me on the way in, after I proved to them who I was. The road's a bottleneck." Jaxon made himself a coffee. "I did think there was something odd about Belinda and Ashton."

"Odd!"

"Brother and sister yet almost like a married couple." He rolled his eyes. "Creepy. That's why I left that stuff in my notes. I knew you'd work it out, Sav. You're like a ferret – when there's a mystery to be solved you're on to it and you don't let emotion cloud the issue."

"I could have been killed."

"Surely that's a bit extreme," he said.

"It was serious, Jaxon." Savannah put her hands to her hips. "Ashton Palmer is an evil man and Belinda is even worse. The police have had their eye on them for a while. They nicknamed Belinda the Ice Queen. I thought her drinking habits were bad enough but evidently she lures men to do her bidding and also likes to use drugs."

Jaxon shook his head. "I'm sorry, Sav. I never expected all this to happen. I'm glad everything turned out okay." He strolled over to the couch and kicked off his boots. "Thanks for looking after the place so well. How did you get on with Ethan?"

Savannah opened her mouth to speak then closed it and shook her head.

"I'm going to have a shower," she said.

When she came out of the bathroom he was watching the TV.

"We're famous," he said. "That's my place there." He waved the remote at the screen. "Your sleuthing sure put Riverboat Point on the map."

Savannah ignored him and went to get dressed. The last thing she pulled on was her hoodie. In the kitchen she wrapped up a couple of Nell's pasties.

Jaxon came to see what she was doing.

"What'd you do to my statue?" he groaned and walked past her to the window sill where she'd left the pieces of broken motorbike.

"I broke it trying to save my life." Savannah glared at him. "Is that okay with you?"

Jaxon gave her a remorseful look. "Yeah. Of course. It's just that it was kind of special. Mum gave it to me."

Just for a moment he looked like a little boy. Savannah wanted to wrap her arms around him.

"They look good," he said poking at the plastic around the pasties. "Are they Nell's?"

Savannah smacked his fingers away.

"There are more in the fridge."

She put the pasties in her backpack then headed to the back door.

"Where are you going?" Jaxon called.

"Out."

"I wouldn't. There are still a lot of reporters and sightseers out there."

Savannah shut the door on him. She had already thought about that. She wanted to see Gnasher. If she went through Ethan's yard and over his side fence she was in the reserve. She could walk through that till she got to Gnasher's boundary.

The minute her feet were in Ethan's yard Jasper was sniffing at her. She gave him a pat.

"Sorry, buddy," she said. "These pasties aren't for you."

"I don't suppose they're for me either?"

Savannah spun at the sound of Ethan's voice. She hadn't seen his bike so she'd assumed he was out. He came out of the shed wiping his hands on a rag.

"They're for Gnasher. I'm cutting through the reserve to get to his place."

"Was that Jaxon's bike I heard?"

"Yes."

"I'm glad he's home."

He held her gaze a moment. He had an unreadable look on his face.

"I'll come with you to Gnasher's," he said.

"I don't need someone to hold my hand."

"I know you don't but I'd like to see Gnasher too. He won't be liking all this noise and the helicopters really freak him out."

"Okay."

"I'll just put Jasper in his yard. Gnasher has a few booby traps that can catch out the unwary."

They set off together. A couple of times Savannah found Ethan steering them in a slightly different direction than she would have taken. She had to admit if she'd been on her own she probably would have got lost. She didn't like the sound of the booby traps either.

She let Ethan help her over the fence into Gnasher's property then she followed him carefully through the bush until they came out halfway along the track that led in from the road.

Ethan paused when they reached the clearing. All the tarpaulins across the front of Gnasher's shed were rolled down.

"Friendly incoming," he called.

They stopped and listened. After all the noise of the last few days it was relatively quiet here.

"Gnasher," Savannah called. "Can we come in?"

"No-one stopping you."

She looked at Ethan. He raised an eyebrow then led the way to one of the tarps that had a loose flap. He lifted it for her and she stooped under and inside.

Savannah put the pasties on the table then turned slowly, taking in the huge space. She'd hardly taken any notice when she'd been here with Li. Where Gnasher stood in the back corner of the shed there was the beginnings of an internal wall but the rest was like a large open-plan house. Each area set out as a room but with no walls. She was glad there were no doors across the front either. It would have felt too closed in after her time in Belinda's shed.

"I like this idea," she said brightly. "You can change the space to suit."

"You're a smart woman," Gnasher said. He put down his hammer to shake her hand. "Not many people understand the potential."

"How've you been?" Ethan asked.

"Keeping busy."

"Are you building this wall?" Savannah asked.

"No-one else around," Gnasher said.

"Gnasher's a carpenter by trade." Ethan rubbed his hand along the beam that would obviously become a shelf. "A darn good one."

"I've got a job for a carpenter," Savannah said. "Well, Jaxon might."

"Is he back?" Gnasher asked.

"This morning."

"He knows when to turn up," Gnasher said. He scratched his chin. "Listen, how's that young girl getting on? The one that turned up here."

"I believe she's doing well. She should recover but I don't know what the future holds for her."

"I never meant her any harm you know," he said.

"I know. It must have been a shock having her turn up out of the blue like that."

"How're you getting on with the TV?" Ethan changed the subject.

"Not watching it."

"Pity to miss all that good footy," Ethan said. "Another cracker of a game coming up this weekend."

"If it was just the footy I would, but all those ads about people's lives and crap and then the ones about car crashes and depression and cancer. It's enough to drive a man to drink. I don't want to watch that."

Savannah inspected the set-up he had. It looked brand new.

"Is your DVD recorder connected?" she asked.

"Yeah but I may as well just listen to it on my tranny as watch it after it's over."

"You could just watch it slightly delayed."

Gnasher frowned at her.

"Set it to record, leave it ten minutes or so and then watch it. When it gets to the ads, press fast forward. It won't be quite in sync with the live game but almost."

Gnasher's frown changed to a grin.

"Why didn't I think of that?" Ethan said.

"You've got no brains. That's why you're a digger." Gnasher slapped him on the back and laughed.

Savannah showed Gnasher the pasties and they left him a happy man.

They didn't speak on the way back but when they climbed into Ethan's yard he stopped and waited for her.

"Mind if I come over and see Jaxon?"

"Do what you like. It's a free country."

Savannah's words were snappish but that's how she felt. Damn the pair of them. They were welcome to each other's company. She sure didn't want it.

CHAPTER
49

Ethan knocked on Jaxon's back door, a sixpack under his arm. Footsteps sounded then the door flew open.

"Ethan, buddy." Jaxon wrapped him in a hug and slapped his back. "Good to see you. Glad you came prepared. It's a bit of a dry show here."

"Thought I'd come and see how your holiday went." It was just an excuse really, another faint chance that he might get Savannah to see reason. He was a bit annoyed with Jaxon himself. It wasn't his fault the Palmers were rotten but it could have been very bad for his sister.

"I spent most of my time on the east coast of New South Wales. Learnt to surf. It was wild."

They popped the tops of their beers.

"Cheers, mate," Jaxon said. "I appreciate the help you gave Sav." He jerked his head over his shoulder and lowered his voice. "She's in the bedroom. Not talking."

"I can hear you, Jaxon."

"You can't hate me too much," he called. "You're still here."

"I've got no car or I would have left as soon as you got home." She pulled open the door. "Is there one of those for me?"

"Sure," Ethan said and handed over a bottle.

She waited for them to sit on the couch then went and sat on a chair at the table.

Ethan stood up and tugged his wallet from his back pocket. "I've got some money from the boats that went out Tuesday," he said. "With everything that happened I forgot about it."

"I'm sure I owe you more than that," Jaxon said taking the money. "I'll sort all that out later."

"You got the boat fixed then?" Savannah said.

"I did," Ethan said.

"What was wrong with it?" Jaxon asked.

"You would have had to clean it by yourself as well," Savannah said.

"The group that were on board when it broke down had done a good job. It wasn't too hard."

"What was wrong with it?" Jaxon repeated.

"Snapped steering cable." Savannah and Ethan answered in unison.

"Belinda delighted in telling me how they'd been sabotaging the boats." Savannah glared at Ethan. "Ashton did the dirty work while she kept watch on the shack from the sundeck of one of the houseboats." She turned to Jaxon. "She told me all this while she was pointing a gun at my head."

"I always did think there was something hard about her," Jaxon said. "She hadn't reckoned with running up against my sister though."

Ethan was still thinking about the sabotage and how he'd thought Savannah was being paranoid.

"I'm sorry I brushed aside your concerns," he said.

"The police found the missing signs in the shed with my car," she said.

"I'm sorry," he mumbled.

"I noticed those homemade ones on the way in," Jaxon said. "Who made them?"

"We did." They spoke in unison again.

Jaxon raised his beer in a salute. "They look good."

He knocked some envelopes from the arm of the couch with his elbow then bent down to gather them up.

"I picked up the mail on my way through town. There are two letters here addressed to you, Sav."

"Who would write to me here?"

Jaxon passed them to her. The first one was quite thick. She turned it over and frowned. "Jan Warner. Why does that name ring a bell?"

"Jan and Fred," Jaxon said. "They've been regular customers."

"Not anymore," Ethan murmured, taking in the look of thunder on Savannah's face.

"Bloody Fred," she snarled.

"What's wrong with Fred?" Jaxon asked. "He enjoys the houseboat life. Drinks a bit much but he's harmless."

"Harmless!" Savannah glared at her brother. "His attitude was bad enough but he lied. He said they'd hardly used any fuel and they had."

"Hope you took it out of his bond?"

"He didn't pay his bond."

Jaxon frowned at her. "Why not?"

"He was my first customer and I forgot. He said he did too. Anyway, that wasn't the worst of it was it, Ethan?"

Ethan shook his head, surprised she had suddenly included him.

"He looked me in the eye," Savannah continued, "and said they'd left the boat in clean condition. One bathroom was putrid and there was a hole in the wall where the toilet roll holder had been pulled out."

"Doesn't sound like Fred," Jaxon said. "What's Jan say?"

Savannah ripped open the envelope. A letter fell out.

"Hell," she said. "There's a wad of notes in here." She held them up.

Ethan studied her as she glanced over the page. She was looking more like her old self. There was colour back in her cheeks and her eyes were bright. He wished he was sitting beside her. He watched as she counted the money.

"Five hundred dollars!"

"Risky to send through the post," Ethan said.

"They've never done that before," Jaxon said. "Always used cheques."

Savannah glanced at the letter again. "Basically she's apologising. Said Fred had overdone things on the last night."

"Got pie-eyed," Jaxon said.

"He'd told her he'd cleaned up the mess he'd made in the bathroom but he'd recently admitted to her that he hadn't and that perhaps he hadn't left enough money for fuel either." Savannah looked up. "I sent him a bill. He obviously didn't show that to his wife."

"Sounds like Fred was a bit naughty," Jaxon said.

Savannah blew out a breath. "You reckon. Anyway, the wall still has to be fixed. I patched it with some cardboard but you'll need to get it fixed properly. I wondered if Gnasher might do it. He's quite handy by the look of things."

"Who do you think did most of the renovations on this shack?" Jaxon said.

She picked up the other letter and Ethan watched her face light up in a smile. She looked across at him. "This is a thankyou card from Emily and the girls."

"Who's Emily?" Jaxon asked.

"The bride-to-be," Savannah said and laughed. "That was such a good weekend."

"What do they say?" Ethan got up and crossed to look over her shoulder.

"Your body gets a mention." She smiled up at him.

"So it should."

"I think they thought I'd hired you specially for the occasion."

Ethan put a hand on her shoulder. She didn't shift away.

"I knew it!"

They both looked up as Jaxon leapt to his feet.

"You two are being so cool but you can't fool me," he said. "You hooked up, didn't you?"

Savannah stood up, knocking Ethan's hand away. She turned to face him, the steel back in her eyes.

"Just a holiday fling," she said.

He stood his ground and kept his eyes on hers. "Not for me."

She frowned.

He took her hands. They were warm and soft, just like the rest of her.

"You were right about all the stuff with the Palmers but not about me. What you see is what you get. I'm not pretending. I love you, Sav."

Ethan put his hands to her face and placed his lips on hers.

"Yes! Yes! Yes!" Jaxon jumped around, pumping the air.

They both turned to him. "Shut up, Jaxon," they said in unison.

"But my plan worked."

"Your plan?" Savannah said.

"I knew if I could get you to stay here for a while you'd love the river, Sav. And you do, I can tell."

"That was why you went away?" Savannah said. "Just to get me here?"

"Yes." Jaxon hopped from foot to foot. "But I also knew you'd have to work with Ethan. You two have so much in common. You've both had tough times in the past. You're both bits of loners. I knew you were meant for each other."

"So this whole holiday and having me help Savannah was your attempt at matchmaking?" Ethan said.

"Pretty much." He grinned at them. "It worked, didn't it?"

Ethan looked at Savannah. "My place?"

"I think so."

He took her hand and led her to the door.

"Hey, where are you going?" Jaxon called. "We should celebrate."

"You celebrate, Jaxon," Ethan said and pulled Savannah closer. "Sav and I have some catching up to do."

"Hey," Jaxon called. "I wouldn't walk away from my business and community commitments for anyone else, you know."

"Talk to the hand, Jaxon," Savannah said.

CHAPTER
50

Savannah sat on the deck while Ethan cooked her breakfast. They'd spent three nights together since they'd left Jaxon to his own devices. He'd asked to come over a couple of times but they'd shut him out. Ethan had even redirected Gnasher to use Jaxon's shower and laundry. They'd devoted their time totally to each other, keeping the rest of the world at bay. Except Jasper, of course. He lay at Savannah's feet waiting for the titbit of bacon she would slip him later.

Savannah knew she couldn't stay at Ethan's forever. Reality had hit when the police had returned her car first thing this morning. Her phone was in the glove box. Now that Jaxon was back she had no reason to stay, apart from Ethan. While it was wonderful living like a pair of castaways in this tree house of his, they had to face reality. He had to work, she had to work, the rest of life had to go on.

A plate of bacon and eggs appeared in front of her.

"Thank you." She smiled up at him. How was she going to leave him? She forked up a mouthful of egg.

"Mmm," she murmured. "This is good."

She gazed out over the river. This morning the clear sky made the water look blue. The light breeze sent small ripples across the surface. Birds swooped and paddled. It was so calming to watch. Jaxon had been right about that too. She had fallen in love with it.

"Best view in the world, isn't it?'

She looked back at Ethan. "It's lovely."

"But?"

"I didn't say but."

"I heard it."

"Jaxon's back now." She gave him a fake smile. "I have to go home, Ethan."

He reached across and took her hand.

"Stay here, Sav … with me."

"What would I do?"

"Help Jaxon with the houseboats, take fitness classes … eat fish." He shrugged his shoulders. "Don't go. I can support us both."

"As much as I love fish …"

"I've got a new job."

"When did this happen?"

"I spoke to the new guy in the garage at Riverboat Point. He's got more work than he can handle. He wants me to join him and see how it goes."

"Congratulations." She squeezed his hand.

"I start tomorrow."

"That's great." She meant it. She was pleased he'd found something local that he enjoyed but taking two fitness classes a week wasn't enough for her.

"Please stay, Sav."

Jasper lifted his head and gave a small bark.

"Jasper wants you to stay."

"Hello." Jaxon's voice carried out to the deck.

"That was an announcement bark," she said.

"Should we let him in?"

The sound of a door sliding drifted out to the deck.

"I think he is already," Savannah said.

Jaxon's face appeared around the doorframe. "Still eating breakfast?"

"Come on out," Ethan said. "Would you like coffee?"

"That'd be good, thanks."

"What about you, Gnasher?" Ethan said.

Savannah laughed as the old man poked his head out after Jaxon. She stood up to make room for the chairs Jaxon was dragging over.

"You two have been hermits for long enough," he said.

"Young fella's a bit lonely," Gnasher chipped in.

"I do feel sorry for him," Savannah said.

"Sarcasm, dear sister." Jaxon put his hand to his chest. "It hurts."

"What can we do for you blokes?" Ethan asked as he put cups of coffee in front of them.

"Nothing for me," Gnasher said. "I'm fine now the hullabaloo's died down in the road."

Savannah focused on Jaxon. He was all hyperactive again.

"What's been happening?" she asked.

"I've got a lot of electrical work coming up. I need help with the houseboats."

"And you thought that someone would be me?" Savannah said.

"You said you liked being here. My electrical work is getting busier. I need someone to look after the houseboats."

Savannah could feel Ethan willing her to say yes.

"Actually, what are you two doing for the rest of the day?" Jaxon said. "I've got two boats going out this afternoon. They're refuelled but they need to be cleaned. I have to go in to Riverboat Point."

Savannah opened her mouth to tell him where he could put his houseboats but Ethan spoke first.

"Sorry, mate. Can't help you. We're busy."

"You can't stay up here forever," Jaxon said.

"Not going to," Ethan replied. "We've got plans for today."

Savannah frowned as Ethan stood up. It was news to her but she followed him anyway.

"You're not leaving me again?" Jaxon yelped. "I've only just got here."

"Sorry," Ethan called over his shoulder. "Keep an eye on Jasper."

Gnasher's laugh followed them down the steps.

"Where are we going?" Savannah asked.

"To the farm. Would you rather we went in your car?"

The thought of riding on a bike was distressing but as she stared into his deep brown eyes what she saw gave her strength.

"No," she said. "Let's take your bike."

She did up the helmet he placed on her head and pulled on the jacket and gloves he offered before she climbed on the bike. He started the engine and the huge bike vibrated underneath her. She wrapped her arms around him and hugged him tight.

The ride was terrifying and yet exhilarating. Savannah loved being cuddled up behind Ethan but for the first part of the journey she couldn't open her eyes she was so frightened. Towards the end of it she began taking in the scenery in small doses. By the time they turned off the main road onto Mal and Barb's property she was keeping her eyes wide open.

Ethan didn't turn towards the house as she'd expected but continued on past and along a track towards the hills that were the backdrop of the property. The ride got rougher. Her stomach did somersaults and she gripped him tighter until finally they came to a stop near the top of a hill.

Savannah felt numb despite the gloves and jacket. Her body felt as if it was still vibrating.

"Hi!"

She turned to see Jenny waving at her from the top of the rise. Then Blake appeared.

"What's going on?" Savannah asked as they climbed off the bike.

"Family picnic," Ethan said. "Hope you don't mind. I was going to tell you about it then Jaxon and Gnasher showed up."

"It's fine, Ethan." She squatted up and down to get her legs moving again. "I like Blake and Jenny."

They walked over the rise. A picnic table and chairs were set out. The view in front was magnificent.

"Welcome to the border," Blake said and wrapped her in a hug.

"Border?" Savannah said.

"Everything this side of the hill belongs to Mal and Barb. Everything that side is mine."

"The whole world divided in two," Jenny teased.

"Why the extra chairs?"

Savannah looked at the picnic setting. Ethan was right. There were six chairs.

"Barb and Mal are coming," Blake said.

"You didn't mention it when you rang," Ethan said.

Savannah took his hand. "It'll be fine."

"Everyone want a beer?" Blake asked. He plucked some bottles from the esky beside the picnic table and they all sat down.

"Ethan didn't tell me," Savannah said. "I haven't brought anything."

"Bit hard on a bike," Blake chuckled. "Anyway, don't worry. Between Jenny and Barb nothing else will be needed."

"Good to see you back here, Jenny," Ethan said.

"I love it here," she replied. "I also love your brother."

The sound of a vehicle turned their attention back to the crest of the hill. The top of a ute appeared and stopped.

Barb waved to them.

"Hello," she called. Mal appeared beside her carrying an esky and some containers.

There were welcomes all round, stilted between Ethan and Mal but welcomes all the same.

They sat down to lunch with the land stretching away as far as the eye could see. Savannah was drawn to the breathtaking vastness of the scene before her. The more she looked at it the more she noticed the subtle differences in colour and texture.

"It's good country."

She turned to see Mal studying her.

"It's looks so vast," she said.

"Good sheep country," Mal said. "Gets in your blood. How are you liking rural living?"

"The river's quite different from the city." Savannah glanced at Ethan. He was looking out across the view. "But it has its attractions."

Ethan turned to her. His gaze locked with hers.

"Jenny's going to work part-time," Blake cut in. "Means she can spend more time here."

"How will that work?" Barb asked.

"I'm going to do midweek in Adelaide," Jenny said. "I'll have a four-day weekend to spend up here with Blake. We'll see how that goes." She leaned into him.

"I'm glad," Ethan said and shook Blake's hand.

"What about you two?" Blake said. "You've had some serious stuff going down."

"Are you okay, Savannah?" Jenny asked. "Blake's been telling me about what happened. I saw it on the news but didn't connect it with you. It must have been terrible."

"A few bumps and scratches," Savannah said. "I've had worse."

"Those rotten people," Barb said, "and they were right next door to you."

"They'll get what they deserve," Savannah said. "It's Li and Hung I'm worried about. How terrible coming to Australia has been for them."

"Not the Australia we think of, is it?" Blake said. "Police, army, they're all doing their best to keep our values. It's a huge task."

Mal snorted.

"What does that mean?" Ethan said.

"People in uniforms," Mal said. "They always think they know what's best for the rest of us."

Ethan pushed back his chair and stood up. "I think it's time we left, Sav."

His face had become a rigid mask. Once more she felt so sad. His family was alive and here with him but they couldn't get on.

Suddenly Barb stood up.

"Don't go, Ethan," she said.

"Sit down, woman," Mal grumbled.

"I won't," she said. "This shadow has hung over us for long enough. You two have to sort this out so the rest of us can have some peace."

"You feel the same way as I do about our son taking up arms."

"I did." Barb stared at Mal. "Things have changed, Mal. Don't make me choose between my husband and my son again."

The breeze ruffled the cloth Jenny had put on the table and a bird called overhead but otherwise there was silence. Savannah's heart went out to this poor broken family. What she wouldn't give to have her parents beside her right now.

"Get up, Mal," Barb said. "Go off the two of you and talk. We'll give you fifteen minutes." She spoke like they were children being sent to the naughty corner. "You're both grown men with different world views but that's okay. Isn't that what you both fought for in your own ways?" She raised her hand in the air making all her beads rattle. "Vive la différence!"

Savannah had to smother an urge to giggle.

Ethan hovered at her elbow.

"I mean it, Mal," Barb said. "I know you want this."

There was a collective holding of breaths. Mal shoved back from the table.

"Let's go," he said to Ethan and stomped away.

Ethan watched him go.

"He wants to make amends, son," Barb said. "Open your heart."

Savannah bit her lip. She could read his inner struggle in the expression on his face. He looked at his mother then strode after Mal.

The whisper of the breeze through the grass and the crunching of retreating footsteps was all that could be heard.

"What made you take the fitness instructor path, Savannah?" Barb asked, turning her back on her husband and son as if nothing had happened.

"Oh … I …" Savannah stumbled over her words, confused by the sudden change in conversation. "I was very overweight as a teenager."

"Really!" Barb said. "Probably just puppy fat, you've got such a trim figure now."

Mothers, Savannah thought. Her own mother had said the same thing.

"I left school determined to change my life," she said. "I started to lose weight and I was looking for a job as a receptionist. I didn't know a place called *Totally You* was a gym. From the outside it looked like a clinic, albeit an upmarket one with lots of plants, mood lighting and relaxing music. Anyway, they gave me a job. Maybe I made the clients feel better. Whatever it was, I was taken in by the fitness thing. It hooks you."

"And you don't do that now?" Jenny asked.

"I was in a car accident. Exercise was my rehab. They weren't sure I'd walk properly again."

"That would have been a long journey," Jenny said. Savannah saw the understanding in her eyes.

"It was. Anyway I didn't go back to running gym classes. I've led a couple of fitness sessions at Riverboat Point. That's been fun."

They prattled on making small talk but it was stilted, the two empty chairs keeping them aware of the important conversation taking place below them. The two men were gone much longer than Barb had suggested.

Blake was trying to lighten the mood with a joke when Savannah saw movement from the corner of her eye. Ethan and Mal were walking slowly back towards them, deep in conversation.

"At last," Barb murmured. "Get the cake out, Blake."

"Sorry, we can't stay," Ethan said as he came to a stop beside Savannah's chair.

She stood up, guessing the talk hadn't gone well.

Barb tried to get him to stay.

"Let them go, Barb," Mal said. "They've got things to do."

Jenny stood up and gave Savannah a quick hug.

"Let's catch up again soon," she said.

There were hasty goodbyes and then Ethan took her hand and walked her back to the bike.

"Where are we going?" she asked.

"Home," he said. "To the river."

CHAPTER
51

The journey back to the river was different from the journey they'd made earlier. This time Savannah kept her eyes open all the way. The wide sprawling country gradually gave way to land scattered with straggly trees and then finally the thicker bush that hid the river.

Ethan rode slower along the dirt road that led to their patch of river. She took in the changes to their little strip of road. There were signs all along the edges that many vehicles had been here. The police were still at the Palmers'. She gripped Ethan tighter as they passed the white gate. The last time she'd seen it was through the rear window of the car as Ashton had shut it. How gullible she'd been.

Ethan cruised slowly down his drive. They climbed off the bike, took off their helmets and patted Jasper. Savannah turned to Ethan. His face gave nothing away.

At the bottom of the back steps she stopped and made him turn. She could stand his silence no longer. She looked into his eyes. They were dark pools of sadness.

"Why did we leave?" she asked.

"I'm sorry. I know it was rude but after Mal and I spoke I couldn't just go back to the picnic and sit there making small talk."

"How did it go with your father?"

"Not easy."

"You seem so miserable."

"Not really. I accepted a long time ago we were different. We both believe in our own causes."

"That's where you're alike."

He frowned at her.

"You might have made different life choices but you're both strong and determined in those beliefs," she said.

"We both bent a little today. You could say we met each other halfway. We agreed to try," Ethan said. "We got a bit of stuff off our chests without coming to blows."

"At least you're talking," she said.

"I don't think we'll ever be close."

"Maybe with time."

"Maybe." Ethan sighed. "There are things I know he wants me to tell him about Afghanistan. He thinks it will make my choice clearer for him but he's wrong. Our beliefs are fundamentally different. I can only talk about what happened over there with people who understand."

"And I'm not one of those people either."

Ethan faced her and took both her hands in his. "Don't be hurt," he said. "I'm glad you don't understand. Maybe in time I can tell you some of it but for now, can you just accept me as I am?"

"What exactly is that?"

He smiled.

"A slightly broken soldier who wants a normal life with the woman he loves."

"Look who you're talking too. I'm the slightly broken woman with her own demons."

"Stay with me, Sav." His eyes darkened and he pulled her close. "We're good together."

She nudged her nose against his and grinned.

"It's tragic you know, but my bloody brother was right. We do make a good pair."

"Does that mean …?"

"I've been thinking too. You're stuck with me."

He lowered his lips to hers. Their bodies wrapped together. She felt herself melt inside knowing she loved him. She trusted Ethan with her body and her heart. It was a wonderful feeling. His lips moved down her neck.

She groaned and pulled away. "Hold that thought," she said. "First I have to make a proper arrangement with Jaxon. None of this coming and going whenever he feels like it. We've got a business to run."

"Let's go and talk to him now. We've kept him in the dog house for long enough."

She laughed then squealed as Ethan scooped her up and lifted her over the fence. Jasper barked.

"Come on then," Ethan said. "You can come too."

Savannah gasped as the dog jumped the fence with ease.

"So that's how he came to me. I thought he couldn't …"

"He knows his boundaries." Ethan ran his hands down her body.

"Unlike his master," Savannah said. She encased one of his roaming hands in hers. "Later," she said. "I've got a business to organise, remember?"

Hand-in-hand they walked down to the river. The four house-boats were lined up along the bank. Jaxon was sweeping the front deck of *Tawarri*. He stopped and watched them approach.

"You've come back," he said with a wary look.

"We have." Savannah gave him a grin and walked the gangplank to the deck. "Thought I'd better come and give you a hand."

"Really?" Relief flooded his face.

"I want to make sure my investment is up to scratch."

"You'll stay?"

"She will," Ethan said.

"You'll live here?" Jaxon threw down the broom. "At the river? Manage the boats?"

"Whoa, whoa," Savannah said. "If I stay we're going to do this properly, Jaxon."

"Yes!" He high-fived her. "Yes we are."

"We might need a name change for a start."

"What's wrong with J&S Houseboats?"

Savannah put her hands to her hips. "Jaxon Smith Houseboats leaves out your partner."

"It's not Jaxon Smith Houseboats, you dummy." Jaxon laughed. "It's J and S ... Jaxon and Savannah."

She gaped at him.

"I did it for the two of us, Sav," he said gently.

Savannah shook her head. She was just beginning to understand the meaning of family again.

Jaxon smiled at her. "There's lots to do. I need my big sister."

"I'm not just doing the shit work," she warned.

"And she means that literally." Ethan smirked.

"I'm going to learn this ticket thing so I can do the fun stuff as well," Savannah said. "I want to be able to drive these boats."

"Whatever you want," Jaxon said.

Savannah knew she did have everything she wanted – a business, a family, the man she loved and all of it together on this magical strip of water, the Murray River.

She crossed back to bank and wrapped her arms around Ethan.

"I'm home," she said.

Behind them Jaxon gave a blast of *Tawarri*'s horn and Jasper barked.

"Now it's official," Ethan laughed.

ACKNOWLEDGMENTS

The inspiration for this story came from several houseboat holidays on the beautiful Murray River. The tranquil surroundings and the company of good friends are very conducive to setting the writer's brain pondering the 'what if' questions. Of course once I'd posed those questions I had to follow up with research.

I would particularly like to thank Jodie Butson who manages FoxTale Houseboats with her husband Michael. Her hospitality and insight into the behind the scenes world of managing houseboats was such a help to me. She happily answered my crazy questions, read an early draft and added to my knowledge of the river.

This story touches on the lives of two fictitious returned soldiers from different eras. I did much reading and asked many questions to delve into the kind of life they might lead upon their return to civilian life. Special thanks to Alex for his frank conversation and early draft read to help fill in the gaps that my reading didn't reveal. I appreciate your willingness to share a little of what it's like to be a soldier and admire your dedication to the defence of our country and way of life.

To dear friends who willingly support the research and writing process and listen to my creative babble, thanks for being there.

And thank you, Joy and Andrew, for providing that tranquil writing retreat.

There are so many fabulous writers out there who support through friendship, mentoring and through simply staying in touch. I am grateful to be part of such a diverse creative community.

Once again it's been a pleasure to work with Glenda Downing who applies her spoonful of sugar to make the hard work of editing fun.

The crew at Harlequin, a huge thank you – to publisher Sue Brockhoff for believing in the early idea, to editor Annabel Blay for her enthusiasm and to all who do their bit to bring the book to life. What a fabulous team you are to work with.

Last but by no means least I am blessed to have a fantastic family who all do their bit to keep this writer afloat and writing. And to Daryl, my thanks and love.

talk about it

Let's talk about books.

Join the conversation:

 on facebook.com/harlequinaustralia

 on Twitter @harlequinaus

www.harlequinbooks.com.au

If you love reading and want to know about our
authors and titles, then let's talk about it.